Blood Exchange

SANDRA HOOD

Published by Sandra Hood

ISBN-13: 978-0-9907006-0-9
ISBN: 0990700607

DEDICATION

For my mom, Eloise,
and my sister, Charlotte,
who waited the longest.

ACKNOWLEDGMENTS

Special thanks to Cheryl, Terri, and Natalie of the
North Georgia Writers Group for your biweekly dedication in
reading the sometimes disjointed pieces of this book, for your
expert editing skills and for the wise and gentle nudges toward
directions I may not have gone on my own. Thanks to Kelly for
sharing my love of books and movies and for always being
interested in talking plots, characters and all things writing, and to
Alex for looking over my shoulder and somehow managing to
make the most mundane sentence I've written sound dirty. Sincere
appreciation to my nieces for letting me borrow your lovely names;
I apologize for anything unsavory that might befall your counter-
characters in the unfolding of this story.

PROLOGUE

I had no idea where I was going until I came to the end. I scrambled backward, pressing myself into the cold wall. Even if I could find a way out, I knew I could go no farther. The weight I carried, the precious cargo I was determined to save, wouldn't allow it. And my choice had brought me to this dismal place.

Silence could have been my ally, yet my breath ripped through me, wheezing against my throat like tiny screams.

Grey-green light filtered through the dirt I'd stirred into the air. One naked sputtering fluorescent. My feet ached, but I clawed at the ground with my toes, felt stone, or maybe tile, cracked and broken. Nothing more than crude sensory input, toes to brain, but still enough to latch onto. I had obeyed my instincts, stumbled through the dark, grasping blindly at the black open space. Now I was trapped in the light, vulnerable, and all I could do was try to recover my breath and possibly my dignity as I surrendered myself and my charge to the demon waiting in the shadows.

I couldn't see anything, couldn't even hear him through the noise in my head. All I could hear was *me*.

Not that it mattered. He had stalked me with aloof surety. I wasn't sure if I had ever heard him, but I had certainly known he was there.

I could *feel* him, lurking, biding his time. Perhaps he was waiting until I had recovered a bit of my stamina. I wasn't sure what rules of etiquette applied to this particular situation, this predator-prey dance that fell so far outside the rules of society I couldn't fathom what would come next. As the prey, I felt sure I was holding up my end of the bargain. I hoisted my shirt over my nose and mouth, filtered air through the cotton, straining to not cough, and stared into the dark as a shiver slid over me. A minute passed, and another tremor shook me. It wasn't fear or the cold at my back. This chill came directly from him.

The air moved as he did, slamming into me like the leading wake of an explosion. It could have been my imagination—I told myself it had to be—except my head actually rocked back against the wall before a frozen draft crawled over my flesh to settle around my feet.

The shock cleared my head. I forced myself to drag in another deep breath, praying it wouldn't be my last.

"Come out of the shadows." The words croaked from my throat, weaker than I intended, but they sent the message I wanted: *Let's get this over with.* "I think you have the advantage." Stupid move? Maybe, but saying something gave me an unexpected twinge of satisfaction, until I saw the shape of a man emerge through the dark.

I braced for another slap of cold air, but something had changed. The shiver that washed over me was gentler, more like a massage of wind on the glassy surface of a northern lake, almost soothing. I didn't understand. Didn't care. My anger flared. *He's toying with me.*

I took a shaky step forward.

"This is all that matters," I said, shielding my cargo with fatigued arms. "I won't give it up."

"I don't want you to," he said. The sound of his voice, sheathed in frost, brought tears to my eyes.

Clay dust drifted toward me as he stepped closer. The fluorescent glow sprinkled down on the man from the shadows, bathing his face in a lifeless pallor.

Blood rocketed through my body in one swift rush, and I swayed precariously. I searched his eyes for some sign of the wholesome, earthy green that had once made my heart swoon, but all I saw was a dark fury.

"Emmalyn, don't move," my husband said, and he lunged toward me, strong arms raised, lips torn back in a snarl.

I opened my mouth to scream, and those strange chilling waves pounded me from every direction.

CHAPTER ONE

The day the world changed was one of the most perfect I had ever seen. The first thing to hit me wasn't the warmth of the sun against my chilled skin or the wispy white clouds floating in an ocean blue sky but the delicious fragrance of honeysuckle. A light breeze jostled the wild growth that nearly blanketed the hole in the ground where I had started my hike. After the dankness of the tunnels, the sweet flowers overtook my senses. For a moment, I closed my eyes and breathed in the sugary scent, remembering how as kids my friends and I would suck the tiny droplet of nectar contained in each flower, moving greedily from bloom to bloom until our taste buds were satisfied and the vines we had attacked were reduced to a green mass surrounded by a discarded bed of the soft petals they had produced for us.

"Wandering down there by yourself again?"

I startled at the voice but climbed steadily from my dirty knees to my feet.

"Scaring the devil out of people again?" I said. My heart pounded an accelerated rhythm I was not pleased about.

The tiny lady before me grinned. "Nice job if you can get it," she said. "Hold on. Let me get a picture of you coming out of that hole. Front page stuff."

I raised my eyebrows in protest but heard the shutter click just before my face broke into a grimace.

"No one needs to see that picture," I said, hauling my backpack aboveground and imagining what the humidity had done to my unruly hair. "You truly are evil."

Anyone who knew Samantha Bedding knew she was about the least frightening person in town. Petite, she reached five feet only with the help of some serious heels. Stark black pixie hair framed her round face. Her reporter's instincts sizzled behind the surface of her eyes, not quite obvious until you got to know her. She, like me, had moved north of Atlanta to the low Appalachian mountains of Graceville for the sake of her husband's career, and we had both floundered a bit before finding that thing that defined us in the community.

Samantha, now the divorced *Ms.* Bedding, had stuck around Graceville anyway, having found her niche at the local paper, a small bi-weekly publication where the most popular recipes around town were often the big story. To give her credit, Samantha was always looking for the next breaking news. Apparently, this week, that was me.

My niche was wandering around underground. During my adolescent years, my father had moved our family to Portland, where I had swiftly become enthralled with the Shanghai Tunnels. I spent practically all of my babysitting money touring the buried maze, fascinated by the trap doors where unsuspecting men, strong but exhausted, who'd gone out for a drink and a break from the hard work that built their strapping muscles, were dropped swiftly and stealthily into the ground and locked away there in cells until they could be loaded onto departing ships as forced slave labor. Shanghaied, those poor men were, along with a few even more unfortunate women. My first real job had been as a tour guide.

When my family had moved back to Atlanta, the closest thing to the musty and mysterious tunnels of Portland was Underground Atlanta—not nearly enough mystery and very little must, only a nice little kiosk or two lain along the cobblestones.

Discovering that Graceville harbored its own labyrinth of tunnels stowed beneath the benign streets and spread of tangled woods was a gift—my own hidden reward for moving to a place that, until recently, barely ranked a mark on the map.

"You aren't seriously thinking you can conjure up a decent story about me wandering around down there?" I lengthened my stride as I passed Samantha, simply for the fun of seeing her scurry to keep up with me.

"Emmalyn, honey," she said, characteristically undaunted and trailing a half-foot behind, "you are the epitome of human interest in this town. It will be a fabulous story."

"Yes, but I've been caving and spelunking and exploring for most of my life. I don't like the idea of some kid going down there and getting lost or hurt."

"Kids are kids. I'm sure they've been sneaking down there for decades. By now, these tunnels are old hat to the folks around here. If kids were interested, the place would be littered with condoms and cigarette butts. The focus will be more on you, your background. Pretty girl dons hardhat, crawls around in the dirt—that kind of thing."

"Wow," I offered with a noticeable tinge of sarcasm.

"Yeah, whatever," Samantha came back. "I just need to *write* something. Give a reporter a break. Graceville is the consummate sleepy little town."

We reached the small gravel parking lot of Graceville's one Baptist church, a quaint white clapboard complete with glowing stained glass and a small steeple rising above the entryway. Samantha's SUV was parked next to my Camry. I popped the trunk and tossed my backpack in while Samantha carefully tucked camera components into a case filled with rippling soft grey foam. It wasn't exactly a fascinating process to watch, but I waited patiently while she settled everything into place.

"So what else is on your agenda for the day?" she said, finally lowering the lid.

"Just heading home," I said, keeping my plans, which were exquisitely simple, to myself.

"See you around, then."

"Lurking behind doorways? Around corners? Hovering outside the entrance to caves?"

Samantha slid her sunglasses on with sinister flare. "You never know what stories lurk beneath the surface of everyday lives."

I laughed and waved as she drove away.

Any lifting of the hot, humid summer air always put me in a good mood. I found myself, for the millionth time that day, humming the chorus of the last country song I had heard that morning. My brain was still crooning its own mangled, repetitive version as I drove into the garage. I circled the house before going inside, pulling a handful of weeds and stopping to cut a small batch of white irises to put in a vase. I'd left the windows open, allowing the soft wind to circulate throughout the rooms. It was fresh and quiet. Birds chirped outside my kitchen window.

I thought about the opening I had discovered in the tunnels.

Branching west off the main shaft, it was practically unnoticeable, the entrance was so small. I had wanted to squeeze through and follow the path, see where it led, but prudence had thankfully taken over. I needed to record the opening as it was before I took a chance on destroying the integrity of it by barreling through for the satisfaction of my own curiosity. Nevertheless, I couldn't wait to add my discovery to the map I was constructing, follow it farther to see how it connected to what I'd already recorded. Even more, I couldn't wait to get back down there with some better lighting and examine the entrance to see if, as I suspected, it had been blocked off deliberately. This had to be perhaps the best day off work since we had moved here.

By six, the smell of my crock pot roast filled the house. When Steven's car rumbled into the driveway, my stomach answered back with a ravenous growl. I grabbed some plates and silverware.

"Hi, hon," I called when he opened the door from the garage.

I'd expected a typical, "Hey babe," but instead Steven didn't answer. That was my first sign something was wrong.

When I peeked around the corner, Steven was perched on the edge of the sofa. He seemed a little pale. My spousal radar went on full alert. I didn't like the confused look on his face.

"Hey, are you feeling okay?" I asked. I had crossed the room in a flash and placed the palm of my hand against his tan forehead. No fever, but his green eyes peered out from under uncharacteristically lazy lids.

"Yeah," he said, pointing a small smile that seemed a little forced in my direction. "Yeah," he repeated more definitely, shaking his head a little. His brow remained furrowed as I pulled my hand away.

"Blood drive," he said, as if that explained everything. His eyebrows popped up for a second. Then his expression relaxed, settling into the face I was more accustomed to—kind green eyes above his sharp but slightly crooked nose, the sculpted jaw set off by the days' stubble, the slight dimple that pierced his right cheek when his lopsided smile pulled up higher on one side than the other.

Even sick, he was gorgeous.

"That was today? I'd forgotten." I lifted my hand back to the dimple side of his face. "I've got dinner. Think that would make you feel better? Or do you want to lie down?"

"Dinner, I think."

I nodded and hurried back to the kitchen. In record time, I transferred meat and potatoes onto two plates, filled glasses with iced tea, and brought it all to the table.

"Comfort food," Steven said, meeting me there. "You sure you didn't remember about the blood drive?"

"Maybe it was in the back of my head." I tried laughing and pushed a plate his way. "Did it not go well? You look kind of peaked."

Steven forked a lump of roast into his mouth. A thoughtful crease formed between his brows.

"I don't know if the nurse wasn't good with a needle or what. It seemed like most of us came away feeling a little off."

"That's unusual. For you, at least. You don't normally have a problem with the medical stuff."

I meant this partially as a joke. Steven's job was related to the medical field in a remote way. Next to the Red Cross, LifeShare weighed in as one of the top non-profits for blood donations. Steven maintained the database, which at first glance might seem like a simple record of in-and-out supply, but Steven had elevated the system to monitor the needs of literally thousands of hospitals nationwide. He monitored their supplies and cross-referenced LifeShare's stock with scheduled surgeries. Two years ago, he had launched a program to gather blood-type information on the populations of major cities. Once he had gathered enough information, he used computer models to cross-reference historical blood consumption related to trauma with the demographics of blood type in a given area in order to anticipate a hospital's needs for accident victims. A lot more went into it than I could comprehend. Traffic statistics, incidence of disease in a given area, stuff like that. In the medical community, Steven's program had alternately been received with excitement and skepticism, but LifeShare saw the same potential that Steven had seen and was the first to actively recruit my husband. Together, Steven and the company had been working diligently over the past year to expand the program beyond the major metropolitan areas. The literal life-or-death importance behind his computer/desk job sometimes weighed heavily on my guy. It wasn't strange for him to carry around some residual fatigue, and I loved him for taking it so seriously.

"I felt great right after. Could've run a 5K," he said, shaking his head again. "By late afternoon, all I wanted to do was take a long nap. Sugar crash from the cookies and orange juice, maybe."

"Good turnout?"

A wry laugh escaped him as he shoveled in more food. Steven seldom scoffed when it came to the company he worked for. Though LifeShare wasn't without its share of office politics, Steven managed to put that aside most of the time.

"Not much choice this time around. They were pushing harder than usual for one hundred percent participation. I mean, they always *encourage* everyone to give, but the campaign came across a little amped up this time. We were beginning to think our jobs might be on the line if we didn't show up. Alyssa practically had herself tied up in knots. Poor girl nearly passes out just thinking about it. She was peeved they scheduled a make-up. They don't usually do that. She can find an excuse to get out of it about every other drive, but I guess it's hard to come up with a plausible excuse when you've got an opportunity to make it up a couple of weeks later."

"I don't know how she stands working there if it bothers her that much." I sympathized with her to some extent. Needles weren't my favorite. I had given up a bit of blood myself recently and when the nurse had inserted the needle into my arm, I had felt my face drain as nausea swam over me. That was a one-time thing with a bad stick. Thinking about it now didn't bother me at all.

"How's Jerry? I know he hates not being able to donate." Jerry Sanford was probably my favorite of Steven's co-workers. He and his wife, Ruby, had helped us settle into our house when we first moved here, recommended a moving company, took us out to dinner. He'd talk to Steven about his work, showing—maybe feigning—interest while some of Steven's other peers made excuses to get out of the room after the second mention of a nanobyte. Jerry had been diagnosed with liver cancer a few months later, a difficult battle but one he was winning.

"Actually, he gave," Steven said, surprising me.

"Why?" It was my understanding that cancer survivors couldn't donate blood.

"His blood won't go into the bank, but the company is involved in some new research. Any blood that doesn't get banked can be used for that. And of course, we're supposed to set an example as employees." He used an official voice, apparently quoting the office memo.

Steven put down his fork and chugged his glass of iced tea. He sat back, looking satisfied, a happy man with a full belly.

"I made sure to get my blood type this time," he said with a grin.

I felt a little guilty. When he had first mentioned the upcoming drive a few weeks ago, I had practically badgered him to find out his type. It was beyond my comprehension that he could donate so often and handle the organization of thousands of donors and not know the type of his own blood. Of course, he argued that he was tuned in to the "big picture" and didn't have time to worry with something as mundane as his own blood type. I didn't believe it for a second. What I did believe was that he enjoyed teasing me with mock ignorance because he knew it drove me crazy.

"Really?" I tried to make my voice sound as if he was revealing something completely unexpected to me.

"Yep." He got up, kissed my cheek, and took his plate to the sink. "Dinner was fantastic. I can practically feel the red blood cells multiplying."

I followed him to the sink. I thought there might have been a little flirting wrapped up in that comment even though he was obviously teasing me about the blood type thing. As far as the flirting went, I hoped I was right and decided to play along.

I brushed my body unnecessarily against his as I added my plate to the sink. There was no need for him to hang around, but he stayed to operate the faucet while I rinsed my plate. That occupied one hand. With the other, he rubbed my back from top to bottom, settling the tips of his fingers inside the waist of my jeans.

I dropped my plate into the sink and turned toward my favorite guy, leaning close.

"Well?" I said, curiosity winning over for the moment.

"O neg. I Am The Universal Donor," he bellowed in a mock superhero fortissimo.

Of course he was, I thought. My husband would give a stranger the shirt off his back—a cliché, perhaps, but in his case an apt description. He was the type to get involved in a worthy cause—soup kitchens, coat drives, you name it. Even his blood type gave him an opportunity to help people.

"So if I needed help, you could rush to my rescue?" I asked

coyly, pressing myself against him and portraying my best version of damsel in distress.

"I could surely try," he said and leaned his lips toward mine.

Later I awoke from dozing, snuggled into Steven's warm arms. The breeze that had cooled and freshened the house when the sun was up had turned nippy as evening settled in.

"The windows are still open. Cold," I murmured.

"I'll close them. You stay put."

Steven started to pull away, but I tightened my grip around his waist, not wanting to let him or his warmth leave me just yet.

"You really are my superhero." I bobbed my eyebrows for effect.

"Want me to use my superhero voice?"

"Not so much," I countered honestly. The teasing bass had certainly been a contributing factor in getting me to this place of comfort and satisfaction, but even I had to admit the Universal Donor Voice was a little creepy.

"Build a guy up and then tear him down," Steven said.

I shimmied toward the headboard so I could give my husband a kiss.

"You don't need building up, hon. In fact, it appears that after much practice, you are officially an expert in this department," I said, patting the sheets to let him know that our bed was the department to which I was referring.

"Well, thank you, ma'am." The corners of his mouth turned down in smug acceptance of the compliment.

I laughed. "What I mean to say is you have accomplished the ultimate goal."

"Well, then, maybe you should thank me."

This time I punched his arm, and the smugness on his face turned to little boy hurt.

"What I *mean* is that through all your noble efforts as my husband and lover, you have given me the gift of a child, and for that I certainly do thank you." My vision steamed over in sudden emotion as I revealed my secret. I blinked, trying to stave off a happy flood.

Steven pulled back an inch, observing my face. "You mean now?"

"Well, no, not now. But maybe a few weeks ago. Or a month,

or two—I'm not really sure when it happened."

"Emmalyn?" Excitement bubbled in his voice. "We're going to have a baby?"

"We are," I confirmed.

Suddenly the covers flew back from the bed and my husband, in all his glory, was jumping around our bedroom like a running back who had just scored the winning touchdown at the Super Bowl.

"Uh. Windows," I reminded him, practicality winning out over my desire not to burst his extremely oversized, newly formed bubble. He certainly would make an entertaining sight for our neighbors at the moment.

"Oh. Right," he said.

Steven scrambled into a pair of sweats and leaned over me for another lingering kiss. I pulled the covers back up to my neck and curled into a ball while he made his way through the house closing and locking the windows. The whooshing sounds of sliding panes and clicks of the locks grew softer as he traveled room to room, his task carrying him away from the bedroom. I closed my eyes and burrowed my head into the pillow. I could feel an involuntary smile play at the corners of my mouth as I drifted back to sleep.

My head had gone fuzzy by the time I woke from my second dozing session. Perhaps a romp through several miles of tunnels followed by one in the sack with my husband, all in one day, was simply too much for a girl in her first trimester. The sounds of the TV sifted in from the living room, finally penetrating my sleepy stupor enough for me to decipher Steven had the baseball game on. After a bout of yawning and stretching, I managed to crawl out of the bed and into a t-shirt and pajama pants.

Steven was laid back on the couch, feet stretched out in front of him, with a bag of Baked Lays propped on his flat stomach. I passed him on my way to the kitchen for a glass of water, rubbing my eyes as I went. This dozing in and out of consciousness was new for me. The little critter inside of me was taking a toll on my energy I hadn't expected. I filled two glasses with ice water, downed one, and took the other to Steven.

"Thanks," he said. "You feeling okay, sleepy head?"

"I am. I assume it's a pregnant thing," I said, unable to keep a silly grin from crossing my face, "but I don't think I could have kept my eyes open if I'd tried, which I didn't, just so you know."

"What about your tunnel trolling? You think that's a good idea now that it's not just you roaming around in there? You think the air down there is healthy for the baby?"

I had to take a breath to keep from getting defensive. Obviously, if I thought exploring the tunnels beneath Graceville was dangerous for the baby, I wouldn't be doing it. But I had to remind myself that this was all new to Steven and put aside my initial reaction—that I was being unnecessarily accused of putting our child in danger—and instead appreciate the idea of my husband's paternal instincts kicking in.

"There aren't any fumes or anything in these tunnels, not even any mold from what I can tell. Just clean, dry earth. Kid needs to get used to getting some dirt between the toes."

Steven squinted at me. There was a definite possibility that something in my body language was projecting exactly that tinge of defensiveness I'd tried to squelch. If so, and if he was picking up on it, he hid it with a smile. "Want to watch the game?" he said, patting the sofa cushion. He rattled the bag of chips. "I'll share."

"Nah. I'm afraid that might put me back into my coma. I think there's a comedy on I might watch in the bedroom."

"It'd have to be on cable," he said. "All the network channels are showing the president's speech."

"Really? I don't remember seeing that scheduled."

"Special broadcast. I flipped over but there didn't seem to be much of a point. Well, I shouldn't say that. He was talking about the growing diversity of our culture and how we all need to be a more tolerant, accommodating nation of people as a whole. Important stuff, I agree, but not the kind of emergency you pre-empt the average red-blooded American's regularly scheduled programming for. You know what I'm saying?"

"Give me a chip," I prompted. He handed me a clump of about twelve. I smiled. A man who can anticipate his wife's needs is a wonderful thing.

"I'll check it out, see if there's anything else on."

My handful of chips had disappeared by the time I plunked back down on the bed and toggled on the TV. The speech was still going on but it sounded like the president would be wrapping up pretty soon so I listened to the last few minutes.

"... not a nation of assimilators. It's time we embraced the true spirit of this great country. To forge ahead, pioneer the territories before us with enthusiasm. We no longer have before us the great unknown frontiers of land that the men and women of our ancestry did. That cannot, and should not, stop us from exploring what does lie before us. And that is an ever-changing population, men and women and children who come to this land of freedom with the same hopes and dreams that our forefathers brought with them when they first stepped foot onto our soil. They come, not to abandon their cultures, not to put aside their ways of life, not to leave behind the customs that make them who they are, but to share their customs with a nation of open arms. A nation that will embrace them. An understanding nation. The greatest nation on earth. We are that nation. Thank you."

The last was spoken with the president's usual authority, but as soon as the words were out, a mask seemed to fall over the man's face. In fact, he seemed paler than usual. I wondered if he had rushed to this press conference without the usual preparation of careful makeup that politicians always wore on television. And why?

I hadn't heard the entire speech, but what I had heard didn't indicate any particular urgency, so hurrying into this press conference seemed very out of character in my limited political opinion.

The message seemed benign enough, almost like a pep talk for the nation. Yet something about it bothered me. I turned off the TV. I had no desire to hear the journalists' questions or the anchor commentaries that were bound to follow.

Instead, I decided to take a hot shower. It wasn't until I had been under the spray long enough to soak my hair and body that I realized what was bothering me.

At the time, I had thought the president ended his speech with his usual sign-off. "Thank you," he had said. Then the typical understated wave. The perfunctory nod of the head.

It was what he hadn't said that made me uneasy.

CHAPTER TWO

I wasn't surprised when the subject came up in our Sunday school class. Steven and I had already heard it talked about on the morning radio driving in.

"He didn't say, 'and God bless.'"

Jim Strickland sat almost directly across from Steven and me in the semi-circle our chairs formed in the room. Having Biblical stories connected to everyday life always brought me more comfort than any other type of Bible study, and Jim was expert at steering most of our discussions in that direction.

Today, for some reason, I didn't have the patience for any type of lesson. My eyes kept straying to the window, to beyond the edge of the woods where that patch of honeysuckle marked the entrance to the tunnels. I was anxious to continue exploring. My mind followed along my line of sight like a shadow, adjacent but not quite engaged. I didn't want to be in this conversation right now. I couldn't put my finger on why, but I was disturbed by the very idea of the president's speech. Was it possible I was one of those card-carrying red-blooded Americans Steven had referred to, irritated at having my regular TV show pre-empted?

I had gone online, found a transcript of the speech, and read the portion I had missed. The message truly did seem to be little more than a rally for us to pull together as a people. Nothing disturbing about that. I had to wonder, then, why for the first time in six years, President Kane suddenly deviated from his usual sign-off of "Thank you and God bless." Perhaps it was a mere oversight. Regardless, I wasn't the only one to notice it.

I needed to pull my focus back into this room. I found Steven's hand, intertwined my fingers with his. There was no need for me to voice the thoughts I was having. Content to listen to the others, I found most of my ideas unfolding in the conversation without my input.

"Okay folks, we can talk about this for a minute but we'll need to move on." Ricky, our leader, obviously saw the potential for a runaway train here. "Putting aside the lack of 'God bless' at the end, do you believe that what the president was saying is in any way part of God's will for us?"

Most heads nodded in agreement. Someone muttered, "Of course."

"It's what our country is founded on, isn't it?" someone else offered.

"Love your neighbor as yourself," Steven said, surprising me. Yesterday, when I'd mentioned it, he hadn't really had an interest in discussing the speech. Honestly, I couldn't be sure he had paid that much attention what with the distraction of the baseball game.

Samantha Bedding, who had until this point appeared characteristically nonchalant, cut her reporter's eyes sharply at Steven, and I found myself irritated by her sudden interest.

"I think that's exactly the scripture President Kane's speech embodied," Ricky said, pointing to Steven.

"Except it doesn't make sense to give that kind of speech but leave off the simple words 'God bless,'" Jim added.

"He did look tired. Maybe he just forgot," someone suggested. I didn't catch who said that, but I remembered thinking the same thing.

"Or his speech writers didn't put it on the prompter." That one elicited a round of laughter.

The discussion went on like that for the remainder of the hour, with Ricky trying his best to steer us back to the lesson. No luck there. Today's topic had taken on a momentum that couldn't be derailed.

Feeling only the slightest hint of guilt, I was glad when class was over.

As weekends usually do, this one passed quickly. Monday morning was ushered in by the intrusion of blaring alarm music being slapped into submission followed by the familiar half-quiet dance of shuffled covers, shower curtain rings sliding across the rod, drawers and closet doors opening and closing. I wasn't scheduled to work until Wednesday so after Steven left, I took a quick wake-up shower and decided to tackle the project of cleaning out our junk room. I opened the door and the enormity of the task hit me. It could seriously take me a full nine months to get the room clean enough to house a baby.

Funny how any thought of the baby seemed to have a direct connection of nerves that brought my hand to my belly. Before I knew what I was doing, there I stood, like so many big-bellied women, caressing the nearly flat flesh of my stomach.

I rolled my eyes and pulled my hand away. I was already imagining painted murals between the windows, and I hadn't even picked up the first piece of junk off the floor. Boxes, I thought. I definitely needed boxes. I could probably find a few at work that hadn't been thrown out. And while I was out looking, it wouldn't hurt to swing by the paint store and check out the no-VOC paint options. Something in a soft green, I thought.

The phone jangled, snapping me out of my daydreams. I scurried back across the hall. It was Steven, calling from his cell.

"Oh hi hon," I answered. "I was about to start cleaning out the spare bedroom. Do you think you could nab some boxes from work? We don't need them right this minute. I'll organize things into some piles and stacks until I have something to put them in. We'll both need to go through this stuff to see if there's anything we can get rid of …"

"Emmalyn." Steven's somber use of my name cut my ramblings short.

"What's wrong?" I recognized his serious voice though I could only recall him using this particular tone twice since I'd know him—once when his dad passed away, the other when he'd come home from work to tell me Jerry had been diagnosed with cancer.

Steven's voice was close to a whisper, as if he didn't want anyone to overhear our conversation.

"Alyssa called in sick. And she called me, on my cell, which is strange. She didn't sound good at all, Em."

"Like a cold?"

"No, her voice was fine. But she still didn't sound like herself. Plus I'm not her boss. I don't have a problem passing on the message, but don't you think it's weird that she called me. She's never done that before."

"Maybe she just called you first without thinking. And she trusts you to get the message to the right person. So there wouldn't be any reason to make another call, especially if she's trying to rest."

"Feels off. I don't like it," Steven said.

"You want me to call and check on her?" I asked.

"Actually, I was hoping you might drive over there. I'd go but something screwy is going on with our database. It almost looks like there's a rogue data module attached to our system. I don't know; I haven't figured it out yet, but I need to get to the bottom of it, make sure nothing's corrupted. Could be just a bug I haven't encountered before. Bottom line—I can't leave. Would you mind?"

I could almost picture Steven running his fingers over the top of his head, working his dark hair into a tangled mass of curls. It's what he did whenever he got stressed.

"No problem." I tried to keep my voice steady enough to not exacerbate Steven's concern. This was difficult because I tended to feed off his emotions. If Steven had a bad feeling, that was more than enough to convince me. I already had my purse and keys in hand and was standing at the front door. "I can be there in ten minutes. I'll call you as soon as I know anything. Don't spend that time worrying."

"I will."

17

"I know."

The air outside had already thickened up for the day, a true sign that summer was imminent. It had been hotter two weeks ago, followed by a cool teaser break; typical Georgia weather, it wouldn't be unusual to switch between A/C and heat throughout the course of a day. I wasn't quite ready to give in, though. The idea of shutting up the house, rendered slave to the processed air, made me feel uncharacteristically claustrophobic. I drove the short distance to Alyssa's with my window down. Somehow the simplicity of the wind against my hair and face helped diffuse my own worry over Alyssa.

Steven and I had been invited to her house several times for dinner. Her boyfriend, Dillon, traveled a lot, but when he was in town, he more or less lived at Alyssa's. Alyssa often confided her ideas about marriage to Steven—and Steven and I, between ourselves, talked a lot about Alyssa and marriage—because Dillon had popped the question enough times that any bubbling excitement they might have enjoyed over the idea had long since settled into an unspoken tension. It crept toward the surface of their relationship like trapped air along the inner wall of a neglected, but not entirely abandoned, bottle of Coke. Alyssa had never revealed her reasons, but she never seemed ready to commit. Steven and I didn't mention it unless she did; all we could do was listen and try to let her see that marriage can be good.

I didn't see Dillon's truck when I pulled up. He was probably out of town, but Alyssa's blue Nissan was sitting in the driveway.

I shuffled my feet for a few minutes after ringing the doorbell. I hadn't thought to ask Steven if Alyssa had called from her house. She might not even be here. It was possible Dillon had taken her to the doctor.

Feeling a little silly, I pulled back the screen door and knocked three times. I hated to wake her up if she was sleeping. But despite all that fresh air and wind and head-clearing, Steven's bad feeling had needled its way into the back of my mind.

Unsure of the protocol for barging in on sick people, I pulled out my cell and called Alyssa's home number. I probably should have done this earlier just to let her know I was coming over, but it was too late for that now.

The phone rang four times before the answering machine picked up. I could hear the announcement through my phone echoed by the same voice on her machine inside the house. I spoke hesitantly. Hearing myself duplicated on the other side of the wall was disconcerting and I experienced an odd moment of shyness, fumbling over my words.

"Alyssa, it's Emmalyn. I'm here at your house, and I'm sorry to bother you, especially if you're asleep, which you probably aren't now that I've rung your doorbell and knocked on your door and, well, I can hear myself on your machine so I know I'm being loud. Anyway, Steven said you called in sick and he was worried about you so he asked me to come over and check on you. I'll hang around for a few minutes. If you're there and if you need anything—"

The click of the phone picking up interrupted me.

"You can come in," Alyssa said in a strained voice.

I waited to see if she would continue, but she didn't say anything else. I definitely agreed with Steven that something was off. The voice on the other end of the phone wasn't that of someone who had been awakened from sleeping. There was no rasp of someone with a sore throat, or even the weak strain of someone with a stomach ache. It was just … wrong.

"Alyssa?" I said tentatively.

Now I really wasn't sure what to do. She had said I could come in. Did that mean the door was unlocked?

I tried the knob, which turned under my hand, so I pushed the door open and stepped inside. Even with permission to enter, I felt like an intruder. Now that my duplicated voice was no longer yelling from the speaker of the answering machine, I realized the house was dead quiet.

The layout of Alyssa's small house was similar to ours, if you took away our downstairs family room and lowered the upstairs bedrooms to the main floor to form a ranch. After passing the boxy den off the front entrance, I peeked into the living room to see if she was lying on the sofa, but she wasn't. In our house, a staircase leading to our bedrooms branched left of the kitchen. Here there were no stairs, but a similar hallway led to the right. I followed it, stopping to check the first two rooms before I got to Alyssa's bedroom.

As I expected, she was in her bed, rolled to one side with her legs curled up to her chest. The phone lay just outside the grasp of her hand, as if it had fallen from her fingers after talking to me and she hadn't moved since.

I rushed over to the bed, my apprehension rising.

"Okay, okay." I said the ridiculous words soothingly. My motherly instincts kicked in, I suppose, because immediately I laid one hand against her forehead while I reached for the crumpled covers and pulled them up over her shoulders.

"What's going on, Lys?"

Cocooned into the blanket, her small frame looked even tinier than usual. Alyssa wasn't the kind of tiny that came with a side order of frail. She was athletic, always running or taking Pilates or yoga classes. I enjoyed the occasional workout, and I could tromp around in Graceville's tunnels forever, but Alyssa was the kind of dedicated exerciser that put us dabblers to shame. Consequently, she had maybe an ounce of fat on her body and looked like a page from a fashion magazine in whatever she wore.

I could find no trace of that vibrancy in the face I was looking at.

It worried me that she didn't answer my prompt. Instead, her eyes turned lazily in my direction. Half the blue irises stayed hidden beneath droopy lids, as if she could fall right to sleep. Part of me wanted to let her, but I had to fight that instinct. We needed to find out what exactly was wrong with her.

I pressed my hand against her forehead a second time, then smoothed back the wisps of blonde hair that had fallen into her face. In a sterner voice I said, "Tell me what's wrong, Alyssa."

"Cramps," she managed.

Okay. I could work with that. Slightly more clinical, I asked, "Did you throw up?"

When she shook her head, it barely qualified as movement. "Not that kind ... oh crap."

Suddenly she threw the covers back. I sprang away from the bed to let her pass, and she took off for the bathroom doorway in the opposite corner of the bedroom. Seconds earlier, I would not have believed she could move that fast, but a second later I heard retching from the other side of the wall. In a bout of selfishness tinged with guilt, I froze where I was. I wasn't sure my newly pregnant body could handle getting any closer for fear of my stomach deciding to follow suit.

I felt a bit braver when I heard water running in the sink. I eased around the bed. I surely didn't care to be one of those hovering types that like to hold your hair back while you're puking your guts out—not even close, I thought, as my stomach lurched into a mini-flip—but I did want to be close enough in case she felt faint and needed my help.

So I purposefully turned my back to the bathroom. Unfortunately, in attempting to strategically place myself in a position that allowed Alyssa her privacy, I realized I could see straight into the master bath thanks to a full length dressing mirror positioned directly opposite the doorway. Perfect view. Of Alyssa.

She was bent over the sink, perhaps to brush her teeth or splash some cool water on her face.

It didn't really matter what she was doing because as soon as I saw her reflection in the mirror, I knew I had to get her to the hospital. I watched, horrified, as a red spot appeared on the seat of her shorts, the outer edges of the stain spreading larger by the second.

Calling an ambulance didn't occur to me until after I had gathered Alyssa into my car. I knew I was driving faster than I should; my heart was pounding with the urgency of getting her to the emergency room. I glanced sideways, then cut my eyes back to the road, unnerved. She seemed unreal somehow. For the first time since I had known her, she looked frail. Slumped against the door, her hands clutched her midsection. I didn't want to think about what the cramps meant. Worse, what the bleeding could mean.

It's just a ten minute trip, I kept telling myself because two-and-a-half minutes in I was beginning to regret my decision to drive her myself. I would never forgive myself if this cost Alyssa …

I forced myself not to think about the outcome. At least Graceville was lucky enough to have a small hospital; without it LifeShare probably would have chosen another location. And with LifeShare came an endless supply of blood; they even had some of Alyssa's in stock. If she needed it. And she might. But hopefully not. Scenarios swarmed through my head like angry bees. By the time my mind had cycled through about a zillion possibilities, we reached the hospital.

I barreled into the parking lot and swung my car into the ambulance bay. I felt sure this wasn't allowed but I didn't think Alyssa could walk from even the nearest parking space. Her complexion literally looked drained of color. And she didn't budge when I slammed on the brakes, just lay there with her damp face pressed against the hard window.

Several wheelchairs were lined up inside the sliding doors. I grabbed one and pushed it back through the doors toward the car.

When I opened the car door, Alyssa slid toward me. I was afraid she might slump completely out of the car and onto the ground, but I managed to push my hip behind the open door and prop her up while I pulled the wheelchair closer.

A moment of frozen panic seized me. My hands were full. The wheelchair was not in a good position. I couldn't reach the car horn. I hadn't alerted anyone inside to the emergency.

"I need help," I screamed, the squeaking crack in my voice both breaking the panic and revealing it to the quiet world around me. I couldn't believe that at the very least someone hadn't come out to scold me for blocking the entrance to the ER.

I hooked my arms under Alyssa's but realized right away that maneuvering her into the wheelchair was going to be a problem. For one thing, I had forgotten to lock the wheels. When I stepped back to pull her, I felt the chair roll backwards away from me.

"I have her." I heard a man's soft but sure voice behind me as strong arms nudged me away from holding Alyssa while he took over supporting her. "Get the chair."

I did what I was told. I allowed the young man to take over and dutifully got out of his way. Gripping the handles of the chair served several purposes. Most importantly, I kept it steady while he shifted Alyssa almost effortlessly from the car. Being able to hold on to something was the only thing steadying my shaking hands.

I stared past Alyssa, past the wheelchair, past the man, into the car. Back at her house, I had grabbed several towels off the bathroom racks and thrown them around Alyssa's waist and legs. I couldn't believe how much blood had soaked through them in the few minutes it had taken us to arrive at the hospital. The grim sight paralyzed me until the young man spoke.

"Let's go," he said, glancing my way. He could just as easily have screamed, "Stop looking at that blood!" my head snapped so sharply in his direction.

His face was pale beneath a sheet of hair black as onyx, so pale that the shade of his lips, almost a maroon red, stood out in an unnatural slash. I only caught a glimpse of his eyes before he turned away, but I thought they might be silver. I had taken a few art classes in college. The angles of his face would make him an intriguing subject.

I shook my head, wondering why I was even thinking about such things. Slamming the car door behind me, I sprinted to catch up as he was wheeling Alyssa through the doors.

A nurse looked up from behind the check-in desk as we approached. To my surprise and hers, the young man bypassed the desk completely and pushed Alyssa straight through a set of doors emblazoned with a wide red stripe. The red stripe obviously meant KEEP OUT, yet I followed blindly, my hands grabbing and catching the swinging doors momentarily before they could swing shut.

The nurse from the desk was quick on her feet. She must have taken a different path than us because she appeared on the other side of the doors as we barged through, attempting to block us. She did not look happy about the situation, nor did her expression indicate any willingness to be helpful.

"You can't just come back here—" she began, then closed her mouth. She was staring not at Alyssa, which is where I thought her attention should have gone, but at the young man pushing the wheelchair.

"No check-in. She will be seen now." His words were calm but authoritative. He shifted his head slightly in Alyssa's direction. She had sunk even farther down into the wheelchair. Once again, he glanced at me. A shiver ran through me as I realized I should tell someone what I knew about Alyssa.

"Bleeding," I managed to get out before my breath caught. I shook my head again, hoping to clear away whatever was threatening to render me speechless. Fear, I supposed. Adrenaline, perhaps.

"She said something about cramps." I felt wide-eyed, staring at the nurse. Then I remembered. "She threw up, too. It's a lot of blood."

"Did she throw up blood?" the nurse snapped.

For a second I didn't understand the question, then realized how I must have confused her. "No. I don't think so. She's just bleeding. So much," I added, my hand drawing a ludicrous circle in front of my pelvis.

"You two go back to the waiting room." A scowl crossed her face as she reprimanded us, but relief swept over me when she took control of Alyssa's chair and began to wheel it away. "I'll come back for her information."

I watched the nurse push Alyssa a few feet down the hall. As she turned right onto a branching hallway, she shot us another scolding look. My feet involuntarily took a series of stumbling steps backwards before my back hit the double doors we had barged through. I had almost forgotten the young man who had wheeled Alyssa in. If it hadn't been for his help, I might never have gotten Alyssa out of the car and I doubted seriously that I would have been bold enough to barge past the desk the way he had. He may have saved her life.

"Thank you," I whispered even before I turned to face him.

When he didn't answer, I looked to my left and then my right. I snapped around, pushing against the doors, and stepped back into the waiting room. A smattering of faces—some bored, some anxious, some angry—looked up to greet me, but the young man was nowhere in sight.

The sight of my car still parked askew outside the sliding doors caught my eye. A different nurse had taken over the desk.

"I need to move my car," I told her.

She looked at me blankly. My thoughts jumbled inside my head. Alyssa's emergency had rattled me in a way I had never experienced before. I wished vaguely that I was more in control; I needed to talk to Steven.

"I brought in Alyssa Davis, the young woman the other nurse just took back." I forced the words out one at a time. That small success seemed to help. I worked to regain my composure as more words spilled out of me.

"I told the nurse everything I know. I apologize. I don't have her insurance information or probably half the information you'll need, but I can get in touch with someone who does. I'll call her boyfriend immediately and I'm sure he can tell you whatever you need to know."

"That's fine," the nurse said.

"I apologize," I said again. I wasn't sure why I felt so remorseful; my polite side seemed intent to take over. "I was a little panicked when we came in and I left my car outside, there." I threw my thumb up to point over my shoulder. "I'll move it, but I promise I'll be right back."

"Come back to the desk when you're done and I'll give you some paperwork to fill out," she said. I must have had a blank look on my face, because she quickly followed up with, "Just fill out what you can," and offered me a soft smile.

Once inside my car, I realized I had left it unlocked with my purse astride the console and the keys still hanging in the ignition. I didn't remember even turning the car off although I must have. I forced my line of vision straight ahead, averting my eyes from the mess of towels on the seat next to me. That curtailed the ominous roll in my stomach, although I couldn't keep the sharp smell of the blood from entering my nostrils. I could almost feel the moist warmth of it in the air as I breathed. The muscles along my ribcage rippled with concern for Alyssa as I threw the car into gear and drove the 20 yards to a legitimate parking space.

Blood or no blood, I needed a moment to recoup before going back inside. I rummaged through my purse for my cell, drawing slow breaths in an attempt to settle my nerves.

Steven's voice brought another surge of emotion to the surface. I fought to keep my voice steady, although I knew he could probably see right through my efforts.

"I need Dillon's number," I said. I wanted Dillon to call the emergency room. I wanted the hospital to have Alyssa's information as soon as possible. And he needed to come home. He should be here. With her.

"Tell me what's going on, Em," Steven said.

I spilled everything in a rush, my voice shaking occasionally as random shivers shook my torso. This must be the shock I'd always heard about, or aftershocks, like the tremors that rattled the earth following an earthquake. I couldn't seem to control my own body, but talking it through with Steven helped. The sound of his voice always calmed me; if he were here, I would throw myself into his arms and hang on for dear life. And I knew he would hang on to me for as long as I needed him. For now, all I could rely on was my imagination, which seemed to do the trick. I began to feel calmer.

"I'm sure Dillon's number is in Alyssa's personal files, or she has it in Outlook on her computer. I'll find it. I'll call him and have him call you back, hopefully right away and then I'm on my way. Will you be okay?"

"I'll be fine," I said.

I needed to get back inside but I wasn't sure if I would be able to stomach the surprise of seeing those bloody towels again when I returned to my car. Better to take care of it now while I was used to the idea. There was a bundle of plastic grocery bags I'd thrown in my trunk to recycle. I grabbed a handful, layered one inside another, and layered another two to serve as a glove for my hand. Without looking down, I wadded the towels into a ball and stuffed them into the grocery bags, tied them off and stuffed that into another bag and then another, tying each one tightly as I went. Finally I shoved them as deep into the rear of the trunk as I could reach and stood back, my breath catching. I would wash them for Alyssa, and if they didn't come clean, I would buy her new ones.

Dillon returned my call five minutes after I reentered the hospital. He was able to provide all of the needed information over the phone. All I had to do was sign that I had brought Alyssa in.

Steven arrived shortly after that and sat with me in the dismal waiting room. I seemed to hurt all over. Either my back muscles had tensed up from sitting in the hard plastic chairs or the aches were some kind of fallout from the ordeal with Alyssa, but Steven wrapped his arms around me and kept me warm until I began to relax and the tension eased. Against my will, I listened as conversations popped up around me. Privacy did not seem to be a concern amongst those waiting.

Story after story explaining how these people's loved ones had wound up in the hospital sprouted to life, one melding into the next, until I couldn't stand it anymore. It wasn't that I didn't sympathize; I did. But each story put me back in the moment of trying to pull Alyssa from my car, the pure desperation I had felt and still felt waiting to know if she would be okay.

The day brightened to its peak, then began to fade toward

evening. The nurses changed shifts at four, so a third face now manned the entrance desk.

"I think I'll check to see if there's any news," I said.

Steven held my hand. "I'm sure they'll call you as soon as they have any information."

"It's been an hour since the new person took over the desk. I'm afraid she doesn't know that we're here for Alyssa. If she's awake, I wouldn't want her to think nobody's here for her."

"I'll check," Steven said and gave my hand a quick squeeze.

"They've admitted her," he told me when he returned. "They gave me the room number. We can go up."

"Thank God," I said.

The sight of Alyssa lying in the bed brought tears to my eyes. At the same time I was flooded with relief. She was alive. The alternative, my fear of the worst, was a thought I had continually pushed to the back of my mind over the last hours. Only now did it seem safe to allow it through, now that I knew it was no longer a possibility.

I approached the bed with Steven standing close behind me.

My hand trembled as I reached out and touched Alyssa's cheek with the backs of my fingers.

"She'll be out for a little while longer," a voice said from the doorway.

A nurse entered the room and began the expedient work of checking the patient's vitals. She wrapped the blood pressure cuff around one thin arm, pumped, released, and yanked the Velcro loose. Alyssa didn't budge.

"What happened?" I asked. "How is she?"

"She lost a good bit of blood, but she'll be fine," she said, her silent smile an obvious indication she would not be offering any further explanation. She hung her stethoscope around her neck, wadded the pressure cuff into her palm, tugged Alyssa's blanket back into place, and glanced at her watch. "Dr. Knight will be by in an hour or so to check on her. You're welcome to stay if you like, but most likely she'll sleep most of that time."

Steven and I thanked the nurse, our voices joining simultaneously.

"Did you eat?" Steven asked me when she was gone.

"Breakfast," I said after a moment, thinking back to the morning when my biggest concern had been clearing a bunch of useless junk away so I could start work on the nursery. My hand automatically went to my belly. I hadn't thought of the baby in all this time. I didn't feel hungry, but I knew I should eat something.

"We could run down to the cafeteria—if it's open. Or go grab something real quick." My husband's eyes followed my hand to my belly. "You need to eat."

"I know. I don't really want to leave her, though, in case she does wake up. She may not remember me bringing her to the hospital. And I don't want to miss the doctor when he comes by."

Steven smiled at me, his lips turning up just enough to make the dimple in his cheek form a crease. "Okay. I'll get you something and bring it back."

Settled into the vinyl chair next to the bed, I was content to watch Alyssa's steady breathing. The rhythm of it had almost lulled me to sleep when I heard her stir. Instantly alert, I stood by her bed.

"Hey," I cooed when her eyes finally opened enough to recognize I was there.

She saw me and then looked around the room, taking in the sterile surroundings.

"Whah?" she breathed. I wasn't sure if she wanted to know where she was or what was going on or even why she was here—probably all three and more.

"You're in the hospital, sweetie." I could answer that much, at least.

CHAPTER THREE

"What happened?" Alyssa asked, voice groggy.

"I'm not sure," I said honestly. "The doctor should be by soon to check on you. Do you remember coming to the hospital?"

"Not really." Alyssa let her head loll to the side and sighed. "I remember I woke up. I had cramps." Something came over her face as she said this. Her eyes widened for a second, then turned pink behind a sudden sheen of tears.

I grabbed her hand. "The doctor will tell us more, but the nurse said you would be fine. You lost some blood so you're probably feeling kind of weak right now." I was struggling with what I should say and what to leave unsaid until we knew more. I didn't like the look of panic on Alyssa's face.

"What about the baby?" she said, and a tear spilled onto the pillow.

For a muddled second, I thought she was talking about my baby and wondered if Steven had shared the news with his coworkers. Then I realized she meant her own baby. The sight of all that blood came back to me and I almost swooned as mine surged through my veins. I was no expert but that amount of blood couldn't possibly be a good sign.

"Alyssa," I said tentatively. "W—" I caught myself. I had been about to say "were." I took a deep breath. "*Are* you pregnant?" I asked, not really wanting to hear the answer.

Alyssa closed her eyes, made a valiant effort at blinking away the moisture, and nodded. A hint of a smile crossed her lips but faded as quickly as it had appeared.

"I don't feel pregnant anymore," she said without a hint of emotion.

Those words tore through my heart. I glanced around, fighting the rise of an enormous lump in my throat. So badly I wished the doctor would come in soon.

"Let's just wait to hear what the doctor has to say." I patted her hand, absolutely regretting the inadequacy of my gesture, but I couldn't think of anything else to do.

Thankfully, Alyssa dozed again after that while I waited anxiously. I had begun to wonder what was taking Steven so long with the food when the doctor finally showed up.

"I'm Dr. Knight," he said, his voice too loud in the confines of the room as he stuck out a lanky arm to shake my hand. He apparently wasn't concerned about waking his patient; what little interest he showed seemed purely clinical.

I discreetly moved as far as I could into the corner of the room and turned my back. I felt awkward. I hadn't been asked to leave and felt compelled to stay as her only advocate at the moment, but I also wanted to give Alyssa the privacy she deserved. I couldn't entirely separate myself from the examination, which consisted mostly of a brief once-over. The doctor did at least pull back the covers to make sure there wasn't any additional bleeding. Alyssa shifted slightly but didn't wake.

"Everything looks good," he concluded.

"What caused the bleeding?" I asked.

"Ovarian cyst. They can cause quite a bit of pain. Most of the time they go away on their own but sometimes they rupture. The bleeding probably looked worse than it actually was."

For real? I thought. Because it looked absolutely horrible. A question formed in my head, but the doctor asked one that made me forget what I'd been about to say.

"Did you bring her into the hospital?" Dr. Knight was already heading for the door.

"Yes. It seemed like a *lot* of blood, Dr. Knight." I scrambled to follow him into the corridor. To my surprise, he actually kept walking.

"That can happen." He tossed the words back over his shoulder. I couldn't imagine anyone, even a double-board-certified-whatsama-ever they bragged about on the medical shows, being so busy he couldn't stop for a moment to discuss a patient. He continued, "Think of it as having a very heavy period in a very short time. The female body is set up to handle this kind of blood loss." The man actually smiled, continuing his haste to get away from me.

"So then, what about the baby?" I spat.

That did it. He stopped and turned. The quick-and-clinical smile was gone.

"There's no baby."

"Alyssa said she was pregnant," I countered. "From the look of things, I'm worried, too. Are you saying she lost the baby, because it seems like that's something you should have discussed with her."

Dr. Knight tucked his bottom lip into his upper in one of those placating half-smiles reserved for the apparent ignorance of people like me. His eyes were dark and impatient.

"I'm sorry. You've misunderstood me. Ms. Davis did not miscarry. She wasn't pregnant. Sometimes a cyst like this can cause a missed period. She may have thought she was pregnant." His eyes crinkled, but at least he didn't smile again. "She can probably go home tomorrow morning."

Dr. Knight walked away from me without entertaining the hundreds of questions that popped into my mind. I had been effectively dismissed.

When I got back to Alyssa's room, Steven was there with the food. My stomach gave a noisy grumble of gratitude.

"She's out," he whispered.

Alyssa was still sleeping, unfazed by Dr. Knight's visit. I couldn't quite reconcile Alyssa's and Dr. Knight's versions of what had caused her bleeding. It was difficult to look at her lying there, and I was more than irritated that I hadn't gotten all of the information I would have liked about what exactly they had done about this cyst. Whatever the procedure, the situation had exhausted Alyssa. At least Dillon was on his way. I felt sure he would have better luck getting more detailed information; no doubt the nurses would fill him in before they released Alyssa from the hospital.

I sat down in the second vinyl chair and devoured the food Steven had brought me. It didn't escape me that the Styrofoam container held a careful balance of lean chicken and grilled vegetables. One compartment held a small amount of banana pudding, which was one of my favorites. He probably figured between the fruit and the milk content it would be a healthy enough dessert. I could picture my husband in the cafeteria scrutinizing the choices and suddenly knew why it had taken him as long as it had to return.

Steven was patient enough while I ate, and I was so absorbed in the food that I didn't pick up on his rapidly tapping foot until after I had downed the last of my iced tea. The same way that running his fingers through his hair was a sure sign of stress (and it looked as though the mop atop his head had seen more than its share of finger-combing today), the tapping foot was another of his barometers.

I reached over to calm his bouncing knee, a guilty smile pulling at the corners of my mouth.

"You didn't have to leave work," I told him. "I would have been fine."

He smiled back. "I really need to get back. I hate to leave you guys."

"Problems with the system still?"

"Yeah, there's still a possibility that it's nothing that looks like it's something. None of the higher-ups seem to be concerned. In fact, they practically shooed me out of there. But since Jerry moved into management and I'm the only one with my hands in the data, I feel like I need to get to the bottom of whatever's going on."

"Does it still look like there's some extra data that shouldn't be there or what?" I truly had only the remotest knowledge of what my husband did for a living, but I made a valiant effort to be supportive and remain interested. He had come to more than one conclusion by talking through a problem with me, even though I hadn't the slightest idea what half the computer jargon meant.

Steven rubbed his eyes and peered through the tangled crop of hair.

"I'm still not sure," he said. "We take huge precautions to encrypt our data, keep donor information and recipient information confidential. It would be disastrous for someone to hack into that. I could be paranoid; there's been a weird vibe around the office lately. But on the off-chance that our data could be corrupted or made public, I feel like I need to keep working until I figure out exactly what's going on."

"You were right. I did need to eat. I feel so much better. And Dillon should be here probably within the hour. He only had to drive from Hilton Head. Why don't you go back to work? I'll wait with Alyssa until he gets here, and then I'll head out." I kissed his cheek. "Please don't get your feelings hurt if I'm crashed in the bed smelling like I've been soaking in a bubble bath when you get home."

I stood up. Steven unfolded himself from the chair, eliciting vinyl squeaks as he moved, and gave me a big hug.

"I can't think of anything I'd rather crawl in bed next to than you snoozing away all post-bubbly."

Alyssa lapsed in and out of sleep over the next couple of hours. I shifted between watching her breathe and checking the path of the sun as it dropped lazily over the horizon. When the line of sky above the treetops turned from deep pink through hazy grey and finally to a deep black, the door to Alyssa's room creaked open and Dillon walked in.

He looked tired from driving, the fine sun-lines around his eyes deep beneath a shag of blond curls. Everything about him screamed overgrown kid and I felt that familiar twinge of sympathy rippling below my ribcage, the same as I'd felt earlier for Alyssa.

He gave me a quick nod before his eyes went to his girlfriend. The mask that fell over his face reminded me that I'd had all this time to adjust to how particularly fragile Alyssa looked compared to her usual athletic gracefulness. Dillon had not had that luxury.

I stood up and moved away from the bed so he could get closer.

"How is she?" he asked, snapping his gaze away from her and settling it on me.

"She's been sleeping a lot. The doctor said she'll be fine. She apparently had some sort of cyst on her ovary. I don't really know what they did to take care of it. She was bleeding quite a bit when I brought her in, but that's stopped, so they must have done something. I got the feeling they didn't want to elaborate since I'm not family. I'm sorry I don't know more."

Dillon leaned over and pressed his lips against Alyssa's forehead. She didn't stir.

"Dillon, can I get you anything? I know you drove a long way. I could get something from the cafeteria, or pick something up from outside."

"I ate on the way." He looked embarrassed, as if he had just said something inappropriate. "When I stopped for gas, I grabbed something."

I stood there awkwardly, weighing what I wanted to do. I hated to leave him with such little information. On the other hand, I wanted to give them their privacy. I had stayed to keep Alyssa company if she woke up, but now that Dillon was here, there might be some things they would want to discuss without anyone else around.

I took a deep breath, telling myself to keep my mouth shut. Of course, even as I coached myself, I knew I couldn't mind my own business. My mouth took over.

"Dillon, Alyssa woke up a little while ago. She asked me something, and I'm sorry if I'm butting in where I shouldn't, but given the nature of her bleeding and ... She told me was pregnant and she was worried about the baby."

Dillon's gaze, suddenly sharp as a knife's edge, cut my way.

"I wasn't sure if you two had talked about her maybe being pregnant," I stammered. "I shouldn't even be mentioning it, except ... well, the doctor said she wasn't pregnant, that the cyst might have made her late, you know. Oh my gosh. I just thought you'd want to know what she was thinking in case she asks about it again."

We stared at each other for a moment, but Dillon didn't confirm or deny any knowledge of whether there was a pregnancy.

"I'm so sorry," I repeated when a full minute of silence passed. "I didn't mean to intrude on your business. I'm sure if she thought she was pregnant, it couldn't have been for very long. She probably just hadn't had time to talk to you about it yet."

His blue eyes softened but squinted to slits. I didn't necessarily get an angry vibe from him, but I felt an overwhelming urge to turn and run away from my own insensitivity.

"The doctor said she wasn't pregnant, though." It might have been a question. It was difficult to tell.

"That's what he said, but he didn't discuss it with her. I brought it up to him as he was leaving. I guess he didn't mention it to her because in his eyes it wasn't part of why she's here. If she thought she was pregnant, though, and now she's not, she may wake up thinking she had a miscarriage. That would be tough on her, I think, whether it's true or not."

My hand protectively grazed the front of my jeans. "I just wanted you to be prepared."

"Thanks, Emmalyn. And thanks for taking care of her."

He seemed to put a lot of effort into not looking at me.

Darkness veiled the parking lot except for the glow of a single street light, which dropped a strange blue cast over my car, altering the bronze paint so that I almost didn't recognize it. The air carried that middle-of-the-night beach ambience—a hint of cool, muggy with humidity, a stiff breeze. The sudden awareness that I had spent the entire day at the hospital brought a fatigue over me that weighed down my shoulders. I stood at my driver's door, fumbling through my purse for my keys. I could hear them jingling, but I couldn't seem to get my fingers around them.

"How is the girl?"

I practically yanked my hand from my purse, fully aware that this was not a logical response to being startled in the middle of a dark secluded lot. The young man who had helped me get Alyssa into the ER was standing on the other side of my car. The blue hue of the streetlight washed his pale skin to an even paler shade, turned the maroon of his lips almost black. He stood perfectly still.

For a second, I was mesmerized, my heart pounding against my ribs. I didn't necessarily feel threatened by him, but I couldn't help but wonder if this was what I would do if someone threatening did appear out of nowhere in a dark parking lot with no one else around. Freeze up and stand there like an idiot and let whatever unspeakable thing just happen? No scream? No fight?

I forced a smile. "She's much better." My purse was in front of me, below the level of the window. I moved my hand around inside, silently renewing my search for the keys.

"Thank you so much for your help," I added. I hoped I didn't sound too distracted, or worse, insincere.

"No problem," he said with a strange formality that didn't suit the phrase. A silent pause stretched between us during which I held the hand inside my purse as still as he stood. The moment seemed to be leaving dangerous behind and instead becoming increasingly awkward.

"A lot of blood," he said finally. His upper lip curled a bit as if he might have been disgusted. I certainly had not seen any sign of that when he was helping me lug Alyssa from the car into the wheelchair, but then again, like me, he had also had time to recover from the adrenaline rush of the emergency. Maybe he was one of those average everyday folk who turn heroic under pressure even though their inherent nature wouldn't indicate it. One of those guys that make the neighbors say, "Didn't think he had it in him."

"She's much better now," I assured him. My fingers finally found the jangle of keys. I pulled them out and smiled, this time with less effort. My big goal in life was suddenly to get away from this place with its blood and morbid stories and weird guys in the parking lot and get back to my house with its locked doors and bright lights and pulsating shower head.

"Thank you again. I don't know how I would have managed without you," I said as I hurriedly unlocked the door on my side of the car and slid in behind the wheel.

I turned the key over in the ignition, grateful for the roar of the engine coming to life. I glanced to my right. He was gone, of course—the quick escape artist.

For the first time that day, I wondered what had brought him to this place.

CHAPTER FOUR

Sleep took over the moment I laid my head against the pillow. The rustling of Steven sliding in next to me some time later wasn't quite enough to drag me back to consciousness, but I was aware of having him cozy in behind me and wrap his arm around my waist.

For a moment I drifted back to dreaming. I was running through the corridors of the hospital, chasing the pale young man. He disappeared around every corner just before I could reach him. He was carrying something. At last, he turned down a dead end. I had time to see that he was carrying a newborn baby before he disappeared.

I was vaguely aware that I made some sort of sound deep in my throat.

"You okay?" Steven whispered, his arms tightening around me.

"Did Alyssa say anything to you about being pregnant?" My words were thick with sleep and emotion. I wasn't completely sure if I said them out loud or if this was part of the dream.

"No," Steven said, hesitating. "Is she …"

"I don't think so," I said. Sleep grabbed me again, pulling me back under before I could elaborate.

Steven and I both overslept so we didn't have a chance to talk before we zipped off to work. My head throbbed. Thankfully, I was only slated to fill in a couple of hours at Michelle's, the local ever-so-small-town arts and crafts store that was about one-tenth the size of the better known big-town Michael's. "Accidentally" calling my good friend Michelle's shop by its masculine counterpart was a bad joke that my boss tolerated in the name of friendship.

"You look like hell," she said distractedly when I shuffled into the shop five minutes late. She had an appointment of some sort, which is why I was filling in for her this morning. Otherwise I would have been content to stay in the bed with a soft pillow firmly secured over my head.

Michelle grabbed her purse from behind the counter and scurried toward the door. She waved her keys in the air, mimicking a mismatched set of wind chimes perfectly tuned to create a head-splitting song. "Back before noon," she said over her shoulder as she fumbled with a fan of forms and paper. "Can you hang around a few minutes when I get back? I need to talk to you about something."

"Sure," I said. My lack of enthusiasm was, I'm quite sure, apparent. I didn't much care.

"Good. Thanks, Em." She pushed through the door, and I sighed in the silence.

Eleven-thirty rolled around without a single customer crossing the threshold. I spent an hour unloading stock and squirreling away the boxes to take home with me. Before Michelle returned, I called the hospital to check on Alyssa and was told she had been discharged. I decided not to bother her and Dillon at home, telling myself she was probably resting. Truthfully, I was relieved at not having to talk to her right away. The idea sent an uneasy quiver across my skin.

I was sure my reticence had to do with Alyssa's pregnancy, or lack of pregnancy, or the bleeding, or the ghostly fellow with the red lips, or the dream about him disappearing with the baby, Alyssa's baby, I assumed, or mine. Okay, I wasn't at all sure where the hesitation to check on Alyssa originated. Perhaps it was a combination of everything. Hormones, maybe. I only knew that not calling to follow up was outside my normal nature. It wasn't like me to shirk compassion, and that bothered me.

Michelle interrupted my self-torture by flinging open the door. "How was business?" she practically hollered across the store.

"Slow," I said.

Michelle wore a peach suit jacket and matching skirt that hugged her body in an expensively tailored silhouette. Her hair was expertly flipped at the ends and perfectly puffed at the crown, even with the carefully placed Chanel sunglasses straddling the top of her head. Her dark brown eyes simmered behind a fringe of extra-long lashes. She came seriously close to appearing richly comical in our sleepy little town, except anything less manicured would have seemed weirdly pretentious on her. This was Michelle—at church, at work, the ball fields, it didn't matter. I massaged my fingertips against my forehead for a moment, hoping to shake my worry and fatigue and climb the energy ladder to somewhere remotely approaching her level.

"What kind of sales?" she asked. She tossed her bag onto the counter.

"Well, none. Like I said, slow morning."

Michelle planted a hand on one hip. "That's what I was afraid of," she sighed. "I'm sorry, Em. I know you love it here."

The look in her eye alerted me to what was coming, so I wasn't shocked at what she said next.

"I can't keep you on, hon." She reached out and touched my hand, which was a practiced gesture but also genuine. "Not with the economy in the shape it's in right now. The ladies in town just aren't able to keep up with their craft projects right now. It's a shame. Lord, but I do appreciate you coming in to cover for me. I suppose I might be able to keep my little store afloat if I throw on the old duds and take care of the inventory myself."

I almost laughed as a picture of Michelle in 'old duds'—wedge heels, crisply creased capris, and drapes of silver bracelets—sprang to mind. Instead I bit my bottom lip, which might have given her the idea that I was sad at the news because she tightened her grip on my wrist.

"Oh hon," she said. "I'm so sorry. I just can't keep anybody on right now. You understand?"

I put my hand over hers. "I completely understand, Michelle. You shouldn't feel bad. I know it's not personal."

I slid off my stool and she hugged me. I hugged her back.

"Things'll get better. Maybe you can come back."

"Well sure," I said. I had intended, sometime in the near future, to tell her that Steven and I were expecting, and that I might not be working after the baby was born, but it didn't seem the time to bring it up now. "Can't keep a good man down."

"Is that a Michael's joke?" she said.

"It might be," I told her.

She giggled and waved, shooing me toward the door.

"Oh yeah," I said. "I set aside a couple of boxes. Trying to pack away a few things at home. Do you mind?"

"No, not at all," she said.

I scooted past her into the back room and returned with my stack of boxes.

"I almost forgot," she said. "Samantha Bedding came by yesterday, asking questions about you." Her voice was suddenly animated with the high pitch of curiosity. "Are you about to be famous in our little paper?"

I forced a smile. "Good heavens. I hope not. I can't imagine what kinds of questions she could possibly have about me." Yes, I was fishing.

"Well, I think she was just trying to get a picture of what you're like in the everyday. You and Steven are such a cute couple. Just a shining example of what a young married couple should be. Maybe she'll be writing about that," she said cheerfully. As ridiculous as it sounded, it wasn't completely out of the question. Michelle was apparently familiar with the typical riveting *Gazette* content.

"That would certainly make for an exciting read," I said, sarcasm dripping, and rolled my eyes dramatically.

"You're so silly," she said, opening the door so I could squeeze through with my boxes. "You'll come by and get your check?"

"Yes, I'll drop back by." I nodded as I left.

. . .

I shrugged off my dismissal from employment with little remorse and decided I didn't have the excess energy to devote to whatever it was Samantha Bedding was up to. I was too worried about Alyssa. By the time I got home, guilt had taken a stronghold.

Steven called within a few minutes to say he would be working late.

"How was your day?" he asked. "You doing okay?"

"I'm good," I replied, which was true on the most basic level. "Any word from Alyssa?"

"Dillon called and said they were letting her leave the hospital. That seems like a good sign, that they're not keeping her."

"Yeah. I called the hospital this morning. She'd already been released. I decided not to bother her and Dillon. Figured they needed some privacy. I want to talk to her though, see if she's okay. But I don't want to intrude. This might be a difficult time for her."

"We'll check in, but I think you're right. We'll give her some time. Do you remember talking to me when I came to bed last night?" His voice shifted gears, humming with trepidation.

"Maybe. I was so tired, and I was having weird dreams. Did I say something about her …" My throat seized up. I couldn't bring myself to say the rest.

Steven understood where I was going. "Yes, but I wasn't sure how much was real and how much was sleep-talking?" He chuckled, but it was a dry laugh.

"I was pretty out of it, but if I said something about her being pregnant, I wasn't talking gibberish. She told me she was pregnant, but the doctor said she wasn't. I'm not sure what to think."

"We'll talk to her. See how things are going."

"I thought I'd bring you dinner since you're working late." I needed the change of subject matter.

"You know I'd love that," he said, "but you're tired. Why don't you stay home and rest up?"

I silently dismissed that idea. I had already grabbed some

vegetables from the fridge. A quick stir-fry would be easy.

"About that," I said, figuring I should let him in on my lack of employment. "We didn't have a single customer at the store this morning, so when Michelle came back from her meeting … well, she kind of … let me go."

"As in let you go home or laid you off?"

"That last one. She likes having someone to crawl around in the boxes for her, but I guess she can't afford an extra employee right now. You think we'll be okay? It's not the greatest timing with needing stuff for the baby and all."

"We'll be fine," he said. "It'll give you a little more time to get things ready, especially if I'm going to be caught up here more than usual."

I sighed. "Let's hope that doesn't become a trend. Meanwhile, I feel like having dinner with my husband, so I'll be over a little later."

"Okay, babe. Can't wait."

Jerry Sanford was the first to greet me when I entered Steve's office building.

"Look at you," he said, offering me a hug. "Bringing dinner to your poor slaving husband. We should all be so lucky."

"How are you, Jerry?" I asked, genuinely glad to see how well he looked. I was also pleased that he didn't bombard me with questions about Alyssa. Note to self: Thank my husband for keeping my involvement on the down-low.

Jerry's chemo treatments had taken quite a toll on him physically. It had taken months, but a healthy glow had finally returned to his once sallow skin. He was still thin, but I could see he was filling out. He looked more like the Jerry I had met on that company picnic at the lake two years ago, before he got sick.

"You really look good."

"Never felt better." He made a show of broadening his shoulders, sticking out his jaw, and comically hiking his pants up at the waist like a country bumpkin trying to impress the ladies.

I laughed. "Is it okay if I go on back to Steven's office?"

"Sure thing," he said. He looked around conspiratorially, as if he didn't want anyone to overhear. "Between you and me, I told that husband of yours he should get on home to his wife, quit worrying about this little kink he thinks he's found in the system, but he wouldn't have any part of it."

"Well, I appreciate that," I said, unsure how to react to the comment. The selfish little part of me that had me pouting earlier agreed. I pushed that side of myself away. Steven obviously felt the problem was much more serious than Jerry did. I supposed it was possible that Steven was hoping to get things running smoothly without raising any red flags within the company.

"He can take things a bit seriously," I whispered back, playing along with the mock secrecy.

"Get back there and feed him." Jerry nudged my arm. "The man needs some nourishment if he's going to work these late hours. Then how about seeing if you can't get him to go home and relax a little. I've looked over the system myself and I can't see any great threat that couldn't wait till morning."

"I'll see what I can do," I said. I popped Jerry a little wink before heading down the hall.

Steven was engrossed in what he was doing, I could tell. He sat hunched over his keyboard, staring at the large monitor on his desk. It looked to me like he had at least four screens open at once. I watched for a moment as he moved back and forth between them, the cursor jumping from quadrant to quadrant, the bars at the top of each one randomly highlighting from grey to blue and back to grey as he entered and exited the screens. A spread of papers littered his desk and the floor next to his chair.

"Hey, babe," he said after a moment. "Come on in. I'll find a stopping place here in a second."

I obliged by finding an empty spot on his credenza and unpacking our dinner.

"How's it going?" I cut my eyes to the monitor and handed him a plate and drink.

Steven scooped a fork full of rice, shoved it into his mouth, and ate hungrily. I was glad I had brought dinner; I wondered if he would have eaten if I hadn't. Funny, I thought. Yesterday he was worried about me not eating and today I was making sure he took time out to eat. Feeding one another hadn't been in our wedding vows, but perhaps it should have been. *For dinner or lunch*, I thought, smiling.

He reached out with his foot and swung the door most of the way shut.

"Let me show you something," he said, pointing to one of the open screens.

I felt my expression glaze over. All I saw were rows of letters and numbers. It meant nothing to me.

"Every piece of data we keep is encoded," he said by way of explanation. "For every bag of blood we inventory, all the information we need is stored in this code. The type, the date we took it in, exactly where it's located, that kind of thing. We don't keep the information on the donor except in the most cryptic format. It's not like we could look in here and say, 'Hey, we're running low on AB pos; let's go find Johnny Brown and see if he can spare a pint.' We do, however, keep the age of the donor, any medications that were taken by the donor preceding, and all of the blood is tested for certain antibodies. That info is in there as well."

I nodded. It didn't make the Greek on the screen any more readable, but so far everything Steven said made sense. I could wrap my brain around the idea of codes for this stuff, and the importance of keeping the data protected. It seemed to me if the codes got messed up, the whole process would come to a grinding halt.

Steven continued after a brief glance at the door. "Everything in that respect is cool." He pointed to a different frame on the monitor. "Here's where the problem might lie, if there is a problem. See these codes. See how they're organized differently than the ones I just showed you. I've never seen these before. They don't follow our normal protocol."

"So you have some bogus information in the system?" I ventured.

"Could be bogus, but I don't think so. I think this data was put here on purpose. The way it was set up, I shouldn't have ever been able to see it. There's no telling how long it's been sitting in the background. I only found it because I took a look at the source programming. There was some code in there that seemed extraneous, but when I broke it down and dug a little deeper, it led me to this database. And it was crafty, the way it was hidden. I tweaked the code to allow user access."

I couldn't imagine deciphering such a thing, but I was impressed. "Why is it there?"

Steven ran his fingers over the top of his head, elbows splayed out like heavy wings. The curls of his hair bunched away from his face for a second before they fell back down to veil his eyes.

"That's the million dollar question. I can't say for certain what the point of it is. I really don't want to even go where my mind is heading with this."

I sat a little straighter as he went on.

"Remember the blood drive last week?"

Of course I did. I remembered it being a really weird day that ended extremely well.

"Look at this code, Em." Steven moved his mouse until one of the codes near the top left of his monitor was highlighted.

"Remember what I told you about donor information?"

I nodded again.

"On the surface, this string of mnemonics may not seem like anything unusual. But when I applied some of our basic protocols to this code and parsed it down into segments, I started to recognize information."

He took a moment to gather together a clump of papers from the side of his desk and shook them as if they held the key. Perhaps they did. I could see that he had taken bits of the code and worked out what looked a lot like some of the algorithms I had forgotten from the single computer science class I had nearly failed in college.

Steven pointed his finger at one of the codes on the screen. "Emmalyn," he said. "I think this is me."

CHAPTER FIVE

"What does it mean?" I asked stupidly. I didn't care for the expression on Steven's face. His eyes had gone wide, not exactly with fright, but I had to admit I had never seen my husband frightened, so I couldn't be sure.

In a whisper, he said, "I tracked myself after the last blood drive." He pointed back to the first set of codes, the legitimate ones.

"This is definitely me." He highlighted a small section of the code, said, "Blood type O neg," then quickly highlighted another segment of the string of numbers. "This is the year I was born, so we have the donor's age."

He nudged the cursor further along the code and highlighted eight numbers.

"This is the inventory code on the pint I donated—03271942. I remember staring at it while they were taking the blood and realizing it was my dad's birthday, which was a weird coincidence—why it stuck in my head, I guess—but it tracks to where the blood is located. There's some other stuff, but never mind that. Look at this other code."

Steven glanced at the door again and swung the cursor back to the quadrant containing the illegitimate codes he had uncovered.

"*This* code contains the exact same information."

I had to stare at it for a moment, because it did contain the same information, but the string was periodically broken and interspersed with other numbers and letters, so the similarities weren't immediately apparent.

"I see it," I said after a moment, "but what does the extra stuff stand for?"

Steven's brow had been drawn into a perpetual frown the whole time he'd been showing me the codes.

"I don't have a clue. Not really. I could be completely off-base. I might even be making the data in this code match things about myself, match the other code … subconsciously, maybe. Except that mine, if it is mine, isn't the only one. I ran a comparison between the two files, and every one of our legitimate codes has a partner code in the hidden database. I've been running it in the background and it's taken three days. That's why I've been hanging around every night till everybody goes home and trying to be the first one in. I don't necessarily want anyone to know what I'm doing until I figure out more."

"I wonder why," I muttered, referring to the longer codes. I didn't really expect more explanation.

"That's what I don't know. LifeShare is expanding all the time. We just started using the new storage wing in the east section of the basement because our inventory has grown so much. If the code needed expanding to track storage, no one talked to me about it, which they should have. That's the only thing I can think of." He rubbed his hands across his face, his fingers digging into his weary eyes for a moment. When he looked up, he seemed to tense.

Through the cracked door, I caught a glimpse of Jerry coming down the hall. I had been under the impression that he was leaving, but apparently he was working late as well. He raised his hand to acknowledge me, and I waved back.

"Sweetie, you're tired." I wrapped my arms around Steven's neck. My eyes, of their own volition, wandered to the highlighted code on the screen. I tried to picture my husband encapsulated in the apparently innocuous string of numbers and letters. Part of me knew that this sort of thing went on all the time. No doubt the database behind my discount card at the supermarket stored something similar. That didn't unnerve me, so why should this?

"Any chance you can call it a day?" I massaged Steven's shoulders, hoping to relax him and lure him home with me. "Sometimes things become much clearer after a good night's sleep."

My concern extended beyond an overworked husband. Somewhere in the back of my mind, I was aware that I just wanted him away from this place. The tone in his voice had seriously freaked me out.

"Come on, hon," I reiterated as cheerfully as possible while I began gathering up our finished plates.

Steven moved his mouse around, closing the windows on his screen.

"Okay," he said. "You win."

It was a small victory, but one I was more than happy to claim.

The phone rang early, stepping in as third snooze to my alarm's first two attempts.

I fumbled for the handset, finally managing to press the talk button.

"Emmalyn? Hi. It's Dillon Evans." His voice sounded strained, weirdly at odds with my visual of his surfer's easy good looks.

I sat up in bed, suddenly alert. Immediately, I was concerned for Alyssa. I should have checked on her. Yesterday's guilt came rocketing back.

"I'm sorry to bother you so early," he continued. "It sounds like you were still sleeping."

"That's okay, Dillon. My alarm was about to go off. Is Alyssa okay?"

"That's why I'm calling. She seems fine physically." Dillon let out a sigh and continued in a softer voice. "She's still having trouble with the pregnancy thing. I mean, we went to her regular doctor to have her checked out. He seems to be in agreement with Dr. Knight—the doctor who saw her in the hospital—that she was never pregnant. I don't know what to do about it. No matter what I say, it's the wrong thing. She gets mad if I try to convince her she wasn't, but it's hard for me to give her sympathy for a baby she just *thinks* she lost. I'm not that good of an actor."

I had no idea how to respond to this. "Is there anything I can do?" It seemed like an empty offer.

"I have to go out of town again. My work—I just can't get out of it, and the doctor assured me that she's not in any danger. Otherwise I'd find a way to stay with her."

"Of course you would."

"I wondered if you wouldn't mind checking in on her. I don't want to push her, but I think it would be good for her to go back to work. Give her something else to think about?" He sounded guilty for even considering this.

The mention of the office reminded me of Steven's problem with the database. I pushed that thought aside and tried to concentrate on Dillon and Alyssa. Whether or not there had been a baby, her trip to the hospital had obviously shaken her up pretty badly.

"I'd be happy to check on her, Dillon," I said, "as long as she's okay with it."

There was a short pause before Dillon responded. "Actually, she's mentioned a couple of times she'd like to talk to you. Maybe because you were there at the hospital. I thought since you were the first person to talk to Dr. Knight, she might believe ... you know, about the baby ... if you talked to her. She thinks I'm the one in denial."

I thought I heard a catch in his voice. I hated for something like this to come between Dillon and Alyssa. This whole situation had an ominous ring to it.

"When are you going out of town?"

"Today. I'll be gone through next weekend. Normally that's not a problem."

"And does Alyssa know you called me?"

"Well, no," he admitted.

"I'm going to give her a call in an hour or so," I said, formulating a plan. "I'll see if she'll go out for lunch with me.

Hopefully it won't be weird for her; I just got laid off at Michelle's so I'll work that into the conversation, take the focus off what she's been through. Maybe getting out, away from her thoughts, will make her feel better. I don't know that I can convince her Dr. Knight was telling her the truth about the baby, though."

Mostly because I wasn't completely convinced myself. Sure, a doctor knew better about these things, but I also knew how I'd felt when I had first conceived. I would have sworn I could feel the difference in myself practically the next morning. Of course, the logical side of me had waited to see the positive results of a pregnancy test. Even without that confirmation, though, I knew. A tiny part of my brain held out the possibility that maybe Alyssa had been so newly pregnant that it hadn't been apparent to the doctors at the hospital. If they hadn't checked her hormone levels, maybe they just missed it.

I wondered if instead of trying to convince Alyssa that she had never been pregnant, it might be better to sympathize with her loss. Maybe all she needed was for someone to believe her.

Three hours later I stood on Alyssa's front doorstep. I hesitated before ringing the doorbell. Being there brought on an odd sense of *déjà vu* so I had to keep reminding myself that I wasn't going to have to barge in on the poor girl and haul her, bleeding, off to the hospital.

Drawing a deep breath, I punched the doorbell. A few seconds later, Alyssa opened the door. Dressed in a smart black ensemble that was sporty without being athletic, she looked like herself again. It was hard to believe she had been in such bad shape only a few days ago.

"Wow, you look great!" I blurted out before my filter kicked in. Relief overwhelmed me. I realized I had been expecting to see a depressed, pitiful version of her.

"Thanks," she said. She looked a little embarrassed, which was out of character for the Alyssa I knew. "Come on in."

"You look like you're feeling better," I said.

"I am." The lilt in her voice made it sound more like a question than a statement.

"You know, that was quite an ordeal you went through," I ventured. "Anybody would understand if you didn't snap back right away."

Alyssa wandered into the kitchen without offering an invitation to follow. She ran some water into a glass and washed down a pill from a prescription bottle. No explanation there either.

"You don't have to do that," she said, suddenly setting the glass down and cutting her eyes toward me.

"Do what?" I took a small step toward her, stopping just inside the kitchen doorway.

"You don't have to placate me. It's not like I'm going to break. I had to go to the hospital. I probably would have bled to death if you hadn't come over here to check on me. And thanks, by the way. I'm thinking I probably didn't say that before."

A half-smile crossed her face before she turned to drop the glass into the sink.

"That's not necessary."

"Yes it is." Her voice was forceful, practically cutting me off. "It's absolutely necessary to thank someone for saving your life."

Alyssa kept her back turned to me. I jumped as a bout of cracked laughter burst from her throat. The laughter, if that's what it was, only lasted a short second. I watched Alyssa's shoulders hitch. After a moment, I realized she was crying.

"Oh, Alyssa," I said and stepped toward her.

"Don't!" she screeched and turned around to face me.

When I saw the look on her face, I was glad that the kitchen island formed a barrier between us. Frown lines drew her forehead into a scowl of anger. I wasn't sure if the anger was directed at me, but I felt the brunt of it like a slap to the face.

"Do not feel sorry for me." She sobbed the order.

I kept dutifully quiet, my hands braced against the island countertop. I knew if I let go, they would be shaking.

"You saved my life and I'm not even really grateful," she spat.

"Don't say that," I muttered.

She kind of staggered back against the cabinets, one hand holding tight to the edge of the sink while she wiped her forehead with the other. Her hand lingered there until she finally looked up at me from under the veil it formed.

"Because *I* should have done something," she finally blurted. "I knew something was wrong and I just laid there. I didn't do anything. I didn't call Dillon. I didn't try to get to the doctor."

"Alyssa," I said slowly, testing the waters of her temper. "I saw you. I saw how sick you were. You were not in any shape to take care of yourself."

"You don't understand."

"Then tell me," I replied steadily, steeling myself for a conversation I really did not want to have.

"I knew as soon as I gave blood at work last week that something was wrong."

I stood a little straighter. "What?" The word came out as a whisper.

"Something happened." She shook her head as if trying to clear some confusion. "I don't know how to explain it."

"Something happened when you gave blood?" I asked, not knowing where this could possibly be going. I knew my voice sounded skeptical, but I couldn't help it. I had been prepared, sort of, to talk about the baby. This turn in the conversation had rendered me as confused as Alyssa looked.

"You're pregnant, right?" she said, squinting at me.

"Steven told you?" I blurted, surprised.

"No," she said. For the first time since I had entered the house, I thought a genuine smile lit up her face. "I can tell."

A beat passed as her expression faded to stone again. "I think we … women, put off a vibe. I can tell just by being near you. It's no different from me being able to tell I was pregnant … before."

I opened my mouth to do Dillon's bidding, to tell her that I had heard Dr. Knight declare that there had never been a baby, but I couldn't make myself say the words. Whether it was true or not, the intensity in her eyes told me that she believed it. Who was I to tell her any differently?

"Dillon doesn't believe me. He filled me in. I know you talked to the doctor," she said, freeing me from making a decision about how much I should say.

"I know what he told me," I said with enough ambiguity to leave her an opening.

"Dillon doesn't know," she said, looking me directly in the eye. "I took a pregnancy test. It was positive."

This was a new development. I couldn't believe I hadn't thought to ask about a pregnancy test.

"I had it in the bathroom, on the side of the tub. I was going to show it to Dillon when he got home from his trip." She sounded wistful and rightfully so.

I suppose the question was evident on my face because she chose to answer what I was thinking.

"I couldn't find it when I came home from the hospital. I looked everywhere, Emmalyn. Retraced my steps a million times, hoping I could come up with some other place I might have put it. Saying I had it and not being able to produce it—it just makes me look crazy, but I'm not crazy."

"Nobody thinks you're crazy, Lys."

The pain on her face struck me like a blow to the chest. Without thinking, I slid around the island and gathered her into a hug.

"I'm sorry about your baby," I said.

She laid her head on my shoulder and cried.

"I can't believe what a relief that was," Alyssa said when we were settled at the restaurant.

She had picked a favorite haunt of hers, a little sports bar in a nearby strip mall, if you could call it that. Basically, the bar occupied the end unit of three attached buildings on the side of the road near a three-way stop. There was nothing fancy about the place, but we were surrounded by television screens covering football, baseball, boxing, and tennis. Alyssa was an avid sports fan and the TVs offered ample distraction. The buzz created by the competing games created a kind of white noise I think we both found liberating.

"What's that?" I was distracted enough by the easy atmosphere that I didn't pick up on her meaning.

"To have someone believe me."

I fumbled with my napkin under the table. "Do you think you'll be able to let Dillon off the hook?" I asked. "He's just worried about you. And he's a guy," I said lightly. "Nothing against men, but I think it's harder for them to accept the women's intuition thing. They're more logical than we are. If I were a man and a doctor told me something scientific that contradicted something more intuitive, I'm pretty sure I'd go with the science. Seriously, he's really worried about you. And he loves you."

"I know," she conceded. "I'll try to give him a break."

Talking about Dillon reminded me of his concern about Alyssa returning to work. Probably nothing more than him wanting things to return to normal, but I felt compelled to mention it since he had brought it up.

"Are you feeling well enough to go back to work soon?" I asked casually after the waitress had delivered our food. I picked up my knife and began cutting my sandwich into quarters.

"Did Steven say something about me not being there? I haven't used all my sick time." Her wide eyes lifted to meet mine for an instant before returning to her plate.

"No, I was just wondering."

"I'm not sure I want to go back there."

"Why?" I wondered out loud. Never mind being rude; I was truly curious. "I thought you liked your job."

"I do. I did," she clarified. "But the atmosphere is different. It used to be this easy-going place, but something's changed over the last couple of months. Everybody's more uptight."

I thought of Jerry and how cordially he had greeted me at the office last night. He had even encouraged me to get Steven out of there; he seemed genuinely concerned that my husband was working too hard.

Of course, that was completely counter to the intensity I felt from Steven. He was equally worried about this problem with the database and the implications it might have. I wondered if Steven was one of the "uptight" Alyssa was referring to.

She went on without any prompting from me. "I can't do those blood drives anymore." She actually shivered, the way I did sometimes when I thought about spiders. For me, it was an involuntary reaction to something I found repulsive. Maybe she felt that way about needles. Steven did say she usually managed to avoid giving blood.

I said as much. "Can't you get out of them for the most part? I mean, I know the company would like all of the employees to participate, but it's not like they're mandatory, right?"

"Steven told you, huh?" Mischief turned the corners of her mouth up into a smile.

"He might have mentioned it. He wasn't saying anything bad about you. I don't want you to get that idea," I added quickly. He had mentioned it strictly in the way one discusses a friend, with no judgmental connotations at all, and I would have hated for Alyssa to think otherwise.

"No way." She dismissed my concern with the wave of her hand. "He's practically my partner in crime. I think he would help me make up excuses to get out of it if I asked him."

I laughed and took a long sip of my iced tea.

One of the TV screens had captured Alyssa's attention. My eyes followed hers. We watched while two teams I didn't recognize bent to face each other in a lineup. I assumed this was a rerun of a prior season game, which I totally could not imagine watching by choice. The quarterback hiked the ball and the players scattered for a moment, then converged back on one another and promptly tumbled into a pile. She shook her head, silently chastising some fumbled play that she apparently understood.

We ate quietly for a few minutes. I remembered Alyssa's

comment from back at her house. "What did you mean when you said something happened when you gave blood last week?"

She caught my gaze. "It wasn't right," she said hesitantly. "I may have passed out there for a second. I guess they weren't watching me that closely because I asked the nurses and they said they thought I was awake the whole time. You know, I'm officially tired of having medical people tell me the exact opposite of whatever I think is going on with my own body."

She looked angry again. I didn't envy the array of emotions she had to be feeling.

"You know what," I said, remembering. "Steven came home that day looking really lethargic and kind of out of it. He snapped out of it pretty quickly after he ate dinner, but I remember he said he thought the nurse taking the blood wasn't very good with a needle. He said a lot of people complained."

"Well, the needle stick didn't seem any worse than any other, but then, I always think it sucks getting stuck. Sorry," she added quickly, apparently for what she thought I might perceive as inappropriate language.

I tried not to grin.

"I hate needles," she said, "but that's not what bothered me, not really. What I mean is I went in to it feeling fine. Well, fine relatively, because I was all bent out of shape about the process as usual. When I came out I felt different."

"Lightheaded?"

"Not exactly. At first I felt weirdly energetic. Then I felt like I was losing something," she said drearily.

The words could have been a bad pun except that she said them without the slightest hint of humor. I wasn't sure if she was referring to the blood, or something infinitely more important.

CHAPTER SIX

Steven got home from work a little early, which was a pleasant surprise. I wasn't hungry after my lunch out with Alyssa so I fired up the outdoor grill and put on a burger for Steven. The evening had turned brisk again and it felt good to be outside in the cool air.

Steven followed me out and plopped into one of the lounge chairs on the patio. He looked exhausted. I was glad he had decided to come home. Maybe a weekend away from the office would clear his mind. I felt slightly unsupportive because I hadn't asked him about the database problem. On the other hand, if he wanted to talk about it, he would bring it up.

I poked at the singed burger and watched the pale red juices erupt from the holes. Call it what you wanted—it was blood. I cringed.

"I had lunch with Alyssa today."

I hated that something as random as a chunk of hamburger brought my mind back to Alyssa. I suddenly remembered the bloody towels I had stowed away in the trunk of my car and had to turn away from the smoldering meat on the grill. The towels were still in there; I had completely forgotten about them. My stomach did a little flip at the thought of even seeing them, much less touching them long enough to put them in the washer. They were probably stained beyond saving now anyway. I made a mental note to ask Steven to put them in the trash for me later.

"Yeah? How is she?" Steven said, blessedly tugging me away from my less than pleasant train of thoughts. "I haven't heard anything about her coming back to work."

"We actually talked about that a little. I don't know exactly what her plans are, but it didn't sound like she was anxious to come back."

"Is she still having problems with that cyst or the bleeding or something?"

I don't know if it was the use of the words *"that* cyst" or the fact that my husband had his hands folded behind his head, eyes closed, way too relaxed, when he said *that*, but I lapsed into an instant bout of reverse chauvinism.

"You think she should be back at work already?" I snapped, instantly snarky. What did he think? That just because she wasn't bleeding half to death, that she ought to jump back on the job, that she might not need a few days to heal emotionally?

Steven opened his eyes to slits. "I'm pretty sure there was some hidden meaning in what you just said, but ..."

"I was just hoping you weren't thinking she should buck up, take it like a man, get back in the saddle, any of that crap."

"Pissed much?" he said.

"Insensitive much?" I countered.

Yes, we were usually the super-in-love semi-newlyweds 'bout to have a baby, but occasionally we did sink down into the Venus-Mars warzone, and that was perfectly normal, I told myself while I steeled my reserves for an argument.

The hands came out from behind the head. So long, rest and relaxation. At least that was something.

"Oh boy," he said a bit too softly, then before I could lash out, "All I did was ask if she was ready to come back to work."

"Yeah, but with ... attitude."

"Attitude?" Steven dropped one foot to the ground as he sat up. The heel of his hand pressed against the corner of his forehead and one visible eye gazed up at me accusingly.

He wasn't really fighting back. And I was starting to feel foolish.

"Why are you looking at me like that?" I yelped. My voice actually cracked. Dang hormones.

"You're brandishing a giant fork?" It was a question, for sure, as if he wanted to know if this was the right answer.

I slipped a look at the fork, which I was holding like a tiny two-pronged scepter.

Tears sprang up in my eyes so I turned and pressed the back of the fork down on top of the sizzling burger. More juices dripped, my stomach lurched, and red flame flared upward, momentarily licking at the edges of the charred meat.

I ran to the edge of the patio and barfed into the grass. Behind me, the barbecue spear that was my weapon clanged onto the concrete.

"Oh boy." Definitely not spoken under his breath this time. Steven was instantly by my side, holding my shoulders. "What's wrong?"

I spit a couple of times and wiped the tears from my eyes.

"Hamburger," I muttered. "Gross." I turned around and dragged my hand across my nose. My other hand went up as a shield, blocking my view of the grill.

Steven bobbed his head in a quick little series of nods, bent and grabbed the barbecue fork, stabbed it into the burger, and lobbed his dinner into the woods the way you might fling a tennis ball for a game of catch with the dog.

"Better?" he said.

Laughter spilled out of me like a dammed-up river finally breaking through a stubborn wall of stone. He just stood there, poor thing, arms akimbo, kind of frozen in place, with this goofy puzzled expression on his face. My river of giggles rushed, then bubbled, then finally smoothed out to a steady flow. By the time I was finished with my little fit, I was bent over at the waist, hands on knees, gasping for breath. I swiped at my eyes again.

"Was that, like, pregnancy?" Steven asked. "Or are you just crazy?"

"Hormones, funny boy. You're really lucky I don't have that fork right now." An unexpected chuckle made my belly contract and threatened to throw me into another laughing attack.

"You may never be allowed to have this fork again." He shifted it behind his back.

I plopped down onto the lounge chair. "So now what're you gonna do about dinner?"

"Yeah, thanks, by the way, for cooking me up that juicy burger."

I waved my hand at him. "Never—ever—say that word again." A moan escaped my lips as I pressed my hand against my belly."

"What? Burger?"

I shook my head.

"Thanks?"

"No, doofus."

"Oh, jui—"

"Naawp!" I blurted, cutting him off. "I said don't say it."

"What? Jui—"

"Don't!"

"Okay, babe, I won't ever say jui—"

"Not funny!" I yelled, but I was laughing and he was right there with me, only louder.

I went to brush my teeth while Steven rummaged through the pantry for a replacement for his banished burger. When I came back, he was slurping on a cup of ramen. Not exactly the most appetizing sound in the world, but my stomach managed to keep itself under control.

"So, you never really answered me about what's going on with Alyssa. Not that I want to set you off again."

"Yeah, sorry about that. The cyst, bleeding, whatever, it sounds like it was a one-time deal. She's fine, physically. Emotionally, I don't know. That part's taking a little longer."

"Makes sense," he said.

"Let me ask you something. Doesn't LifeShare have a policy against letting pregnant women give blood? From what I've read online, most agencies don't allow it."

"So you believe her now?" he asked, the outside corners of his mouth turning down as if he didn't know what to make of it.

"I don't *not* believe her. She said she took a pregnancy test and it was positive."

"Hmmm. Well, yeah, I'm pretty sure it's on the list of ineligibilities, but maybe not in the first trimester. I'm a guy; I've never paid attention to that part of the pamphlet. Did she know she was pregnant before she donated? It's ultimately up to the donor to let us know. We wouldn't let an obviously pregnant woman give blood, but if we can't tell…" He trailed off.

I shrugged. "She didn't say. I don't know if she did the pregnancy test before or after giving blood. I assume after. I can't imagine her donating if she knew, except I think she did know, even without the test, so that doesn't make sense. She was kind of confiding in me today about the whole thing. Talking about it seemed to make her feel better. I hated to ask too many prying questions. I especially didn't want to say anything that might make her think she did something to cause a miscarriage."

"God no," he agreed. "It's weird, though. She usually finds a way to get out of the blood drives. Of all times, it sounds like this might have been the one she had a legitimate excuse for."

"You did say the company was pushing employees pretty hard to participate this time around. Is it possible she could have felt so pressured that she would have given blood, even knowing she might be pregnant?"

"I can't imagine. Alyssa's never been one to stand down on an issue. But if she was pregnant, it being so early and all, I can see her not wanting the whole office to know about it yet. The whole thing doesn't add up, though, does it?"

I had to agree. I'd wish-washed so many times over the past couple of days about whether she was pregnant, or wasn't pregnant, I just couldn't be sure anymore.

"You really think there's a chance she might not come back?" Steven asked.

"It sounded that way. She doesn't like the atmosphere there— more intense, I think she said. Something like that."

"Well, she's right about that. I thought it was just my imagination. I don't like this situation for her, but I'm glad to hear I'm not the only one who's picked up on it."

"I was thinking about that," I said after a moment, wondering if I really wanted to head down this road. "I talked to Jerry for a few minutes before I came to your office last night. If anything, he seemed to be more easy-going. He encouraged me to try to get you to go home, quit worrying about the problem with the database. He definitely didn't seem to be taking it as seriously as you are."

Steven looked uncomfortable. He got up and tossed his ramen cup into the trash and threw his fork into the dishwasher.

I tried to catch his eye, but he wasn't looking at me. "Did I say something wrong? I didn't mean to imply that you shouldn't be taking it seriously."

Steven looked up at me, biting the inside of his lip—another stress indicator.

"What are you thinking?" I prompted.

"Before Jerry took his medical leave, this is exactly the kind of snafu he would have taken seriously. But now that he's back—and my boss ..." He trailed off for a second. "I've tried talking to him about it. Half the time he brushes it off. He doesn't seem to think it's a big deal, and he's adamant that he doesn't think our system's been breached, which is exactly what I do think, although for the life of me I can't figure out why or how."

"Maybe his heart's not in the job anymore. Do you think that's possible? I mean, he's riding a pretty big high right now as a cancer survivor. Maybe he's shifted his priorities."

"Well, then, he needs to step aside and let somebody do the job who can get his head in the game."

For a moment, I just stared at Steven. Those were quite possibly the harshest words I had ever heard him speak. The fact that they were about a friend was even more disturbing.

Steven must have picked up on my disapproval.

"I can't believe I just said that," he amended. "I'm way too stressed over this."

Stressed, yes. Enough to make a comment like that—I thought not. Once again, I felt as back and forth as a kid on a high-flying swing, and it felt dangerous.

CHAPTER SEVEN

For all my pregnancy-induced sleepiness, I was surprised when my eyes popped open just as dawn was breaking on Saturday morning. I made a valiant effort to go back to sleep but couldn't ignore the sounds of Steven's annoyingly peaceful snoozing and the chipper song of those early birds we all love so much, except when they stage their musical production right outside your bedroom window.

I gave up and climbed out of the bed, gobbled down a bowl of cereal, and was pulling on some grub clothes for tackling the mess in the nursery when Steven's cell rang and vibrated across the nightstand.

After a couple of groans and some lengthy stretching, he rolled over and grabbed the phone. I heard a few uh-huhs and a yeah or two, then he finally hung up.

"What's going on?" I asked.

"Jerry," he said. "He wants me to come in to the office for a little while."

"What for?"

"I don't know." His voice was thick with sleep but he was already moving, sliding into a slightly used pair of jeans.

"Well, I mean, is it just you coming in? Does it have something to do with the database? Do you think they know what you're up to looking at the codes?" I was rattling off questions and I had a million more.

Steven stopped me. "It's okay, Em," he said, giving me his best nonchalant face. "The boss has called in a group of us. Apparently there's some kind of press release coming out involving LifeShare and the company wants to make sure we hear whatever it is firsthand. I don't think it has anything to do with the codes or me. Probably another bogus lawsuit somebody's trumped up. I'm sure they just want to make sure we're prepared in case we get approached."

"Approached by who?"

"Journalists? Attorneys? LifeShare will take an 'official' position on whatever's going on, and we'll all be required to adhere to that. It's normal protocol."

I followed him into the bathroom.

"How long will you be there, you think?" Selfish me—my lazy-day Saturday nursery cleaning with the help of some hunky muscle was slipping away too quickly.

"No way to know." He pecked my cheek with a quick kiss. Almost as an afterthought, he added, "What'd you have planned for today? You look like you're ready to hit the tunnels?" That little lilt of a question held a ton of skepticism, as if he didn't approve, which pretty much cinched my sudden decision.

"Yep," I said, and continued on as if I'd had this plan all along. I wondered if pregnancy hormones could account for a whopping case of juvenile rebellion. "I found a new opening on the west branch last time I was down there and I'd like to hike it before I run out to the university. A couple of hours with their equipment and I could lay down a pretty accurate map of the part of the system I've been through. And I'm sure Dr. Kendall would love to see an update."

"You think Kendall will be on campus on a Saturday? You don't want to make the drive out there for nothing." Steven obviously didn't have time to raise a proper protest since he was heading for the garage by way of the kitchen, where he grabbed a bagel and a pint of orange juice before jumping in the car.

"I'll check in with you before I head out," I said. Which meant I'd be out of reach while I was underground, which he didn't care for. I gave him a little wave and closed the door to the garage. I wasn't in the mood for his passive disapproval of my work in the tunnels. He didn't have to like it, but he needed to respect that I did.

All of a sudden, I was rather excited about my plans for the day. With my attention focused on Alyssa this past week, I had almost forgotten the small opening I'd seen the last time I'd gone exploring in the not-yet-famous, or maybe the used-to-be-famous-but-lost-their-appeal-for-everyone-except-me tunnels of Graceville. Now that I'd allowed the discovery back into the forefront of my mind, I could picture the sliver of an opening. It would be a tight fit getting through, the kind of dirt-hugging side-slide that cavers thrived on. The only way I'd make it through that crack, short of opening it up with a chisel or a sledge hammer, would be to dump every last ounce of air from my lungs in order to squeeze my chest through, and I wanted to make sure I accomplished that before my growing belly made it impossible.

I was a little disappointed that the sweet smell of the honeysuckle had peaked and abated in my absence, but being underground with the scent of wonderfully neglected earth and the sound of my own breathing was a welcome escape from LifeShare and blood drives and emergency hospital runs. Before I knew it, I had traversed the main tunnel to the point where I remembered seeing the opening to the west. Training both my headlamp and flashlight on the wall, I searched for the crack, excitement building in my pumping veins.

When I saw it, I came to a swift halt. Only then did I realize how fast I had been moving. I usually liked to take my time, enjoying the seclusion these tunnel hikes brought me, imagining the people who had built them, and hunting for clues as to the purpose of the old ruins. But this morning, my eagerness to see what I might find beyond that crack had me moving at a near sprint. My heart pounded a strong rhythm as I ran my hand gently over the zig-zagged edges of the crack in the wall.

A mound of dirt lay at the floor, having fallen away and revealing what might have been an attempt to seal off this corridor. Immediately, my mind questioned why. Why, and when? I dropped my backpack, fished out a sample bottle, and filled it with a scoop from the mound of dirt. Digging into it wasn't anything like putting a shovel into loose sand. The dirt was crusty and dry, much like an abandoned anthill, which made me think the dirt had not fallen away recently. My small Canon in no way compared to Samantha Bedding's professional equipment, but I snapped off a photo and drew a quick sketch with measurements in case I disturbed the integrity of the opening when I went through.

I checked the gap again, running my hands along the earthen wall and probing several spots with a thin rod. The mere fact that some of the dirt had fallen away was reason to be cautious, but after a few moments of safety checks, I deemed the remaining borders to be structurally sound.

First, I shoved my backpack through to the other side. Then I followed, turning profile to better squeeze through the small space. As I had anticipated I had to push all the air from my lungs in order to collapse my ribcage enough to press through. The walls bore simultaneously against my back and breast, leaving dry smudges across my shirt but nothing more. Not even a brief rain of dust fell around me.

Once through I faced the new tunnel and took a moment to draw some deep breaths, spiraling my flashlight across the fresh surfaces. I knew what most people would say—another tunnel of dirt, woohoo, looks just like the last one. Even Steven couldn't figure what enjoyment I got out of the tunnels. A trek through the mountains, with streams and waterfalls, and changing colors of autumn leaves was so much more beautiful, he thought. I thought we got to see that anytime we wanted, with no more effort than to hop in the car for a Sunday drive, but this ... this was something hidden, almost secret, something we didn't get to see unless we were willing to go deeper and give ourselves over to the body of the earth for a short while. It wasn't about stalactites or stalagmites or water dripping through the ground. I could never quite explain to people the personal satisfaction I felt from being below the surface like this.

I reached down to retrieve my pack, and a shiver ran over my skin as I felt an unexpected chill. I held my hand out to the crevice, feeling for a draft, but the air was still as night. The temperature on this side of the wall didn't feel any different from that in the main corridor. I pulled the straps of my pack over my shoulders and rubbed my hands against my arms. My skin was tight, constricted by gooseflesh. I grabbed the bottle from the side of my pack. Maybe I needed some water. Now that I paid attention, my t-shirt was damp from sweat. I had, after all, just hoofed over a mile at a pretty good clip. It wouldn't hurt to take it little easy as I explored this new branch.

Upon closer examination, the space was a little tighter than that of the entrance tunnel. It was as if this channel had been burrowed rather than mined, a hurried, crowded route narrow in width, not much wider than a large man's shoulder span. I followed along, randomly dragging the palms of my hands against the roughly excavated sides until the passageway suddenly ended in an abrupt wall that loomed before me, flat and strangely smooth.

That was it—my search along this path had ended almost as quickly as it began, but I was intrigued by the way this end wall was completely out of sync with the walls that had led me here. Even the floor beneath my feet was rough, rocky in places, with pits and bumps. Not this wall. There was an unnatural softness to it. I backed up several steps to chronicle this find with another photo, hoping I could capture the juxtaposition between something that seemed, not manmade, because obviously the tunnels themselves had been crafted at the hand of man, but perhaps newly manmade, and done with very little effort to disguise the freshness.

I dropped my pack to the floor and felt around inside for my camera. I couldn't take my eyes off the structure, for lack of a better word, for that's what it felt like—a piece of construction, one unnatural to its surroundings, the way a city's first skyscraper must look against a maze of humble homes scattered along meandering streets and lawns.

For a while I just stared, taking in the subtle nuances of the dirt wall. It wasn't quite smooth enough to have been laid with a trowel. There were no telltale markings like one might find in stucco. I held out my hand again, compelled to touch the formation, to feel the makeup under my own fingertips. As I ran my hand across the surface, I could sense the soft gradations, as if my hands belonged there, as if someone else's hands could have actually rubbed this wall into place.

The more I stroked the wall, the more the minute distinctions revealed themselves. It was not as smooth as I had first believed. A web of tiny cracks ran through what I decided was not much more than caked mud. Without thought or planning I began to pick at the cracks like a child picks at a scab, almost unaware or if so, unable to resist the urge. At first only a trickle of dust fell away, but I continued to claw until eventually the dirt began to cascade against itself, breaking away in a steady stream, sometimes falling to the ground in stubborn clumps.

I worked, scraping and tugging and clawing at the formed earth, not even realizing until after a moment of digging against hard barrier that my fingers had found a new unrelenting surface. My chest rose and fell with the effort. For a moment, I dropped my aching hands to my side, then reached up and adjusted the lamp strapped to my forehead so that it illuminated the hole I had created.

First, I was a little appalled at what I had done. I had practically vandalized what could be considered a piece of history. My raw excavation was nearly four inches deep and six inches wide.

I leaned forward and blew a steady breath into the cavity. Traces of dirt flew away, revealing the concrete I had unearthed. Not old brick, or bedrock. I couldn't be sure, but this didn't even appear to be the kind of concrete block that would be mortared together. This appeared to be a poured structure, a foundation, perhaps a basement.

Ironically, I found myself harboring a swift case of contempt that modern man had found the nerve to lay a structure that interrupted these old tunnels. I thought I knew what might be on the other side of that concrete wall, and I was impulsively angry that I had been denied the chance to follow this tunnel to the place it should have traveled.

Frustrated, I turned back. I had been expecting much more out of my big discovery. I certainly hadn't bargained for a dead end. When I got back to the crack where I had entered from the main tunnel, I found my breathing was labored, but not from exertion. This was me being pissed off. I would need to calm down before I went back through the opening. Part of getting through without causing any more damage was being able to empty my lungs enough to squeeze through, but I couldn't do that if I was huffing and puffing like I'd just run a marathon. The irony wasn't lost on me either, as I stood there with my eyes closed, taking slow, deep breaths, trying not to think of the thing that was racing around in the back of my mind. I had, after all, just clawed a hole in a wall with my bare hands, and I had no idea what had made me do such a thing.

For the second time I stuck my backpack ahead of me through the hole. I was still keyed up but also ready to get moving again, so I did a little jiggle-and-shake shoulder dance accompanied by a long exhale and said thanks that no one could see me right now. Nerves weren't my style.

I felt the cold again, a flash of it as I stuck my arm through to the other side. Goosebumps rippled over my flesh. It was just a variation in temperature between one area and another, but I found it disconcerting nonetheless. For whatever reason, being down here today wasn't having its usual therapeutic effect. I suppose it was possible that trekking off underground to spite my husband could have something to do with that, but I wasn't in the mood to analyze that particular train of thought right now.

Mirroring my earlier movements, I squeezed my chest between

the unrelenting edges, happier than I should have been to be standing in the main tunnel. The wider corridor felt like freedom, but to my relief it also held a spark of possibility. Ultimately my reason for venturing around under here was to find out something new. At least I could walk away with questions. I turned to head back to the entrance behind the church and glanced back over my shoulder. I had an idea about what I might find down that corridor if I paid better attention to the clues.

But there was something I wanted to check out before investigating any further.

From the edge of the woods, I saw the tell-tale SUV belonging to Samantha Bedding once again parked next to my Camry. Maybe our small town reporter needed a new moniker—cave stalker? This was only the second time she had been waiting for me at the end of my trek and already I missed emerging unnoticed from my little adventures. I considered this an invasion of my privacy and seriously hoped it wasn't going to become a trend.

Samantha had been lounging inside the back of her car, using the rear hatch for shade. Her short legs dangling childlike from the platform were at odds with the hunter's instinct behind those inquisitive dark eyes. She hopped down when she saw me.

Feigning celebrity chased by the paparazzi, I stuck out one hand to hold off this news hound and yanked my backpack up to partially cover my face.

"No pictures," I yelled.

"No cameras," she whispered, and held her hands up beside her face to prove she was unarmed. "Got everything I need, except a signature so I can print what I got."

"I have a phone, you know."

"Yeah, sure, but this is more fun when I'm bored."

I opened my car door and dropped my pack onto the seat. "Maybe you need to move on to the next big story," I said, emphasizing my sarcasm with air quotes. Her career was headed downhill fast if I was her "big story."

"Worry not, my friend. I have a feeling there's a whopper of a story coming down the pike as we speak. Although we could talk about why your fingers look like you just dug your way out of a shallow grave."

Instinctively I wiped my hands on the legs of my jeans. My fingertips throbbed; my nails were caked with dirt. "No big," I said, smiling. "I'm not much of a glove person, even when I'm gardening. I like to feel the earth with my hands. I connect better that way. Don't say it's weird—I've already heard it. I guess I got a little carried away."

"To each his own."

I popped the glove box, pulled out my phone and wiggled it at Samantha. "Great way to get in touch with people," I said.

"Okay, okay, I get it."

"I do need to give Steven a call." I was throwing hints left and right that I wasn't really in the mood for this surprise rendezvous, but she wasn't in message receiving mode. Must be a stubborn journalistic thing.

"Post-spelunking check-in with the hubby?"

"It's not spelunking, since these aren't natural caves. They're tunnels."

Samantha offered me a brief tight-lipped smile. "I know. I promise the article uses only the proper terminology. So where is the hubby today?"

"Work," I said.

"On a Saturday? Something up?"

I took a couple of steps to my left, positioning myself so that in order for her to look me in the eye, Samantha had to stare almost directly into the sun. Perhaps that was evil on my part, but her showing up here had been enough to seriously irritate me. Now with the questions? She put her small hand over her brow as a shield and squinted.

"Not that I know of," I said casually. There I was being suspicious again. Was she actually fishing for information? "Just a meeting."

"I heard all the department directors were called in. That sounds ominous. Are you worried?"

My first thought was how in the world she could possibly have heard anything about the meeting, much less which employees were involved, but I decided very quickly not to take that bait if indeed that's what she was offering.

"You really are bored, aren't you?" I laughed. "What's to worry about?"

Samantha shrugged. "Well, it is Lifeshare. That place is filled to the brim with human blood. Don't you ever worry about biohazards?"

"I guess if it was the CDC, I might. But this is healthy blood. They aren't storing deadly viruses. I'm no expert but I don't think people would actually be called *in* to the building if there was a threat like that."

She tossed her head in apparent agreement. "I guess you're right."

Yep, I thought. "Hey, did you say you had something for me to sign?"

She had shifted sideways so she wasn't staring into the sun anymore, but she narrowed her eyes nonetheless. "Yeah, right over here."

I followed her to the back of her SUV, where she pulled what looked like a legal document out of a briefcase. It was short, but I still didn't care to read it. "Legalese," I stated with disapproval.

A pen appeared before my eyes. "You don't need to read it. It's the paper's standard release so we can use your photo, that's all."

I took a second to scan it anyway and concluded it was what she said it was, gave it my John Hancock of lesser importance, and handed back her pen.

"There you go." Holding up my phone again, I reminded her, "I really do need to check in with Steven."

"Sure. I've got to get going too." Samantha reached high and slammed down the back door of the SUV.

I turned back to my car, already punching in Steven's number on my cell.

"Say, how's your friend?" Samantha had one hand propped against the back window, leaning casually, other hand planted on her tiny hip. A living oxymoron, she could not have looked more nonchalant or more probing.

I merely raised my eyebrows in response.

"I heard you had to take Alyssa Davis to the emergency room. She okay?"

I really, *really* wanted to call my husband, and then I really, *really* wanted to get on the road to the university so I could follow my lead on the tunnels. What I really did not want to do was have this conversation. There was no way she was getting any information out of me about Alyssa.

"She's better. Thanks for asking," I answered in my lightest Southern-Belle-just-this-side-of-bitchy voice. I'm not sure if it was my tone or the fact that my expression read like a giant sentence-ending period that put an end to the questions, but I was infinitely glad when Samantha Bedding got into her giant car and drove away.

"You hear a lot, don't you?" I said into the dust stirred by her tires. I dialed Steven on my cell and got his voicemail.

Patiently, I left a message.

Then I borrowed the church's outdoor faucet and washed the dirt from my hands.

CHAPTER EIGHT

Normally I enjoyed the drive to the university—beautiful mountain scenery, banked curves in the road, the leisurely pace of cruising into town, down oak-canopied streets lined with Victorian-style houses. However, between not being able to get in touch with Steven and the lingering annoyance of Samantha's ambush, I was in a bit of a mood. Thanks to Samantha, I now had Alyssa on my mind. I hadn't checked in on her the past couple of days and was, once again, feeling a little neglectful.

The combination of summer and Saturday had rendered the campus fairly empty, which was fine with me. I had my choice of parking spaces and picked one that would let me walk through the quad, a brick-lined circular opening tucked into a perimeter of cherry trees which, aided by the cooler mountain temperatures, were still adorned in lingering blooms.

The old brick of the buildings reminded me of the clay walls of the tunnels. I pushed through the front doors of the two-story that housed history and archeology and breathed in the mustiness of the old halls. Another reminder of the tunnels. Dr. Kendall's office was tucked in the back corner. A drab yet exhilarating space, every wall was lined with crammed bookshelves, including the window that should have looked out over the gardens. It was a good thing the university had figured out how to retrofit the old building with central air or Alan would have suffocated long ago from the book dander. I moseyed up and tapped at the open door.

Dr. Alan Kendall, my favorite hand-me-down from a life-long

friendship with my father, peeked up at me from over his wire-rimmed glasses. A loose curtain of grey hair flopped near crinkled eyes as he smiled. He looked exactly the way I always remembered him, even from childhood, decked out in faded jeans and wrinkled oxford shirt with the sleeves rolled halfway up his forearms, bulky silver watch ever-present on his thick wrist.

He waved an arm at me, gesturing me in, as he pushed himself to stand behind the book-cluttered desk.

"Emmalyn. Come in, come in."

I scooted around the desk to give him a hug, after which he placed his big hands on my shoulders. "What's in the pack, Explorer?" I smiled at the familiar nickname. My dad had called me that when I was a kid.

"A little dirt. A lot of questions," I said, swinging my pack off my back. I pulled out the vial of dirt. "Something to test, although I don't expect to find anything interesting. What I need is a map."

Kendall slipped back into his chair and tapped at the keys of his computer. "Google Earth, at your service. What're you looking for?"

I dragged a chair around so I could see the screen. "That'll do for starters. Can we take a look at the aerial of Graceville?"

"Sure thing," he said, bobbing his head to look alternately over and through the glasses on his nose. "Anything in particular?"

"Yep." I pointed. "That big building there."

"Ah, the infamous LifeShare."

"Now, where is First Baptist?" I said, and followed the familiar streets to the little church behind which I began my hikes through the tunnels.

From above, the church was surrounded by a forest of trees, with nothing to the rear of the building until the trees stopped abruptly at the giant LifeShare rectangle and its array of parking lots.

I pulled a large piece of paper from my pack and unfolded it onto the desk. I had drawn a crude sketch of the church, the entrance to the tunnels, and a rough estimate of the maze of corridors below the ground that I had traversed so far. I took a pencil, quickly added the short tunnel I had hiked that morning, and drew a harsh straight line to indicate the abrupt end to that tunnel.

Then I pointed back to the screen.

"Steven tells me that LifeShare recently opened a wing in the basement for storage." I ran my finger along the east edge of the roof outline. "Is there any way to tell if the basement ends here at the edge of the building we can see or if it extends underground?"

Kendall gave me a sideways glance and began to punch keys. I bent over, pretending to tie my shoe. Kendall wasn't only a respected professor of both history and archaeology, he was a sneaky fellow with access to things I had no business knowing about. After a moment, a set of blueprints appeared on the screen. "Ventilation system. Best I can do."

"Whatever you got."

"Okay," he said, indicating a square filled with a web of tunnels I assumed to be the heating and air system of LifeShare. "This appears to correspond with the aerial image we were just looking at."

He punched a few more keys and the prints shifted left on the screen. More keystrokes and the image spun back and away, changing view so that we were looking at the building from the side. At the right edge of the original square, the ducts dropped a level possibly twelve feet deeper than the system they were attached to. The twelve feet above the ducts appeared to be void.

"Looks underground to me," Kendall said.

"That has to be the storage basement Steven told me about. No floor above?"

"Not from what we're seeing," he agreed.

"And scale? How long would you say this wing extends?"

"I'd say a hundred yards. Football field. About that size, actually."

"Wow. I knew it was big, but … Can we go back to the Google Earth shot?"

"Sure." Kendall clicked the first tab on his browser and the overhead of LifeShare came back onscreen.

"The football field. It's here, right?" I traced a rectangle off the edge of LifeShare.

"Yes, if you could see it, that's where it would be. What's your thinking, Emmalyn?"

I grabbed the sketch I had spread across the desk and followed the paths with my finger as I spoke. "These are the tunnels I've been through. They start here behind First Baptist church, stretching these three miles with several corridors branching off. A week ago, I noticed this corridor, almost sealed off but with just enough of an opening for me to get through. It went a quarter of a mile and then stopped, dead end, just like you see here. Look at the map. If I scaled my drawing down to match the computer image, I'd say that dead end puts me right about here."

I poked at the screen.

"Right about at the end zone," Kendall said, referring to LifeShare's hidden underground football field of storage.

I let out a deep breath, exasperated. "LifeShare cut off my tunnels."

"You need some iced tea," he said after I had exhausted a tirade against LifeShare for interfering with my pet project.

He pulled a pitcher from the small refrigerator in the corner, grabbed two glasses off a shelf, and poured.

"Don't worry 'bout the little one. It's decaf."

"What?" I was confused, then shocked, then a broad smile crossed my face as my hand went involuntarily to my stomach. "How'd you know?"

"Wife of forty-two years. Three daughters. Four grand-daughters." He took a long sip of the tea and laughed. "All those women and I still don't know bunk. I do know you're usually a lot calmer."

"I know," I agreed and matched Kendall with a swig of my tea. "But I wanted so much to see where those tunnels led. They had to have had a purpose, and no one in town seems to know the history, or they don't care. That's worse, I believe. It irritates me that I might never know why they were created or what they were used for. I can't believe I've hit a dead end."

"Dead end? Only if you let it. That tunnel you were in this morning was only cut off in the physical present. Its history still exists."

"Not unless you've got a tome stashed on one of these shelves outlining the history of the Graceville tunnels. Nobody around here seems interested in talking about them, which could mean there's nothing interesting to talk about. Wait. You don't, do you, have a book?"

Kendall tipped his head. "Sorry, no. But here's my suggestion. Being an explorer doesn't always mean following the footpath."

I raised my eyebrows. "That sounds like something you would have told me when I was eight years old."

"Still true. So explore."

"Ugh. I hate it when you try to get me to think." I downed another swallow of tea and marked a few short paces across the crowded room. My eyes landed on the Google Earth map on Kendall's screen.

"Maps." I quietly tested the theory, then convinced myself, stating more firmly: "Maps!"

I picked up my crude drawing. "I need to know what the land looked like before LifeShare built on it. Maps, if they even exist, old photographs, whatever. I guess I always assumed there was nothing there before, just a big field or something, but that might not be true. If LifeShare built through the tunnel system, they could have destroyed other entrances. Tunnels like the one I discovered this morning might even continue onto the other sides of the building. It's something I'd like to see."

I remembered my comment to Samantha earlier about connecting with the land through my bare hands. Maybe I could do that by studying the land from above the ground; it was certainly worth a try, and now that I had thought of it, I wanted nothing more than to immerse myself in what used to be the topography of Graceville—before LifeShare.

In a moment of clarity, I closed my eyes for a moment before I chanced another look at the grinning Ph.D. sitting on the edge of a desk that had developed its own topography by way of mountains of books and papers. I imagined the inside of Kendall's brain to be just as crowded and jumbled.

"Spill it, Kendall," I said as sternly as I could manage. "What have you got in the archives and why haven't you already given it to me?"

"Well, let's just go take a look. And to answer your second question, it's up to the explorer to find the way."

"How very Indiana Jones," I teased, completely unsure if the reference was accurate or not. But I felt very much like an impressionable student and Alan Kendall seemed very much my hero at the moment.

I looped my arm through his as we strolled underneath the thick tree canopy that led to the library. Towering shelves surrounded us, but whatever Kendall had in store for me was tucked away, once again, in a back corner. It seemed a lot of important things on this campus were relegated to the farthest reaches of these brick buildings.

He pulled out a step-stool and climbed to the top shelf while I waited anxiously for him to tug a sheath of papers from the surrounding volumes.

He held out a weathered file folder, bound together by elastic nearly atrophied with age. When I didn't reach for it right away, he gave it a little shake.

"Might help. Might not," he said with a mischievous wink. "But I'm pretty sure you'll learn something."

"Are you trying to sneak a history lesson in on me?" I said, finally grasping the folder. I carried it to the nearest table. "Can we take a look?"

"Absolutely."

Carefully, despite my excitement, I pulled back the elastic strap and took out the first item. It was a photograph of an old house, front porch wrapping around two sides, gravel drive. I flipped it over to see if anything was written on the back, thrilled to find a name—Johnson—and an address. I didn't recognize the street name, but underneath it read "Graceville, Georgia." I felt a surge of excitement just looking at the ancient home that had existed somewhere in my town. Much like my adventures in the tunnels, the sight of it sparked so many questions. I thought I understood, in the smallest way and possibly for the first time, my old friend's enthusiasm for archaeology and local history.

I was reaching for another page when my cell phone rang in my pocket. Reluctantly I checked the screen.

"It's Steven," I told Kendall. "Meeting finally over?" I said into the phone.

"Where are you?" Steven said. His voice held a mixture of annoyance and what I could only describe as exuberance.

"I'm at the University, with Dr. Kendall. I tried calling you," I said, aware that my tone was defensive.

"Can you come home?"

"Well, sure," I said, "but Alan just pulled a file for me with some really nteresting stuff. I want to spend some time looking through it."

"It can wait. I want you to come home."

I glanced at the folder with its possible historical treasures. It probably could wait, but that didn't mean I wanted to. "Maybe in an hour or so," I said.

"Emmalyn, trust me when I say whatever you're doing can wait."

I frowned. "What's going on, Steven?"

Kendall tapped my shoulder. He had put the photograph of the white clapboard back in the folder and secured the elastic. "Take it with you," he whispered.

"Really?" I mouthed the word, then returned my attention to the phone.

"Okay, I'm on my way, but you've got to clue me in. What's so important that I need to stop what I'm doing and get home right away?"

Steven let out a little whoop of laughter. "Oh boy, Em, you won't even believe it. And I'm not telling you over the phone and ruining it because it's too freaking unbelievable. I'm one of the first people in the world to know something huge, and I want you standing right here beside me when the news comes out."

"Okay then," I said and snapped my phone shut.

Kendall handed me the folder. I gave him another hug.

"Thanks, Professor." I said.

"Enjoy the journey," he told me and waved a quick hand in the air.

The drive back from the university dragged slowly on, as if time had added a few undiscovered seconds to every minute. The clutch of maps and photos lay on the seat beside me, taunting me because I wanted more than anything to find out what kind of goody package Professor Kendall had put together for me. I hadn't thought much of it at the time he'd given me the folder, but I had the distinct feeling he'd been doing a little research of his own on my little town of Graceville and her mysterious tunnels. True to form, though, he enjoyed being a bit mysterious himself. That explained him holding out on me until I came up with the idea of maps and photos on my own.

The thought made me grin.

My cell rang and I had to dig blindly in my purse while I kept my eyes on the road.

"How far away are you?" Steven said when I answered.

I glanced at the clock. "Probably forty-five minutes. Steven, you have got to tell me what's so important. You obviously found out something this morning at work. What in the world went on at that meeting?"

"I did, but I can't tell. Not yet. Forty-five minutes is good. You'll be here in plenty of time."

Exasperated, I sighed. "Okay, if you won't tell me, then I'll guess. This morning you said something about a possible press conference. Something new LifeShare has in the works?" I ventured.

"Not exactly, but kind of."

"So there is a press conference."

"There is."

"In, what, a little over forty-five minutes?"

"Very astute."

"And you're excited about it so it must not have anything to do with the database problem."

"Completely unrelated."

"And nobody's suing the company, because while incredibly exciting, not exactly *that* kind of exciting."

"Nope. Not exactly."

"I'm getting nowhere," I said after a pause. "This is so very intriguing, hon—kind of like these winding roads. And since we're down to me being there in not much more than a half hour now, how about if I just savor the anticipation and enjoy the surprise."

"Perfect," Steven said. "But don't stop at the gas station and strike up a lengthy conversation with any of the townsfolk. Trust me—you're going to enjoy this so much more firsthand than you would through the grapevine."

"You *are* the grapevine!"

Steven bounded through the door to meet me when I got home. He couldn't have been more jittery if he had downed back-to-back double espressos.

"Okay," I said. "You've got to tell me what has you in such a state."

"It's history, Em. History is happening right now, right here where we live. Where I work!" He grabbed my hand and tugged me toward the couch.

I dropped my purse and Kendall's folder onto the coffee table and plunked down next to Steven. "Just watch," he said, and turned up the volume.

A panel was already assembled, a row of men and women lined up in chairs behind a podium.

"Is this a Presidential press conference?" I muttered.

Steven didn't need to answer because at that moment President Kane walked onto the stage, his face a curious display of calm behind a carefully contained smile.

"Good afternoon, my fellow Americans," he began. "Today marks a day like few others in the history of this nation. It is a day that will, in some way, change the life of every person on this planet. I want to keep my remarks brief, because these men and women gathered behind me have incredible news to share. Over the course of the next few days, months, possibly even years, stories will abound, tales will be told, the scientific community will be questioned, scrutinized, doubted, and regaled. Like our forefathers before us, we are entering unchartered territory, forging forward into a new age of possibility. What I ask of you as a nation, what I ask of the world, is that we march together into this new age that is upon us—with a sense of cooperation, trust, and faith, with the spirit of our ancestors inside us as we embrace a world forever changed for the better.

"At this time I would like to introduce two award-winning members of the medical research community. Please welcome, from Johns Hopkins University and Hospital, endocrinologist Dr. William Bentley and oncologist Dr. Randall Anoud."

President Kane held his arm out to welcome the two men to the podium and shook each man's hand in turn.

I let out a little sigh. "Our President really has become the master of the ambiguous, hasn't he?" I scoffed, remembering the similar speech he had given the week before.

"Just wait," Steven said. He tapped his fingers impatiently against my leg, but his eyes never left the television screen. "It's all about to make perfect sense."

The two doctors glanced at each other, then both faced the camera with practiced composure that nearly belied their eagerness to share whatever news they were about to present.

Dr. Bentley spoke: "It is our pleasure today to share with you the results of an extensive research project. Dr. Anoud and I, along with this elite assemblage of physicians behind us, have worked diligently in the medical field for a combined seventy-three years, dedicating unending hours of time and energy to the hope that one day we could stand before you and, in one-hundred percent confidence, tell you that we have solved the mystery of mankind's most dreaded medical anomaly. It is certain. It is definitive. It is the end to one of our greatest fears. Cancer can, and will, be cured. We have found the way."

I missed whatever was said after that because I slapped Steven's arm and began to jabber. "Seriously? Are you kidding me? You knew about this and didn't tell me. *Why* do you know? What's this got to do with LifeShare?"

Steven laughed. "Very serious. Not kidding. Admit it, you're glad I didn't tell you. I said it would be better to hear it like this, and I was right, wasn't I?"

"Maybe, but I can't believe you didn't spill."

"It's kind of my job not to."

"Okay, see, and exactly what does this have to do with your job?"

"LifeShare is on the cutting edge with this, Em. We're setting up clinics immediately to start administering the vaccines."

"Vaccines?" I asked dumbly. "Like a shot? They're going to cure cancer with a shot?"

"It's a little more complicated than that, but basically, yes. And LifeShare has the facilities in place already."

My eyes dropped to Kendall's folder on the coffee table.

"Like a giant football field of blood storage?" The words popped out of my mouth before I could stop them. They had nothing to do with this monumental moment, but hearing Steven mention LifeShare's facilities struck a nerve, and suddenly I was irritated again by the possibility that their building had cut a chunk out of my tunnels.

"What?" Steven looked completely confused.

"Nothing." I shook my head as if to leave it at that, but continued on despite myself. "Professor Kendall and I were looking at some maps of the area and it's possible that LifeShare's new storage facility was built right in the middle of the tunnel system."

"And?"

"And nothing. But you know I wanted to explore those tunnels and I can't do that if there's an underground building the size of Sanford Stadium sitting in the middle of them."

Steven took a deep breath and let it out in a slow whistle. "Seriously, Em, I am not trying to minimize that the tunnels are your thing, but I think you're missing the big picture here. We're talking about curing cancer. Cancer, Em. Gone—the way of smallpox, and Polio. Imagine, just for a second, what it meant to the world when people didn't have to worry about those diseases. Cancer is our Polio, hell, it's our black plague, the worst disease we have, and it's about to be eradicated, wiped out."

"I know. I just—"

"And the company I work for gets to be a part of it," he interrupted. "*I* get to be a part of it. In what world does something this phenomenal fall under the shadow of your cave-trolling adventures, Em?"

Every word he said was true, and his less-than-diplomatic delivery was well deserved, and yet I felt the ridiculous urge to correct his erroneous description of the *caves*. Instead I allowed my eyes to go wide with the apologetic disparagement I had earned.

"I'm obsessed, I know. I'm sorry, Steven. It's just that all I've thought about all day was the tunnels and I just found out I may not be able to explore them the way I wanted, but …" I waved my hand in front of my face hocus-pocus fashion and snaked my arm around my husband's, snuggling close in a blatant play for forgiveness. "… my irrationality is gone. I'm excited about this, and what it means for you. I really do want to know more about LifeShare's involvement in this."

Steven ran the fingers of his free hand through his hair, and to give him the credit of the sainted, I could see that his anger was already beginning to dissolve.

"Maybe we should just watch," he said, using the remote to crank the volume up another notch.

By this time, the doctors who had made the announcement were gone and another had taken their place. The caption at the bottom of the screen identified the man speaking as Jameson Clark, MD. I recognized him as one of the doctors standing in the background while Bentley and Anoud were making the big announcement.

"… this new breakthrough. All the progress put together over the last fifty years is miniscule in comparison to what we've discovered. Never mind free radicals or cell mutation. Those things still occur in the human body, but they don't hold the key to curing cancer. They never have. What we have discovered through extensive research over this past year that *is* key is what's *not* occurring in the human body. You see, a very small, very elite segment of the population have never shown signs of cell deterioration on any level beyond normal aging. Further, these individuals have an ability that was never before believed possible. They can actually heal themselves, reversing damage at the cellular level. Imagine the knitting together of a cut on the skin but faster and without the process of scabbing over, no scarring. Then imagine this on the molecular level, happening within the body.

"We have completely changed our viewpoint on cancer based on this new knowledge. Cancer isn't a disease; it is the natural state of the human body …"

"He can't be serious," I said, but Steven either didn't hear me or chose to ignore me.

"Given enough time," Dr. Clark continued, "enough progression of age, every person alive would eventually get some form of cancer. The easiest way to describe it is that most of us are missing a specific chromosome—the chromosome that allows us to regenerate and replicate—key word, *exact*—duplicates of the cells we are born with. In most of us, over time, cell division becomes inaccurate. These continued inaccuracies eventually turn our cells against us. The mutated cells then duplicate at a much faster rate than stem cells were designed, replicating themselves without check, eventually crowding out normal cell growth. That is the part of what we already know about cancer that remains the same. But now everything has changed. We have the ability to isolate the chromosomes necessary not only to destroy the growth of cancer but to reverse the process, returning malignant cells to the benign state. Furthermore, we have the ability to transfer that chromosome onto the DNA strand of any individual."

Here he paused, a serious smile coming over his face.

"We no longer need the cure for cancer. With this new breakthrough, we can prevent cancer from ever occurring. And, the process is as easy as giving blood."

These last words sent a chill down my spine. My mind was suddenly bombarded with memories of Alyssa's cyst/miscarriage and Steven's problems with the database at LifeShare. The concept of donating blood had played such an overwhelmingly large part in my life over the last few days, my mind automatically wanted to make a connection where I knew there couldn't possibly be one.

Dr. Clark's image split to one half of the screen while his interviewer, Barton Spencer, appeared on the other half. He had been speaking so long on his own I thought perhaps this was still part of the press conference.

"So this miracle population that's been hoarding the cure to cancer. Who are these people?" the anchor asked crassly.

This was why I hated watching the news. Even the most serious subject became a farce with these so-called journalists. I supposed this was the beginning of the backlash the president had alluded to in his opening remarks.

Dr. Clark's lips tightened for a moment. Then he went on as if he has been expecting exactly this type of treatment and was prepared for it.

"The research community has gone to great lengths to protect the privacy of the people who make up this incredible segment of the population. The level of testing necessary to make this breakthrough a possibility required an enormous sacrifice on the parts of these individuals. For obvious reasons, it would be unfair to publicize their identities."

"What obvious reasons are those, Dr. Clark?" Spencer shot back, unperturbed. "It wouldn't be that the medical community wants to keep this secret for monetary reasons? Assuming the community as a whole embraces this idea, there will be storms of people wanting their—what shall we call it—vaccine? Who benefits here?"

"Well, obviously, humankind benefits, Barton."

"Yes, but who profits?"

The interview appeared as if it was spiraling into a sparring match. I wondered if we would get any more useful information.

"Actually, Barton, there is little opportunity for profit here other than the cost of the chromosome transfers. As I mentioned, the process of inoculating people against cancer is no more complicated than going to your local Red Cross to give blood. In fact, select clinics have already begun obtaining the equipment and medical personnel are being trained, as we speak, to offer this service. We expect the first clinics to be up and running within the month."

"So soon? After years of researching a cure for cancer, you're saying that we can simply walk into a clinic sometime before the summer's out and get a dose of No-More-Cancer."

"If you want to put it that way, Barton, yes. The treatment will be available that soon. Now that we have the cure, we want to make it available as soon as we possibly can."

Barton Spencer turned directly to the camera, leaning conspiratorially forward with his elbow on his desk, the corners of his mouth turning up ever so slightly. If that grin had been delivered courtesy of Charlie Rose from behind the round table, I might have fallen into a trusting spell of unquestionable belief, but this guy—this Barton Spencer—seemed intent on conveying pure mockery. His next words validated my thought like no others could.

"The cure for cancer," he said, four little words dripping with sarcasm. Spencer abruptly straightened his back, slapped the desk with the palm of his hand, and let out a little snort. "After the break. Join us for more on this legendary development when we return with Dr. Jameson Clark."

Steven muted the television. We sat for a moment in silence. For my part, I was afraid anything that came out of my mouth might be considered disrespectful on the part of my husband. However, the stretch of quiet finally got the better of me.

"Are you sure this isn't some kind of 'War of the Worlds' joke?" I said.

"It's real. I promise you that," Steven said. His face still beamed with the enthusiasm of being involved through LifeShare, though I could tell he was awed by the news even though he had been privy to the information beforehand.

"Is this even feasible?" My words were whispers. I guess I was awed as well.

"The end of cancer," he said by way of confirmation.

"That would be a miracle from God," I said.

When Steven and I finally went to bed that night and I began to drift off to sleep, that thought played over and over in my head.

CHAPTER NINE

When I finally fell asleep, I crashed hard for a couple of hours, then found myself tossing and turning, lapsing in and out of incoherent dreams that were lost to me the moment I stirred. Adrenaline had taken hold of my body so I couldn't relax. Sometime in the middle of the night, I slid closer to Steven's side of the bed in the hopes that being close to my husband would help me settle down. When I found the right side of our bed empty, I came fully awake.

Quietly, I folded back the covers and grabbed the throw from the end of the bed, wrapping it around my shoulders. I crept down the stairs, navigating by the soft bluish glow coming from the den. My bare feet barely made a whisper of sound as I padded down the carpeted steps.

Dim white light came from the small lamp on the bookshelf behind Steven's desk. The blue tint was provided by the computer screen that formed the backdrop behind Steven's silhouetted head.

My husband's monitor was filled with smaller versions of the same four screens I had seen on his monitors at the office.

Steven's fingers flew intermittently across the keyboard, tapping out sequences I knew would be meaningless to me, the results popping into various quadrants of the screen. It looked like he was still trying to decipher the codes he had shown me at work a couple of days ago.

"Can't sleep, huh?" I finally said.

Steven jumped and pulled both hands through his dark hair as he swung his desk chair around to face me.

"Looks like I'm not the only one. Did I wake you up?"

"Nah." I sidled over and slid into his lap, wrapping my arms around his neck. "I imagine there are a lot of people wound up tonight. The cure for cancer—it kind of rolls around in your head, doesn't it? It's amazing, but then it just seems crazy, like it can't possibly be true. Then I imagine that our baby could be born into a world where he—or she—doesn't ever have to worry about this scary thing."

"I know. I try to think what it would be like to be in school forty years from now and learn about this disease that used to be so terrible. And chemotherapy? That'll probably seem like some horrible archaic torture. Our kids will probably think doctors were idiots. They'll look back on it the same way we look back on leeching or bloodletting as ridiculous treatments for people who probably just had the flu."

"It's crazy, right? Never having to experience seeing a loved one waste away like that." I was suddenly overwhelmed by the thought of people I had known, and the millions I didn't, who had either overcome or succumbed to cancer, and how bravely most of those had fought against it. I blinked away the tears that threatened to form. "It'll be like the eight-track—just a vague memory."

"What's an eight track?" Steven said, furrowing his brow in convincing confusion.

"Exactly." I bent my head for a lingering but simple kiss.

When we pulled apart, I squinted down at him. "Working on the database in the middle of the night?" I was aware that my voice carried a somewhat accusing tone.

Steven rocked us back in the chair and glanced over his shoulder at the screen behind him. "I've got to figure this thing out, Em. Once the media gets wind that LifeShare will be one of the clinics administering the vaccine, they're going to rake us over with a fine tooth comb. And this is a problem. If the press even suspects we have any kind of problems in the company, it won't matter if it doesn't have anything to do with the vaccine. They'll find a way to make news out of it, or try to use it to discredit us, maybe even discredit the whole idea of a medical breakthrough. I can't imagine it would be pretty."

"Did Jerry or anyone mention it at your meeting this morning? Did they ask you to work overtime on it?"

"Nothing about the database. They explained how this got through FDA approval so quickly, but the main focus was on what's coming down the pike, how we'll need to prepare for when the vaccines are available, the best way to notify the public about getting inoculated, how to handle the press if we're approached."

"Well, I can see not talking about it in a meeting with everybody present. But did Jerry say anything in private? To you? He has to know this is an issue that could blow up in your faces."

"No, and I get the feeling that they'd rather sweep this one under the rug than risk bringing attention to it by devoting manpower to solving it. And why not? If it truly is a problem and the press finds out and decides to make something of it, I figure I'll be the one to take the fall."

I shook my head. "You don't think they'd make you a scapegoat. Your research is one of the main reasons LifeShare is in the position it's in. Surely they won't forget your project played a huge role in them being on the A-list for administering these vaccines. It's why they brought you in."

"And who better to blame if a problem with the database comes back to haunt us? The database is essentially mine—it's founded on my research, I maintain it, I designed the schematic for storing the data. And I'm pretty sure that if it happens to make LifeShare look bad, I'll be the one it'll backfire on."

"So you have to work on it at home, in the middle of the night?"

"I have to figure out what it means. That's the bottom line. And I need to do it fast. It's what's best for LifeShare, and for me."

For all of us, I thought.

I climbed back into the bed, my mind whirling with too much

information and too much worry. Eventually, sheer boredom and fatigue took over, blissfully suppressing the adrenaline flowing through my veins, and I slept again.

At eight o'clock the alarm sounded and I slapped it silent with the back of my hand. If it had crossed my mind during the night, I would have turned the stupid thing off so we could sleep in. The sky was clouded in grey and a steady rain was coming down. To my relief, Steven was in the bed beside me, breathing heavily in his sleep. The alarm hadn't even penetrated, apparently. I lay there, listening to the sounds of him sleeping and the soothing rhythm of the rain and wished I could fall back to sleep. But my mind had started its relentless churning the moment I had smacked away the indistinguishable song on the radio. I gave up—no falling back to sleep for me—and quietly crawled out of bed.

An hour later I walked into our Sunday school class, dropping my umbrella into a pile of wet shields inside the door. The patter of rain had blossomed into full pounding, hammering steadily at the roof so that the room felt muffled and damp, the air claustrophobically thick.

"Where's Steven this morning?" Ricky asked as he made his greeting rounds.

This was the fourth time I had been asked the same question, and already I was weary of answering with my half-truth. I had to remind myself everyone here had likely heard yesterday's grand news story, but people didn't yet know about LifeShare's connection.

"He didn't sleep much last night," I said. Neither did I, I realized, as a wave of fatigue swept over me. I was starting to regret my snap decision to pop out of bed this morning. Not much more than an hour in and I was wishing I was home again, snuggled against my snoring husband, basking in the warmth of mingled bodies and thick covers.

"Anything we need to worry about?" Ricky's frown of concern was sincere enough, but he looked like he was chomping at the bit to get to the front of the class and begin today's lesson. He glanced toward the podium for the third time since he had greeted me.

"No," I said, dismissing him with a slight push of my hand against his arm. "Everything's fine."

Ricky was already moving away. "You'll let us know if we can help?"

"Sure," I said. "Thanks."

I took a seat on the far side of the circle of chairs and glanced around. Samantha Bedding, from across the room, caught my eye in her unrelenting reporter's stare. I stretched my mouth into a quick smile in acknowledgement and looked away. She had that familiar inquisitive look in her eye—the look of questions. I turned my gaze to Ricky, while mentally I began to plan an escape from the room that would avoid answering even one of those inquiries.

Ricky stood before the podium with his hands clamped on either side, making eye contact with each of us.

"I'm sure I don't have to tell you what's been forefront in the news since yesterday evening," he finally said.

Chatter broke out amongst the group. The level of excitement was palpable.

"I know I speak for most of us in this room when I say that we have never needed a miracle to validate the faith we have or the truth that we know. And yet that's exactly what we're seeing. A true miracle."

I zoned out as the discussion began to echo every thought that had plagued my mind during my few hours of fitful sleep last night. I wasn't sure how much time had passed or how much had been said when I snapped out of my blank state.

"What if it's not a gift from God?" I blurted.

Every pair of eyes in the room pierced me, and I had a snapshot in my mind's eye of what they were seeing—a tired young woman who seldom contributed slumped down in her seat, arms folded tightly across her chest, a scowl etching her face. Too late to pull the impulsive words back. Unable to explain myself—I could not have rationalized where they came from if I had been threatened.

A chorus of questions, scripture, outrage barraged me:

"What are you saying?"

"...end to cancer. How can that not be a miracle?"

"Tell that to my mother."

"What else could you call it, Emmalyn?" Ricky asked, breaking through the chaos. The room fell silent.

Slowly, I unfolded my arms and pushed myself up straighter in my seat. I wondered how appalled Steven would be if he were sitting here by my side.

"A *gift*," I said, emphasizing the last word, "especially one from God, doesn't come with a price tag. I guess I'm wondering what the cost will be."

I couldn't explain my doubt, but it didn't go over well.

I decided it was wise to step out of the debate and let the others hash it out. As soon as class was over, I grabbed my umbrella and headed for the car, opting to skip the service. I had a good idea the sermon would center around the same topic and since I had thoroughly branded myself as a doubter during Sunday school class, I didn't think the congregation would miss my presence.

The rain had lightened to a steady drizzle. I sat in my car for a moment, my eyes roaming involuntarily to the woods behind the church. I was torn between wanting to be out of the rain and wishing it wasn't too muddy and wet to climb down into the ground. The tunnels would be dry. More importantly, they offered a solitude I simply couldn't find anywhere else. I would have to be satisfied with the folder Professor Kendall had given me.

The house was quiet when I arrived. I left the umbrella open in the garage to dry and dropped my keys and purse on the kitchen counter. I couldn't help wondering if I would find Steven once again entrenched in the den, amidst a glow of computers and foreign codes. But the office was empty and silent; I found a strange sense of relief in that. I wasn't crazy about the idea of my husband as a workaholic. I had no problem admitting I didn't always take well to change, and I didn't care for this metamorphosis, whether or not it was a necessity. Whatever level of commitment Steven thought he had to put into his job right now, I reminded myself it was temporary. It was only a matter of time before he got to the bottom of the database problem and then he would go back to being the guy I could count on to be home for dinner, the guy who was energetic and fun and didn't have dark circles under his eyes and permanently unruly tufts of hair sticking out from his head.

The image actually made me chuckle until I thought more about why he was spending so much time in front of his computer, agonizing over those mysterious codes. He wouldn't back down until he figured out what the extra information in the duplicate codes meant, no matter how long it took. My thoughts effectively squashed my own laughter, especially when my mind wandered to last night's newscast. At the same time that I could imagine people all over the world rejoicing, I couldn't help but wonder why I didn't find the news of an end to cancer such an exciting prospect. I needed normal. I needed nothingness. I needed to take my husband out to a movie.

Since he was up half the night, I assumed he was still sleeping, so I padded quietly up the stairs only to find he wasn't sleeping at all.

I suppressed a giggle when I rounded the corner to our master bathroom and discovered what Steven had been doing while I was off at church.

He was laying half in-half out of one side of the cabinets under the sink, his back arched and knees bent up at a funny angle. He was swinging the adjacent door open and closed.

"Whatcha doing there?" I asked, leaning against the door jamb.

He jumped. I seemed to be good at making him do that lately. The door he was swinging slammed almost shut, but a piece of plastic kept it from closing all the way.

"Crap," Steven shouted, yanking his hand away as he simultaneously jerked back, his head banging against a box. Several shampoo bottles toppled over, bouncing and rolling off his face.

My hand came up to cover my mouth.

"That hurt," he said, deadpan. "I think I might be stuck in here."

Squeezing my lips tight, I reached down and grabbed the two naked feet in front of me. After a series of pulls and tugs and him shifting and wiggling his arms around a bit like Houdini in a straight-jacket, we managed to dislodge him from the man-eating cabinet.

I collapsed on the floor next to him, biting my bottom lip to contain what could have become a malicious grin.

"Freedom," he sighed, leaning back on his hands.

"So," I said, still unsure of what he was up to, "what exactly are you doing here?"

"I am making the world a safer place for our baby girl," he said dramatically. It wasn't exactly the O-Negative superhero voice, but it was frighteningly close.

I raised one eyebrow, hoping for an explanation. Inside I was tickled that he had assigned the female gender to our baby. It was too soon for that, but adorable nonetheless.

"Those door latches that keep kids out of poisons and deadly falling shampoo bottles?" These were the actual words that came out of his mouth, but the rising tone of his voice as he said it translated into, "Duh! I'm installing some extremely sophisticated safety equipment here. Isn't it obvious?"

I leaned forward, climbing over his gangly legs, supporting myself by placing my left hand in the one clear spot between a spray of screwdrivers and drill bits and some other stuff I didn't recognize. I pushed the cabinet door closed, then pulled as if to open it and was surprised to find that it opened only an inch before catching on a little serrated piece of white plastic that stuck out from the back of the door.

"That is so cool," I said, my admiration genuine. "Good job, Dad."

I tested the safety latch several times, pressing down to release the little hook so the door would open all the way, closing it back, and watching it catch again at the one-inch mark when I pulled on the door.

Satisfied that I indeed had conquered the child-proof gizmo, I backed up and crawled onto my husband's lap, my legs straddling his.

"Baby girl, huh?" I looked down into his eyes and grinned.

"Or boy." His voice sounded silly. "You know?"

"You know," I echoed in a silly voice of my own. I put my hands on either side of his grubby face and kissed him hard, my lips lingering for a moment against his when the actual kiss had finally played out.

"Any reason why you picked today to install safety latches our baby won't need for a good year?"

Steven rolled his eyes toward the ceiling. "Just trying to get a jump on things."

"Uh huh, because if you were thinking I'm mad about your working in the middle of the night, that would *not* be true."

"Wasn't thinking that."

"Uh huh, and if you were thinking I'm a hormonal mess and am likely to go a little crazy on you at the drop of a hat, that *would* be true."

"Definitely wasn't thinking that."

"And if you were thinking that you were planning to spend the afternoon in your office and this incredibly sweet gesture would take my mind off of it, you would be right."

"Might have been thinking that."

"And if you were thinking that since it's raining outside, I might want to spend the afternoon sifting through the maps and stuff that Kendall gave me yesterday, so I wouldn't even notice that you were fretting over the database anyway, but that I would make you something delicious for lunch first, and after several hours, no matter what, we could take a break from our respective obsessions and go see a movie? What about that?"

"I think that sounds like a perfect deal," he said.

"Get in the shower, goofy." I jumped up and turned on the water to start it warming up. "I'll reorganize the killer shampoo bottles."

"I was hoping I could count on you," Steven said, cutting a wary glance toward the cabinet.

"And thanks for this," I added. There was no way he could have known this was just the dose of normal I was longing for.

"You're very welcome," he said while stripping off his shirt and pajama pants.

I took a moment to admire the perfectly muscular view before he disappeared behind the shower curtain.

The weight of the folder Dr. Kendall had given me transported me blissfully back to the place I wanted to be. I tucked the package against my chest and stole away to the bedroom, where I would have plenty of room to spread the contents across the bed. And where I would be out of earshot of the continuous news updates on the cure for cancer streaming from Stephen's office. The vaccine, or whatever it was, had overnight acquired its own acronym: CURE, which stood for Cancer Undergoing Responsive Eradication. Whoever had come up with that was reaching about as far as possible to fit something meaningful to a set of letters, but I supposed if any threat of the twenty-first century deserved that particular moniker, it would have to be a cure for cancer.

I found I still harbored a tiny grudge toward Steven for forcing me away from the University without a chance to "explore" this new find with Alan. I felt certain the professor's perspective would move me along at a much quicker pace than if I were left to my own devices.

Of course, chances were pretty good Alan would have lent nothing more to my questions than his rugged grin, and perhaps an urging to find out for myself how my research would unfold. So in that respect, I supposed it didn't matter that I had not had the opportunity to look through the file in his presence.

I glanced toward our master bath as I plunked cross-legged onto the bed. Steven had, after all, won me over with the installation of the baby locks, so I spared a deep breath toward letting him off the hook for interrupting my endeavors into the mysteries of tunnels.

I pulled the first item from the pouch—the photograph I had barely had a chance to glimpse, of the old clapboard house with the partial wrap-around porch—and laid it next to me on the comforter. I felt the muscles along my brow immediately tense into their typical response to curiosity. I would have some serious crevices in my forehead by the time our baby was old enough to say "wrinkle." At the same time my mouth twitched into a small smile. I pulled the next document from the folder and examined it.

The page showed what appeared to be a listing of property transfers in Graceville starting in August of 1932 and spanning a short two-month period. I perused the first few names—Arthur Blackshear, Henry Caldwell, Nathan Smith—and tried to imagine who these fortunate people could be who not only survived the Great Depression but also the crash in bond values around that time and were not only able, but brave enough, to purchase new homes in the middle of an economic crisis.

That idea flitted away as quickly as it had formed when I decided, after a second look, that the addresses I was seeing did not appear to be purchased property but rather properties that had been sold. In a column next to the names and addresses, the county was listed. Most of the homes were in Rabun, a few from neighboring Habersham and Stephens counties. Another column—there were no headings—contained the initials I.J.

I.J., I imagined, was either the person who had purchased these properties, or the short signature of the person assigned to keeping track of the sales. The rightmost column contained a two-digit number that I thought at first might have represented the sale value, but I couldn't reconcile any way of turning the two digits into a price that made sense for the era. And if these poor people had found it necessary to sell their homes for under one-hundred dollars apiece, much less for prices in the teens, then I had to wonder what sort of man—or what entity—had benefitted from such meager transactions.

My former admiration for the sturdy stock of America was replaced by a surge of pity as I imagined Mr. Blackshear's family forced from their home. A tear sprang unexpectedly to my eye.

"Oh, good grief," I muttered, picking up the picture of the white clapboard. I loved the dirt drive that crossed in front of the house, and the faded grey clumps of weeds that had sprung up along the edge of the yard in the black-and-white spring when this photograph had been taken.

I glanced toward the bedroom door, hoping Steven remained busy in his office, as I ran a finger beneath my eye to erase the evidence of my wimpiness. Hormonal or not, I wasn't in the mood to either explain or to be teased for going all soft-hearted over some victims of circumstance I had never even met.

I slid the photo toward the foot of the bed and picked up Dr. Kendall's folder. I rummaged through the contents, flipping gingerly through the aged, fragile pages. About two-thirds of the way through, I found a tattered map, hand-drawn not quite to the precision of a blue-print, but it was obvious enough that this was a layout of a small neighborhood. The streets were nearly straight and the strips of land on either side had been divided into small evenly-spaced parcels. Penned neatly in the center of each rectangle was a two-digit number. Small calligraphic script spelled out the date in the bottom right corner: February 3, 1932. Beneath that was an underline, curved ever so slightly, and underneath that, two other numbers connect by the scrolled letter "x" that I thought might represent a longitudinal and latitudinal position.

I kept a pad of paper on my nightstand, usually reserved for to-do and grocery lists, flipped to a clean page, and sketched a rough copy of the map. I grabbed the list of property transfers and smoothed it out in front of me. I ran my finger down the record of numbers along the right side of the paper. The first number, chronologically, turned out to be 11. Eleven had been assigned to Henry Caldwell. I scrawled his first initial and last name into the first empty lot outline on the first street. Eleven. One-one. I searched the list for the name corresponding with lot 12, and filled in my second square. I couldn't say why, but it lightened my heart to see those names begin to occupy the squares one by one, knowing that Nathan Smith and Jeremiah Channing and my friend, Mr. Blackshear, hadn't been without homes after all.

Hunched over my pad until the small of my back began to ache, I methodically matched names to square plots until I finished by printing C. Stancil into the last square of the leftmost street, left side of the road. Charles Stancil was number 88 in my quaint little neighborhood of sixty-four houses, houses I imagined to be prototypes for an oncoming age of cookie-cutter subdivisions.

Ultimately, though, my neighborhood remained incomplete. I had given each of the square plots an owner, but the space at the top end of the map remained empty. The original map showed a plot of land, more sprawling than the others, that sat along a thin meandering road at odds with the severe lines of the neighborhood below it. I hadn't included it in my original sketch because it did not seem to be part of the planned development, but looking at it now, I felt compelled to sketch the piece of land into the area just north of what I had already drawn.

Making use of the barest of artistic talents, I had managed to turn what had probably been a beautiful country lane of smooth dirt, perhaps even gravel, lined in the spring by a smattering of daffodil clumps and a lazy dog or two, into something that looked more like the bottom curve of an umbrella, with geometric yards raining down from its edges like perfectly aligned giant square raindrops.

I turned my map sideways and for perspective, drew a light line along the midpoint of the neighborhood, then began to divide the right half of the neighborhood into what I equated to twenty five-yard segments. To the left of the midpoint, I sketched a light version of the huge building Professor Kendall and I had looked at on Google Maps. Even with my skewed dimensions, the community appeared to take up roughly the area of LifeShare's grounds, plus an additional plot approximately the size of a football field. Of course it was possible I was forcing my sketch to match what I wanted it to reflect.

I stared at the map for a long moment, then reached across the bed and picked up the photograph of the white clapboard once again. My eyes remained glued to the picture as I fumbled open my nightstand drawer and poked my hand around inside, finally wrapping my fingers around a pair of reading glasses I used to keep from straining my eyes on the rare occasion I dallied in a cross-stitching project.

The glasses, a whopping three-times magnification, served the purpose. I slipped them onto the bridge of my nose and let my eyes focus on the blurry wooden mailbox at the edge of that unpaved drive.

My hand trembled. I flapped it back and forth at the wrist, hoping to shake away the nerves tingling there, and picked up my pen. With great care and a deep breath, I drew the tip of the pen down and across the empty space at the top of my page, mimicking as best I could the slanted calligraphy of the original map.

I wrote *I.J.*—letters intricately rounded, perfectly centered—a crown on the community.

It was a bit of a drive on the main highway to the nearest small movie theater, and when we got there, we found the parking lot as full as I had ever seen it. We weren't alone in thinking that a rainy day was a good time to hang out at the movie theater. Or perhaps the rest of the county, like me, needed a break from the continual rehashing of the latest big story on the CURE. The thought was cynical, I knew, and I felt momentarily ashamed. Every time I heard a report, though, the doubts and worry I had been experiencing came rushing back to the surface. I couldn't seem to quiet my mind. The rest of the world was certainly more excited to hear the updates than me.

Our top three picks were sold out by the time we weaved through the roped-off line to purchase tickets. By default for the foreseeable time frame, our choice was either an animated flick that, according to the poster, had something to do with puffins and ostriches and a giant mansion on the precipice of a mountainside, or what looked like a futuristic mystery neither of us had seen the trailer for. It starred Keanu Reeves and since Steven and I were fans of *The Matrix*, I felt like it was a safe enough bet.

We found our seats and I volunteered to go for the popcorn and drinks. The lobby was swarming with people but the line was surprisingly short. Within ten minutes, I had our goodies in hand and headed back down the corridor to our theater. The theater opposite mine let out as I rounded the corner and for a moment I felt like a salmon swimming upstream. A group of three girls headed right for me. Caught up in giddy commentary of their movie, they leaned into one another, giggling. From the looks of things, they seemed intent on not splitting apart. I tried to dodge to the left to avoid them but the crowd was too tight. The blonde one on the end gave a dramatic flip of her long hair as she passed me. She must have put her whole shoulder into it because she managed to clip my elbow in the process.

My arm went up. I felt the popcorn bucket leaving my hand, but I managed to fumble it around on the tips of my fingers before regaining my grip. I lost a handful of kernels to the process, which was a lucky break, considering. The straws for our drinks hit the ground and I was immediately glad they were paper-wrapped. I glanced around, contemplating whether it was safer to try to bend over and pick them up or turn and join the crowd, get some replacements, and hope the crowd emptied by the time I headed back this way.

Before I had time to make my decision, someone dropped down in front of me. He scooped up the straws and handed them to me. I reached out to take the straws, my eyes slowly moving from the white paper to the hand that held them. I felt a chill flutter over my entire body as my fingers closed around the straws.

The hand, barely revealed under a dark sleeve that fell long over the fingers, was unnaturally pale. A flashback hit me, an image temporarily burned against my retinas. I had only seen skin that pale one time before, when the young man had helped me with

Alyssa at the hospital.

I shook my head, forcing my eyes away from the straws in my hand. By the time I looked up to see if it was him—could it possibly be the same guy? —all I saw were a few unrecognizable faces, the last stragglers leaving the theater.

I spun around. He might have been the one with the dark hair, buried in the crowd turning the corner at the end of the corridor, just tall enough so I could see a pair of hunched shoulders inside a dark shirt. It was impossible to tell from the back with so many people moving as one.

I stared after the crowd until they finally dispersed. The air around me turned weirdly quiet and still. When I realized I stood alone in the hallway, I backed my way into the theater.

When the movie was over, I hesitated, forcing Steven to watch most of the credits roll before I got up to leave. The incident with the popcorn and straws still had me unnerved. The idea of exiting leisurely, separate from the rest of the crowd, held infinitely more appeal than spilling out as part of the herd.

"You okay?" Steven asked when we reached the lobby.

"Fine," I said, my answer clipped. I hadn't even realized I had stopped in the middle of the lobby. I forced myself to start walking toward the exit doors, but my eyes drifted to the bank of video games on the right side of the room.

A group of boys—young men, maybe, it was difficult to tell what age they were because their faces were at once distinct and nondescript, ageless. They looked as if they could have been brothers, or a clan, or a cult—same black jeans and jackets, same dark hair, the same pale skin ... the same maroon lips.

They had clumped around the game closest to the windows at the front of the lobby. Two teenage girls were playing at the machine next to them, and they kept glancing over at the boys, laughing playfully.

A couple of the boys sauntered closer to the girls. I saw one slip his arm over the brunette's shoulder, and she reciprocated by nudging him with her hip.

Three remained in the original group, two carrying on a dour conversation, from the looks of it. The third guy kept his head lowered, as if he was only interested in his own feet, oblivious to whatever the other two were pointing at through the window in the parking lot.

Steven tugged at my hand. I followed, forcing myself to smile up at him as we passed more closely than I would have liked to the small gang.

I observed the whole interchange of their behavior as a snapshot, but it was the young man staring at his feet that had captured my focus.

As we walked past them, that one, the palest one with the deepest red lips, looked up at me. His silver eyes gazed into mine for a long second before I caught myself staring and turned away. The muscles around my mouth twitched and I realized I was thinking of speaking, of asking him why he had disappeared so quickly from the hospital.

I drew my mouth into a taut line, cutting off the half-thought I had been about to voice. I wrapped both my hands around Steven's arm, pressing myself against him. Suddenly I felt very cold.

"You didn't say if you liked the movie." Steven drove. I was tucked into the passenger's seat, slumped down with my arms crossed over my chest. It took me a beat to register that he was talking to me.

"It was good. Weird." I turned to look out the window. My surreal transparent reflection stared back, as if a curious clone of me peered in from the other side of the window. The image made my nerves tingle so I turned away, looking at Steven instead.

"You don't look so good," he said. "You probably shouldn't have put that greasy movie butter on the popcorn. You know it doesn't sit well with you."

"It's not the popcorn," I said, my voice a drone. My mind was so preoccupied I couldn't seem to find the energy to add inflections to my words.

"What then?" Steven alternated looking at me and turning back to watch the road. "It's not the baby?"

"No," I answered quickly, forcing some attitude into my denial. "No. The baby's fine."

"Tired?"

I knew Steven. He didn't like to push, but I wasn't doing a very good job of hiding my feelings. He wouldn't give up until he figured out what was bothering me, even if it turned out to be nothing. Just like he wouldn't give up until he figured out what was wrong with his database at work.

I hoped beyond hope *that* problem turned out to be nothing. The alternative had way too many implications. What reason could anyone possibly have for creating a database that stored unauthorized donor information? And if there was truly nothing clandestine about the extra database, why not let the administrator in on it? Why go to lengths to hide it and make Steven dig through the programming to try uncovering it? And who at the company or outside could be responsible?

"Did you see those guys in the lobby of the theater?" I blurted, making an unconscious decision to tackle the most recent of the many things needling at my brain.

"Which guys?"

"Over by the video machines. There were five of them. They all looked … alike. Dark hair. Pale."

"Dark clothes?" he verified. "What's that called these days? Goth? Emo? I can't keep up with the latest teenage trend. Not even sure of the difference. Having a baby is making me sound like my father," he added with a grin.

"I'm pretty sure I've seen one of those guys before." I squirmed in my seat, jammed my hands into my jacket pockets. "At the hospital. I told you about the guy who helped me get Alyssa from the car into the wheelchair and into the hospital. He had that same look, but I don't think I realized it till I saw that group tonight."

I took a deep breath and held on, reluctant to let the air escape through my pursed lips. "Maybe it wasn't him."

"It could have been." Steven glanced over at me, a frown crunching together the space between his eyebrows. "This town's small enough you probably run into the same people all the time and don't even realize it. Did he say something to you? Do something?"

"No, he just looked at me, that's all."

"Well, he probably recognized you too."

I had no doubt the young man had recognized me. I was convinced he was the one who had picked up the straws and handed them to me. If he was playing some kind of game, what could possibly be the purpose?

"You know?" Steven said. He reached over and poked at my wrist until I took my hand out of my pocket and intertwined my fingers with his. That simple gesture made me feel better somehow.

"Think about it," he continued. "You see the same faces at the grocery store, the doctor's office, the gas station. But most of the time, nothing's happened to trigger a memory. But this guy you said helped you at the hospital—that's a memory-maker—of course you're going to recognize him if you see him again. And that makeup? I mean, come on, who could forget that freaky lipstick. If that doesn't make an impression, nothing will. And if he's the one who was staring at the floor, he's probably not much of a social dude, so I wouldn't worry about him staring at you, Emmalyn. You are a beautiful woman, after all."

So Steven had noticed the look-alike crew of five. And he was trying to lighten my mood by throwing me a compliment. I couldn't fault him for insincerity; I knew he meant it. I also knew in my heart that the way I looked, whether beautiful or haggard with worry over a friend bleeding profusely, had nothing to do with why the man with the silver eyes had been watching me at the movie theater tonight.

CHAPTER TEN

I surfaced from sleep long enough to gauge whether it was still raining. The birds were at it again, chirping their morning songs outside the bedroom window, and I could detect a hint of sunshine burning through the leftover fog of yesterday's downpour. Happy with the knowledge that I could get outside today, I sunk back to a dreamy state until Steven gave me a departing peck on the cheek.

The humming of the garage door closing brought me fully awake. In short time, I had donned my loosest jeans and hiking boots, yanked my hair into a ponytail, and had my backpack sitting before me on the kitchen table as I gobbled down a bagel full of nice soothing carbs and a glass of orange juice full of something I seemed to crave. Sugar or vitamin C, I supposed—whatever it was made me happy.

I had already thrown a few items into the pack beyond what I normally carried. I rummaged through a storage bin in the garage, digging through the proof of mine and Steven's various athletic interests—helmets and bats, gloves, a catcher's mitt, two sets of in-line skates, the recommended knee and elbow-pads for such endeavors, several tubes of tennis balls—until I found what I was looking for tucked in the back corner under a badly misshapen yoga mat.

I got to the tunnels early. The church lot was empty, the underbrush leading to the tunnels still wet. Sunlight trickled through the trees in slivers, carving the damp ground into slices of sparkling green and brown. My feet and three inches of my jeans soaked up the dew, but four feet inside the entrance, the earth was dry and familiar. I breathed the cool air, pulling the scent of clean clay through my nostrils. I was faintly aware that my heart was beating rapidly. Not from exertion; from anxiety, maybe. Each time I came here, anticipation quivered in my bones. It's what kept me coming back.

I sifted through my backpack for the pedometer I had fished out of the storage bin and clipped it to my belt. Next, I pulled out the sheet of paper I had stuffed inside and held my crude drawing of the 1930's subdivision under the beam of my headlamp. After the movie, I had spent a few minutes at the computer, taking a cue from the wise Professor Kendall. The numbers in the bottom corner of the original map had indeed been longitude and latitude coordinates, ones that corresponded almost exactly to where the church stood. I didn't pretend to fully understand what that meant, but I had taken a moment to draw a square with a steeple in the bottom right corner of my map. Inside my square were three words, First Baptist Church, neatly stacked and centered.

I began to walk the tunnels, knowing exactly what I was looking for, occasionally glancing down at the pedometer, which I had configured to measure distance in relation to the length of my stride. I knew before I actually saw it that I reached the crevice— the one I had discovered on my last trip down here—and came to a stop, indulging in a few settling breaths before I turned to stare into the opening. My jeans, a pair a bit baggier than I would normally wear, had grown only slightly snug over the past weeks, but it was enough to bring back the memories of squeezing through that tight space.

Never mind. I wasn't interested in going inside this corridor to explore. I had seen all I needed to on my last trip. I dropped my backpack to the ground and drank water in big gulps, finishing off the swigs with follow-up gulps of air, and once again fished my neighborhood map from the front pocket of the pack. I drew a faint pencil line starting at the church, stopping when my line ran parallel to the lot—lot 11—where the home of Henry Caldwell would have stood in the 1930's. I took off my pedometer, read the distance, wrote it along the line I had just drawn, and marked the line with a short perpendicular stroke leading to the center of the lot.

I cleared the pedometer and began walking again, purpose tensing the muscles in my calves. The signs would be faint, I felt sure. Perhaps nonexistent, so I alternately kept an eye on the pedometer as I scanned the walls on either side of me for even the smallest tell-tale clue. The lots on the map had been fairly small, measuring only about seventy feet from center to center. After traversing that distance and noticing nothing out of the ordinary, I stopped and dipped into my backpack once more. The large flashlight I carried, one we had used on our honeymoon when we had gone SCUBA diving at night, was too heavy for hiking, but it cast a strong broad beam.

I switched it on and the dirt wall flashed into existence. I felt an irresistible urge to look behind me and glanced over my shoulder. The weaker ambient glow lit the clay to a deep red backdrop marred only by a looming silhouette shaped in a grotesque elongated version of myself. Somehow eerier than seeing the tunnels through the narrow isolation of my tiny headlamp, having the beam dissipate from blinding to black along the walls around me produced a shiver of vulnerability in me that I hadn't expected. Though I had never been in such a situation, I thought this must be what it feels like to be thrust onto a stage, blinded by the harsh lights, knowing that just on the other side of those beams, people were watching from the dark, their secret faces obscured by shadow. I had a desperate urge to turn the lamp off, to feel the comfort of the dark close back around me like a protective cloak, but resisted.

For several long moments, I stared at the slab of dirt, allowing my eyes to adjust and scanning for variations or imperfections. There had to be something. There needed to be. Alan's maps had planted the seed of a theory in the back of my mind, but I hadn't truly allowed myself to believe it until now. With a pang of guilt, I remembered clawing away at dirt in the side tunnel, finding the concrete foundation hidden behind that façade, how I had scratched into the formation with my bare fingers and yanked away clods that thudded around my feet. And how I hadn't even been aware of what I was doing until afterwards.

I could feel that desire coming over me again, wanting to know so badly what, if anything, was on the other side of the dirt. I let my eyes close and raised my hands in front of me. Stepping forward, my palms met the barrier of dirt and I began to trace the rugged terrain with my fingertips—blind, it was like reading a well-known history for the first time in Braille, or caressing every curve and valley of a familiar face, learning to recognize it in a new way.

And I found it—a place where the caked dirt under my left hand felt slightly different than that under my right. I opened my eyes to let the light back in, to prove to myself that there really was no visible difference, but let my fingertips continue to graze the surface. The red clay spread seamlessly from one hand to the next. The texture had been meticulously copied. I had walked through this section of the tunnels dozens of times and never noticed anything out of the ordinary, but now I could *feel* the difference.

I rubbed the space under my left hand, round and round, like buffing the wax from a car. It was softer somehow, the surface silkier. It made me think of a vessel that had been formed by its sculptor and allowed to dry but never baked to a hard shell. I had sculpted a few pieces in an art class and I remembered that soft dusty feeling, the way the vase had felt vulnerable, as if it could crumble back to nothing if I applied too much pressure.

I took a deep breath and stepped back, my eyes never leaving the spot where my left hand had just been.

I reached into my back pocket, wrapped my fingers around a cold handle.

With barely a twinge of apprehension, I took the small pick-axe and swung it into the wall, then bent it forward to create torque and yanked it back. The sculpture broke and crumbled to the ground at my feet. I brushed away the loose dirt and waited for the swirling storm of dust to settle, then leaned forward until my face nearly filled the hole I had created. My headlamp revealed what I expected. My heartbeat ratcheted up a notch.

There was another small corridor, almost identical to the one I had found on my last trip down here, branching perpendicular to the main tunnel, with rugged curved walls again not much wider than shoulder width. I drew my gaze away and switched off the big lamp, so that I could focus the beams of my headlamp and flashlight into the hole. It took me a moment to direct the lights exactly where I needed them, but suddenly I saw the unnaturally flat wall at the end of that corridor.

I stared, momentarily mesmerized, my chest heaving as my grip closed tighter around the pick-axe. I knew there would be a stronger, unnatural barrier behind that carefully crafted veneer of dirt—one that had no business in a tunnel system that had been here first.

I had a hard time tearing my eyes away from the dead end at the length of that corridor. Still peeping in from my crude window, I twisted the axe in my hand and shoved it into my back pocket. I reset the pedometer with a push of my thumb, grabbed the flashlight from the ground, and turned back toward the main corridor.

The pounding of my heart beckoned me to break into a sprint, but I forced myself to walk as closely as possible to my normal stride, to allow the pedometer to measure my steps. I needed normalcy and my carefully metered stride was the best I could manage as the beam of the flashlight opened up the path before me and darkness engulfed my back.

This time I could tell the difference in the texture of the corridor wall when I approached it. I told myself my eyes were attuned to the subtleties somehow, but deep inside I thought it was probably more of a feeling than anything that brought me to a stop.

With a lack of reserve or respect I would not have believed I was capable of, I drew the pick-axe from my pocket and swung.

My muscles twitched with the desire to rip the wall apart. I wanted to clear a hole, to pass through, to gouge that flat surface at the end of this capillary, to uncover whatever stood behind the façade of dirt that had been layered there and drive my small pick-axe into it until I had ripped through ... to what?

An underground storage facility? That's what Dr. Kendall's schematic had indicated would be there. Air conditioning ducts. Refrigerated compartments, perhaps, containing rows and rows of blood, some donated by the people I lived around, people my husband worked with, Alyssa's blood.

The shudder that traveled up my spine reverberated down my arms, raising goose bumps, and my fingers tightened on the grip of the small axe. I didn't want to think about anything connected to Alyssa's blood—not the trails of it dripping down her legs, not the bloody towels stowed away in the trunk of my car, a trunk I hadn't been able to bring myself to open since that night at the hospital. Most of all, I didn't want to think about the small life that losing so much blood may have cost her.

I shook my head. I wouldn't let these disconcerting memories distract me. Setting my mouth in a hard line of determination, I swung again, and again. Dust engulfed me as clods and chunks of dried mud fell about my feet. A coughing fit seized me and I stepped back, dropped the axe to the ground and folded my elbow over my mouth and nose until I had cleared my lungs of the flying particulates.

Tears streamed over my cheeks from the effort.

Bent at the waist, I rested my hands on my knees for support and pulled a few more breaths until I felt sure the threat of breaking into another coughing spasm had passed. I wiped the tears from my face with the heels of my hands and gazed at my destructive handiwork.

It wasn't a hole so much as a gash, a dark jagged wound in the shadowy wall. For a moment, I found myself oddly confused by the grey surrounding me. I yanked the headlamp from my head. A crack scaled the surface of the lens—I had no idea how that had happened—the bulb behind it clear and void, the filament fried. I stuffed the elastic band into my pocket and resurrected the flashlight from beneath a pile of dirt, frantically brushing debris from its lens, still mercifully intact.

The wall sprang back into focus, the gash harsh and gaping. And big enough for me to get through.

I crouched so my head cleared the top overhang, put one leg through to straddle the bottom ledge, and pulled the flashlight, heavy in my hand, through the hole with me as I turned and backed in my other leg.

The corridor was almost identical to the first one I had traveled, slim enough to almost graze my shoulders and clear my head by only inches. The beam of my light wavered ahead of me as I marched forward, intent on reaching the flat wall I knew would be at the end.

I hesitated only a moment when I reached it, then brought out my weapon once more. Turning the axe on its side, I tapped it against the dirt and watched scales of it flake to the ground. I had dug into the dirt in the first side-tunnel with nothing but my fingers. I didn't expect this covering to amount to much more than a thin façade, like stucco over mesh, and I was right.

Another tap with the side length of my tool sent a second spray of dirt cascading to the floor. A third and the clang of metal rang in my ears. I flinched. I had been expecting to find concrete.

Using the knife-like edge on the back of the axe, I began scraping, pulling chunks from the wall. Metal against metal, the growing silver slab before me rang out at each touch of my axe. The clangs echoed behind me like tiny screams, and I had an image of ripping flesh from bone that threatened to halt my actions.

But stronger was my curiosity of what this meant, this metal barrier. If what I was uncovering was the outside of LifeShare's underground storage wing, I would have expected poured concrete foundation or cinder blocks at the very least. A surge of my newfound anger seized me, and I scraped harder at the dirt, not caring that the metal screeched and squealed in protest.

I knew in my heart what *should* be on the other side of that wall. A basement, or a cellar, more likely, underneath the home of Henry Caldwell. That was the discovery I was supposed to be making, except that LifeShare had barged in and destroyed the history I so wanted to uncover and replaced it with blood and technology and its secret databases with secretive codes and this ridiculous metal ...

My axe hit a groove and caught. Startled by the change, I paused to scoop up my shirttail and swipe it across my sweaty cheeks and forehead. I yanked back on the axe, then reached out to touch the edge of the metal. I turned the axe on its side, pressed the edge into the groove, and pushed up. A ribbon of dirt fell from the indentation. I pulled down and released a longer finger of the packed mud. I felt the rough edge of concrete butt up against the slab of metal.

I picked up the flashlight and trained it on the crack between the concrete and metal.

"It's a door," I whispered, and a hiss echoed my voice from behind me.

I whipped around, swinging my light in a tight arc.

There was nothing there, nothing at all but a sudden burst of a breeze that started at my feet and rose along my body. It seemed to come from nowhere, yet it lifted the loose strands of my hair and slapped them softly against my face. A trail of dust blew up off the floor just in front of my feet and slithered away from me over the tunnel floor in a dusty wave.

I began to shiver as cold crept over my skin in tendrils.

My hand fell open and the axe thudded to the ground, mimicking the heavy thud of my heart against the wall of my chest. I wanted to run. I wanted to stand my ground. I couldn't turn back toward that door. I wanted to scream, and I had no idea why.

Finally, I began to walk in slow, measured steps, making sure I stayed a foot behind the swirling layer of dust moving along the floor. When I saw it settle, I stepped forward, one foot placed carefully after the other until at last I reached the main corridor. I wanted to look behind me, for that's where the cold was the most intense, against the back of my legs and neck and creeping through the small spaces between my shoulder blades and the pack I wore, but I didn't dare. At least not until I was out of this tiny tunnel that had served what purpose? What had it meant to the Caldwells? Henry Caldwell, his family, the Smiths, the Channings—what had they needed these tunnels for?

I squeezed back through the hole, into the main corridor. Immediately a sense of safety washed over me. False or real, I didn't care. The cold wrapping my limbs edged away so quickly that I thought I must have imagined it. And yet everything inside me begged me to look back, to find the source of that frigid breeze.

Had it come from underneath the door? From around the door? I remembered the refrigerated compartments I had speculated might be on the other side. There was no way that door could have opened without me hearing it. And yet if it had, cold air would have gushed out into the warmer tunnels. Hot air rises, so the cold would have been forced downward. That would explain the dirt swirling across the floor. It would even explain the cold against my back, snaking up from my ankles and clenching my neck. I reached up and pulled the elastic band from my ponytail, letting my hair fall down my back like a blanket over that exposed skin.

I would have heard it—the clanging of a door handle, the screech of hinges, a dry scraping of metal across the dirt pathway. Something. Wouldn't I?

I closed my eyes for a second, unsure of what to do. I felt frozen to this spot. Torn between wanting to go back and find out if the door had opened—*who had opened it*, my mind taunted—and the sound of my husband's voice telling me that I shouldn't be down here alone.

Alone, I thought.

But I wasn't alone, was I? Not anymore. Every time I stepped into these tunnels now, I brought my child under the ground with me. Anger—at Steven for being right—and guilt—at choosing anger as a response to his concern—gripped me. And the need to get my baby out of here. That's what finally made me turn and run.

That and the faint howling screech that echoed from the darkness behind me.

For the first time since I began exploring the tunnels, I felt a sense of relief to climb out of the small hole in the ground behind the First Baptist Church of Graceville and feel the warmth of the sun sifting through the overhead branches. I collapsed onto my knees at the edge of the opening, my hands planted on my thighs to support me, and sucked in clear heated breaths perfumed by freshly cut grass laden with the tang of wild onion.

When I felt like I had purged my lungs of dust and clay and darkness and the smothering weight of hidden secrets, I pushed to my feet, arched to stretch my back.

Breeze pressing against my damp skin, I took a minute to absorb the woodsy chatter—rustling leaves, acrobatic squirrels, chirping insects, *life*, not thoughts of people who had been gone for decades. I was able to push aside the panic that had started me running. That howling? I asked myself. That was probably nothing more than the air conditioning system inside LifeShare cranking on. If that were true, why then had I never heard it before? I had, I reminded myself, single-handedly destroyed two walls that no doubt acted as insulation against the sounds coming from that building. In fact, it was entirely possible that protecting the tunnels was the reason those walls had been constructed. Maybe there was something about the sound or vibrations from the mechanical systems of the building that would threaten the structural integrity of the tunnels. Or perhaps the acoustics of the tunnels would magnify any sounds from LifeShare's equipment, causing some kind of noise pollution throughout the surrounding area. There were still homes and businesses close enough by to be affected if that were the case.

A small laugh escaped my lips, and I took a deep breath.

I didn't believe any of my own half-baked theories, but at least positing them was helping me get a grip on myself, and more importantly, it helped me shovel to the back of my mind any more speculation over that weird iciness that had slid over my skin.

I looked toward the parking lot. More welcome relief. I had half expected to see Samantha Bedding, perched like a tiny gnome against her giant SUV, waiting for me. But the lot was empty.

My jeans were filthy with dry dirt and my hair could certainly have used a good brushing. My mother would have told me to get home and tidy up before anybody saw me out in public. But I knew an empty pantry awaited me at home. Dirty or not, I had to stop at the grocery store. I decided to skip the Ingles four miles down the road and drive the twenty-four to the smaller market that serviced the other side of town. The chances of running into anyone I knew were less there.

My appearance was incentive enough to justify the extra miles, but the drive would also give me more time to detox and refocus on the tunnels themselves. I wanted to contemplate logistics, measurements, ponder questions about the plots of land that people had once inhabited aboveground, decide what and how to best investigate. I was afraid idle conversation would destroy my momentum. I didn't want to talk about the beautiful weather, or the upcoming ice cream social at church, and I certainly didn't want to talk about the CURE. I wanted to live in my own little mind for a while until I could figure out if the things I thought I had learned could be true and what implications they held.

The trip to Rosie's Market gave me time to organize my thoughts, none of which were wasted on what to buy when I got there. I arrived in the potholed parking lot with no plan at all. My mental grocery list was empty.

I grabbed a cart from the corral and went inside. I wasn't familiar with the layout so I found myself perusing the aisles slowly, lingering over selections instead of grabbing items out of habit.

After several trips up and down, my cart was filled with unusual items I had no idea how to put together to form a meal. At the Ingles, the produce section was located to the far left side, so it was usually the last thing I hit before checking out. Already I had a pile of the summer's bountiful fruits in my cart, including two small kiwifruit, a mango, a clump of firm nectarines, a small seedless watermelon, and a bundle of fat black cherries. Too soon for my taste, the selection would reduce itself to apples and oranges, so I wanted to get all the variety I could.

The chill from the freezers at the middle of the store worked its way into my neck and shoulders, cranking tension into knots. I quickened my pace, grabbing a few essentials to get out of there. Meats lined the left-most wall. I stopped to look at the chicken but moved on quickly when my stomach lurched. I stood motionless for a moment, taking deep breaths. I refused to share my second bout of morning sickness with a store full of strangers.

When the storm of my stomach settled from the choppiness of deep-sea waves to more of a Gulf shore lapping, I picked up a package of flank steak, thinking Steven might enjoy my recipe for pepper steak with sticky rice tonight. I tilted the package to stuff it into one of the sanitary plastic bags I had pulled from the roll overhead, and a spill of rich red-velvet blood ran from underneath the meat, pooling and sloshing in the corner of the cellophane wrapped package.

Suddenly I felt lightheaded. My fingers tightened around the handle of my cart. I had grand intentions of staying upright even as I felt my knees buckle and glimpsed the shining linoleum floor coming toward me.

Blood. The thought drifted through a cloud of cotton stuffed inside my head. *Not again.*

"Wake up, sugar."

The languid voice echoed through dark space, hitting my ears before I was able to peel my eyes open. The minute I saw light, I was pushing myself up off the floor.

"Easy does it there." A pair of hands grabbed my forearms, steadying me as I slowly climbed to my feet.

"I'm so sorry," I said thickly, vaguely aware of a smattering of curious faces watching me.

"No need for that," said the woman whose hands held mine firmly. Her voice flowed like southern silk. She gently transferred my hands back to the handle of my cart.

I held on tightly, my eyes glued to her beautiful ordinary face and its halo of puffy yellow hair.

"Good thing you didn't conk your head," she said seriously. "That fellow hadn't caught you, you'd have a goose egg for sure."

I saw a stock boy standing back a couple of feet to my right. "Thank you," I told him, cutting short the nod I intended to offer because fuzz threatened to fill my head again.

"Oh, not him," the yellow-blonde lady whispered in my left ear as she nudged me and my makeshift walker toward the front of the store.

"That fellow caught you was one of them weird ones, you know, face all painted up white with the dark all around their eyes. There seems to be more and more of them freaky types around here these days. I ain't got nothing against being a rebel or expressing yourself, but I just can't stand the idea of a man, I don't care how young or stupid, putting on that dark red lipstick, you know what I mean? It's creepy."

I shivered involuntarily. Creepy was one way to describe it.

The yellow-haired woman helped me all the way to the front of the store, her hand lightly steadying me by resting just above the small of my back.

"Don't you worry, hon," she said. "I sent Jason off to the vending machine for some crackers and we'll get you a Coke to drink. I bet you ain't ate nothing, have you?"

I nodded. I couldn't possibly explain the chain of events that had led up to my squeamishness at the sight of that blood. Agreeing seemed so much easier, and truthfully crackers and Coke sounded like a fine idea.

She chattered all the way to the registers about how the youth of our country was going down the tubes, commenting on everything from belt chains to muffin tops, belly piercings (and even those in them "other" places) to Mohawks, then turning a page in history to headbands, bell bottoms and shag haircuts. The poignant sing-song of her rants took my mind off all things related to fainting. I finally glanced over to spy her name tag.

"Thank you for helping me, Lillian," I said when we reached the check-out lane. "I'm feeling a whole lot better."

"Well, you just lean there and keep steady," she ordered. She pulled a bottled Coke from the small fridge at the checkout lane, twisted off the top and thrust it at me, motioning for me to drink up. I took a swig, and she nodded her approval and began grabbing items from my cart and lining them up on the conveyor. "I want to make sure you're steady on your feet before I let you drive away, now."

She gave a little forward tilt of her head, cutting her eyes at me from beneath a serious brow, so that I knew she meant business.

Jason came back with the crackers and held them out at arm's length, as if he didn't want to get too close. I took them. Lillian bobbed her head, a "well, go ahead" motion, so I ripped the cellophane and ate obligingly.

"I really appreciate your help," I said.

"Don't you worry your pretty little head about it," she said with a smile, moving to the end of the conveyor to transfer my groceries into plastic bags.

Meanwhile, I practiced standing on my feet without support. My head felt perfectly clear, my stomach almost normal. I didn't think I would have any trouble getting home.

While Lillian loaded up the rest of my bags, I ran my debit card through the reader to pay. Lillian pushed my cart for me, keeping a keen eye trained on my steps.

I tried to smile.

"You just walk here right along side of me, hear. If you start to feel even the teeniest bit woozy, you reach right out and grab hold of me. I don't mind."

I followed obediently alongside her and the cart. To my relief, I never needed to reach out and grab hold of Lillian. Not that I wouldn't have taken her up on her offer, but I was infinitely happier making it through the parking lot under my own control.

"You want these in the trunk?" Lillian asked. The sky had gone slightly overcast but she still squeezed one eyeball to almost closing, as if the sun were beaming her directly in the face.

My keys were in my hand. By habit I put my thumb on the button to pop the trunk, but jerked my thumb back at the last second, stopping dead in my tracks. Alyssa's towels were still in there. My stomach roiled threateningly.

"Oh, we'll need to put them in the backseat," I said.

"Not a problem," she answered.

I opened the car door for her and reached for a couple of bags from the child-seat section of the cart.

Lillian shook her head at me. "You go on and sit down. I'll take care of these," she said, another order to which I complied, although I felt ridiculously self-indulgent sitting behind the wheel while she loaded my groceries behind me.

"Okay, then. You drive extra careful. If you start to feel dizzy, promise me you'll pull over and call somebody?"

"I promise."

Lillian closed the back door. I watched her through my rearview mirror as she scurried about the parking lot, collecting a short train of carts to push back into the store. She gave me a little wave as she passed.

I waved back and stared into the rearview mirror as she disappeared from view and a black SUV filled the frame in her place.

It was parked three lanes away, its overly-darkened windshield facing directly toward my car. Any other day, I might not have given the car another thought but my fainting spell had me feeling paranoid and the tunnels had launched me into over-analysis mode. If it had been silver instead of black, I might have suspected Samantha Bedding of following me to the boonies. Except for the super-tinted windows, this was just a run-of-the-mill SUV, noticeable only because it was parked off by itself. A Porsche I could understand; I would have chalked that up to self-preservation.

I stared another moment into the mirror, my nerves on alert.

I could feel the eyes behind that dark glass, the eyes I couldn't see, watching me. This was ridiculous, I told myself. I should leave. Drive. Unfortunately, my internal battle between logic and instinct didn't sway toward my rational side.

I blundered out of the car and headed his way, intent on confronting whoever was behind the dark tinted windows. It occurred to me halfway there that Steven would kill me for acting so foolishly, but that thought wasn't enough to break my stride.

"Stop following me!" I screamed at the black window.

Panting, my shoulders heaved from the outburst. I stood there, inches from the stealth black car with its opaque, no doubt Georgia-illegal, windows, with nothing but the sound of my own ragged breathing filling my ears.

Nothing happened. The rise and fall of my chest and shoulders slowed.

I wondered again about the state of my paranoia. Was I so wound up over a bunch of coincidences that I was screaming at empty cars now? I looked down at my feet and shook my head. With a sigh, I turned to walk back to my car, hoping no one had witnessed my bizarre behavior. I should have my head examined.

Then I heard the buzz and whoosh of the window lowering behind me.

I stopped mid-stride. A quick breeze caught my hair, swirling it around my face. Just keep going, I told myself, and whipped around.

"Why are you following me?" I asked. For all my bravado, I couldn't bring myself to look at the person inside that car. My core tensed, pulling against my planted feet.

"I'm not."

It was his voice—the one from the hospital—soft, almost

inaudible, yet clear as the ring of crystal in a silent room. Only two simple words and I knew it was him.

I forced myself to look up.

The window was cracked open three or four inches, revealing little more than his dark eyes below the rain deflectors. No, that was wrong. The eyes themselves were silver—although no one really had silver eyes, did they?—if you looked closely at them. The dark was smudged on in the circles underneath, across the shadows of his lids, black contrast to the rest of his alabaster face. I had no bleeding friends to attend to, no distractions to pull my attention away. I couldn't help but stare. There was something tortuous about that face that made me want to memorize every nuance.

"You are," I murmured, intending to argue my point.

His head swiveled ever so slightly, side to side, two times.

"This is just the way it works," he said.

I had never heard more ambiguous words. I should have been annoyed by this punk, this … kid, who was playing with me. I felt myself lean forward, toward that cavernous black window.

"The way it works?" I repeated, forcing each word from between my lips.

He blinked, looked back at me once, then set his gaze forward, somewhere beyond the windshield. I could see the white of his knuckles grip the steering wheel.

Suddenly the engine sprang to life, roaring.

I jumped, stepping back an inch.

He cocked his head my way again, reluctant but determined, as if looking at me pained him. The intensity of his silvery eyes bore into me, and I flinched.

"Don't let them take your blood," he said, the muted words so lost in the revving engine noise I wasn't sure I heard them correctly.

Before I could open my mouth, he threw the car in gear and tore away, the cracked window sliding shut as he went.

A spray of dust and pebbles scattered around my feet.

. . .

I climbed into bed early, body exhausted, mind spinning, and waited for Steven. He had met me at the door when I came back from the grocery store, taken the bags I had draped over my arms, and in that moment I had decided to keep the events of my strange day to myself. So we had put together a quick dinner and afterward he had gone off to his office to indulge in more database detective work. I had propped his pillow behind my back and tried to read the latest suspense novel everyone was raving about.

Thirty pages in, I was barely intrigued by the fictional plot. My imagination was running so wild within my own life, I couldn't seem to give in to the characters or their impending dilemmas. Instead I drew a mental picture of those three side tunnels. I felt sure I knew where they would have led if LifeShare had not dropped its sprawling foundation into the labyrinth I might have discovered back in the 1930s. One tunnel leading to the home of Henry Caldwell, lot eleven. The second, today's revelation thanks to my brutal attack at that wall, led to lot twelve, where Nathan Smith had lived. Another to lot thirteen.

The more I thought about it, the more certain I became, and the more questions I formed. If those tunnels led to the houses, the obvious question was why. Were the tunnels some kind of storm shelter? A way of getting to safer ground? And if so, where?

The questions cycled through my mind, and cycled again, until I finally grew sleepy. When Steven slid over and pulled me against his chest, I let my body meld into his, grateful for the warm distraction.

His arms wound around me. Large hands slid underneath my thin shirt, pressing against my back, almost completely covering my bare skin. He placed little lingering kisses on my nose and my forehead and my cheek and finally his lips landed on mine. I opened my mouth to his, hungry for this connection, for the heat of him, and savored his warm, wet lips and tongue against mine. I wrapped my leg over his back and pulled him to me, our bodies searching each other's with a need that dulled all thoughts of blood or cures, underground mazes or young men with freakishly pale faces. One by one these things faded from my mind until all I could think about were Steven's taut muscles working against mine. Together, we found a rhythm that built and quickened until my entire universe consisted of him and me and nothing else.

For a long while, we lay in a bundle of arms and legs, letting our heavy breaths slow back to normal. With his elbows, Steven propped himself over me, smoothing my damp hair back away from my face.

I kissed the edge of his chin. My lips curled involuntarily at the corners.

"So," I said, "did you sneak in here to lull me into a stupor before you head back downstairs, or are you here to stay?"

"I'm not going anywhere," he said on a cross between a groan and a sigh, and he flopped against my side like a dog lazy with sleep but in need of a warm body to lean into.

"You figured out the database?" I said. Only a hint of excitement painted my voice. I was too far gone to muster much more than the faintest interest.

"Not yet," he said, absently stroking the bony edge of my hip with his thumb. Any other time, my ticklish nerves would have sent me into a laughing fit, but sleep had me in its grip and my senses were numbed. "But I can play the game as well as whoever put in that hidden code, so I wrote in some code of my own. It would take a genius to find it, but I'll be alerted if any of that extra data is activated or accessed in any way. If it makes any connection to the rest of the system, I'll know it."

His slurred voice held a note of confidence that I latched onto. I needed something—anything—that I didn't need to worry about. This would do for tonight.

CHAPTER ELEVEN

The phone beside my bed rang too loudly, jarring me awake. I was shocked to find it was after eleven o'clock. I smacked my lips and stretched my dry mouth through a yawn before answering, but the heaviness of sleep was evident in my voice.

"Wake up, girl," my Mom sang cheerfully into the phone. "Are you feeling okay? It's a little late for you to still be in the bed. You're usually up with the chickens, putting the rest of us to shame."

"Mom," I managed, croaking the word, which halted her for a moment. I made a vain attempt to clear my throat. "Where are you?"

A fuzzy memory came back to me. Before Steven left for work, he told me she had called yesterday. He had probably even thought I comprehended. Little did he know my overworked neurons had barely registered his words, until now. Mom passed through town every few weeks and always made a point of stopping by. She usually called at the last minute, never sure until the day before when she would skip through our little town, and I was always tickled for her to visit.

I forced myself to sit up. "Where are you, Mom?"

"I stopped by the craft store, thought you might be working. Michelle said she had to let you go. I'm sorry about that, hon. Hard times these days, especially for a small business like that. I was hoping for some shopping and lunching, but if you're not up to it, I could swing into Clara's on the way over. I bet I could snag you a leftover breakfast scone. Some iced tea. Be good on your stomach if you're feeling a little iffy."

"No thanks," I said, rubbing my eyes. I had a lot more waking up to do if I had any hope of keeping pace with my Mom today. "I'm good. I'll grab a piece of toast to hold me over, jump in the shower. Come on in when you get here if I'm still in the shower," I said and put the phone back on the nightstand.

Before my mom even spoke, she dropped her purse from her shoulder at the front door and placed her hands on my belly.

"Kicking?" she asked, a twinkle in her eye.

"Yeah, a little." It was funny. Steven and I hadn't been the kind of impending parents to anxiously feel for the pounding of tiny feet and fists under my flesh. It seemed too soon for that anyway, but now that I thought about it, the little tyke had been fluttering around in there quite a bit over the last few days.

"Well you look fantastic," she said, "although maybe a bit more toast might do you some good."

"Thanks?" I said, recognizing the light mocking quality of her voice as something I had always loved. I was still stuck on the flutter of my belly and how that was an actual baby wiggling around in there. How had I not made the connection before? The corners of my mouth curled involuntarily.

"Don't look so goofy," she said, somehow managing to tear her hands away from my belly and heading past me toward the stairs. "Let's see what this nursery looks like."

It's a square room filled with boxes and two unopened cans of icy green paint, I thought, but I let her go. My mother had a knack for everything domestic from cooking to gardening to decorating, but she started every project with a silent pondering stretch of time where, from my perspective at least, all she did was stand very still and stare at the space, *feeling* it. I had watched her do this in various stages, from disheveled bed-head to earthy tree-hugger to the oh-so-put-together chic woman with just the right touch of grey in hair that would have otherwise been too obviously dyed, donned in the perfect layering of cashmere and denim so as not to come across as pretentious.

From the time I was a child, I watched her process in wonder, always anxious to dive in haphazardly but instead indulging her method. After all those years of impatient observation, I accepted that it worked for her, so I gathered my jacket and purse while I waited.

Five minutes later, she returned down the stairs. "Let's get," she said cheerfully. She stooped to pick up the purse she had dropped on the way in. "We'll take my car."

We spent the entire day shopping and lunching and browsing and planning and reminiscing. It was exactly the right medicine for me. Steven jumped up from the couch and hurried to meet us when we came barreling into the house, our arms overloaded with packages, our laughter booming over the television.

I noticed that the television was tuned to the evening news. A crowd was gathered in protest. I knew that certain groups were pushing to make CURE available first to the unfortunate population already in the end stages of cancer. Others wanted to give the first doses to those with the most incurable forms, like ovarian and pancreatic cancer victims. Efforts were being made to push the project timeline forward, but as far as I knew, approval was still weeks away. Still, I thought, mere weeks and this disease would begin the great disappearing act. Eradicated, just like the acronym said.

Weeks. Days. Months. Years. It really didn't matter to the person who wasn't able to hang on to his last threads of life for that long. No matter what day the first doses were administered, there would always be that person who missed the life-saving deadline, possibly by hours or even by mere minutes.

I kissed Steven and discreetly strolled to the coffee table to mute the remote while he gave my mother a hug.

"Ready?" she said, and immediately began pulling items out of bags, displaying each one for his review.

Steven stood with one arm around my shoulders, the other

hand stuck deep into the front pocket of his jeans, nodding at intervals he perceived to be appropriate. I had to bite my lip to keep from laughing.

The last thing she pulled out was a small book, covered in almost the exact same icy green that I had chosen for the baby's room.

"This is for me," she said. "For now."

"What is it?" Steven asked.

"A baby book." Mother and I spoke in unison, and this triggered another bout of giggles.

"Mom's going to start it for us by putting in some old photos of my family, kind of like a family tree. Then maybe we can get your mom to work on your side of the family for us."

"That's nice, Margie," Steven said. It still freaked me out to hear him use my mother's first name, but her hippie side had insisted on it, and it really did suit their relationship.

"Well, now that I've thrown everything all over the place, I'm going to split," she said. It didn't escape me that she reverted to a phrase from the flower-child era. Using it personified one of her mottos—look to the future but never forget where you came from.

"Don't worry," Steven joked. "I might be able to help get some of this stuff upstairs."

Mom—well, at that moment she was definitely Margie—poked Steven in the stomach with her index finger, causing him to fold over like a five-year-old being tickled.

"Thanks, Mom," I said, hugging her at the door. "Today was great."

"Yes it was. Thanks for including me," she said, as if I were the conspirator of this particular outing instead of her. Silly. She held the beautiful green book in the air, touched my stomach again, and then she was gone.

Steven had plopped down on the couch in the middle of our newly acquired baby booty when I returned to the living room. I picked up a sheet set covered with little baby lambs and stuffed it back into a store bag. When I reached for another item, Steven grabbed my hand and pulled me down onto the couch beside him, deftly snatching the stuffed lamb I was about to sit on and popping it into my arms.

I laughed and leaned against his shoulder.

"Hanging out with your Mom make you feel better?" he said.

"Oh my gosh, yes," I said, then it hit me. I peeked up at him. "Wait a minute. What makes you think I needed to feel better? Did you instigate this?"

"Instigate might not be the right word," he said, sounding every bit the instigator. "Margie called. I might have mentioned that a shopping spree could snap you out of your funk."

I sat up. "Funk?"

Now Steven had that deer-in-the-headlights look in his eyes. The desire to backpedal was so apparent I almost felt sorry for him, but unfortunately my newly acquired quick-to-the-defensive temper seemed to be the main thing in control these days.

His hands went straight to his hair. He pushed it back and left his fingers there, elbows in the air. "Come on, Em. Something's going on with you. I know you were in those tunnels again yesterday."

That stung. I had always been ready, especially since I became pregnant, to defend my explorations as a safe, healthy, legitimate hobby, but this time I had to admit I'd been a little freaked out by my latest trip down there. A clear vision of that metal door, caked over in dried mud, the dusty draft along the floor, and that scream—but of course it wasn't a scream, it was something else, something logical, it had to be—sprang to my mind.

I forced myself to settle in against my husband, to seek shelter in him instead of fighting him. In my heart I knew he wanted the best for me, and arranging for my mother to take me shopping was a sweet gesture, not one I needed to jump all over him for.

He let his arms fall down, relaxing, and wrapped them around me. "What's going on, Em? I didn't say anything last night, but I could tell something was bothering you."

Something. Everything. Too much.

Between codes and blood and hidden metal doors, I couldn't even pinpoint what it was that bothered me the most. The tunnels or the CURE? Alyssa or my new extremely pale goth/emo friend? The fact that I hadn't made as much as a dent in the nursery I should be decorating because finding out what had possessed my long-ago neighbors to carve tunnels beneath their land preoccupied my mind. I needed to give him something, so I picked what I considered to be the most benign of my choices, leaving out the encounter with my hospital buddy in the parking lot at Rosie's market. Steven was already on alert. Mentioning Rosie's would not go over well.

"Well, I did almost pass out in the grocery store yesterday, but other than that …" I threw in a little laugh as an attempt at deflection.

I felt the muscles of his chest tense beneath my cheek. "What exactly do you mean by pass out?"

"Dizzy. Woozy." I drew a spiral in the air with my finger.

"It was the blood in the stupid meat package," I said, and immediately wished I hadn't let that thought into my head, much less voiced it. In a flash, I pushed myself up off the couch and ran for the bathroom.

Mom's visit inspired me. I spent all day Wednesday working in the nursery. I moved boxes, and packed and moved more boxes, and carried them one by one to the garage, trading the mess in the baby's room for another pile of disarray in the spot where Steven normally parked his car. He wouldn't be able to pull his car in until we moved the boxes to yet another area, but I felt sure he wouldn't mind. It wasn't as if I had much choice.

Each time I sat a box down next to my car, I glanced at the trunk, shrugged off the nasty little flip that threatened to turn my stomach, and went back upstairs. I really needed to ask Steven to take Alyssa's towels out of my trunk for me. It was ridiculous that they were still stuffed inside, and even more ridiculous that I was avoiding dealing with them.

Not the only thing I was avoiding dealing with, I told myself. I had taken great pains to make sure I didn't catch any updates on the CURE. That meant no radio, so I had loaded the CD player with some of my favorites. When I plunked down at lunchtime in front of the TV with my sandwich and lemonade, I found myself changing the channel to HBO before I even turned on the set. I didn't care anything about watching a movie, but I wanted to make sure I didn't accidentally catch a special update, a talk show, or even a trailer for the six o'clock news.

Of course the main thing I was trying to avoid was thinking about the tunnels, the metal door, the squealing screech stretching out of the darkness, what had made the dirt slink across the ground in that cloudy wave. Admittedly, I wasn't having much success since my mind continually returned to the idea of getting back underground to see if there were more side tunnels to each of the houses that had once stood there. I toyed with calling Dr. Kendall, but rejected that course. He'd already given me the satchel of documents. I still had leads I hadn't completely followed through on.

By the time Steven came home around eight, I had completely exhausted myself with scenarios and plotting and diversionary tactics, plus thirty or so trips up and down the stairs, and fallen into a deep sleep on the couch. He woke me long enough to encourage me to slurp down a bowl of chicken noodle soup. Then I went back upstairs and crawled into bed for the night.

I heard the answering machine pick up when I stepped out of the shower. Dr. Sherman's office reminding me I had an appointment on Friday afternoon.

I dragged the towel across my hair, rubbing out the moisture. I had completely forgotten. I hadn't even mentioned it to Steven, which was just as well. With all he had going on at work, I doubted he would be able to get away for the appointment anyway.

I stood in the nursery doorway, staring at the progress I had made yesterday. The floor was nearly clean. Two cans of paint sat alongside a drop cloth, paint tray, rollers, and extension poles. I thought about the baby book my mother had bought us and how I would love the serenity of these walls once they were painted in that new-spring-leaves shade of green.

Painting was not on the agenda for today. Curiosity was. I needed to get out of the house.

I drove straight to the church. My backpack was in the back seat, along with my 1930's neighborhood map. I had traded my broken headlamp for the spare that worked and brought an awl and a couple of wedges, all lighter than the pick-axe and less destructive, for chipping away the dirt over the metal doors, assuming there were more metal doors. There would be. I knew it in my heart, although even after an entire day of self-imposed distracted contemplation, I still couldn't pinpoint what purpose they served. All I could figure is they were emergency exits from the underground storage facility at LifeShare. But why were they camouflaged as part of the tunnel walls? Maybe LifeShare didn't own enough of the land to completely shut down the tunnels, but for safety reasons they needed to keep the exit doors concealed so no one would try to get in. No one but me, that is. I remembered a time when I would have chewed out another person for daring to destroy a part of the tunnels, and now I was wielding axes with nary a care. Of course, I reminded myself, the "tunnel walls" I had destroyed weren't part of the original structure.

At the last second my churning brain registered that the traffic light at Broad Street was shining red. I slammed on my brakes, skidding to a stop. First Baptist was only another mile down Main Street. I had been so intent on getting there I had almost run the light.

An old tan Impala pulled through the intersection in front of me. The man inside gave me my well-earned dirty look and cruised on through. Thank God it wasn't anybody I knew, and thank God I hadn't hit him. My chest heaved.

I made a snap decision and turned left, toward LifeShare.

The gated section of LifeShare's rear parking lot began a little over a half mile down Broad. At a quarter mile, I turned onto a side road that wasn't marked. In all the times I had gone to visit Steven at work, I had never been down this road before but I felt sure it had to lead to the back of LifeShare. It seemed to run parallel to the main entrance. About a hundred yards along, the pavement gave way to dirt. I felt an instant security—it was a familiar sensation, one that usually came over me whenever I was surrounded by the simplicity of earth and nothing else—as I bounced along the rutted pathway, raising a funnel of dust behind me. The road wasn't maintained. Deep crags made my wheels drop at odd angles. I began to worry about the oil pan and carefully maneuvered the car to avoid rocks. Foliage along the sides of the road thickened, creeping inward, the branches clawing gently against my doors like woody fingers. The high scratching squeals reminded me of the eerie howl that had resonated from far back in the tunnels, for I had convinced myself in the darkness of my dreams that it was indeed a howl, or scream, or some other call of distress that had nothing to do with contracting heat ducts or air compressors.

A shudder worked its way over my shoulders and slid up my neck like ice. I took a deep breath and concentrated on keeping the damage to my car's paint to a minimum, rolling slowly along, until the woods alongside the road opened up to reveal a smoother path, a strip of loamier soil cut down the middle by a two-foot swath of green weedy growth. The road dead-ended into scrub after another thirty yards. Reluctantly, I parked and stepped out.

The area in front of me was less overgrown than the woods I had just driven through, as if someone had made an attempt to keep it cleared up until maybe the last year. What might have once been a pasture was now knee-deep in short brush, small pines, dandelions, and a spray of yellow butterweed.

After a moment, my ears tuned to the sounds of rustling leaves, chirping birds, the rattling of twigs as a squirrel darted in front of me and up a nearby oak resplendent with age and gnarled branches. Dust lingered in the air behind my car. I saw nothing but nature here. I could hardly detect the opening in the woods where I would need to retrace the path back out.

I sighed, and my own voice sounded cavernous and disconcerting in my head, like an intrusion on this space.

The wind kicked up, rattling the mounds of bushes and weeds in front of me. Sweet gardenia road the breeze and filled my nostrils. I knew exactly which way to go. I tucked my keys deep into my jeans pocket and followed the scent.

Walking through it, I found the brush wasn't as thick as I had thought. I could still make out the original road by keeping my eyes trained on the ground in front of my feet. Each time the wind gusted, the scent of gardenia became a bit stronger, until finally I saw the glossy bushes smattered with white blossoms.

The gardenias formed a hedge across what was now a rotted wood porch sagging under the weight of time and neglect. The rest of the house had pretty much caved in on itself, leaving a pile of rubble memorialized by twin brick fireplaces at either end. I experienced mixed emotions over what stood before me. I was excited that I had found this house—it was the only home remaining from the neighborhood that had once occupied this land. At the same time, I felt a poignant sense of regret for the decay of that stately white clapboard from the photo Dr. Kendall had given me.

Not quite ready to trespass—this had, after all, been someone's home—I turned slowly and surveyed the spread of land behind me. The overgrowth came to a height that reached somewhere between the short brush close to the house and the older wooded area heading back toward Broad Street. The area had definitely been neglected, not so much as the thicker woods, but longer than the plants that had once been a part of the house's landscape. Between the trees, a glint of chain link caught my eye. I guessed it sectioned off the flat barren area beyond because that land belonged to LifeShare, and concealed directly below that land was the new underground blood storage facility. I had no interest in that area right now. The idea that the homes from my map had probably once occupied that space brought a wave of anger over me. I realized I had already formed a personal attachment to my 1930s neighborhood in the same way that I called the tunnels my own. Never mind. Probably if I poked around enough, I would find a No Trespassing sign anyway, so I turned away and focused my attention on what was left of the white house.

Steven would not approve, but I would have to worry about that later. Right now, there weren't any signs telling me to keep out of the house, so I began picking my way through the rubble.

I felt like a kid again. The sense of doing something I shouldn't intermingled with the hope of finding some treasure and keeping a secret that was all mine, although I really had no way of knowing who else might know about this place. If it didn't belong to LifeShare—and I assumed it didn't since it hadn't been leveled along with the adjacent land—it belonged to somebody. Maybe one of I.J.'s descendents, I thought, remembering the initials on the mailbox in the photo.

The sun angled slightly west of overhead. Its rays cut through slats of wood that had formed the rear exterior wall, parsing the tattered floors into shadowy stripes. Already heated up from my trek over the rolling hills, I was intensely aware of the thin sunbeams stinging into the skin on my neck and arms. I had been planning on exploring underground, not a day out in the sun. I hadn't bothered with sunscreen. Even the partial shade of that back wall looked irresistible. I began picking a path in that direction.

I stepped gingerly over the boards, testing each one before putting my full weight on it. Staring down at my feet, I became acutely aware of just how much the bump of my stomach had grown, seemingly overnight.

"Don't worry, baby," I muttered into the empty space. "We are not falling through any floorboards today."

As if to mock me, the next board I stepped on groaned menacingly and gave unexpectedly under my weight, throwing me off balance so my other foot came down with a crash when I tried to steady myself. The plank screeched in protest, sagging beneath me, but held as I buckled full force, rolling to minimize my impact. I came to a stop and wrapped my arms protectively around my folded knees until I caught my breath.

When I looked up, I realized that what I thought were floor planks was really a cellar door built into the floor. Without the support of cross beams, the trap door was less stable than the actual floor, and I imagined that at one time there had been a rug, or possibly a small table, over the door that would have minimized traffic over the weaker area. The wood hadn't broken, but the door had twisted on its hinges when I had fallen into it and now sagged precariously on one side.

I reached out, snaked my fingers through a cutout near the edge, and pulled up. The ancient hinges had bent, either from time or neglect or from my impromptu vandalism—perhaps a combination of the three. At any rate, the door resisted so that I had to climb back to my feet for leverage. The hinges screamed in protest, but with my back and leg muscles behind my effort, I managed to pull the door all the way up, revealing a crude set of stairs constructed of bricks laid into the hard clay.

I found myself glancing around, then thought how ridiculous I must seem if, by chance, anyone could actually witness my solitary intrusion on this space.

"This is not some bad movie," I told myself. Feigning more resolve than I actually felt, I rubbed my hands against the legs of my jeans, wiping away the sweat lingering there, and stepped onto the bricks.

The steps descended in a spiral. I followed the outer edge, where the risers were wider. They curved sharply back toward the front of the house, and the thin sunlight streaming in through the western wall didn't cast much in the way of light once I had descended halfway down. With no handrail, I put my hands against the dirt walls to steady myself and tested the edge of each step with the bottom of my foot before stepping down. The smell of the damp earth quickly engulfed me along with the darkness. The feel of the carved dirt beneath my fingertips triggered a familiarity, reminding me of the side tunnels leading to the foreign metal doors I had discovered and how I had trailed my fingertips along those rough walls in the same exact way. There was nothing to hold onto, but the connection with the clay was comforting nonetheless.

There was no metal door at the bottom of these steps. Even before my eyes adjusted to the lack of light, I felt and formed the image in my mind—strong thick wooden door, iron hinges, heavy handle. It was so normal, so befitting the rest of the house that had nearly fallen to ruin, so exactly what I should find beneath a century-year-old house, that I was filled with relief and actually laughed.

After a moment, my eyes adjusted and I could make out a dim version of the door. Rough wooden slabs banded together by iron straps, it was so wonderfully unexceptional that it instantly established itself as a favorite discovery. Wasn't this the kind of thing I had been hoping to find—something out of history, something that held the promise of revelation, of purpose or origin? My only regret was that the cellar door was sealed tight by a heavy lock that hung from the handle. I grasped the lock and tugged, disappointed to find it held fast against the possibility of rust and decay. The living area above had been stripped bare, providing not a hint as to who had lived here or what kind of lives had transpired within these walls. Even though I had enjoyed that space for the relic it was, I realized I had felt as let down by the lack of artifacts there as I was intrigued by what might be hidden behind this door.

But, I told myself, I could not, and would not, be breaking any locks, and I was practically overjoyed to find I hadn't completely lost my respect for such places after all.

I put my palms against the door, leaned forward and laid my cheek against the wood, relishing the tactile sensation of being one with a space. The kids at school had made fun of me for such unusual behavior, which was probably why I enjoyed exploring alone so much. Having no one around to observe my zany quirks suited me just fine.

The door was cool to the touch, and I closed my eyes, imagining the foods that might have been stored inside. My thoughts took over my senses, wandering away, until a thump, soft but solid, reverberated through my face and hands. I jerked away from the door. Shivers swept up my arms and creepy-crawled over my scalp, tingling, as waves of cold air crept through the tiny cracks between the planks of the door and around the edges.

Recoiling, I scrambled backward, forgetting the steps behind me, and tripped into the bricks. The small of my back landed hard against one sharp edge. I cried out, but my voice betrayed me, restricting itself to a guttural groan trapped in my throat. Grappling for purchase on the crooked steps, I scuttled backwards up the curving bricks, clawing with my hands to get back to the light.

CHAPTER TWELVE

I didn't go home, didn't want to be alone in my house. I felt like a spooked kid and sought out the closest comfort of a parental figure I could think of. I drove to Professor Kendall's house.

Liz, Alan's wife, took one look at my grimy skin and immediately ushered me into the shower, where I stood until my fingertips pruned. I had cranked the temperature to about one degree short of scalding. The spray beat into my burned shoulders like tiny knives, but I couldn't shake the feeling of that cold air from the cellar. It had come out of nowhere. It didn't belong, didn't make sense.

Eventually, soaked and safe, a welcome trace of defiance began to conquer my unease. Venturing, exploring—that's what I did. It had never rattled me before. Removed from the scene, I now wondered if I'd had any real reason to be frightened in the first place. If I thought logically about it, what had happened that was so out of the ordinary? A bump? A puff of air? The scariest thing about all this, I decided, was how easily I had freaked out. I didn't care for that version of myself.

Towel-dry and back in my clothes, I padded into the living room, feeling surprisingly awkward.

"Ah, there she is," Alan called from the kitchen. "Just in time."

I forced a smile, suddenly embarrassed at having chosen his house as my refuge.

"Don't be like that now," he said. He thrust a steamy mug at me, and I sniffed. Hot chocolate, a treat that would normally seem odd when the temperatures were already reaching the mid-eighties outside. But he knew me, didn't he? Had for a very long time. And the warm brew was the perfect salve for what was bothering me.

I sipped, relishing the warm slide into my empty stomach. Alan sank into the end of his overstuffed couch, sipping at his own cup, which I was pretty sure contained black coffee laced with a shot of aged whiskey. I smiled again, genuinely this time, and plopped onto the cushion next to him.

"Thanks for the shower," I said, pulling at the ends of my wet hair.

"Well, you looked like a sad little orphan caught out without her coat."

"Such a terrible thing in this Georgia humidity, too," I joked. My eyes fell to my flaming pink shoulders. I had the sunburn to prove that coat or no orphan's coat, I was certainly in no danger of succumbing to any frigid temperatures.

"How're those shoulders feeling?" Alan asked, following my gaze. His expression hovered somewhere between sympathy and revulsion.

"I'll probably be okay as long as I don't touch them for the next week or so."

"You know they've got this amazing new invention called sunscreen," Alan quipped, flashing eyes disappearing behind the rim of his mug.

"Haha. I'm usually *under*ground? I didn't plan on hiking out in the sun, you know."

"And yet you were. How'd that come to be?"

The patio door hissed on its track. Liz came in carrying a tray covered with aloe leaves.

"Don't scold, Alan," she said, lugging the tray to the coffee table. She began expertly stripping away the outer layer of one cutting with a vegetable peeler. It wound up looking something like a slimy paintbrush, which she held out to me. "We all get caught out in this sun unprepared from time to time. Go ahead. Just paint that right onto your sunburn. You won't believe how much it'll help."

I obediently took the aloe brush and began drawing stripes of the cooling juice over my skin.

"This was pretty stupid of me," I said.

Liz was busy peeling another leaf. "Ah, at least you're not too fair. I'll send some of this aloe home with you. Couple doses and you'll start tanning up in no time. As for being stupid, let me guess. You had a hankering to follow a lead and took off without thinking it through. I'm familiar with the type, you know."

She cut a quick glance toward her husband, and I stifled a laugh.

"Hmmm," I said, "I suppose this could be considered his fault, now that I think about it."

Alan had raised his coffee mug for another sip, but stopped midway. "You two ladies aren't going to gang up on me, are you?"

"Remember when we looked at the LifeShare space on Google maps? I didn't think much of it at the time, but I must have noticed the dirt road, the one that runs around the LifeShare storage area. I've driven by that road a hundred times, but I never really wondered where it might lead until I found that picture of the white clapboard house in the documents you gave me. When I realized it bordered the north edge of the 1930s neighborhood, I decided to drive out and see if anything was left of the house."

"Dog with a bone," Liz said nonchalantly. Alan and I caught each other in hangdog grins.

"All right," he said. "So what exactly out there got you so spooked?"

I recounted the story as best I could. I felt silly, too much like that little girl Alan had described for my liking, and insecure when it came time to tell them about the cold air coming from the cellar. And since the stand-alone fact that I had freaked out over a bump and a breeze sounded so ridiculous to my own ears, I spilled the whole story of how I had gouged away walls of dirt, revealing both concrete and metal hidden beneath the ground, finishing up with the way I had bolted from the tunnels after cold dirt stirred and swirled itself around my feet, my fear boiled over by the voice I thought had screamed at me from the depths of the maze.

"I thought it might have something to do with the refrigeration in LifeShare's blood storage facility," I added hopefully, grasping onto what felt like the only rational possibility left in my story. "I guess that's where you come in, Liz."

Elizabeth Kendall was the only actual physicist I knew, although at this stage of her life, she preferred to tinker in the garden, create culinary wonders of the hot chocolate variety, and dote on her semi-workaholic history-geek of a husband.

"Well," she said after a contemplative pause, "if the metal doors you're talking about are directly connected to a cooled storage facility underground, and they were relying on the faux walls of the tunnel as an insulation or sealing agent, then removing the earthen barrier could theoretically allow a displacement of air to occur if that were the only outlet, kind of like the way the back door will slam when you swing open the front door. Now, having said that, I can't begin to fathom what type of engineer would come up with a system that utilizes these tunnels as part of their schematic."

Alan stuck a finger in the air. "Unless LifeShare was able to purchase this particular tract of land, which was big enough for their purposes, but they couldn't secure the entire area that included the tunnels. Putting metal doors in the middle of a tunnel system practically screams, 'See if you can break in here.' Hence the mud walls. Civilizations have been constructing …"

"That's exactly what I thought!" I rudely interrupted with little regret, since Liz and I exchanged a knowing look, both realizing that Alan could quickly travel down a historical tangent from which there would be no return.

"If they don't own the land," I continued, "that would explain why the tunnels are still open. LifeShare didn't have the right to seal them off completely, so they just sealed off as much as they could. Of course that raises the question of who does own that land. I know part of it is on the church property. That's where I enter, so unless the church decides to seal off that entrance, I assume there will always be access. What about the cellar at the house?" I blurted, changing directions. "I'm pretty sure the metal doors are located right where cellars to the old houses would have stood. What if the clapboard is connected to the tunnel system, too? Is there any way the air displacement could travel that far?"

Liz shook her head. "I don't see how. Maybe if the tunnels were sealed, and that were the only point of escape, but since the tunnels have an opening in the opposite direction, any air, after leaving the side tunnel you mentioned, unless it were acted on by some opposing force, would travel equally in all directions. I can't imagine a refrigeration system creating enough airflow to cause a reaction that far away. Unless the building has a built-in design that vents through the tunnel system. Have you noticed anything like that in the main tunnels?"

"No," I said. "Nothing like that, not until that one time after I uncovered the door. And I can't even say for sure that clearing the dirt away left any kind of breach or crack or opened any kind of seal around the door where air could come through. I just felt the cold air behind me and saw the dirt swirling on the ground. I should have stayed put and examined it more closely, I guess, but the willies got the better of me."

"Could have been a ghost," Alan chimed in his deep, logical voice, and I jerked around to face him.

Liz reached over and tapped his arm. "Stop that, Alan, That is not helpful."

Hearing such a southern-belle, motherly instinct come from the former physicist's mouth brought a smile to my face. I suspected she meant it to render Alan's ghost comment absurd. It almost succeeded, but I could not honestly say the crazy thought had not crossed my mind. I also thought it was interesting that Alan, not having been allowed to venture down a historical path in the conversation, had gracefully turned it over to us ladies until the chance to seize an irresistible opportunity to tease had presented itself.

In an effort to take the paranormal out of the equation, I asked, "Can you think of any other reason the cellar door would have cold air flowing from behind it? And there was that thump?"

Liz's mouth turned down at the corners as she thought briefly. "That thump could have been anything, I suppose. A rat, some other animal. As for the cold air—and I hope you know I don't mean to diminish your experience at all—but is it possible that you've turned that into more than it actually was?"

"What do you mean?" Even though I tried to disguise it, I didn't have a knack for the nonchalant like Liz. I felt sure she could detect my instant defensive streak kicking in.

Spreading a soothing smile across her face, she said, "I'm a scientist, so try to keep in mind this has more to do with my scientific method than what it sounds like to you, which is probably that I don't believe you. That's not what's going on here."

"It's really not," Alan offered, shaking his head in confirmation.

"Consider," Liz went on after an appreciate glance at her husband, "that you previously had an unusual experience involving this mysterious flow of cold air in the tunnels, a confined secluded place, and this is probably foremost in your mind. It is, after all, the reason you decided not to go back into the tunnels but to drive out to the house in the first place. So whether you were conscious of it or not, I'm sure it was on your mind."

I couldn't argue with that, and gave her a little nod.

"The cellar is underground, like the tunnels. It's meant to be cooler, for storage—reminiscent of the LifeShare blood storage facilities, I'm sure. There's a door. It's not metal, I'll give you that, but do you see the similarities?" She went on without actually soliciting an answer. "The house is open, it was breezy today. Could it be that a bit of breeze dipped down the cellar stairs, stirring the cooler air, and with all that's going through your head, you reacted more intensely than you normally would have? It's how they get us in the horror movies—build up the anticipation in our minds. Then, bam, any old thump in the dark sends us screaming."

I let out a little laugh. "Physicist, psychologist, and movie critic, are we?"

"Nah, just trying to set your mind at ease. Being pregnant will do enough to your head without throwing conspiracy and local mysteries into the mix."

The mention of my pregnancy snapped me back to reality. I hadn't told Steven I was driving out to visit the Kendalls, and as much as I was enjoying playing the baby bird in this intellectual nest, it was probably time for me to go.

"And you have," I said. "I think I needed a voice of wisdom to ground me. I'll be the first to admit the hormonal swings have definitely got my brain twisted about lately."

Alan grunted, as if the mention of a lady's hormones deserved a male counterpoint to keep the conversation worthy of mixed company.

"Being pregnant might make you a little goofy from time to time," Liz said, "but don't let it get in the way. I believe you're on to something. It might turn out to be more of a *historical* mystery," she said, glancing at Alan with a twinkle in her eye, "but a mystery just the same. In fact, when you find out who this I.J. person is or why the houses in that neighborhood had tunnels beneath them, I know Alan and I both want to hear the whole story."

"Thanks for being my sounding board. And for the shower. And for the hot chocolate … and the aloe," I added, laughing. When I stood up, Liz jumped to her feet and took the mug I had been holding. At some time during our conversation I had finished off the hot chocolate. It and the aloe had worked double magic, soothing the chill inside me as well as the chilling burn across my shoulders.

Liz placed the mug on the coffee table and picked up the remaining aloe stems.

"Put another coat of this on before you go to bed tonight," she said clinically, like a doctor administering orders that were not to be refused. She held out a small cheesecloth pouch containing leaves and cinched at the top with string. "Tomorrow morning try this tea. Brew it up, let it cool, then soak a couple of washcloths, and put those on your shoulders a couple of times during the day. This is a special blend I put together, but if you need more just use straight green tea."

She glanced at Alan, who eyed the pouch suspiciously. I wondered how many of Liz's natural home remedy experiments he had endured over the years.

Liz slapped his chest playfully with the back of her hand and passed the pouch of tea to me. "Stop giving her that look, Alan," she told him, then whispered confidentially to me, "It works. Even some tough guys are sensitive to the sun. We've dealt with our share of sunburns over the years."

I took the pouch, carefully avoiding looking at Alan lest I burst into laughter. They made an adorable couple.

"First thing in the morning," she reiterated. "Don't forget. I think you'll be feeling better in no time."

I hoped so. I also wondered whether Liz was referring to my sunburn or to the fact that she thought I'd gone a little crazy.

"What happened to your back?"

I whirled around at the sound of Steven's voice and yanked the clean t-shirt down over my waist. Still preoccupied with my day, I hadn't heard him drive up, come up the stairs, not even the garage door lifting or the door to the house close. Anyone could have walked in on me. Not exactly a comforting thought.

"It's just a bruise," I said, reaching for the clean shorts laid across the foot of the bed.

Steven leaned against the door jamb, a move that seemed easygoing but seethed with irritation. I had a pretty good idea what was coming next.

"Yeah, I see that. What happened, Em?"

"Well, I wasn't in the tunnels if that's what you're wondering." Defensive again, my voice nearly squeaked the retort.

"Okay," he said reasonably. "How'd you get the bruise?"

"I just tripped and fell back against some … stairs. It's fine. It doesn't even hurt."

"This happened today, and it's already black and blue. It has to hurt." Frowning, he stuck his right hand out, planted it against the other side of the door, creating a human blockade. The gesture ticked me off. I felt trapped and wanted nothing more than to fling myself against that arm and break through to the hallway. *Red Rover, Red Rover, send Emmalyn right over.*

Instead, I picked up my dirty clothes and carried them to the hamper.

"Okay, it hurts," I admitted, "a little, but only if you touch it. So don't," I added, glaring at him momentarily.

"I won't," he countered.

We sounded like a couple of brats.

"Where'd it happen?" he asked, and when I didn't immediately answer, "Where were you?"

Sorting laundry suddenly seemed like a great way to avoid my guilt. If I looked at him now, I would see the accusation written on his face. It was apparent enough in his voice, so I dug into the hamper and began tossing colors in one direction, whites in another.

"I found an abandoned house and wanted to check it out," I finally said. "It was nothing. There were some stairs leading down to a cellar. I lost my footing at the bottom and kind of fell back against the steps. That's all."

"That's not nothing, Em," Steven scolded. "This is exactly why I don't want you wandering around in tunnels by yourself—"

"I wasn't in the tunnels." I cut him off.

"Tunnels. Abandoned houses. Doesn't matter," he huffed. "You were there by yourself. No, wait—you weren't alone. You had our baby with you."

"Low blow," I said, beginning to fume a little. "As if I'd put our baby in danger."

"Isn't that exactly what you're doing?"

I was growing extremely tired of being talked to like an irresponsible teenager, but that didn't stop him from continuing. "Did your phone even work wherever this house was? Did you think to let me know where you were going? Was there anyone around to help you if you had gotten seriously hurt?"

Steven's last remark, obviously meant to slap me into some kind of rational reality, accomplished quite the opposite. I thought of the guy from the hospital and how he had appeared out of nowhere to help me get Alyssa from the car and into the building, how he'd been there when I passed out at the grocery store. In fact, he seemed to have appeared out of nowhere each of the handful of times I had seen him. Maybe *he* would have come to my rescue if I had needed him.

I threw down the jeans I had just pulled from the hamper, jammed my fists on my hips, and looked my husband directly in the eye.

"No, Steven. There was no one around. Nobody but me, out in the middle of nowhere without a thought of safety for our unborn child, thinking only of myself and what I want to do, whenever I want to do it. Is that what you want to hear? You know I'm careful. I've been doing this sort of thing for as long as you've known me, long before that even. I didn't check my phone, but I'm sure it worked. I wasn't more than a mile and a half from Main Street and Broad, fifty feet from that stupid fence that borders LifeShare. If I'd screamed loud enough, you might have heard me from your office," I added.

"Settle down," he said, clearly astonished at my outburst. Granted, we hadn't had many, but this wasn't the way we usually handled our disputes. He reached toward me, lowering the muscle blockade, and I took that moment to barge through the door and down the stairs.

He didn't follow me.

We spent the next hour stewing in separate rooms, Steven in his office and me in the kitchen throwing together an impromptu dinner. Having abandoned the laundry upstairs, I opted for the therapy of chopping vegetables. When I had finally decimated two bell peppers, an onion, and three carrots, I threw them into a pan and started in on the chicken. The sizzle of veggies in oil made a soothing sound that demanded my attention and eventually accomplished what Steven had wanted. Of course he had said *settle down*—maybe not the best phrasing under the circumstances—but the outcome was the same, which was the settling of my nerves.

I poured the stir fry over some quick-cook rice noodles and forced myself to walk down the hall to Steven's office.

"Dinner's ready," I said softly, barely poking my head around the edge of the door.

Without hesitation, he planted the splayed fingers of both hands in his hair and turned to face me. His bottom lip was drawn up into a knot that told me he was trying to put our little spat behind him.

"It's not crow," I said with a tease, "so come on."

He sighed and pushed himself out of the chair. "Don't care for the crow."

"Who among us does?"

We ate quietly, still not fully recovered from the tension. Afterwards I rinsed the vegetable peeler and took it into the living room to whittle back the outside layer of the aloe Liz had given me. I had just finished slathering it over my shoulders, chest, and the back of my neck when Steven appeared with two cups of vanilla ice cream.

"Peace offering?" he asked

"Thanks," I said, and grasping for a counteroffer, said, "You know I've got a doctor's appointment tomorrow."

His eyebrows went up. "Did you tell me that?"

"I might have mentioned it when I first made it. I can't remember, but I didn't remind you, so I'm not going to be mad if you can't come. I can ask the doctor whether hitting my back poses any danger to the baby while I'm there."

He paused as if thinking over the best response, finally settling on, "I think that's a good idea. I wish I could go with you, but I don't think I can get away from work."

"What's happening at LifeShare?" I asked, grabbing onto the change of subject, even if I wasn't crazy about the subject matter. "Have you figured out what's going on with the database? You haven't mentioned it lately."

He stuck the spoon in his mouth, shook his head, and pulled the spoon out clean. "I've done about all I can do on that," he said. "There haven't been any hits on the database since I embedded the program to trace activity, at least nothing that would trigger an alert. We could have a hacker who's laying low. No evidence the data's being used outside the company, and the legitimate database is functioning as it should."

"So it's a waiting game?"

"Pretty much," he said

"Aren't you finding that frustrating?" I asked. He had gone after the problem like a dog after a bone in the beginning. Now he had lapsed into wait-and-see mode, a strategy I had difficulty understanding. In my mind, Steven's pursuit of the database glitch paralleled my ventures in the tunnels, and I was certainly frustrated by my own lack of answers.

"Yeah," he said, "but I've got my hands full right now. We're going to have trainers on-site tomorrow to help us get geared up for the first steps in implementing CURE."

"So soon?" I slurred around a mouthful of ice cream.

"Em, how can you not know what's going on with this?" he said with a smidge more vehemence than I thought was necessary.

I decided to treat his question as rhetorical, but just the same, it was a good thing I had my mouth full. I shifted, folding my feet into the space between me and the overstuffed chair arm.

As if to prove that I was lacking in a proper CURE education, he flipped on the TV and toggled through a series of news channels, each one offering updates on the progress of the cancer vaccine. When he glanced over at me, I smiled sweetly, ignoring what I perceived as a reproachful attitude.

"I get your point," I said. "Why don't you just tell me how this thing is unfolding, since you're at the hub of it."

If he thought I was being smart, he didn't let on. "Well, there's going to be a press conference early next week to give the public more information about how the vaccine actually works. The main reason LifeShare's been chosen as one of the first sites to administer it is because we already have the storage capability in place."

"Blood storage?" I asked rather weakly, unable to keep my peripheral thoughts about LifeShare's intrusion on the tunnels from creeping back into my brain.

"Yes. Turns out that the vaccine involves a series of steps, starting with donating blood. Not for public use. The donated blood gets treated with the vaccine, its earmarked solely for the patient that donates it, and it'll be kept in our new underground storage facility until we've stored and treated enough for a transfusion. That's the final step."

"A full blood transfusion? How much blood does that take?"

"Not a full transfusion, but close. The human body, average, contains ten pints. The collection will be nine pints treated."

"At a pint per donation, wouldn't that take eighteen months?" I said, shocked. I may not have been following the news, but I was aware enough to know people probably already thought this was going to be a quick fix, not a year-and-a-half commitment to receive the treatment.

"Normally, yes, since we're only allowed to donate every fifty-six days, but there's a saline-based replacement solution available now that'll allow us to donate one-and-a-half pints and reduce the waiting time between donations to thirty days. That shortens the whole process to six months."

"That's still a long time," I said. "Disappointing for a lot of people. And I would think you'd have to be in good health to donate that frequently. What about the people who already have cancer?"

Even though I had made a valiant attempt to keep CURE as far off my radar as I could manage, I found I was honestly distressed by this new revelation. My distraught expression must have read as nausea to Steven.

"Are you okay talking about this, Em?" he asked, sitting a little straighter and wearing a sudden should-I-grab-a-wastebasket look on his face. "You're not going to ..." he trailed off, drawing an explosive barfing gesture in the air by quickly fanning his fingers.

I was definitely digging deep into the last of my reserves to stay in the conversation without getting queasy. The ice cream, cool on my stomach, was helping for the time being.

"I'm fine," I said. I couldn't help wondering how long LifeShare had been privy to this new-found cure for cancer before the rest of us knew anything about it. The expanded storage facility had barely completed construction. And the employees had been "encouraged" to donate blood more frequently over the past year. I found myself calculating the number of pints Steven had donated during that time. I thought we had both believed that blood was earmarked for hospitals. Now I wondered how much of it was being stored underneath LifeShare. Were Steven and his coworkers intended to be the first recipients of the vaccine? Was my husband going to be a human guinea pig?

I decided to keep my questions to myself for the time being. Steven was already defensive about the part he played in the CURE project. He was upset with me for not being more interested. It didn't seem like a good time to start peppering him with my conspiracy theories.

"Something as big as CURE is always going to have some controversy attached to it," he said. "I admit it's ironic that we'll be able to treat healthier patients first. The process will be different for people who have cancer. It'll take longer to collect the blood necessary for the transfusion. Some of them won't make it that long. Others won't be healthy enough to donate at all. It's sad, but we can't let one element overshadow the fact that, once this is in place, the human race will be cured of cancer going forward."

"Collateral damage," I muttered absently. I already had so much going on in my head, it wasn't likely I could add anything intellectual to our conversation. Now a new idea swirled in the mix. Maybe my suspicions were rooted in the fact that the government was involved. Maybe it was because CURE was being rushed. I had never been one to lend credence to conspiracy theories, but I realized that in my ignorance I had allowed myself to think of this cure as disreputable, possibly even a hoax. Turned out it was anything but a hoax, and my husband had now become a key player.

We.

Steven had used that word at least three times in the last thirty seconds. To my suspicious mind, the people behind CURE were *them* and, warranted or not, I had labeled *them* as the enemy. Now my husband was referring to *them* as *we*, and he clearly included himself in the group.

CHAPTER THIRTEEN

I stood in the doorway to the nursery, surveying the progress I had originally thought would take me most of my pregnancy. The carpet still needed cleaning, the walls painting. Once that was taken care of, I could concentrate on the fun of shopping for the big items. My mom and I had gotten some cute decorations and some adorable outfits, but we still needed baby furniture—crib, dresser, changing table, maybe a rocking chair, bedding for the crib, a colorful mobile to hang over the baby's head, light willowy curtains over blinds to keep the light out when the baby was sleeping. The blinds, of course, would need some kind of safety feature—none of those loose strings a baby could get caught in. The possibilities were endless. Each addition I thought of prompted an array of other items, and each of those was a springboard for a dozen other items we would need.

It occurred to me that maybe I should have been a little more concerned about losing my job.

It also occurred to me that standing here daydreaming might be my way of sabotaging my doctor's appointment. If I was late, I would have to reschedule. If I had to reschedule, I could avoid giving a blood sample, at least for another few days. Maybe that would give me time to think, enough time for me to figure out why giving blood was not a good idea.

And maybe the last thing I needed was more time to think. I was at least pleased to find that the rational part of my brain still existed somewhere in there.

I closed the door to the nursery and was in the car on my way to the doctor thirty minutes later.

My doctor's office, like most of the medical practices in town, was in a stretch of small buildings across the street from the small hospital. I caught a glimpse of the ambulance bay in front of the emergency room doors as I drove past. Averting my eyes, I turned left into the parking lot on the opposite side of the street.

Only a couple of women were seated in the waiting room as I entered. They both glanced up at me when I walked in, identical smiles crossing their faces before they returned to the magazines in their laps. It was impossible to tell if either of them was pregnant. They could probably say the same about me. I could definitely feel a difference in the shape of my body, the slight outward curve of my profile, the way my jeans didn't want to button over my abdomen, but it wouldn't be readily apparent to anyone who looked at me that I was pregnant, especially in this age of the muffin-top. It seemed like everyone had a little paunch hanging over their too-tight jeans these days.

I took a seat and waited, my magazine open in my lap, while the other two women were called back. Another who had already seen the doctor came out the same door a few minutes later. She was obviously pregnant, last trimester it appeared, although I was a poor judge of how belly size related to how far along someone might be. I tried to sneak a peek at the crook of her elbow, to see if a cotton ball was taped across the vein, but she had a sweater draped over her arm so it was impossible to know.

The door swung open again, startling me. The nurse shouted my name as if I wasn't the only person in the room.

I followed her into one of the examining rooms, where she perched me on the end of the exam table. My dangling feet swung nervously from the end, palms and underarms growing sweaty, while my eyes drifted across the posters lining the walls—mostly pictures of in-utero babies in various stages of development.

"Okay, we're just going to get your blood pressure," she said, slapping on a cuff. After a moment, she gave me a slightly disapproving look.

"What's wrong?" I asked.

"Just a little high," she said, turning away to jot the numbers onto my chart. "It's not uncommon. New mothers tend to be a little nervous on their first trips to the obstetrician. We'll keep an eye on it. Having any problems?" she continued, looking at the chart and not at me.

"No," I said, "like what?"

"No spotting. No cramps. Anything out of the ordinary."

"No," I confirmed, then remembered my back. I had promised Steven I would ask the doctor about it. "Except I bruised my back yesterday."

"Hmmm." She glanced my way at this, and made a little note on the chart, but didn't inquire further. "You can show it to Dr. Knight when he comes in." She reached for the door.

"Wait," I blurted, and she turned around. "Dr. Knight? I'm supposed to see Dr. Sherman."

Her eyebrows creased into a frown. "I'm sorry. The ladies at the front desk should have told you. Dr. Sherman was called to the hospital for an emergency C-section. Dr. Lamp usually takes Sherman's patients when he can't be here, but he's out of town, so Dr. Knight agreed to come over so we wouldn't have to cancel appointments. It's okay. These early visits don't really entail much—mostly measuring your uterus. Gauging how far along you are."

I apparently did not respond with the appropriate reassured expression she was hoping for, because she tilted her head and forced a little smile, as if talking to a child. "Don't worry," she said, "when it comes time to have your baby, Dr. Sherman will be there. And if you go into labor during regular business hours, any patients with appointments that day will be seen by either Dr. Lamp or Dr. Knight, depending on who's available that day. It's a good system."

My hands were balled into fists. I got the feeling she would have liked to have added, "... so deal with it." Lucky she didn't because I had a disturbingly satisfying fantasy of throwing a jar of tongue depressors at her.

I inched toward the end of the table, contemplating leaving, but Dr. Knight popped through the door seconds later, thwarting my escape plan.

"Hello there. I'm Dr. Knight. Let's see how this baby's coming along," he said all in a hurried stream, scanning my chart while he washed his hands. He swiped a paper towel across them, then turned and stuck his right hand out toward me, offering to shake. His hand was moist and clammy in mine. Without much decorum, I wiped my palm against the leg of my pants. I couldn't take my eyes off the nondescript average man standing before me. He was definitely the same doctor who had seen Alyssa at the hospital, but he was nothing like I expected from my distorted memory. No horns. No pointy red beard. His hair was light and thinning, his thick glasses drooped down over a round nose, his chin all soft, lacking any angles. A half-smile crinkled his cheeks against the bottoms of his eyes. I had obviously never formed a true visual of this man. The stress of Alyssa's situation had apparently assisted my mind in conjuring up a much more sinister persona.

"Sorry about that. I guess I didn't dry well enough. Lie back and we'll have a look." He reached underneath my calves and yanked out an extension for me to prop my feet on as I laid back on the table.

He pulled some kind of contraption from a drawer, squirted some gel from a bottle onto my abdomen, and held the end of what looked like a microphone against my skin. After a few seconds of moving the apparatus around, a light thumping beat its way through a steady stream of static.

I couldn't help but smile.

"Heartbeat sounds good. Strong."

He grabbed a measuring tape and held one end to my belly button, stretched the other down to my pubic bone over my open jeans.

"Progressing nicely for four months," he said.

I popped up onto my elbows.

"What? No," I grumbled. "Four? That can't be."

He picked up the chart and flipped a few pages back and forth.

"How heavy was your last period?" he said.

"Not very," I said, confused. First he tells Alyssa that she isn't pregnant when she is, and now he's telling me I'm more pregnant than I am.

"Periods pretty regular before that?"

"Sometimes. Not always. Sometimes I could go six weeks." There were a couple of times after Steven and I got married that I thought I might be pregnant, only to have proof to the contrary pop up a couple of weeks later.

"Happens," he said simply. "Sometimes you can have what looks like a light period even after conception. Sometimes it's just a little heavy spotting that you might mistake for a period."

"You mean I was pregnant before my last period."

"That's right. Of course, we can confirm with an ultrasound in a few weeks. That will give you a more accurate due date."

"Is that bad?" I asked. "That I didn't know, I mean? Bad for the baby?"

He crossed his arms and leaned back against the counter.

"Not at all. You eat pretty healthy? You don't smoke? Any drinking?" The questions rattled off the end of his tongue.

I nodded or shook my head at all the appropriate times, mutely answering the questions.

"Then you're fine. Just make sure you take your prenatal vitamins, and we'll see you again in a few weeks. The ladies at the desk will set you up an appointment."

"That's it?" I said.

"Oh, unless you have any questions," he added hastily, as if he couldn't believe he had forgotten to ask.

"What about blood?"

Dr. Knight's expression fell slack. I thought for a moment he might be confused by my question, but then his little smile returned.

"No need for that today."

"You mean I don't have to give a blood sample today?" The octave of my voice was keyed a little high. I wondered if he noticed.

"Afraid of needles, huh? You're off the hook today. No blood. No urine."

I shook my head in acknowledgement and he turned to leave.

"Dr. Knight," I blurted, for the second time.

"Yes?" he said.

"I'm just curious. Can pregnant women give blood? You know, like donate."

For the first time, the smiling crinkles beneath his eyes faded.

"We don't recommend it." His voice had taken on a purely clinical tone. "During pregnancy a woman's blood volume is increased, to nourish the baby. Donating blood is a noble thing to do, but I have to recommend you wait until after the baby is delivered. Then you can donate all you want."

I stared him in the eyes, hoping to read something from his expression, but I was getting nothing.

"What if you gave blood before you knew you were pregnant? You said women can have a period even after they've conceived, so they wouldn't know they shouldn't donate blood, right?" I could see the hurt on Alyssa's face as clearly as if she were standing in front of me.

Dr. Knight crossed his arms again. Whether I was right or not, I read the gesture as standoffish. Of course he could just be anxious to get to his next appointment.

"First of all, the extra period, while normal, isn't all that common," he said. "And if a woman donated blood that early in her pregnancy, it shouldn't cause any complications. Of course, she would need to inform her doctor and then we would need to take a blood sample to monitor red blood cells, iron count. If you gave blood, Mrs. Trew, you should say so. I'm sympathetic to anyone who doesn't care for needles, but this is not the time to let your fear stand in the way of the well-being of your baby," he said, a scolding tone taking over.

I shook my head. "No, no. I didn't mean to give you the wrong idea. My husband works for LifeShare, that's all. They do a lot of blood drives there, and I wasn't sure what the policy was for giving blood if you're pregnant."

The doctor leaned forward a bit. "Yes, I understand LifeShare holds blood drives every six weeks or so. An excellent organization. They provide the hospital with most of its blood needs. Relax, Mrs. Trew. We may have to prick your finger here a time or two, but that's no big deal. The hospital is always in need of blood, but you have the perfect excuse for not participating in the next six or seven blood drives, at least. No big needles for you," he said, the crinkles returning to his eyes.

I had been gearing up to ask about Alyssa. I still couldn't help but wonder if the blood drive had contributed to her losing the baby. The problem, I remembered, was that Alyssa and I were in the minority as far as believing she had actually been pregnant. This man had certainly been adamant that no pregnancy had ever existed.

"I do have a confession to make," I said, wishing I had kept my curiosity about blood donations in check.

Dr. Knight raised his eyebrows.

"I fell and hit my back against something yesterday," I said, my hand going instinctively to the bruise just above my hips.

He walked over and raised the back of my shirt. "That's quite a bruise you have there."

"My husband is worried that falling might pose a risk to the baby," I said, staring ahead while he pressed tenderly at the outside of the bruised area.

A little laugh escaped into the air behind me. "You're feeling fine otherwise, no cramping, no spotting. That baby of yours is well-protected inside your body, so unless you experience any difficulties, there's really no need to be concerned."

Even though I had asked about the fall for Steven's benefit, I couldn't help feeling relief that the baby had suffered no ill effects.

He let my shirt fall back over my hips and stepped back toward the door but kept his eyes trained on me.

"You might want to think about staying out of those tunnels, though."

My heart gave a guilty thunk. "What?" I said, voice trapped in my throat.

Dr. Knight lifted the corner of the current issue of *People* lying on the counter and pulled the community paper from underneath. He unfolded the paper and displayed the picture of me climbing, wild-haired and dirty, out of the tunnel entrance behind First Baptist Church. Samantha Bedding's article about me and my adventures were front page news in Graceville.

I felt a huge sense of relief to get out of the obstetrician's office and away from Dr. Knight. An urge to check on Alyssa came over me, but I decided it would be better to call her casually from home than to show up at her doorstep with inquisitive panic written on my face. We had played out that scene once before and it hadn't turned out well.

Instead, I drove another two miles into the town square and parked in front of City Hall, which was not much more than a slice of red brick façade in a line of conjoined buildings occupying the south side of the square.

My skills as a researcher were limited to which way to turn in a maze of tunnels, so I had no idea if I could find any information here, but I figured it was worth a try.

I approached the counter, thankful that the place was empty except for me, and tapped the bell sitting there.

I recognized the girl who answered the bell from church, but I didn't know her name. I plastered a smile across my face and got ready to do the you-look-familiar-where-do-I-know-you-from dance.

"Hi," she said, eyeing me vacantly, "can I help you?" Young, maybe in her early twenties at best, she obviously had better things to occupy her interest at church than an old married lady like me, since she showed no signs of recognizing me. That suited me just fine. I might be on the front cover of the *Graceville Gazette*, but at least I hadn't acquired local celebrity status.

"Yes," I began. "I'm doing some research on the property that LifeShare owns. I wondered if you might have any real-estate records from that sale, who owned the property before LifeShare bought it."

She hummed thoughtfully. "We could look at the tax assessment. Do you have the address?"

I gave her the address I used when filling out Steven's employment information. Her fingers tapped across the keyboard for a moment.

"Here it is. Lists LifeShare Corporation as the owner, previous owner is First Bank and Trust. That help?"

I shook my head. "What about older records? I believe there used to be an old neighborhood on the property before LifeShare took it over."

"How old?" she said, looking skeptical.

"Nineteen-thirties. I don't know how long the houses stood, whether they were there up until the time LifeShare bought it."

"Nah," she answered, boredom written on her face. "We don't keep anything that old. Five years is about all we can store around here. The older stuff gets moved to storage, but our storage facility flooded a few years back and most of our records were destroyed. Big mess."

"Hmmm," I said, thinking. I really had no idea what I was doing. "Any ideas on where to find that kind of information?"

"I don't have a clue. We've only gone to putting records in the computer here about … two years ago?" she said noncommittally. "And I don't ever remember anything about a neighborhood that old around here. All I remember is a big field. We used to play Frisbee and tag football over there when I was a kid."

"Really? Where LifeShare is now?" I asked.

"Yep." She glanced around. "High school. Great place to park, I mean, hang out. Nobody ever mentioned a neighborhood. If it was there, it must've been torn down or something before I was born. You know who might know, though, is Mrs. Wheaton over at the library. She knows everything."

There was trace of grudging awe in the girl's voice, as if she'd grown up enough to now appreciate elderly wisdom but hadn't quite put her days of interacting with the librarian behind her.

I got back in my car and drove to the library.

I asked for Mrs. Wheaton and waited patiently until a woman in her late eighties slowly worked her way out of a back room. I instantly felt guilty for dragging this woman from whatever she did behind those hidden walls and wondered why in the world she was here instead of at home knitting in front of the television. Her skin was as delicate as lace, her hair a yellowing ochre, and she ambled along by shuffling her feet one before the other without really lifting them, but after looking into the steel-grey eyes draped by so many tiny folds, I believed it was possible this woman could recite the reference numbers of every book in the building.

"Can I help you?" she said, craning her bent neck to look up at me.

"Um, perhaps," I said and introduced myself. If the girl at City Hall had had a healthy respect for this woman, the feeling was certainly contagious. "I'm doing some research on the property that LifeShare owns. I believe there used to be an old neighborhood there. The houses were built around 1930, and ..." I hesitated, unsure of how to proceed. "... and well, it looks like this may have been one of the first subdivisions in the area, so I'm interested in who the people were who lived there, what made them decide to buy the smaller homesteads, that kind of thing."

"I remember the houses you're talking about," she said. "Most of that area was destroyed by a tornado that came through the area forty or so years ago. The rest were torn down. Small homes, not much interest in rebuilding, I guess."

"So you knew the families?" I asked, intrigued. I showed her the list of homeowner names I had jotted down in the car. "I was hoping I might be able to find some family members to talk to." I had scoured the small Graceville phone book and, other than Smith, hadn't found a single surname to match the list from my map, which I found unusual. All I could assume was that the daughters had married and thus lost the lineage, which was no help to me.

"You won't have much luck there. That bunch kept to themselves. A few kids back in the older days, but not much in the way of grandkids as I remember. A lot of them worked at the tanning factory over in Moseby. I guess they were the beginning of that generation where working was more important than raising families, DINKs I think they call them."

A little chuckle escaped her lips, as if that was the most ridiculous thing she could fathom. I rather agreed with her.

After a moment, she continued. "The few that were left when the tornado came, they took the insurance money and moved on. Never heard anything about where they wound up. Hmmm," she said, as if only just considering something she hadn't thought about in years.

"Do you have any idea why those families decided to buy houses in a neighborhood like that? They all seemed to have owned bigger tracts of land before they moved here."

"Oh, no, honey. I was nothing but a tyke when all that happened. Who knows why people do the things they do? Could've been the economy. Times were hard back then. Could've been the newest fad, I guess. Not much has changed in that respect, if you think about it."

Mrs. Wheaton's efficient nature couldn't be held at bay for long by nosy folks like myself. While I worked on forming my next question, she wandered over to the magazine display cases and began sifting through the stacks, shuffling the issues until they were arranged in order with the most recent issue on top.

"What about the white house out behind LifeShare? Old clapboard. It was kind of at the head of that subdivision, only it must have always had dirt road access. It's fallen down now. Do you think that happened in the tornado too? If so, it wasn't leveled the way the neighborhood was. Of course, that could have been LifeShare's doing. They own that land now. Covers over their underground storage, although ..." I caught myself, realized I was rambling. "Although, I'm not sure if that's common knowledge. My husband works there."

Mrs. Wheaton glanced up and grinned. "About everybody's husband works there, honey. Small town like this, not a lot of versatility in the job market. We've become a sort of new variety of the factory town, I suppose."

She went back to her magazines for a moment, leaving me to wonder if we were done with our conversation. Then she looked back up at me with a tilt of her chin. Her eyes narrowed.

"That house didn't fall down from the tornado. No," she said, as if suddenly remembering. "I do recall that fellow owned that house, and his family. Nice folks. The mother, she taught Sunday school over at the First Baptist. Not my age. I was still in grade school. Johnsons, I believe."

I nodded, thinking of the initials on the mailbox in the photo Alan Kendall had given me.

"Yes, that house fell into ill repair along about the time the son died, him in a hunting accident. Young fellow had just started a family, too. I remember my mother talking about it, how sad it was that they lost him right when his wife was about to have their first child."

"That is sad," I said, my hand automatically touching the small swell of my own baby.

Mrs. Wheaton's gaze drifted to where my hand lay. I thought I saw a flash of acknowledgement cross her face.

"They lived there in that clapboard with his parents," she went on, with a chipper note in her voice. "Not a lot of room for that many people, by today's standards, but we made it work back then."

"What about the tunnels?"

"Tunnels?" she asked. She picked up another stack of magazines and began thumbing through the issues.

She obviously hadn't seen the current edition of the town paper and Samantha Bedding's story regaling my underground adventures. Still I had a hard time believing she didn't know anything about the tunnels. No one had any information about them, yet everyone was completely nonchalant about their existence. Weren't there any curious people in Graceville?

"Yes, the tunnels. I thought they might have connected to the cellars of the homes in that subdivision. There's an entrance in the woods over behind the church. The paths have all been cut off by LifeShare's underground building, but it looks to me like at one point those houses were connected by the tunnels."

"Well, that's just silly," she said, the skin around her eyes crinkling in amusement. "You pointed it out yourself. If you stood between any two of those houses, you could practically spread your arms and touch both at the same time. Not that uncommon nowadays but back then, kind of unusual, at least in this area where people liked a little sprawl in their land. Why on earth would they need tunnels underneath their houses to get from one to another?"

"I don't know," I said honestly, having no answers of my own. "Do you know if the tunnels existed before the subdivision was built? Maybe they chanced upon them and decided since they were there, they'd use them to connect to each other? In case of emergencies or something? Weather? Ice?"

I took a deep breath and let it whistle out into the quiet space of the library. "These are stupid questions, aren't they?" I asked.

Mrs. Wheaton shook her head ever so slightly, but the way she dropped her chin and pursed her lips was a better indication that she agreed with my last statement.

I raised my eyebrows in surrender to my own stupidity. "Not much in the way of investigative skills," I said. "My husband and I haven't been here long. I find the tunnels … interesting. I also find it odd that nobody seems to know anything about them, or that nobody cares, or nobody is ever down there, or wants to go down there, except me, of course."

"All I can say is this," she offered, still working through her magazines. "That hole in the ground behind the church opened up not long ago after a big storm came through. Nobody thought much about it. It's on the church property, and the church depends on tithing, as you know, so there probably hasn't been a whole lot of money for closing it up is my guess. And the parents around here, they've told their kids to stay out of there. I'm not so naïve to think all of them have obeyed, but I've found that the bigger a deal you make out of something, the more the kids want to do the complete opposite of what you say. So the fact that there're some passageways under our little town—I suppose we don't think it's all that interesting. If there were giant rubies hanging from the walls, or veins of gold, now, you'd have a different story altogether. But if that were the case, I imagine such a source of wealth would have been very well known and tapped itself out years ago. And Graceville would have staked a little claim to fame from such a thing as that. Say you've been exploring down there?" she asked. She lined up the edges of the stack of periodicals with her aged hands. "Have *you* found anything particularly exciting going on down there?"

A snapshot visual of the tunnels flashed behind my eyes—smooth clay walls, a suspicious lack of exposed granite, which I would assume typical of the bedrock of the area, a lack of wood supports suggesting a structural integrity that couldn't be accidental, side tunnels closed and carefully concealed, a labyrinth that echoed the layout of the houses above it, and a complete lack of interest by the townspeople. Yes, I thought I had stumbled upon something *particularly* exciting down there.

"No," I said. "Nothing exciting at all."

I thanked Mrs. Wheaton for letting me take up her time and went back to my car. Frustrated with my inadequate detective skills, I dialed Steven and got his voicemail. He must still be tied up in meetings at work.

"Hey babe," I said into the phone. "Good checkup. Everything's great with the baby. I asked about falling on the steps, too. The doctor said there's no need to worry. The baby looks fine, and aside from a sore bruise, I'm fine too. I thought you'd want to know that." A small laugh escaped my lips, and once it had, I knew I needed to spill the beans. I snapped the seatbelt across my lap, pushing the strap down to ride just below the small swell. "I have a couple of surprises for you though. First one—uh, the little bugger is a wee bit older than we first thought. Seems I'm four months along. The doc gave me an explanation about missed periods and all that, but the bottom line is we're getting this critter a little sooner than we originally planned. How about that? Oh, and the second surprise? I'll let you in on it when you get home."

I snapped my phone shut. Having quickly emptied my bag of investigative tricks, I drove home.

When the whirr of the garage door signaled Steven coming home, I sneaked a quick peek at myself in the foyer mirror, ran my fingers through my hair to fluff it, and hurried toward the kitchen. A sampling of emotions urged me on—guilt at being an unsupportive wife; the newfound knowledge that, at least temporarily, my sexy days were coming to a close more quickly than I had realized; and a confusing mix of frustration and exhilaration stemming from what I had and had not learned from Mrs. Wheaton today.

Feeling slightly foolish, I leaned my back against the door jamb leading into the living room. After a second's thought, I bent one leg and placed my spiky heel strategically against the wall, hoping the curve of my bare leg would distract Steven from the fact that I had squeezed more tummy than I probably should have into the tight red dress.

Steven swung open the garage door and came to a halt, staring at me with an expression that told me I had achieved exactly the success I had hope for.

"Whoa," he said. "What's the occasion?"

The way his eyes scanned my body from head to toe managed to erase any silliness I had been feeling. I took a few slow steps toward him, letting my hips sway a bit more than was absolutely necessary,

"I'm really sorry about last night," I said, tilting my chin down playfully and drawing my bottom lip into a loose grip between my teeth.

"What exactly happened last night?" he said, a grin crossing his face. He shifted his briefcase from his right hand to his left and sat it on the kitchen counter but his eyes never strayed from my gaze.

"I was a bad girl. Temperamental. Kind of a brat," I teased, rolling my eyes up and to the corner to convey how entirely embarrassed I felt at my terrible behavior.

"I wouldn't say that."

"No?" I crossed one leg in front of the other, closing the distance between us ever so slightly.

"Not at all," he said. "You were … taking a stance. Not nearly as impressive as the one you're taking now," he added, "but very admiral nonetheless."

I twirled a lock of hair around my finger. "Are you sure? Because I was afraid you thought I had been naughty."

"You're being naughty now," he said, all playfulness disappearing from his voice. He grabbed my hand and pulled me toward him. "Get over here."

I let him draw me against his chest and wrapped my arms around his back as he bent to kiss me. When he finally broke away, my breath shuddered through my lips, swollen from a desire that was swiftly travelling to the rest of my body. I planted my hands on his hips to steady myself.

He held my face with his strong hands and looked at me. "I'm not upset about last night," he said, suddenly serious. If he was questioning my motives, that was okay. I'd already shown him I had put our fight behind me and it was good to know he had as well. "We're not exactly on the same page about CURE, but that's okay. You're probably right to be skeptical about something this big, especially since it was sprung on the world so quickly and we don't have all the information about how it works. I don't have the luxury of being as reserved as you being involved through work. We can disagree on this and still be okay, can't we?"

"We can," I said. "In fact, if this thing turns out to be the miracle everyone thinks it is, I'll relinquish my role as conspiracy theorist with glee. I don't exactly like the part of me that finds it hard to believe that this whole CURE won't somehow come back to haunt us. Is that horrible?"

"Definitely not horrible," Steven said, smiling as he ran his hands down the length of my arms. "Even if CURE turns out to be everything it's supposed to be, I'm not so naïve I think we're going to solve the world's problems."

"Let's go dancing," I said, grasping his hands as they touched mine.

"Dancing, huh?" He narrowed his eyes at me. "Is that your solution to solving the world's problems?"

"No, dancing is my solution to taking your mind off the world's problems."

He narrowed his eyes at me and leaned back an inch or two, allowing himself the ability to scan my dress a second time. "I'll change my clothes," he said.

It felt good to be out on the town, or rather out of the town. The closest nightclub was twenty miles up the interstate—really more of a restaurant that broke out slightly louder music after ten—but the drive was nice. We had dinner at a booth tucked into a dark corner while we waited for the latecomers to filter in and have some drinks. The crowd grew thicker as the music built to a deafening roar. Within half an hour, I had fully given myself over to the pulsing lights, pounding music, and the swaying, bouncing bodies on the dance floor. I spun and waved my arms in the air, forgetting for the moment that my tummy might never fit into my tight little dress again. Although I couldn't hear him, I knew Steven was laughing at me when I swung my head wildly, sending my loose hair flapping around my face.

I pushed at his chest playfully, wiggling my hips and then my shoulders. Steven picked me up and spun me around in circles until I screamed with laughter.

"Whoa," I sighed when the throbbing music settled into a slower rhythm. I let my head hang back, enjoying the little-girl freedom of having my weight supported completely by another person.

Steven leaned over me, swinging me back and forth so my hair dangled behind me. Cocking his eyebrows, he bent and planted a little kiss on my neck.

"I'll get us something to drink." He shouted the words next to my ear, the music not quite swallowing them up before they traveled the short distance.

I nodded and watched him push his way toward the bar. I bundled my hair on the crown of my head, baring my neck to cool down, and fanned my face with the other hand. Taking great care not to get knocked down or accidentally pushed, I worked my way through the pulsating bodies. At the outer edge of the crowd, the breeze created by so much movement swept over me. I let my hair drop.

I looked around, surveying the room for someplace to sit. The space had filled to near full capacity, it appeared, but I spotted two stools at the counter that lined the south wall. I scurried over, bobbing my head in time to the music as I went, pulled loose the tiny purse strapped over my shoulder and tossed it onto the counter. I was sure my makeup could use a touchup, but I didn't want to give up the seats for a fresh coat of lipstick. I rummaged to the bottom, found my lipstick and swiped it across my lips, maneuvering strictly on faith.

Just as I pulled the lipstick away, I felt a nudge.

"That could have been a disaster," I called, holding up the lipstick.

I held out my hand for the drink and gave myself a little push-off from the counter, spinning my seat to the right.

When I saw the face in front of me, I reached out and grabbed the counter, cutting off the spin. A surge of anger flamed up from my chest, crawled along my neck.

His face was like porcelain, fragile with a sheen that reflected the club lights, ever-changing as flashes of blue, red, green, white, and gold bounced off his skin. The silver eyes all but disappeared within the display. Lips, blackened by the shifting lights, drew an unwavering slash, something steady my eyes latched onto.

"What are you doing here?" I meant to shout the words, but my throat strangled them to a whisper no one could possibly hear. I could hardly detect their presence inside my own head.

"Watching you," he answered. His dark stroke of a mouth barely moved. There should have been no way I could hear him above the buzzing din of music and shouting voices, but his words reached me just the same.

"Your red dress is irresistible," he said before I could form a reply.

I stared into his still face, not believing what I was hearing. Was he actually flirting with me? He couldn't be older than mid-twenties. That alone rendered the idea completely absurd. On top of that, my husband was only yards away.

I narrowed my eyes. "Thank you?" I said. This time I heard myself more clearly, as if the resonance of the nightclub, though still loud, had faded to background noise.

"Irresistible is not good," he said plainly. With a jerk of his chin, he seemed to notice something from across the room and his eyes cut in that direction like swinging daggers. I tried to follow his gaze, thinking I might see Steven coming toward us, but I couldn't make out anything significant within the crowd.

"Compliment? Insult? Make up your mind," I muttered, seething sarcasm.

"You are having a child." It was not a question but a full-on, no-doubt statement of knowledge.

Had he followed me to the obstetrician? I thought, appalled, even as my hand darted automatically to my belly.

"Who are you?" The space between us buzzed like a charged conduit. I felt as if I could just as easily have thought the words and he would have heard them. My head grew thick. The fact that I was even carrying on a conversation with this guy should have been enough to prove I had lost all sensibility.

"Isaiah," he answered simply.

I drew air in through my nose, slowly, as if preparing to meditate, hoping to clear the cobwebs that had taken over my mind.

"Isaiah," I echoed softly, testing the name while interjecting a touch of wrath. "Who *are* you?" I repeated my question, trying to make myself understood. It wasn't his name I was looking for.

"I am not in agreement," he said, leaning forward a fraction of an inch, intensity joining the flashes of light around his eyes.

I had no idea what that meant. "You need to stay away from me," I said, reaching for my purse.

His hand shot out and encircled my wrist. My arm froze in position, my fingers inches away from the strap of my bag.

Mesmerized, I couldn't move my arm. Numbness wrapped itself around my wrist, hand, and forearm like a frozen drink being poured over my skin. Unfolding each pale finger, he eventually pulled his hand away from mine. I was not even sure if he had ever touched me.

"I cannot," he said, his body angling slightly toward the counter. My hair had fallen over one side of my face, mercifully concealing my eyes, yet with a slight tilt of his head he was able to capture my gaze. I thought he was studying me.

"*I* am not in agreement." I repeated his cryptic words in a failed attempt at scathing mockery, cutting my eyes to look at him through the curtain of my hair. The corners of his blackened lips turned up at the corners—apparently he appreciated my dry sense of humor.

"What did you mean?" I said, turning to face him directly. I actually felt my face go void of expression as I remembered what he had said to me the day I had run into him in the grocery store parking lot.

His eyes never wavered from mine, save one slow blink as the shadowed lids slid shut, momentarily hiding the silver behind them.

When he spoke next, his deadpan words drifting through the pounding din of too-loud music and straining voices, a shiver traveled the length of my spine, possibly because even though my thoughts had completely shifted gears, he understood exactly what I was asking.

"You cannot let them take your blood."

He spoke very slowly, and as if his body worked in conjunction with his voice, he raised up away from the counter until he sat rod-stiff before me. For the first time, his eyes lowered from my face. I felt an almost palpable sense of release, as if I had been tied to a post and someone had suddenly cut the ropes that held my hands. The relief that washed over me was fleeting, however, as I realized he was staring at my abdomen, the place where my baby was growing.

Somewhere deep inside me, I wished I had the fortitude to reach out and slap this Isaiah, or at least to get up and walk away, but the impulse never fully reached the conscious part of me. I remained glued atop my stool, speechless.

A flash of familiarity caught my eye from somewhere in the crowd. I turned to find Steven coming toward me, two drinks in his hand. He had to shift his shoulders from side to side to avoid bumping into the throngs of people.

My head swam as the music roared against my ears. The thrumming bass rocked my body.

"Sorry it took so long," Steven said, and held out my glass.

I blinked several times and took the glass of ginger ale, wrapping my fingers around the cold wet glass.

Steven plopped down upon the stool beside me.

Right where Isaiah had sat only a second before.

"I think I'm ready to go," I said. I felt very tired.

Steven bent sideways and laid his large hand over my smaller one. Until that moment, I hadn't realized that my hand stretched protectively over my small belly.

"Too much?" he said, his lips brushing lightly against my ear.

The gentle concern was evident even though he had to shout to make himself heard.

I looked down at the two hands, his and mine, lying against my stomach. A rush of emotion overwhelmed me. The idea that, together, we would have to protect this baby against the big bad world, even things that would be so cleverly disguised as good, was as strong as a premonition.

My other hand was still clenched around the drink Steven had bought for me. Embarrassed at the moisture that sprung to my eyes, I used the back of one knuckle to blot at my eyes, hoping to keep the threatening tears from overflowing.

"Too much fun," I said, forcing a strained lilt of cheerfulness into my voice. I nodded toward the door. "Do you mind?"

"Not at all," he said. His hand squeezed mine. "As long as you've gotten a proper grip on the world's problems, we can declare this mission accomplished and call it a night."

"I don't understand the world's problems one iota more than before we left the house, but I had a blast dancing. Is that good enough?"

"Good enough for me," he said.

I flinched when he broke contact with me, as if my panic hovered in the nearby shadows, waiting to pounce. Steven stood up and held out his hand. I placed mine in his, palm to palm, grateful when his fingers wrapped around mine.

As hard as I tried, I could not keep from scanning the room as we left.

Isaiah.

If he was there, he was lost in the sea of faces.

Steven was quiet for most of the drive, his concern evident only by the fact that he kept glancing over at me every few seconds.

"I'm fine," I told him after about the tenth time he looked at me.

"You sure nothing's bothering you?"

"Nope." By that I meant to convey that he could stop worrying.

At the same time, the simple negative answered his question in a completely different way. No, I wasn't at all sure that nothing was bothering me.

While I waited for Steven to unlock the kitchen door, I tugged at my dress zipper but couldn't get a grip. "Can you get this? I can't wait to get out of this dress."

He opened the door and half-blocked it, forcing me to squeeze by him to get through. "You look great in that dress."

'Not irresistible?" I said with not the least hint of flirtation. My arms crossed my chest reflexively. The standoffish nature of my gesture did not escape me.

Steven pushed several dark strands of hair away from his face. "You could definitely be considered irresistible," he said. "But I can read between the lines." He slapped my bottom as I passed by.

"Go put on those ugly pink sweats of yours. You're irresistible in those too."

My arms relaxed.

I conjured up a dirty look, threw it his way, and headed upstairs.

CHAPTER FOURTEEN

Isaiah's stare, so pale, so intense, bathed in the flashing club lights, morphed into Alyssa's sweet angelic face. She looked down toward the tail of her oversized t-shirt, saw the jagged lines of blood streaking her legs, and began to laugh, and laugh, and laugh, as she turned and ran through a field of wheat and weeds and wildflowers, trailing her fingers along the passing stalks and petals, snatching one here and there, then letting them float to the ground. I smelled the sweetness of gardenia and wanted to follow her into this perfect scene, until she glanced back at me over her shoulder. Her smile was gone. Her eyes had narrowed to slits, the space between them cragged with worried lines. The wheat collapsed around her, darkened, folded together to form tunnel walls. Alyssa's fingers trailed against the dirt, scraping. Dust fell like rain, pounding in my ears, and the tunnel walls closed in on themselves, drowning her in shadow as she shook her head violently from side to side. Somehow she was wearing my red dress. I tried to wonder if I had lent it to her, but the sides of the tunnels kept getting closer and closer, and the impending darkness numbed my mind. Just before she disappeared, she reached down and touched the red fabric. Blood came away on her fingertips and she began to scream.

I woke gasping, clutching the sheets, my body damp from sweat.

Steven was gone for the day.

LifeShare was embarking on phase one of the CURE.

I was going to visit Alyssa.

184

. . .

Dillon picked up when I called Alyssa's house. The conversation was awkward and short and ended with him asking me to give her a couple of hours before stopping by. Rather than kill those two hours doing something productive at home, I decided to cruise by LifeShare. A scheduled blood drive, not unlike the dozens of other blood drives LifeShare had held since we moved to Graceville, was on the calendar. Nothing interesting about that. But with CURE on the horizon, curiosity got the better of me. I couldn't help wondering what was going on over there.

I wasn't disappointed, or maybe I was. The parking lot was overflowing—not an empty spot anywhere in the back lot. I weaved my way back out and took advantage of Steven's parking sticker to grab a space in the staff lot.

I heard Jerry's voice, before I rounded the corner of the building, trying to shout above the crowd.

"Folks," he said in a stern voice that somehow embodied the loving concern of a grandfather figure while demanding respect in return.

"Unfortunately, we aren't prepared to accept CURE donations for each of you today. CURE donations require a longer appointment than a routine blood donation, and that's all we're set up for today. I understand your desire to get started on the process, but we're going to have to turn most of you away anyway. I'm afraid we don't have enough staff on hand to handle this many people."

A buzzing roar welled up from the crowd, with a few discernible comments standing out:

"We were here first!"

"Yeah, first come, first serve."

"We drove two hours to get here."

"You don't *need* it; I do." This one held a choked hint of desperation.

Jerry held up his hands, inadequate shields, in an attempt to quiet his audience.

"Look," he said, straining to be heard, "LifeShare is as anxious as you are to get these treatments started. But we are bound by certain federally regulated protocol. Because demand for CURE is so high and because there is some controversy as to who will receive the treatments first—and believe me, LifeShare only received this information earlier this morning—the government has decided to put each recipient on an appointment schedule."

"What does that mean?" The question came from the far side of the crowd.

"It means," Jerry said, "that each of you will be receiving notices letting you know when and where to report for the required three appointments."

"But we live right here, and we're ready now!" another voice shouted. I might have recognized this one, but the collective roared up in support before I could place it.

"I understand," Jerry continued calmly. "But I'm sure you all agree that residential proximity to a CURE facility can't be the determining factor in who has access to the treatment first."

"When can people expect to receive these appointment notices?"

This voice stood apart from the rest with a professional air I recognized right away. It belonged to Samantha Bedding, our hometown reporter who was more famous, at least to me, for always appearing in the church parking lot whenever I decided to explore the tunnels. I was not remotely surprised to see her here.

Jerry scanned the group, finally settling his dark eyes on Samantha. He seemed relieved to have a more dispassionate question to address.

"As I understand, the first letters have already gone out. They will be issued on a staggered basis over the next few months, so if you don't receive your schedule right away, you will in the near future."

"And how is the government deciding who will get the treatment first? How do they know who needs it right away and who can wait?"

"I can't answer that. However, CURE has set up a website which will contain an application for anyone seeking special consideration. I cannot tell you what the criteria are because I haven't had a chance to look at it myself, but from what I've been told, for those who meet certain requirements, there is an application you can submit to request having your appointment schedule moved up. I encourage each of you to go to the website and read the information for yourself. It will answer all of your questions."

Another round of protests and questions bubbled up from the group, but Jerry had apparently had enough of crowd management.

He held up one hand and shook his head.

"As I said, LifeShare had hoped we would be able to begin the first stage of treatment for some of you today. I apologize that we did not expect the turnout we have here. On top of that, we now have to adhere to the scheduled appointments."

Jerry turned to go back inside, even though the crowd did not seem satisfied, but then he turned back and stared out over the faces for a moment.

"I look out here," he said finally, his demeanor switching from professional to that of confidant, "and I can put a name to ninety percent of the faces in front of me. Most of you know that I fought my own battle with cancer last year, so don't expect me to stand here and be Mr. Clinical and not say I don't sympathize with every single person's desire to get this treatment and put fear behind you. I get it, and I expect I'd be right out there with you if CURE had come along when I got my diagnosis. I would have done just about anything to move myself to the front of the line. It's a legitimate thing to want to do. But let me ask you, as friend to some of you, and to the rest, as someone who's been there. Do it the right way. Fill out the application. Go home and do it today. And when you come back, we'll be here, ready to help."

He gave smiling an effort, an expression that consisted of tight lips that only managed to stretch limply to one side.

"If you want to stay, hospitals are still in need of blood. You can still help another person by donating."

He paused for a moment, then turned back through the LifeShare doors. I watched as the crowd broke up, some small groups remaining to hash out their grievances amongst themselves, others heading back to their cars. Not one person followed Jerry inside.

Only Samantha Bedding lingered in place, taking a moment to jot some notes on her tiny spiral pad. I skirted the edge of the disbursing crowd, avoiding eye contact, and pushed through the doors. Jerry was still standing there, just inside, dolefully peering out through the glass at the neighbors and friends he had just turned away.

"Emmalyn," he said when he saw me. He held out his arms for a hug. "Good to see you."

"You too, Jerry," I said. "I still can't get over how amazing you look." It might have been inappropriate to say, but each time I saw him looking a little stronger, I had to remind myself of the picture of him lying gaunt and sickly in a hospital bed not that long ago. In case he wasn't, he should have been an inspiration to everyone who had stood in that parking lot today that CURE or no CURE, cancer could be beaten.

Behind the recovered strength, though, was a hint of forlornness in his eyes. "Well, that's something I didn't consider," he said.

"What's that?"

"That this thing would impact our normal blood drives. Nobody's going to want to give a pint of blood for someone else if it means having to wait longer to store the blood they need for their own CURE treatment."

I glanced back at the dispersing crowd. "The selfishness of humanity?"

"Hmmm. I suppose. Hopefully temporary," he said, and shook his head a little. He turned to walk the hallway toward the interior of LifeShare and I fell in step beside him. "I heard you got laid off at the craft store," he said, practically grinding gears as he switched tack.

"Yeah, Michelle felt bad about having to let me go, but she didn't really have a choice. I hope she knows I understand that."

"I'm sure she does," he agreed. "You know, if you're interested, I could offer you a little something around here. I guess you've heard Alyssa hasn't been back since her …"

His voice trailed off, as if he didn't have the words to describe what had happened to Alyssa. I was right there with him; I couldn't completely explain it myself, and I had witnessed it firsthand.

"We were thinking of hiring a temp, but if you'd like to get in a few hours, we'd love to have you fill in for a while. We could pay you a little more than a temp since we wouldn't have to go through an agency."

Surprised, I remained silent for a second. If the truth were known, it would be nice to have a few extra dollars to stock up on the things we still needed for the baby.

"I doubt I can match Alyssa's computer skills. I don't know how helpful I could be." It was the honest truth, even though saying it might sabotage the offer.

"Don't worry about that," Jerry said with a wave of his hand. "Mostly, I'm just looking for someone to help me catch up on the filing. And as soon as we start seeing our first CURE patients, I'll need someone to help catalog that information into our computer system. It could be boring, I'll warn you. Not much more than data input, really. After we take the blood, we'll run some tests and then it'll need to be coded into our system. The data entry screen will walk you right through the process."

I realized I hadn't responded when I felt Jerry touch my arm.

"What do you say, Em? I can train you to handle that part in less than an hour, and you'd be doing me a big favor."

I smiled up at him.

"Sorry," I said. I'd gotten sidetracked processing one component of his pitch. "I was just wondering if you had discussed this with Alyssa. Any word on when she's planning to come back to work?"

"She won't be back for a while, and that's if she decides to come back at all. But either way, we can still use the extra hands for a while, especially during the first onslaught of the CURE donations."

"I wouldn't want to step on any toes," I said, false diplomacy since I had already made up my mind to come on board. LifeShare might just be the next place I needed to explore. Jerry had convinced me without even trying.

"No danger of that, I promise," Jerry said. "Alyssa's job is here if she wants it, whether or not you take the temporary position."

"Well, that's good to know. Steven and I could use the extra income right now," I said, glancing down at my growing tummy. "And I guess you know temporary is fine with me."

Jerry glanced at my tummy and smiled. "Then it's settled. How soon can you start?"

I felt reassured knowing my working at LifeShare would not impact Alyssa's position, but it was Jerry's mention of coding the blood donations that had convinced me. The instant he had said it, Steven's mystery computer codes had sprung to mind.

"How about Monday?" I said. Might as well jump in feet first.

"You should have talked to me first," was Steven's reaction when I told him about Jerry's offer. He didn't exactly come across as angry, or offended, or overly worried, but some combination of all three, I thought.

"It was so spur of the moment, and informal," I argued. "This could be a good thing. He said I would be 'coding' the blood donations into the system. That sounds like the perfect opportunity for me to find out if this has anything to do with your problem with the database codes. I could help you."

Steven reached out and swung his office door shut, then gave me a reproachful look.

"You are absolutely not going to help me with anything," he said.

. . .

I left and drove to Alyssa's house, Steven's words ringing in my ears. I was annoyed with myself for letting my husband put me in my place, but I tried telling myself that LifeShare was ultimately his workplace and I was tagging along. I had hoped we could attack this coding problem as a team, but I guess I was wrong. That wasn't going to keep me from finding out whatever I could.

When Alyssa answered the door, I was shocked in a good way. I don't know what I had expected, perhaps some pitiful version of the sickly woman I had discovered the last time I stepped into this house. I did detect an awkwardness, though, in her eyes and wondered if that was something I was projecting or if she might still be embarrassed by the forced intimacy of our relationship. Neither of us could erase the fact that I had seen her at her most vulnerable or that she had confided in me when people who were closer to her didn't believe her story. Thinking about the baby she might have carried, I resisted the urge to place my hand on my own belly, which had expanded since the last time I saw Alyssa. I didn't want to draw attention to my pregnancy.

"You took my job," she said suddenly.

So much for trite greetings. I had no idea what to say to that.

She motioned me in and headed for the kitchen. "Jerry called to let me know he was hiring you part-time."

"Is that a problem? I wanted to talk to you first before I accepted the job. If you have a problem with it—"

"I'm never setting foot in that place again," she said bluntly, meeting my eyes straight on.

"I don't understand," I said honestly. I did wonder if she would be okay with me filling in for her, but I didn't think she would be angry enough to quit. "Does it bother you that I'll be working there? I didn't really take your job; I'm just helping them catch up, mostly with the filing. I probably won't be there that long."

"Good. Good," she repeated, a sudden blank look crossing her eyes. "That's good. You should get out, Em. You know, before."

I began to reevaluate my first assessment of Alyssa. Physically she looked fine, but what she said was odd and the vacant look in her eyes worried me.

"Alyssa." I couldn't worry about offending her. "You're not making any sense."

"I'm sorry. I guess I'm a little keyed up."

She looked anything but keyed up. "But you're okay. You're feeling okay?"

"I feel fine. But they can take that letter and shove it."

"What letter?" I said, although I thought I knew.

"It came this morning," she said. "I can't believe the nerve, like they can just come up with some cockamamie healthcare scheme and make us do whatever they want."

"Who are you talking about?" I asked carefully.

"The government. That stupid CURE thing," she said, and I gathered from the way she emphasized the word "cure" that she held at least as much skepticism for our new miracle as I did. "I got a letter."

"What letter?" I repeated, even as I remembered Jerry's speech outside of LifeShare. Alyssa hadn't had the privilege of hearing the explanation about scheduled appointments. I could see how receiving such a letter without warning would set off some alarms.

"*My* letter. It's very official. I assume everyone is getting one. They act like we don't have a choice. They're forcing this on us, Em, like a smallpox vaccination or something. Can you believe that? Like what are they going to do if I don't get this CURE vaccine, keep me from going to kindergarten?" She let out a little snort, but her hand was shaking as she pressed it against the countertop. "We should have a choice about this. Maybe some of us don't want to be *cured*."

"Tell me about the letter, Alyssa." My voice, surprisingly, was very calm compared to how I felt at the moment. Her description of the letter, if accurate, was not what I would have expected based on the information Jerry had announced to the crowd outside of LifeShare.

"It's this official government document, a mandate or something. Three appointments already scheduled out for me."

The timbre of Alyssa's voice had risen a note or two. "They didn't even ask me if I wanted to participate. There is no way I'm going into that clinic at LifeShare. Especially not there. Never again. They already killed my baby."

I thought I heard a catch in her voice before she went on. "I'm *not* giving them any more blood. And I am *not* letting them inject me with anything. I don't care if I do get cancer, they're not touching me."

I waited a moment while we both took a couple of breaths.

"Do you have the letter?" I asked. I wanted to see this notice for myself.

"I haven't tossed into a lit fire yet, if that's what you mean."

I winced but kept my voice steady. I had hoped she would offer to show it to me, but she hadn't, and it didn't seem exactly appropriate to ask outright.

"And there are three appointments?" I was thinking about Steven's description of the CURE process. "Does it say what happens at these appointments?"

Alyssa let a long sigh. "There's a long insert with the letter, but it's all a bunch of jargon no one without a medical degree is going to be able to slog through. But from what I can tell, you go in for three appointments and they take some blood, but it doesn't sound like we're talking about a small sample here. From what I can tell, you have to give more than a pint. Then after they've taken a bunch of your blood, at your last appointment that's when you actually receive whatever it is that modifies the chromosome they're talking about. I'm not clear on what taking the blood is for."

"Making room?" I muttered, unaware that I had spoken until Alyssa repeated my words.

"Making room for what?" she said.

"I don't know," I said, thinking it would be nice to know exactly how this thing worked. And wondering why the medical community didn't just spell it out. "For the treatment?"

"Why in the world do they need to make room for the

treatment? This is the craziest thing I have ever heard of. I don't like it, Em. It feels like a government train wreck bearing down on us."

I had to admit: If Alyssa was telling the truth about the letter, I didn't like the idea of being railroaded into a treatment, especially before researchers knew the full ramifications.

"Didn't you get a letter?" she asked, drawing me back from my trailing thoughts. I must have been speechless for a minute there.

"No," I said. "No letter."

"I must be one of the first," she said thickly. "Guess I'm just special."

"When are you supposed to go in for your first appointment? According to the letter," I modified.

"This Tuesday. But I'm not going. I don't care if they put me in jail."

"I can't imagine anything that extreme would come from missing an appointment," I said, trying my best to minimize Alyssa's state of panic without out-and-out dismissing her concerns. She seemed very adamant about her interpretation of the letter. Without seeing it for myself, it was impossible to judge whether her reaction was warranted or not.

"It's probably in the fine print," she said.

CHAPTER FIFTEEN

By the time I got home, I was completely on edge. And if I was being truthful with myself, I was more than a little annoyed with my husband's head-of-the-household, foot-down response to working at LifeShare. Instead of making dinner, I spent a good twenty minutes rummaging through the small stacks of mail in the kitchen. I rifled through our magazine basket and then moved on to Steven's office to see if there was any possibility that I could have missed my own CURE notice.

Part of me wanted to completely dismiss Alyssa's talk of this letter as pure fabrication, but since I had basically heard Jerry announce the same thing outside of LifeShare, I couldn't do that. I glanced down at the small mound of my belly. I could picture all too vividly the blood streaming down Alyssa's legs, the pain in her eyes at the loss of her baby, and I knew if there was a letter, I would have no problem helping her build a bonfire. Her words nagged at me, along with those of my new shadow, Isaiah. There was no way I was going to let LifeShare or anybody else take my blood.

My mind took a left turn, venturing into a place I knew better than to go. What exactly did Steven know about all this?

I finished my search of Steven's desk and slumped into his chair, spinning it to face the study door just in time to hear the garage door open. I hadn't found any letter in my search. That was a relief. Unfortunately, I'd been stewing. With the search over, I had nothing to focus on but the anger that burned in my every nerve over Steven's ridiculous chauvinistic statement.

I heard a tap and looked up. Steven's typical lopsided grin sprang to his face as he rounded the office door, but its usual effect was lost on me. Irritation boiled up so fast I had no hope of taking my temper off the flame.

"What do you mean?" I spat, picking up the conversation from his office as if no time at all had lapsed. "'*You are absolutely not going to help me with anything?*'"

I should have felt guilty to see his grin lose its shape. After all, that smile had popped onto his face because he was happy to see me. But I had conjured up way too much animosity over the last hours to be tamed by boyish charms.

"Emmalyn," he said, resignation lurking beneath frustration. Instead of coming into the room to drop his briefcase as he usually did, he leaned into the doorjamb. "We do not need to get in a fight about this."

"Not sure we have a choice," I said. "All I'm trying to do is help."

His fingers combed back his dark hair, stretching his scalp tight before letting go. I pictured his eyes rolling behind the veil of his hand. Completely unwarranted on my part, but my blood seethed anyway. When he looked back at me, his face held more anger than I had been prepared for.

"And I'm saying that you don't need to be involved."

"Why? Why shouldn't I?" I raised my eyebrows, petulant, daring him.

A second passed and the flash of surprise gave way to practiced composure. "I wish you had talked to me first, before you told Jerry you'd work there."

Uh-huh, I thought, my fingers gripping the arms of the chair. His calmly reprimanding husband act hadn't worked on me, and neither would redirection.

"I'm sure you do," I barked, "but why? That's what I want to know."

"Because I can handle this on my own. And because that's what people do. They don't just take jobs without talking about it to each other."

"They might if it's no big deal. So again, why? What's going on over there that you don't want me involved?"

Finally, he crossed to where I sat and reached across me to set his briefcase in its customary spot. Instead of pulling his arm back, he tried to take my hand. I swung my own in an upward arc, attempting to bat his away. He countered in a flash, whipping his hand around to clamp down on my forearm. His grip was firm but didn't hurt. I yanked back on principle, but had no hope of breaking his grip.

"Whatever it is, I'll figure it out," he said, staring down at me. "You don't need to be in the middle of it."

"And yet I am," I defied, meeting his glare evenly. The warmth of his hand was seeping into my skin. There was something in his eyes I had never seen—a lurking danger—that threatened to melt me to the core. My reaction surprised me. I could feel my anger shifting precariously toward lust.

"Get up," he said.

"What?" I asked, taken aback.

"I said get up, Em. I'm pretty sure this anger of yours is somehow tied up in hormones, and even though I understand that, I might yell. I do not plan to stand over you and yell down at you. If we're going to have this fight, we're going to do it face to face."

Aware that I was doing exactly what he had demanded of me, and in a vain attempt to channel my anger back into the fight I had started, I bounded to my feet, sending the chair rocketing back behind me. I managed to stop my forward motion, landing with my face an inch away from Steven's chest, my wrist still locked firmly in his grasp. My mouth tensed, but the effort to not speak lasted only a few seconds.

"You do not want to yell at me, Steven. What happened to working as a team?" I fumed, turning my face up to his.

Eyes unwavering, he continued to glare at me. "We *are* a team at home, Emmalyn. We are *not* a team at LifeShare."

"Fine," I said, wrenching my arm. "Then tell me why. Tell me what you know."

He hadn't let go of my wrist and gave it a firm shake. "I don't know what I know. That's the point."

"So there's no good reason for me not to work with Jerry. You just want to boss me around. 'No working at LifeShare.' 'No exploring the tunnels.'"

A trio of dark strands flopped onto his forehead, partially shielding his eyes, now narrowed to slits. I no longer wanted him to let go of me; I wanted him to take hold of more than my wrist. Who cared if it was the hormones talking?

"Because it's dangerous," he said firmly, giving my wrist another tug that pulled me off balance. I knocked into him, my breasts suddenly plastered against his chest. His free hand snaked around my waist, pressing my hips closer. I pushed against him with my free hand, but he drew me in tighter. Angry heat ran off him in waves, simultaneously frightening and causing fire to course through me.

"Which one is dangerous?" I managed to say.

"It doesn't matter," he said.

It did matter, and I wanted him to admit it, but I wanted him more.

He knew it, too. The thin lines of his eyes softened, relenting to half-mast, shining green beneath the dark lashes, staring me down, and I knew he could read right through my angry exterior.

I opened my mouth to protest, and he clamped his down on top of mine, his lips bearing down, forcing me to respond, coaxing the truth out of my body. I dug my fingers into his bicep, and he retaliated by freeing my wrist long enough to reach back over his shoulder. He grabbed his shirt in his fist, yanked it over his head in one motion, daring me further, but instead of fighting I used my newfound freedom to find enough space between us to unbutton the top of his pants, strained with desire.

His lips never left me. I was only vaguely aware of my own

clothes disappearing until I became caught up in the sensation of his skin sliding against mine. I smoldered inside and out.

We found ourselves crumpled in the office floor, our bodies slick with sweat, both exhausted by this unchartered type of passion. His arms were wrapped protectively around me, my heart banging against his in a last effort at rebellion. I didn't want to move. I couldn't.

When our breathing finally slowed to a pace where speech was possible, Steven kissed the space below my ear and whispered, "You're still going to take the job, aren't you?"

A shiver ran from the spot where his lips seared my neck, traveled like a surging current through my veins. My pulse picked up.

"I am," I said.

My body was still infused with hypnotic languidness when the thin morning light crept through the bedroom window. I blinked and dozed, indulging in the warmth of Steven's body nestled against mine until the rusty cogs of my mind slowly rolled into a state of consciousness capable of memory.

I bolted to sitting, throwing the covers away, and slapped Steven's naked backside. He thanked me with a belabored groan.

"Get up!" I shouted, awake enough now to enjoy the idea that I had turned Steven's words from the night before on him. "We're late."

He jabbed a knuckle into one eye, rubbing away the sleep I had callously interrupted, and rolled onto his back, stretching overhead so the muscles along his ribs lengthened into detailed definition.

"Late for what?" he mumbled.

I grinned, stunned momentarily into a snapshot pause. This was no time for my libido to crank up, but our out-of-character tryst from last night combined with the sight of his muscles all relaxed and elongated, partially revealed by wavering drapes of the sheet, acted like a firing mechanism within me.

"Vacation Bible School kick-off," I said. "I'm supposed to be making hot dogs or … something. In thirty minutes. Up, you!"

Instead of cooperating, Steven stretched some more and casually flung the covers completely off with a kick of his leg. The crooked smirk that crossed his face was laced with pure mischief.

"Are you sure church is where you want to be after a night like last night? You're not afraid the whole town will be able to tell what you were up to?"

"Oh, hush," I said. A searing blush bloomed over my face and neck, but I refused to give him the satisfaction of seeing me grin like a schoolgirl.

I turned my back on his laughter and headed for the shower.

Being late to church turned out to be a very good thing. His teasing nagged at me; on the drive over I had practically convinced myself that my clothes were sporting some tell-tale letter that branded me as a married, pregnant slut for my husband. Steven abandoned me with a playful upturn of his mouth and headed off to attend Sunday school, leaving me to fend for myself among the lunch crew.

I followed the scent of barbecue around the left side of the sanctuary, where hot dogs and hamburgers were already charring away on the grill.

"Oh my gosh. We've missed you around here. You look great." Camille Bellows, glistening southern-belle style, more or less grabbed me, shoved a bag of buns and a box of foil sheets into my hands, and planted me behind the table next to the grill. My job was to load the cooked hot dogs into the buns and wrap them in the foil sheets for easy pickup when church let out.

Everyone seemed too busy to involve me in the conversations that were already underway, which suited me just fine. I realized that I had been avoiding church for the last few weeks, ever since the town buzz had lit up with talk of the CURE. My eyes wandered to the woods, my thoughts to the tunnels. They had an almost palpable pull on me that I might never be able to explain. Steven was probably right to be concerned, at least in that regard. If given the choice, I would abandon my post as hot dog wrapper and gladly run for the tunnels this very moment.

There was a box of latex gloves on the table, so I snatched a pair and wiggled my fingers inside. I could hear the children singing inside the church and forced myself to focus on the sing-song rise and fall of their tinny voices as a platter of cooked franks was slapped down in front of me.

Five full platters later, I had amassed a mountain of lumpy aluminum cylinders waiting for hungry hands. Almost on cue, a wave of voices rounded the corner from the front of the church. I stripped off the latex gloves and quickly tidied up the dusting of crumbs I had created.

"Hi, Ms. Emmalyn."

Josh Garrett was in the second-grade class I sometimes substituted for. "Hi there, Josh. Are you going to have one of my hot dogs? I wrapped them up special just for you."

"Can I have two?"

I was fumbling for an answer when Josh's mom, Selena, intervened. The last time I had seen Selena was in Sunday school class a few weeks before, when I had so eloquently announced my doubts that CURE was the miracle everyone believed it to be. I couldn't help wondering what kinds of debate that had prompted. I steeled myself for some advice I wouldn't want, but Selena seemed content with patting Josh on the shoulder. "Let's just have one, Josh, and see if that doesn't fill you up." Josh reluctantly moved on with his one hot dog, grabbed some chips and ran off to sit with his friends. Selena lingered a moment, gathering condiments and napkins.

"Congratulations to you and Steven," she whispered conspiratorially. "I heard the good news, and I do believe you're showing the tiniest bit."

I smoothed the front of my shirt to loosen it from clinging. There wasn't much point in hiding it; word of my pregnancy had apparently gotten around.

"Thanks, Selena. I guess I am."

"Just the teeniest bit," she said, holding up her thumb and forefinger to indicate the exact degree of teeny she meant. "Other moms can pick up on these things."

"Yeah?"

"Oh, of course. Past your first trimester, huh? It's about time for you to start taking it easy." She gave a polite little wiggle of her eyebrows and moved down the line, pulling my gaze after her like a magnet. I was gearing up for a smart retort when another voice in line broke the spell. And thank goodness. Even considering a smart retort was outrageous, much like my anger toward Steven last night. Who knew pregnancy hormones would unleash the smarty-pants I'd never known was lying dormant inside me my whole life?

"Yes, you'll be needing to take it easy now, Explorer." The familiar voice belonged to Professor Alan Kendall. He picked up two hot dogs, balanced them on separate plates, and moved toward the bags of chips and drinks, fixing me with a stern eye. "Put your feet up. Get that husband of yours to feed you grapes—no that's too healthy—make it bon bons."

"Alan," I said, and maneuvered to the opposite side of the table to give him a hug. "What are you doing here?" I took the two drinks from his hand, and grabbed a foil bundle for myself.

"Ah, Liz's sister is here for the week. She brought her granddaughter, and we all thought she might enjoy spending the week in VBS. What better place than here?"

"Well, sure," I said. "You're going to drive her up every day?"

"Why not?" he laughed. "Classes are over. We came today to let her check it out, but if she wants to attend the whole week, I've got nothing much better to do."

"Did Liz come with you?" I glanced around. I spotted Steven across the lawn heavily involved in a conversation that consisted of men rocking on their heels and breaking into sporadic bouts of deep laughter.

"Nope, just me and little Keera." Alan sidled up behind a tiny girl with a shock of blonde curls and tapped her on the left shoulder. When she turned her head that way, he slipped the plate between her and the girl to the right, the trick sending Keera and her new friend into a fit of giggles.

"Thank you, Uncle Alan," she squeaked.

"You're very welcome. Gobble up," he said.

Alan and I wandered away from the kids' table to where the first line of tall forest pines cast blessed shade over us. A warm breeze kicked up, stirring a faint scent of damp earth that seeped through the headier perfume of freshly trimmed grass. Unable to help myself, I cut my eyes toward the spot not far away where the ground opened up to the tunnels underneath.

"One guess as to where you'd rather be right now," Alan said.

"That obvious?"

"Well, you've only looked into the woods about a dozen times since I ran into you. Anything new turn up in your research?"

"Not a lot," I said, remembering my venture to the white clapboard house from the photograph Kendall had given me, and my unproductive follow-up attempt at detective work in town. "Around here, the most interesting thing about those tunnels is that no one seems to be interested in them."

"Except you."

"Yes, but people are beginning to get irritated with me for my need to wander the bowels of the earth," I said.

"People? Like Steven?"

"Especially Steven."

"Don't tell me he shares the concerns of the chipper housewife?" He chuckled softly at his reference to Selena Garrett's comment about me taking it easy.

"Why does everybody think that just because I'm pregnant, I should stop moving?" I said with a grunt. My ears picked another familiar voice out of the crowd, and I followed the serious-with-an-attempt-at-playful cadence to its owner. Samantha Bedding was here with her camera, snapping candid photos of the crowd, pulling groups of children together to pose. On another mission for the local paper. She raised the camera for another shot. From behind the lens, her eye caught mine and the cheery look on her face hardened for a split second. A quick, almost imperceptible nod of her head sent my eyes back to the woods.

"Perhaps the folks in this town are more interested in those tunnels than they let on," Alan said.

That grabbed my attention away from Samantha, her roving camera, and ... a signal to follow her? Or was I just looking for an excuse to get down there?

"What do you mean?" I said, trying to refocus.

"Sometimes people reveal more by what they don't talk about than what they do."

Alan's simple perspective on humanity always intrigued me. Any other time, I would have loved nothing more than to indulge in a little philosophical exploration with him, but I noticed that Samantha was in the act of skillfully separating herself from the crowd and her duties as photographer. In less than a minute's time, she had faded into the forest like mist on a breeze. I glanced around the group; no one else seemed to have noticed where she was heading. I hoped when I followed her I could be as furtive.

"You might be right about that," I told the Professor. I held up the forgotten hot dog in my hand, still wrapped in foil. "I need a drink. Can I get you or Keera anything?"

"No thank you, hon. We're fine. I might see if I can catch an audience with that husband of yours for a moment, if I can lure him out of this blazing sun." He fished a handkerchief out of his pocket and dabbed at his forehead. "You run along. Do what you need to do," he said.

"Samantha," I called. No need to whisper, I thought. The chatter and music from the church would prevent anyone who wasn't in the tunnels from hearing me. "Where are you?"

Samantha took a step toward me, from out of the shadow where the light from above had filtered to darkness. Despite knowing she was there, I flinched when she appeared so suddenly, and so close.

Her eyes narrowed. "I want to know what you know," she said, with no trace of the playful spirit she had used in her ploy to elicit carefree pictures from the kids.

"What are you talking about?" Not much of an actress, I glanced back over my shoulder toward the ragged hole that led aboveground, paranoia settling over me like a heavy cloak. Something about the intensity behind Samantha's eyes worried me—I had a sudden notion that either I knew more than I realized, or that I needed to know more than I actually did to satisfy this reporter's hunger for a story. Whichever it was, I felt sure Samantha was going to be disappointed. All I had to work with were disjointed pieces; I had barely assembled the outline of the puzzle, much less gotten to the heart of anything that made sense.

She edged toward me till I could feel her breath float across the still space. "You spend all your spare time down here. Your husband works at LifeShare. LifeShare sits right on top of this place. What's the appeal, Emmalyn? What's the connection?"

An overwhelming urge to back away came over me, but I stood my ground. "You can't make a story where there isn't one, Samantha," I said through gritted teeth.

Even in the dim grey light, I thought I saw a challenge in her staring eyes. Without a word, she turned and began tromping blindly into the depths of the tunnels.

"What are you doing?" I barked.

A light appeared a few yards away, the beam of her flashlight bobbing behind the outline of her tiny silhouette.

I hesitated, watching the light grow dimmer. Samantha didn't seem the least bit intimidated by the tunnels or the dark, or by whatever secret she thought I might be keeping. I huffed and grudgingly took off after her.

With her short legs and my longer stride, I caught up in a matter of seconds.

"How many times have *you* been down here?" I said, matching my pace to hers.

"Very perceptive," she said with a harsh chuckle.

"Have you been following me?" The images of her "waiting" by her car in the church parking lot those times when I had finished my underground hikes came back to me. Now I had to wonder if she might have been down here with me, shadowing my moves. It took a healthy allotment of willpower to suppress the anger that was churning through my core.

"Not exactly," she said. She was marching along at a pretty good clip—much faster and she would have broken into a slow jog—and the breath in her voice reflected it. Still, she spoke with a nonchalance that perturbed me even further. "But after I did that profile on you in the paper, I got more curious so I decided to wander down here myself to see what all the hullaballoo was about."

"Find anything interesting?" I countered, attempting an indifference I couldn't quite achieve. My voice was steady as a steel bridge, though. At least my level of fitness could still override the irritation of having this small, rude woman invade my space. I hadn't liked her doing a story about me and the tunnels, I really didn't like finding her skulking around outside the tunnels waiting to talk to me, and I especially didn't like having her down here with me, now or ever. Sure, it probably made me seem superior to even think it, but she didn't belong. She didn't appreciate the tunnels the way I did.

Abruptly she stopped. She glanced up at me, her eyes filled with a wicked twinkle that might have been nothing more than a reflection of the flashlight's beam, but I thought not. That evil glimmer exuded from within, pure get-the-story Samantha Bedding. I knew exactly where we were, and my lips tightened with resolve not to give anything away.

"Ready to head back?" I said without much hope.

"You want to tell me about this?" she said. She didn't wait for an answer, and turned toward the crack I had found that led into the small corridor. At the end of that corridor was a flat wall created out of mud and dirt, concealed behind the dirt a door that probably led into LifeShare.

I wanted to tell her exactly nothing about this.

A quizzical tilt of her head, a ten-second standoff, and then an eye roll. "No?" she said, and stuck one arm through the crack. She was shorter than me but also a little heavier. She maneuvered her body sideways, emptying her lungs to squeeze through. When she reached the other side, she shined the light back in my direction. "Come on," she said.

Not much time had passed since I had last gone through that crack, but the way my belly had suddenly started expanding, I wasn't sure how easily I could get through. It wasn't as if I could reduce the size of my womb the way she had sucked in her abdomen to get through.

"Oh," she sighed, "might be a tighter squeeze these days?" Without warning, she turned the heavy Maglite on its heel and slammed the handle against the crack at waist height. Clods of dirt fell away, crumbling like a red avalanche.

"Stop that!" I yelled, appalled that she had no appreciation for the integrity of these tunnels. I grabbed for the flashlight.

She yanked it back, just out of my reach. "I think you can make it now."

"That is not the best way to get me to follow you," I said through clenched teeth. The air moved behind me, a slight hiss of wind that raised the fine hairs on my arms. Not a sound accompanied it, but I felt it inside my head as if I could hear the wind. I remembered how the air had moved inside the small corridor when I had first discovered that metal door I believed to be part of the underground labyrinth of LifeShare. That unexpected cold breeze had cascaded to the floor, causing the loose dirt to roll across the ground like a low fog.

I looked down at my feet, where newly disturbed dust swirled. A shiver ran up my spine.

"Yeah, I guess I can't force you," Samantha said. "You've not your own light, right?"

So I wasn't the only smartass in town.

She swung the flashlight back into the slim tunnel, leaving me in shadows.

With a glare aimed at the back of her head, I turned sideways and slipped easily through the bigger opening. As hard as I tried, I couldn't think of a way to keep her out of the tunnel. And as much as I didn't want her to see that metal door caked in dirt that would greet us at the end, I had to assume we wouldn't be heading this way if she had not already discovered it.

Reluctantly, I followed along behind her, trailing my fingertips against the walls on either side. The touch of the earth against my skin somehow helped subdue my anger, until after a few moments I almost forgot Samantha was there. I noticed something I hadn't on my first trip through this tunnel. I'd already noted that the entire interior of the tunnel system was unnaturally smooth, nothing like the cragged and ragged surfaces of most excavations, but I now realized an even smoother stripe ran the length of the main corridor, polished to a silky trail my fingers always seemed to find. For the first time, I wondered what had created that sleek band. Had someone else trailed their fingers along the walls the way I did now? How many years would that take?

Samantha or no, I became absorbed in the tunnels—the dry clay beneath, around, and above me, the comforting closeness, the basic scent of clean earth, the pure lightness of a silence that allowed the simplicity of our padding feet and the whisper of my fingers against dirt to create its own soothing musicality.

The spell was broken when Samantha halted in front of me. The beam of her light was trained on the flat wall at the end of the tunnel. The section of bared metal door reflected the flashlight's beam back at us, illuminating Samantha's face in the ambient rays.

Her eyes were locked on the door, most of it still encrusted in clay, but I could still detect the greedy glimmer that came over her eyes. She dropped the beam to the floor. When I saw what she had stashed there, a kind of horror came over me. I stole a glance behind me, into the smothering darkness.

"Samantha," I said. "You can't do this."

Samantha picked up what looked like a large awl and held it out to me.

"We," she said, correcting me. "You can chisel around the door with this. I'll knock down what's caked over the surface."

"No *we*," I said, holding my hands up and away from the tool. "What are you thinking?"

"We're going to uncover this door. Don't tell me you don't want to see what's on the other side?"

She had already chiseled away some of the dirt disguising the right side of the door. A small jagged line of metal peeped out from the deep clay bordering it. She planted the tip of the awl at the spot where I had knocked loose a bit of dirt around the edge of the door, intending to finish her work, and pulled down with a yank. A snakelike clod fell to the floor, exposing another twelve inches of the metal perimeter.

"Stop," I said, threat of a higher octave creeping into my voice. "We both know it's LifeShare. And even if we uncovered the door, we can't go in there. I'm not getting thrown in jail for breaking and entering."

She planted the awl again and heaved downward, lengthening the naked metal by another foot, revealing a small rectangle that had to be a deadbolt. Her eyes darted my way, then back to the task.

"You mean to tell me you've been crawling around in these tunnels ever since you moved here, you found *this*," she said, waving frantically at the door, "and you're not even slightly interested in why it's here, what's behind it."

She fixed me with a knowing smile. The truth must have been written on my face. "Of course I'm interested, but I'm not doing this. You said it yourself. My husband works for LifeShare. And you're a reporter. This is no way to get a story, assuming there's even a story to be had. We need to leave."

I turned back toward the main corridor, ready to find my way out. I didn't need light. I knew the tunnels well enough I could find my way without it.

"Do you know how long I've been waiting for a *real* story? This is it. It may not be these ridiculous tunnels of yours," she said, "but it might be the CURE. If LifeShare is in any way not on the up-and-up with those treatments, I will bring the company down. Sorry," she added, throwing an insincere glance my way, "that wouldn't be so good for your husband."

I stopped. Drew a deep breath. And there it was—Samantha had her suspicions about CURE the same as I did. If it hadn't been for the crazy edge to her voice, I would have been relieved to find an ally. As it was, my allegiance shifted automatically to Steven. Ninety percent of the LifeShare project was founded on his research. No way this little twit was going to bring down anything having to do with him.

"You can try," I said, very calmly. "I'm leaving. I have no intention in being a part of whatever this ludicrous plan of yours is."

She reached to grab me when I turned, but the swinging arc of the flashlight beam gave her away. I dodged to the left and her hand jutted past me to the right. The space in the tunnel was tight. I had thrown myself against the wall to avoid her. She twisted, raised the flashlight, and swung it at me. Shocked—*did she actually try to* hit *me?*—I bent sideways and slid along the wall. Wherever she was aiming, I felt lucky when the metal cylinder only connected with my bicep. Still, I let out a scream of pain and kicked out with my right foot. She went down, but I didn't flatter myself that I'd done anything more than cause her to trip.

"Shit!" she said harshly, climbing to her feet. She had cracked the lens of the flashlight when she fell, and the bulb flittered sparks of unfocused light when she shone it onto the hand she had landed on. Deep scratches marred her palm, courtesy of the awl she'd been holding. Beads of blood seeped from the shallow wounds, tiny maroon-red wet droplets pushing through the rusty-red clay that coated her hand.

I could see she was hurt, if only superficially, but couldn't conjure up any sympathy. She'd swung a stinking flashlight at me. All I wanted was to get out of this tunnel, and away from her.

I didn't care about the darkness. I'd been down here enough

times to find my way back without benefit of light. But she stood between me and the length of the tunnel. The only thing behind me was the LifeShare door, still encased in its mudded shroud.

Steven's warnings rushed into my memory. A dry laugh escaped my lips, an eerie sound in the confines of the earth, as I thought of all those times he had warned me not to be down here by myself. I wasn't alone now, and look where it had gotten me.

Samantha took a step toward me. I shifted back and my foot knocked something metal against the door. One of her tools.

"Samantha," I said as calmly as I could. "This is crazy. You need to clean up that hand so it won't get infected. We need to get out of here."

"No," she said, the word stretching upward at the end so I wasn't sure if it was a question or a statement. She bent and grabbed the awl, rearing it up as if ready to plunge. For a panicked moment, I thought she intended to stab me with it. "We're going through that door."

My arm throbbed where she had hit me, my back ached with the cold of the door pressed against it, but I didn't dare move. "You know that's not going to happen."

"That's my call."

I started to argue, prepared to push past her and run, when she lunged. I still couldn't be sure whether she was planning to attack the door behind me or if she was angry—or crazy—enough to plant the stupid thing in me. Whatever her intent, she never made contact with either me or the door. I cringed, threw my arms over my face, heard scraping followed by silence. One second she was there, the awl raised to strike, her wet eyes gleaming in the half-light. Then the flashlight fell to the ground, flickered off and sputtering back on as it rolled, and she was gone.

I froze. Long seconds passed while I couldn't seem to bend my arms or legs, then I forced myself to move, squatted, fumbling for the light, my hand shaking so badly I couldn't close my fingers around the shaft, wishing more than anything I didn't have to hear the whooshing, scrubbing sound that slid away from me at lightning speed and the disappearing murmur that could have been a scream if it hadn't sounded so much like the desperate wheeze of air squeezed from the lungs of someone too frightened to find her voice.

I fell to my knees, groping for the flashlight, my numb fingers sending it rolling from my grasp several times until I was finally able to wrap my hand around it. I clutched it to my chest, where the metal and the extending light rose, fell, and trembled against the red walls in unison with the frantic cadence of my heartbeat.

I squeezed my eyes shut for a moment, willing myself to move. Finally, I trained the beam out in front of me, focusing the dwindling light down the corridor so I could see the cracked opening at the far end. Between here and there, no sign of Samantha—nothing but two rutted tracks that trailed along the ground as if someone's heels had been dragged across the dirt. Those two lines in the dirt made me want to scream.

Tears stung at my eyes. I fought the urge to cry, bore down the panic boiling inside me. I should find Samantha, I told myself, but I *had* to get out of here.

Deep breaths.

After a long moment, my heart settled back into a rhythm blissfully short of insanity. I liked where I was just fine. Staying crammed into the dead end of the side tunnel with my back against the wall gave me a preposterous sense of safety. The mere idea of walking over those shallow ruts on the ground riddled me with repulsion.

My stomach lurched as I folded my feet underneath me, but I dragged myself up on my quivering legs, shined the light straight ahead, and walked—methodically, *you can do this, one foot before the other, don't look down.*

The crack in the tunnel wall, bigger now, its edges sprinkling newly disturbed dirt, almost stopped me. I drew deep breaths, willing myself to pass through. Until I stepped into the main corridor, I at least knew there was nothing behind me. Once I left this slim side tunnel, I could only shine my fading light in one direction. I would be completely vulnerable to the cloying black of the tunnels closing in on my back.

Decision made, I sucked in another breath and let it shudder from my body. I put the flashlight through first, then shifted my body sideways, pushing through the opening. The desire to run was so great, I had to cling to the wall for the strength not to bolt wildly. I knew these tunnels, I told myself, digging inside for the comfort, the *oneness*, I had always felt with them.

I reached back and felt that smooth strip rubbed into the wall, reassuring, familiar, my guideline to safety. I stepped to my right, angling my beam of light slightly in that direction. Several yards, and I stopped to listen. A few feet further, and there—I thought I heard something to my left, quiet as imagination. I forced myself to aim the light back that way, knowing if I saw something—anything—connected with that whisper of a sound, I would go insane.

I also knew that in order to keep going, I had to prove to myself there was nothing lurking in the shadows. I swung the light around, cutting frantic lines through the darkness. My breath seeped from my tight chest in relief. Nothing there but my imagination, I told myself.

I slid further along, maybe twenty yards this time. Again, I thought I heard something, a whisper of movement hidden within the sounds of my own breathing and the soft sigh of my shirt rubbing against the ragged dirt. I stopped, but if there had been any sound, it disappeared into the silence I created. The flashlight sputtered and dimmed, like it had been cranked down a notch. I could barely see the ground at my feet.

Stop spooking yourself. The sound is you! It's you sliding against the tunnel wall.

Summoning as much courage as I could, I took one pace forward, putting a few inches between myself and the wall to eliminate the sound of my shirt dragging against dirt, and with a tentative step, a pause, another careful step, continued working my way back toward the church. If I could just get to the exit, see blessed daylight filtering into the end of the tunnel, I would be okay.

It couldn't be far now, I thought, forcing away the image of those ruts made by Samantha's shoes, an image that squeezed into my mind like a tightening vice. Another step, another pause, and I heard something—faint, but horribly audible. I was not imagining this. My mind scrambled to connect the sound to something, any innocuous image, and came up with a squealing leak of air hissing through the tiniest tell-tale breach of a hole in a wet inner tube, whistle and sputter intermingled. I knew exactly what that sound meant out on the lake. It meant get off the water, get to safety, and I was overcome by the exact same reaction now—to get out of these tunnels, leave, find Steven, forget I had ever been stupid enough to follow Samantha Bedding inside.

She came into view then—barely revealed by the stammering Maglite—as if thinking her name had conjured her into being. Breath halted in my chest. It wasn't just her. A figure hovered over her, shifted, jerked its head toward me. Black dagger eyes stabbed out at me from behind a curtain of matching stringy hair. I had time to capture a glimpse of Samantha, limp, lifeless, blood smeared across her chest in an angry blaze. The hissing, Lord God, I didn't want to know, but that horrible hissing, the small wet gurgling—could that sound be coming from Samantha?

The figure lunged toward me, and three thoughts scattered through my numb brain in the time it took the flashlight to fall from my hand to the hard ground:

Run.

Scream.

Fight.

I did none of them.

The form—*Animal? Man!?*—flew at me in a swift blur, reaching me before I could blink or act, pushing a wave of chilled air so close to my face that my breath stopped. At the last second, I prepared to close my eyes, seeing myself as I had seen that still shot of Samantha, lying dead in these tunnels—my ironic fate.

214

A second figure shot out of my periphery, slamming into the first at the same time that the scent of fresh warm blood filled my nostrils. I tried to follow the movement, but I felt suddenly sluggish, as if I couldn't keep up with my surroundings. My ears worked slower even than my eyes, failing to decipher the unnatural speed with which the skirmish, inches from me a mere second ago, disappeared into the black. I froze in place, and my senses did a fast-forward. All of a sudden I could detect every sickening lightning-fast growl-snap-tear of the fight. A moment of silence passed, followed by a thud. The space around me was at once stiflingly silent yet deafening with the sheer terror that comes from listening to death in progress. I wondered if I was going to faint, and felt my knees begin to buckle.

Steven, I thought, but it wasn't Steven's hand that clamped over my mouth and scooped up my body before I hit the ground. So fast, *so fast*, we crossed the darkness, away from the flashlight's failing beam, from Samantha, from the blood, *her* blood.

He—*not Steven, it's not Steven*—hit the wall with a blow that would have broken my bones, and I felt the dry earth of another tunnel wall fracturing. The force reverberated through me, shaking my skeleton. He sat me down and cradled my head to rest against the dirt.

"Do not speak," he said, soft as breath.

Isaiah.

"There could be others."

I smelled a hint of copper, sharp but faintly sweet like the beginnings of decay, on him.

At the back of my head, through the dirt wall, I could hear children laughing.

CHAPTER SIXTEEN

I struggled to look up, expecting to see Isaiah's pale face, but instead another set of familiar eyes, surrounded by the weathered crags of age and wisdom, stared down at me.

"You're okay, Emmalyn," Alan Kendall said. "You just fainted."

"Wha—?" I tried, confused by the cool patches of grass pressing through the dirt against my back, not understanding why the bright sunshine stung my eyes.

"Shhh," he soothed. "Don't speak."

Don't speak. The same words, but a different voice, echoed through my mind.

"You're okay," he repeated. He spoke again, but not to me. "She's fine. Get Steven. Let's give her some space."

I followed his voice to find a clump of faces hanging over me. I jerked as they came into focus. Alan waved his hands in dismissal and after a moment, the worried faces backed mercifully away, carrying the hushed murmur of concern with them.

"What?" I tried again, but found my voice limited to little more than a sigh. The white siding of the church, gleaming in the sunlight, came into focus, the canopy of the tent, blinding in its whiteness, a flash of the sun's rays reflecting from a line of cars— why was everything so *bright?*

The lingering aroma of burnt charcoal and singed meat invaded my nostrils. I nearly gagged, cutting off the many questions that raided my thoughts.

Alan glanced around. There was something frantic about the way his brows bunched into knotted lines. Panic surged inside me.

"The baby!" I pushed against the ground, attempting to sit up, but rising even a few inches made my head swim.

"The baby is fine," Alan said sternly, leaning closer and pressing gently against my shoulders to keep me from sitting up.

He stole another quick look around, then settled his gaze back on me.

"Listen to me, Emmalyn," he said, his voice strict with a desperate demand I had never heard from him before. "We will talk later. Not soon, necessarily. It may be a while, before we can. But you must remember." He paused, ever so briefly, and his brows furrowed down again, intensifying the severity of his words. "What you believe happened—Did. Not. Happen."

A moment of confusion swept over me, interspersed with flashes of dark anguish, as if my mind was wrestling to both latch on to and abandon a memory wrought with misery. Dizziness washed through me again. I focused on his eyes, fighting my own spinning mind, wanting nothing but to believe what he said.

"Em." Steven dropped from out of nowhere beside me and sudden relief ran through me like a flood. We grasped for each other. I managed to wrap a wad of his shirt into my fist. He framed my face in his large hands. "Are you okay? What happened?"

The question might have been for me, but Professor Kendall answered.

"I think she's fine, Steven," he said, clapping my husband on the shoulder reassuringly. "The heat may have been too much for her, I'm afraid."

The mention of heat conjured a frost that suddenly coursed outward from my core. I shivered involuntarily and read the alarm in Steven's expression. Anxiously he looked me over, his eyes and fingertips performing a spotted scan of my body, as if some explanation could be found written over me in code.

"You're not hurt?" Steven said.

My gaze eased from Steven to Kendall, who stood behind

Steven now. The Professor gave an almost imperceptible shake of his head, and I found myself mimicking the movement.

Alan clamped his hand on Steven's shoulder again.

"Lucky for Em, I haven't lost my reflexes altogether," he said. The smile in his voice was missing from his face. "She was only out a few seconds. I caught her on the way down, or she surely would have bumped her head a good one."

Steven gave a cursory nod of approval and glanced up at the older man in gratitude.

An instant smile, perfectly humble, lightened Kendall's face. He gestured away any thanks with a wave of his hand and wagged a playful finger at me. "I wouldn't recommend relying on these old arms as a rule, were I you, Emmalyn. Let's let this be the last time this happens, what do you say?"

I let him hold me with his gaze for a second longer before I sought refuge in Steven's eyes.

The words Professor Kendall spoke, together baffling and comforting, ricocheted through my drowsy mind, threatening to send me into a spiral of bewilderment. How much fantasy could play out in one person's mind in the time it took to black out and reawaken?

Lying on the cool ground, shrouded in light, with the strength of Steven's hand wrapped around mine.

Or that other, darker vision that felt like reality.

I couldn't be sure which one was the dream.

I startled awake, shaken once again by the images that plagued my sleep, images that vanished in an instant so I could never latch onto any tangible memory. Whatever the dreams were, they left in their wake an unexplainable burden of distress that lingered for too long.

If not for my insistence against it, Steven would have hurried me directly off to the emergency room. Confused as I felt, I was certain of two things. The memory of Alyssa and everything surrounding her bloody encounter with the hospital was one I desperately needed to keep in the recesses of my mind for the moment. Secondly, I couldn't bear the thought of crossing that emergency room threshold, with its cold antiseptic promise of help, and take the chance of being remanded into the care of Dr. Knight.

What you believe happened did not happen.

The Professor's words echoed through my head. I couldn't precisely remember him saying them; they may have come from one of my dreams, but they felt so very real. Horribly real, in some way. And equally baffling. I couldn't help connecting the strange advice to Alyssa and her lost baby, which made no sense. There was no reason Alan would even know about Alyssa, much less my connection to that sorrowful day.

What you believe …

I thought I believed the same as she did, about the baby, but the nagging words of Dr. Knight were always there in the background. *Not pregnant.* I was appalled to find that I still had doubts, even after I thought I had determined Alyssa had to be right. Surely she knew her body better than anyone else. Alan's words, whether real or conjured from a nightmare, meant nothing if I didn't know what it was I did believe.

I shuddered and burrowed back against the pillows of my bed. I nuzzled my palms against the small bulge of my belly, hoping to reassure myself that I was making the right decision. It was nearly nightfall now, and Steven had since given up trying to persuade me, but I was still grateful when the baby rewarded me with a ripple of movement that bolstered my resolve to steer clear of Graceville Regional Hospital.

Bed rest was my compromise, one I was gladly willing to make. A chill had snaked its way into my bones and I felt as if I had been steeped in ice water, yet I knew I wasn't ill. Occasional quivering spasms seized me, aftershocks of fright I couldn't seem to rid from my system. Steven had noticed my bouts of shaking and had taken my temperature a number of times. Each time it had been perfectly normal. Yet when he had pulled the winter comforter from the linen closet where I had only recently stored it away for the summer, I accepted the extra source of warmth with subdued eagerness.

I heard his footsteps on the hall stairs a moment before he strode lightly into the room for his thirty-minute check. His attempt at a smile didn't completely disguise the lingering concern on his face. And something else, I thought. His green eyes were slightly widened in a way that reminded me of the day he had asked me to marry him. Remembering that day, and how he had worn that boyish fear-stricken gaze for hours before getting up the nerve to finally make his request, made my lips curl at the edges. My would-be smile straightened, however, when I wondered what he could possibly be thinking that would bring about that familiar odd expression of fear and nervousness, different only in that the stern set of his jaw erased any undercurrent of excitement.

He thrust a large mug in my direction. A whisper of steam rose from the brim.

"Tea," he said, a little self-consciously, and eased himself to sit beside me on the bed without creating too much of a disturbance. "No caffeine. I thought you might like some."

I scooted up and took the tea, more for the comfort of wrapping my hands around the warm cup than for the drink itself.

"Are you sure you're okay?"

He had given up asking me what had brought on my fainting spell, since I had offered no reasonable explanation, but he was still skeptical as to how I was recovering. I had lost count of how many times he had asked. I still had no idea of how to answer.

"Are *you*?" I said, staring directly at him.

He flinched slightly. The muscles of his face contracted mildly, attempting to gather his expression into one of nonchalance, but the effort failed.

His hand lay stiff against the top of his thigh. I slid my upturned palm underneath it, and his fingertips curled in reaction, folding mine into a locked grasp.

"What's going on?" I said, tightening my grip.

He ran his free hand through his hair, pushing the dark waves over the crown of his head, then laid his hand on top of mine, forming a protective cocoon.

His gaze dropped to our hands. "It can wait," he said. "You need to rest."

"I really don't need any more rest," I said, a hint of impatience sneaking into my voice. The cold aftereffects of my dreams still lingered. The last thing I wanted was to appear ungrateful, even though the last quiet hours confined to my bed had allowed unlimited questions to ramble through my head. As much as I appreciated my husband's loving attention, I didn't necessarily want any more time alone with my thoughts. To prove my point, I set the tea on the bedside table and pushed myself to sit up a little straighter.

If it weren't for the persistent flutter in my abdomen, I would have been concerned over bad news about the baby. With that worry dispelled, I couldn't imagine anything that I couldn't handle.

"Whatever it is, just tell me," I said, turning the tables. I felt suddenly protective of him, but the feeling did not come without some selfishness. Focusing outward on him carried for me its own relief, freeing me momentarily from the loitering uneasiness of the day.

"Something's happened," he said. He paused, still looking at my hands. "I didn't want to tell you today."

"What is it, Steven?" I said. A million ideas as grim as his voice raced through my thoughts. My mother? His father? I had thought I could handle anything as long as the baby was okay, but I immediately knew that was a ridiculous notion. There were so many possibilities capable of tearing my heart apart.

"That reporter that did that story on you."

What might have been an image of Samantha—a gruesome snapshot—flashed against the backs of my eyes.

What you believe happened ...

I shook my head involuntarily and snapped my eyelids shut, willing away the picture in my mind. My heart instantly leapt in my chest. I listened as intently as I could through the sound of my body's blood pounding out a suffocating backbeat to Alan's words.

Did. Not. Happen.

"They found her in the woods near the church," Steven continued. "A couple of teenagers, the Dalton's daughter and Cameron—I think his name is—Spencer. They were helping out with some of the games for the kids after lunch. They wandered into the woods, just being kids, and they found her there."

Steven paused, as if this was enough explanation. He hadn't noticed the reaction that must have shown in my face, but he had to have felt the jerk of my hand enclosed in his because his fingers tightened around mine. He looked up but couldn't seem to meet my eyes directly.

"What do you mean, found her?" I asked, not wanting to know.

"She's dead, Em," he said, and that terrible image blazed against my retinas again. I clenched my eyes shut, but the image was burned into them like a relief drenched in deep sepia tones, a dark shrouded scene from one of my dreams. Blood. Somehow I knew there was blood.

"What happened?" My voice quavered.

"No one is sure. Who knows why she was out there, in the woods. It might have been an animal. People are saying a coyote." He looked square at me then, his green eyes swimming behind a sheen of impending tears. "It happened so close to those tunnels, Em. There could have been coyotes down there with you any of those times. Do you understand that?"

I couldn't explain to him that there had never been any coyotes in the tunnels with me. No matter how sure I was, he would never believe me.

"How?" I said, the question riding on a whisper.

He knew what I meant. He didn't want to say it, but my eyes gave him no choice.

"Her throat was ripped ..." he said, unable to elaborate further. "It was over very quickly, at least."

"At least," I repeated, the two words a quiet drone.

. . .

This time, when my body woke me with a jerk, Steven's arms tightened around me, pulling me into the comforting curve of him. My eyes opened grudgingly to find the bedroom swathed in the fading darkness of early morning. So much for my bold statement about not needing any more rest. The news about Samantha had weighed down on my chest like a cinder block. Sleep had been the only way to catch my breath.

"Where in the woods?" I said, quietly voicing the latent thought that had been with me even while I slept. The words drifted across the air like fragile vapor.

Steven stirred behind me. I felt the rhythm of his breathing change, but he didn't answer. After a moment, I thought he hadn't heard me, but then he let out a sigh that drifted over my shoulder.

"Close," he finally said, and I was instantly grateful that I didn't need to elaborate. "But not that close. The other side of the church, about a half mile away. The creek runs there. She was—"

I squeezed his arm and he stopped. I had no way of knowing, yet somehow I did. It took little imagination to picture Samantha there, the rushing waters of the wide creek having cleansed away her blood and with it, evidence that held the answers to her death.

We lay there for a while, quiet, while the light outside filtered from dark to grey.

"She was at the church," he said. "Taking pictures of the kids. Wasn't she?"

"Yes."

More silence. I could offer no more unless he asked. And he would ask, now or eventually. I thought it would be now and prepared myself for it. Because whenever he did decide to ask, he deserved the truth—as much truth as I could give him. The need for answers buzzed like an electric current under his skin.

"You went into the tunnels ... yesterday?" he said after a bit. He hadn't moved except to gather me as close as he could.

"Yes."

"She was with you?"

"Yes," I said again, and waited.

He was in no hurry, and after more moments passed with the only sound in the room our synchronized breathing, said, "Why?"

I paused before answering, not sure what to say.

"She thought I knew something I didn't."

"About the tunnels?"

"And about LifeShare," I admitted, understanding fully that this brief statement could open a door between me and my husband that barricaded mysteries we weren't meant to solve. Like the doors in the tunnels, I thought. The parallel was not lost on me, and a fresh surge of hatred for LifeShare's blatant disregard for the history of the tunnels simmered inside me. Warranted or not, I now blamed them for Samantha's death, and for whatever, if anything, might go wrong in this room right now.

Steven's next question did not surprise me.

"*Do* you know something, Em?" he said.

"All I know is that the tunnels were there. Then LifeShare was there." I paused. I had promised him the truth, if only in my heart, and now was the time to keep good or betray him in a lie he would never know existed.

Gently, I unfolded his arm from across my chest and slipped from the bed. My backpack was inside the closet, my crude map rolled up inside. I brought it back to the bed and smoothed it as flat as I could. Steven sat up.

"This neighborhood stood where LifeShare is now."

"This is the church?" He pointed toward the steeple-topped rectangle in the bottom right corner.

"The opening to the tunnels would be here," I added, pointing to an area not far from the rear of the church. "Once inside, the main tunnel seems to run around the perimeter of where this neighborhood stood. There are side corridors—I've discovered two, but I believe there are more—that branch toward the center of where these houses stood. The two small tunnels I found were closed off, made to look like they had never existed, by a façade that was almost undetectable. I knocked away the barrier of one and followed it. It ended here."

I took a pencil from the nightstand and lightly drew a line along the back side of the house at the bottom right of my grid, the house closest to the church, then drew my pencil back and forth along a short section of the line, darkening it for emphasis.

"There is a door here, Steven, under the ground, inside the tunnels. It has to lead to LifeShare because the building sits right in the middle of this space." I didn't bother to extend my new drawing, but traced my finger in a rectangle that encompassed the whole of my neighborhood map and the houses within it.

He studied the map for a moment longer, then looked at me.

I went on. "Samantha found what I had found—the side tunnel, the door. Maybe she followed me, I don't know. She wanted to go through it, into LifeShare, but I refused."

He pressed his lips together. "What then?" he said.

"Then she was gone."

"What do you mean, gone?" he asked.

Our legs were touching where we sat, and the heat from that one small section of his skin burned against mine with something more intense than the temperature of his body. I felt tethered to him, for the strength I needed, for the truth I needed to give him but couldn't explain.

My eyes stung with surprise tears I wanted desperately to hold back, but I met his gaze head-on so he would know I meant what I said.

"She was with me one minute ... and then she wasn't," I said simply. It was the truth as I knew it. I had run it over and over in my mind as I lay in my bed the day before, trying to decipher memory from dream. I remembered leaving the small side corridor and working my way back toward the tunnel entrance, but what I remembered was so clouded it had become little more than an afterimage, something I suspected I might have experienced while knowing I might never be certain whether I had experienced it at all. I had no better explanation.

With methodical precision, Steven took the map I had laid across the bed, rolled my drawing to the inside, and placed it behind his back as he shifted on the bed to face me. Much like the sieve that was my memory, the part of my leg where he no longer touched me simmered with the missing heat of him, like a pillow that trapped, if only momentarily, the warmth of the person who had lain there.

"Does anyone know you were down there with her?" he asked, his green eyes dark as emeralds at night.

I thought of Alan. If he knew, he would never say.

What you believe happened ...

I didn't know what I could believe, but I knew what I couldn't.

"No," I said, weighing my decision carefully.

Steven gave a little nod of his head, accented by faint music that suddenly drifted from the alarm into the silence between us, and the facets of his eyes lightened.

CHAPTER SEVENTEEN

I stood outside the walls of LifeShare, hesitant but resolved. Today was the day Jerry and I had arranged for me to start my temporary job, and I intended to keep that arrangement, despite Steven's attempt to have me postpone. Jerry would understand, Steven kept insisting, and while I felt certain that might be true, the thought of mundane data entry or filing or whatever it was that Jerry had planned for me was infinitely more appealing than rambling around my house alone, or worse, falling asleep knowing that when I woke up, Steven wouldn't be there.

I found myself glued to the pavement. I couldn't shake the correlation between the entrance door that loomed in front of me and those other hidden mudded-over doors buried beneath the earth at my feet. I wondered dismally if the secret of them was mine and Steven's alone to keep, now that Samantha was gone, and felt my palms go clammy.

Summer had officially pulled its thick blanket up past the foothills of Georgia and over Graceville's modest mountains. Even the early morning sun bore down on my fair skin with searing intensity. A wave of nausea stirred in my stomach. The light sweat that broke out on my skin reminded me too clearly of the previous day and my reaction to the heat. I didn't want to find myself lying on the front stoop of LifeShare. Fainting here would likely earn me that cracked skull Professor Kendall had saved me from. I was here. I couldn't avoid going inside forever.

I took a deep breath and stepped through the doors.

The cool air was instant relief, with the added effect of helping to clear my head. Jerry met me in the lobby within minutes and ushered me through hallways I was familiar enough with, though being here in a capacity other than visiting Steven somehow lent a more clinical atmosphere to the space.

Jerry opened the door to a small room piled with mounds of paperwork.

"I wasn't lying when I said this wouldn't be the most exciting work," he said apologetically.

"It's okay," I said with a laugh. "I knew what I was getting into."

I surveyed the stacks of papers, imagining hours of tedious sorting and filing. I had kind of latched on to the hope, at least, that tackling the mundane work might magically keep my mind occupied enough to ward off the frequent invading thoughts of Samantha. It wasn't the original reason I had agreed to take the job, but it seemed like a good enough diversion for the moment.

"I hate to say it," Jerry said, pacing a circle around the room, "but no one has touched any of the filing since Alyssa left. I think it's only fair to show you the task you're up against. The good news is it'll have to wait."

He picked up a stack of folders, tapping them with his forefinger. "Ah ha, here they are. Follow me," he said, and I obeyed by trailing him down the hall to a different office.

The second office was much neater—empty really—and one I had seen before since it was connected to Jerry's by a glass partition. It consisted mostly of a desk with computer surrounded by plenty of space to work. He plunked the folders down next to the keyboard and motioned for me to take the desk chair.

He yanked another chair up beside me, gave the mouse a little wiggle, and the monitor sprang to life.

"I guess you've heard that the new scheduled appointments for CURE begin today," he said.

"I knew about the appointments, but I didn't know they were starting today," I said.

It made sense, I supposed. Alyssa had said her appointment was scheduled for Tuesday. I just hadn't fully registered that Tuesday meant tomorrow. I wasn't sure which unnerved me more, the actual CURE procedure or the wild slant to her eyes when she assured me that was one appointment she had no intention of keeping.

"Yep, first one's in a half-hour." He tapped the folders again. "Before we went on this scheduling system, though, we had already administered the first stage of the treatments to this group, who we thought would be our first recipients."

Jerry clicked his way through several stages of the software I would be using. I tried to follow his movements but he maneuvered much too fast for me to catch anything useful.

"So first things first, I need you to get the data from these patients into our system. Once we get caught up on these, I'd like to get on a schedule to have every patient's codes in the system within a day or two of when they donate."

Jerry showed me how to input the first patient's data, then supervised as I input the next few. After that he left me to fend for myself.

This is what I had been wanting all along, to get inside LifeShare and see if I could help Steven with the mystery behind his duplicate codes. Somehow, though, that second hidden database had become intermingled with blood drives and CURE donations, with Alyssa and the loss of her baby, the hospital, Isaiah, the tunnels, and the death of Samantha. Instead of the work helping to clear my mind, my brain rebelled by thumbing through this Rolodex of ideas in a never-ending loop.

I tried to focus by paying close attention to the codes as I typed them into the computer interface. It was one thing to think of the codes as unexplainable numbers, another to know they represented actual patients giving up their blood for the promise of a life without cancer. The implications were daunting, and my stomach tingled with apprehension.

Each patient's data was grouped into a collection of reports.

Consisting mostly of figures, they looked to me like test results, although I could find nothing to identify the type of test or any indication of who any particular patient might be. After scrutinizing the data of the first five or so patients, I finally settled into a groove and gave up trying to find meaning in the figures.

Several hours later, my stack of folders had dwindled down to one last set of reports and my swirling thoughts had stirred themselves into a kind of murky soup that made it difficult to concentrate on anything other than transferring statistics from printout to database.

Jerry reappeared as I was inputting the last patient.

"Looks like you've made some good progress here," he said.

I glanced up and smiled, then punched in the last few figures. My back ached from sitting hunched over the keyboard. For a split second I longed for the tunnels—the trapped cool air, the earthen smell of the clay, the solitude. Then I thought of Samantha and how she had intruded on that space and what it had cost her. I gave an involuntary shake of my head. Despite the images that invaded my sleep—crazy, impossible visions—I didn't want to believe that her death had anything to do with the tunnels. Or LifeShare, for that matter.

I realized my brow had furrowed into a frown and tapped the folders into a neat stack, hoping Jerry couldn't read the distress behind my expression.

I forced a smile and handed over the hard copies.

"On to the filing now?" I asked a bit more cheerily than I had planned.

"Nah," he said. "I think you've tackled enough for your first day. Let me show you where to pick up the data from the clinic and then we'll call it done. What do you say?"

I hadn't known Jerry that long, but he had always presented a fatherly persona to me. His weathered skin and thick grey hair were part of it, but there was something in the deep gravelly voice that cemented the paternal image. I found myself wondering if he had children, and why I had never thought to ask.

But now wasn't the time to ask. Jerry swung around the glass partition, deposited my stack of folders into a file on his desk, and ushered me down the hall. As we walked, I tried to imagine how the corridors in front of me related to the tunnels below, and mentally laid out the tracts of land and houses that had once stood here.

Every step I took bolstered the irritation building inside me. Walking in stride with the man who had dismissed Steven's concerns about the database problems, I had to concentrate to keep my anger directed at LifeShare. It wasn't fair to blame Jerry. Like Steven, he simply worked here. He himself hadn't destroyed a historical structure to build this place.

The clinic opened to the outside on the west end of the building. I knew the location from the parking lot, but it took a long time to walk there through the wide tile corridors. The air seemed to grow colder with every turn we made and the hard floor clacked against our shoes, eliciting tiny echoes that trailed close behind us like shadows.

Finally we reached another set of glass doors. Jerry pushed through and held the door for me. We approached a counter shielded by even more glass—glass seemed to be everywhere, why had I never noticed that before—behind which sat a scrub-suited young woman who might have been a nurse or a receptionist, I wasn't sure which.

"Hi Jerry," she said, voice muffled by the thick partition. Her blonde hair gleamed unnaturally under the fluorescent light.

"Lucy," Jerry said, making introductions, "this is Emmalyn Trew. She's going to be helping us out part-time."

Lucy beamed up at me, smiling cheeks pushing her doe-brown eyes into a slant. "Trew," she said thoughtfully. "Any relation to Steven?"

I smiled back. "Yes, actually."

"Yep," Jerry confirmed. "Emmalyn just happens to be the one and only Mrs. Steven Trew," he said a bit theatrically. He shot a crooked grin in my direction.

Lucy's gaze fell to the small swell of my abdomen and her smile wavered.

The muscles of my mouth threatened to draw my nice-to-meet-you smile into a humorous smirk. Jerry's paternal side was showing, and perhaps a little possessiveness as well. I got the distinct feeling that he was marking my territory for me, and I had a sudden notion that Steven's trips to the clinic for blood donations had been overseen with precision by a certain petite blonde nurse. He'd never mentioned that part to me.

"Emmalyn will be stopping by from time to time to pick up the paperwork from the CURE donations," Jerry said, getting back to business. "You'll be sure to help her get the correct forms, won't you, Lucy?"

Lucy's eyes hesitated as she stared at me, then bounced gleefully from me to Jerry. "I surely will," she said, and motioned for me to come around to her side of the glass. From this vantage point, I could see a hallway lined with examination rooms. Apparently LifeShare had added on more than the underground storage space. I had only given blood once at LifeShare, shortly after Steven had started the job. At that time, there had been five beds lining one wall in a common room. I remembered Regina Haskins lying next to me, our blood flowing in unison into matching pint-sized bags while she regaled me with the layout of the town, including the best places to buy fresh meat, have my clothing dry-cleaned, and which garage I should visit if my car gave me trouble.

Down the hall, a man clad in neat blue scrubs that matched Lucy's glanced at me and disappeared into one of the rooms. Lucy pointed to a rolling file cart, regaining my attention. "We put the reports in here when they come back from the lab. You can come by any time and pick them up. They'll be ordered numerically here on the tab. Record the series, first to last, on this clipboard and sign to show you've picked them up, and they're all yours."

"Thanks, Lucy," I said. "I appreciate your help. Should I tell Steven you said hello?" I added.

"Oh sure," she said, "although I believe we're expecting him back in the clinic this week."

The lines along Jerry's forehead deepened for a second, and Lucy's eyes widened slightly in response. Aware that I was on edge about so many things, I decided that the non-verbal exchange between them—assuming it actually was an exchange and I hadn't imagined it—was something I wasn't ready to completely dismiss, but something I'd need to think about later.

On the way back to the offices, Jerry gave me a sidelong glance that lingered for an uncomfortable moment.

"I heard about what happened yesterday," he said.

News travels fast, I thought. I geared up to assure him that my fainting spell was nothing and that he shouldn't be worried about health issues interfering with my work.

Before I could answer, he added, "Samantha Bedding. Were you friends?"

Friends?

I had never thought of Samantha as a friend, I realized.

"Kind of," I said noncommittally. "More like acquaintances. She did that piece on me in the *Gazette*."

"I heard about that. I haven't seen it yet," he said.

I waved my hand dismissively, wishing I hadn't mentioned it. I had never exactly been crazy about having an article written about me, but for the first time, I had a wild desire to hunt down every issue in town and set fire to them all. I suddenly didn't like the idea of Jerry or anyone else at LifeShare seeing that story about my explorations of the tunnels.

"Well, I wouldn't go to any special trouble," I said, forcing lightness into my voice. "Other than a picture of me on a really bad hair day, I'm afraid it's not very interesting."

"Hmmm." The sound, little more than a buzzing in his throat, did not seem to be a comment on Samantha's article, interesting or not. He watched his feet as we continued to walk, then looked back at me after a moment, his mouth stretched into a thoughtful line. "Terrible tragedy," he said.

"Yes," I agreed. "Terrible."

. . .

The air had grown muggy, the sky a grey blanket while I had been inside, and my head felt as thick as the low clouds.

I drove away from LifeShare, my mind filled with more meandering thoughts than when I had arrived. A cute blonde nurse, or whatever she was, seemed to have taken a shine to my husband, although I considered that the least of my worries. The codes, although seemingly innocuous and delivering on their promise of mind-numbing data entry, were chinking away in the recesses of my mind, the cogs of their meaning moving steadily closer to forming a connection that might get a new set of wheels turning. And of course, Jerry's mention of Samantha had brought that horror bubbling back to the surface.

I found myself revisiting the previous day's events. The more I thought about it, the less I was able to differentiate between what was real and what I hoped beyond hope truly were horrific visions from my dreams.

If not for Professor Kendall's words, I might have been able to draw a more definitive line. If Alan had meant to reassure me, he had only served to raise more doubts.

What you believe happened ... did not happen.

Of what I could remember, those words were the most vivid. What exactly did he mean? Why had he said them? Had he said them at all, or were they just another one of the things I had imagined?

A dump truck pulled into the lane in front of me, forcing me to slam on my brakes and jarring me out of my reverie. Clods of red clay showered from the back of the truck, bounced, and spattered against my windshield. I saw, as clearly as if I was standing there, the dust that rained to the ground when Samantha had heaved her flashlight against the opening to the side corridor.

Was that really what had happened? What I believed had happened?

Or part of the dream?

The truck, or perhaps just the possible memory it had triggered, had shocked my heart rate into overdrive, reduced my breath to wispy jags.

I took the next left and drove to the church. Vacation Bible School must have ended about the same time I had left LifeShare. If Alan had brought his niece back today, there was a possibility I might catch him.

The parking lot was empty, though, except for a scant collection of cars. I recognized a couple of them, but none belonged to Alan Kendall. I pulled into a parking space, meaning to dig my phone out of my purse, and froze at what I saw.

Two thick tracks had been cut into the grass behind the church. They led straight into the woods. Fresh indentations pressed the grass into serrated flat grooves across the short green lawn. The stripes in the grass were smattered with a trail of red mud clots squashed flat by the weight of whatever vehicle had driven there. Where the grass met the parking lot, two bands of terracotta started out thick and red, then faded and thinned along the asphalt.

I thought of the truck that had pulled into the road in front of me, the red dirt that had cascaded from its bed as it clamored into my path, scattering the loose remnants of a full load of soil, and my heart began to pound all over again.

I bounded from the car and sprinted toward the woods, my low heels twisting and catching on the uneven ground. The tracks blazed a path through the grass but I didn't need any markings to find my way. I knew exactly where they would lead, and the idea of it churned through my stomach with a sickening rage.

A mammoth mound of dirt had been piled along the tree line where the woods started, only yards from the opening to the tunnels.

A small backhoe sat parked nearby, ready to push that dirt into the entrance, to close it off for good. There was no other explanation. I bent over, grasping my knees with my hands to steady myself, and forced myself to take in deep breaths. The freshly dumped earth reeked with a damp stench, foreign and overwhelming with the sheer disturbance of it. I trudged farther into the woods, longing to smell the familiar clean dry fragrance of my tunnels.

Why? I wondered, but I knew. It was because of what had happened to Samantha. It had to be. Coyotes, I thought, disbelief squirming like a virus inside my head.

Who had the authority to order such a thing? The church? Did they own the property back this far? I had never bothered to even wonder.

Or LifeShare? Certainly they had no respect for the historical value of these tunnels. That much they had proven already.

I stood at the entrance, staring down into the rich darkness. The pull was almost palpable, but I knew I couldn't go in. I wasn't dressed for it. I had no idea when someone would be back to begin filling in the hole. Steven would completely freak out.

All logical reasons, but the real one, of course, was Samantha.

Even still, anger surged inside me thinking about the mound of dirt and the backhoe.

I might never be able to go inside again, I thought.

I forced myself to leave the tunnels, purposefully turning away from the mass of dirt as I trudged from the woods back across the church lawn.

"Oh hey!"

My eyes had been locked on the ground, I realized as I snapped my head up to find Selena Garrett hauling a plastic bin toward her SUV. Her son, Josh, ran across the front lawn toward the playground equipment.

I forced a smile. "Here, let me help you with that," I said.

"No no, but thanks!" She held fast to the bin while skillfully dislodging her keys from the waist of her capris, and the SUV's hatch popped obediently open.

"How are you feeling today?" she said. "We were all very worried about you passing out like that yesterday."

"I'm fine," I said, hoping my increased heart rate didn't make me look like I was about to put on a repeat performance.

She stole a glance down at my shoes. My eyes followed hers

involuntarily. The toes and heels were caked with the red dirt.

"Have you been in the woods?" she said nonchalantly, then when I didn't answer right away, "I saw the article about you digging around out there."

I couldn't be sure whether her voice carried a note of disapproval or if it was only my imagination. I seemed to project that onto anyone these days who mentioned the tunnels.

"Yeah," I said, not interested in elaborating. "What's up with the dirt?"

She nodded vigorously, even as a veil of sympathy fell over her eyes.

"It's to close up that hole back there. What happened yesterday was so awful. Pastor Bill has been looking into closing up that entrance for a while now, I hear, but after what happened to that poor woman, he finally decided we shouldn't put it off any longer."

Selena pulled down the hatch and called for Josh.

"Does the church own the land that far back?" I asked.

"No, it actually belongs to LifeShare."

I winced. No surprise there.

"Our committee got in touch with them this morning, and they agreed that in light of yesterday's … events, it really did pose a danger to have the tunnels open so just anyone could venture down there."

"Do we even know Samantha Bedding was down there yesterday?"

"Whether or not she was, it's the coyotes everybody's concerned about. If they have a den down there—"

"Has anyone ever actually seen any coyotes around here?" I blurted, still annoyed by the ludicrous idea of a pack of coyotes living inside the tunnels. Why had no one ever bothered to ask me if I had ever seen any signs of wild dogs down there? Because my answer would be no, I thought, and that wasn't the answer they'd want.

Josh zipped around the back of the building and slammed against me, arms wrapping around my legs for a brief hug.

"Hi Miss Em," he beamed.

"Hi Josh."

Selena patted his head and pulled her son protectively toward the car.

"I don't think proof is the issue at this point, Emmalyn," she said. "We really just want it to be safe around here."

I decided to let it go at that, waved at Josh as they pulled out of the parking lot, and went back to my car.

Leaving my door ajar to let the breeze circulate, I picked up my phone and punched in Alan Kendall's cell number. It rang four times before tripping over to voicemail. I disconnected and called his house instead.

Liz answered.

"Hi Liz," I said. "I was looking for Alan. I thought I might be able to catch him at the church after VBS. I don't suppose he's made it home yet, huh?"

"Change of plans," she said. "Alan decided to take Keera down to Disneyworld for a few days instead. She enjoyed the VBS kickoff yesterday, but after what happened to that poor woman, Alan thought it might be a good idea to find something else to do. I hope you're not offended."

"Not at all," I assured her. It wasn't as if I had invited Alan, and he certainly had no obligation toward me to bring Keera for the whole week. "He mentioned something yesterday that I wanted to ask him about. I tried his cell."

"Well good luck with that." She laughed. "I haven't heard hide nor hair from him since they left this morning. He doesn't like to talk while he's driving, so don't take it personally if you don't hear back for a while. Of course, if we hear from him at all, it'll be a small miracle. Sometimes he can be a bit rebellious about checking in."

What was the other thing he had said? That we would talk soon, when we could? It almost seemed as if Alan had known at that moment he would be unreachable. If he had been planning to take Keera to Florida, then why had he even shown up at the church yesterday?

I had to wonder if Liz was trying to discourage me from trying to contact Alan. He had obviously told her about Samantha's death; I wondered if he had also shared with her his cryptic words of advice to me.

"How are you feeling, hon?" Liz said, almost as if she could read my thoughts. "Alan told me you fainted yesterday. Is everything okay?"

"I think I'm fine," I told her. "I suppose he was right about the heat getting to me."

"Well, these summer days are only going to get hotter, and the bigger that baby grows, the more you're going to feel it. So you take it easy, you hear me?"

"That's some advice I'm happy to take," I said, keenly aware of the sweat that had sprung out along my temples. I ran my free hand over my belly, still small compared to what it was destined to become, but now that I had "popped," as my mother called it, the round curve seemed to be swelling noticeably with every passing day.

Guilt wafted over me, subtle but challenging what might be my lack of motherly instincts. The child I was carrying could very well be playing in this churchyard, even in these woods, in the very near future. It might be time for me to start thinking a little more like Selena Garrett and embrace the concept of safety instead of my own curiosity.

Steven arrived home to find me in his office again, seated in front of the computer. He rounded the corner, then stopped abruptly in the doorway. When I glanced up, I thought I saw a flicker of apprehension cross his features. No doubt he was afraid of a repeat of Saturday night, when I had allowed my anger about LifeShare and the tunnels to take me over like a woman possessed. The evening had turned out surprisingly well. However, I knew neither of us cared for a repeat of the spat that had preceded our lusty end-product.

"Safe to come in?" he asked, raising his eyebrows quizzically.

"Promise," I said. "Come here. I want to show you something."

"Uh-oh. Sounds serious," he said, but wandered obediently over to the desk and reached across me to drop his briefcase in its habitual spot.

"First things first, though," he said. He grabbed the arms of the chair, spun it toward him, and leaned down to kiss me. The kiss was warm and sweet and lingeringly exquisite. I laughed a little and tried to refocus. In his own way, Steven had sufficiently established that we were absolutely in no danger of reenacting our most memorable fight to date.

"Okay, what've you got?" he said.

"Well," I began. "I spent all day putting codes into your computer system at LifeShare and at the time I thought none of it made sense. I mean, I could tell I was transferring some kind of test results from reports. None of them had anybody's names on them, though."

"That would make sense," Steven said, skepticism sharpening his words. "We've always used codes to identify our blood supplies, never names."

"Okay, then I can understand the names not being on the reports. Confidentiality. But the reports themselves seemed awfully cryptic to me—there was nothing to indicate what type of tests they might be."

"Blood type," Steven suggested.

"That was definitely part of it. Makes sense for donations— more so, I think, than if the donor is also the recipient. Regardless, there was a lot more data than blood type would account for. I wish I had a copy of those reports so I could compare—"

"You don't, do you?" Steven glanced around, alarm apparent on his face.

"No," I assured him, "but look at what I found ..."

I trailed off and pulled up one of the websites I had been looking at.

"I've been going over it and over it and I think I've figured out what type of tests they're running on this blood. Look, blood glucose." The screen showed an example glucose level. I wrote it on a sheet of paper, and clicked another link.

"Cholesterol," I said. I wrote down another set of sample numbers, representing total cholesterol, LDL, HDL, and triglycerides.

I clicked another tab.

"The last is the CBC. I didn't have enough data for this one, but I think the results may be pieces of a complete panel. The figures I saw seemed to fit white blood cells, red cells, and platelet count."

I wrote down three more figures and looked at Steven. "Can you show me the codes again? The legitimate ones and the ones from the rogue database?"

Steven gave me a speculative stare, then shifted the keyboard toward him. With a few clicks of the mouse and a series of keystrokes, he pulled up two nearly identical sets of data. Side by side like this—and probably because he had pointed it out to me—it was easy to see that the list on the left contained the same, but not all, of the data in the list of lengthier codes on the right.

"What are you thinking, Em?" he said.

"Look at the first code."

I copied the first code from the left data set, but instead of copying it exactly, I broke it into sections, so that the sample test data fit neatly into the gaps.

"The extra data," I said. "The test results, interspersed with the birthdate, the inventory codes, the blood type of your legitimate codes. It doesn't explain everything. There are still a few digits I can't account for."

"Lord, Em," Steven said, running his hand through the loose, dark strands of his hair. "You could be on to something here. Remember I told you I wrote in some code that would alert me if the rogue database was being used?"

"You're kidding. You saw activity yesterday?"

"Yep." He gave me a look and grabbed the mouse again, clicked on a module that allowed him to search, and typed:

03271942. His father's birthday; it was the reason he had remembered the inventory number from when he had last donated blood. A number he would recognize and never forget.

The code containing Henry Trew's birthday sprang to the top of the screen.

Steven surveyed the string of data. "There are only five digits we haven't accounted for."

"And the M," I corrected. It seemed crucial that we find an explanation for every part of the code, and each of the codes in Steven's database began with either an M or a V.

He took the pen and scribbled a thick slash through the M at the beginning of the code.

"The new storage facility is divided into two sections. Nobody ever mentions it, so you tend to forget. But I swear, there are little signs outside the entrances. They're called ..." He paused, dropping his chin toward his chest, coughing out a choked laugh before he continued. "The wings are named Mars and Venus. Ridiculous. I don't know why I didn't think of it before. M and V—Male and Female."

"Female," I said softly, and my stomach turned a little flip. It was a very inopportune time for images of Alyssa or Samantha to pop into my mind, but they flashed before my eyes like twin bolts of lightning. Alyssa—blood streaming down her legs. And Samantha. I could imagine her all too vividly, blood draining across her chest. The thought of her throat cut—not cut, but *ripped*, that was how Steven had described it—made my head swim.

I forced myself to concentrate on what Steven was doing.

He scrawled the long code onto the paper, then scratched through the segments we thought we knew the meaning of, which now included the leading M. That left only the five characters he said we hadn't yet identified, but also a four-digit section of what he had told me was the inventory control number, the number that, for him, corresponded with his father's birth date.

Then he wrote the remaining numbers on another line, this time in backward order, placing a hyphen after the first three, then after the next two, and finished with the last four numbers.

He peered over at me. Dark wavy strands of his hair had fallen back over one eye, but I could still see the raised eyebrows. Together we looked back at the number he had written.

"I always assumed the blood bags were pre-coded with an inventory number," he said. "But this suggests that the inventory number is specific to the donor."

One second before, I had meant to ask what the first and last two digits of the inventory code might represent, but the series of numbers Steven had written on the paper completely erased the question from my lips.

"That's your social security number," I said, my voice a strangled whisper.

His mouth tightened into a severe line before he spoke. "No name identifier, but something to make sure the donor is matched to the recipient at the last stage."

"For the transfusion," I whispered. I almost couldn't bear to think about the actual process of how the CURE was administered. I hated talking about it even more.

"But—" I started.

Steven cut me off.

"These are old codes," he said. "Codes from our regular blood drives. Codes from before we ever learned about CURE."

I nodded. He had verbalized my thoughts as if he knew exactly what I was thinking.

"Do you think LifeShare has been collecting this data all along? Storing it in this second database? Why?"

Steven shook his head. His eyes remained locked intently on the puzzles written before him on screen and paper.

"I don't know," he said.

CHAPTER EIGHTEEN

Tuesday morning, I awoke to find the sky darkened by clouds and impending storms. My mood matched the gloomy weather.

I had thought about the codes all night, excited by the possibility of uncovering something more related to Steven's duplicate database. After two hours at the office, I had discovered nothing more than the fact that inputting this data was extremely tedious and boring. I sincerely hoped that Alyssa's position at LifeShare had included some more versatile duties.

When my stack was completed, I traversed the sterile grey halls by memory to pick up more test results from the clinic. I walked slowly, studying the layout, wondering which innocuous side door, if any, might lead to the underground wings where the blood was stored.

I spotted Lucy right away as I passed through the clinic's glass entrance. She didn't notice me immediately, though, and I thought her engrossed expression carried a dark concentration that contrasted sharply with her bubbly demeanor when we had met yesterday.

I tapped on the glass between us and her head popped up.

"Oh hi," she beamed, instantly chipper, as if my appearance had shocked the somber countenance off her face. "You know you don't have to knock, right? You can just come on back and get what you need."

I rounded the desk obediently and began pulling the latest CURE test results from the files.

"I didn't want to startle you. You seemed pretty engrossed in what you were doing."

"Oh, yeah," she laughed, crinkling her eyes before letting her facial features relax into a lackluster droop. "I guess I do kind of get that zoned-in look on my face when I'm working on something. But trust me, I'm not thinking as hard as it seems."

I glanced around conspiratorially. "Well, you looked sufficiently dedicated to your work to me," I said.

"Oh, I am dedicated to it," she retorted with the breezy swiftness of innocent idealism. She might have been insulted by what I had said; I wasn't sure. "I fully support CURE and I want to do whatever I can to be a part of it. Don't you?"

Blunt? Okay. Innocent? Not so sure anymore. Rather than respond, I decided to change directions. I motioned toward the hallway of doors, each one with a small window.

"So these are the examining rooms? When did this happen?" I said lightly. "The last time I gave blood, I sat on a cot along with about 5 others in one room. Sort of old army hospital style."

Disapproval seemed to drift like a thin fog over Lucy's expression. If so, it lifted immediately. The girl might not be good at initial reactions, but she was master of the quick recovery.

"Well, that was fine for the occasional blood drive," she said. "But CURE demands a higher level of confidentiality. Everything runs a little longer—from first consultation to final treatments— and the patients have so many questions. Something this delicate deserves privacy. It really shouldn't be conducted out in the open."

No, no, I thought, we wouldn't want anything about LifeShare, CURE, database codes, or historic tunnels to be out in the open, would we?

"LifeShare must have known about CURE long before the rest of us, then, if they were able to remodel this section so there would be private examination rooms in time for the treatments." I said, fishing.

Lucy was definitely not an easy catch. This time her reaction remained confined to the narrowing of lids across her brown eyes.

"More of a lucky coincidence, I'd say." She picked up the clipboard and thrust it toward me. "Did you sign out the test results?" she added with fair mix of cheer and dismissal.

"Thanks, Lucy," I said. "I was just about to do that."

Looking somewhat official with my armload of fresh reports, I headed back toward my office, strolling a little more leisurely this time. I smiled and offered cursory nods to the occasional person who passed by, while stealing quick surveying glances at every branching corridor, recess, and doorway. Mostly it was the same uninformative monotony—nondescript beige doors, some with keypads, most without.

I wasn't yet brave enough to venture down any of the side halls and, although the doors with keypads interested me most, there was little point to investigating those any further.

Pausing, I leaned against the wall and fiddled with the strap of my shoe for a moment, using the time to scope the length of the hallway. Finding it empty, I slid into one of the recesses and let my fingertips graze the doorknob. A vision of the clay-caked doors in the tunnels below invaded my memory, and I felt my hand begin to tremble. Just like I had no way of knowing what exactly was sealed behind those secret doors, I had no inkling what might lay on the other side of this one—conference room, executive office, banks of computers, or nothing more sinister or revealing than a janitorial closet—but my fingers ached to turn the knob and discover something … anything.

"Curiosity killed the cat!"

I jumped at the intrusion of Lucy's voice. In the time it took for my hand to recoil reflexively, a horrible scene played out in my head—Samantha, cornered in the shadowy depths of the tunnels, thrashing against red dirt saturated to deep burgundy by darkness and blood, a pack of growling coyotes ripping and shredding her throat as she forced her last screams through the tattered flesh.

"Ah, you scared the devil out of me," I said, and before I could help myself, decided on a strategy I seldom used—the outright lie.

"This isn't the ladies' room?"

A smile crossed Lucy's lips but her brown eyes gleamed bronze with distrust. We both knew I was up to no good.

"Nope," she said, voice once again bubbly. "A little farther down. But you might not want to take those reports into the restroom with you. Wouldn't want them to get wet."

I loosened my grip on the stack of test results in my hand, and gave back my most innocent smile.

"You're right, of course," I said, forcing a little laugh. "I don't know what I was thinking." I lowered my voice to the level of confidentiality and lightly touched my rounded belly. "I didn't think being pregnant would affect my bladder already, but I guess this is just the beginning."

"Hmmm," she said, stealing a quick glance downward. "You need any help finding your way back?"

"No, I think I'm okay from this point. But I'll be sure to get specific directions before I head out for the restrooms again."

Our exchange had become petty, but I didn't really care at this point. I gave Lucy a parting smile and listened for her footsteps between mine.

Jerry had been in meetings all morning, but he was back in his office when I returned, so I stopped by his desk to say hello.

"You already finished the stack I left this morning, huh?" he said, motioning to the new reports I held.

"Yeah, I just picked up this new batch from the clinic. I'm surprised at how many patients we're seeing so quickly."

"Back to back appointments," he confirmed. A wistful look washed over his face. "It really is an amazing thing, isn't it?"

"Amazing," I repeated, weighing the connotations of this word. I found I neither agreed nor disagreed with Jerry's assessment.

"You're skeptical," he said. Apparently I read like an open book. My own husband had said the same thing about me, hadn't he?

"I guess I am. I'm sorry, Jerry. I suppose you and I have very different perspectives about CURE."

Jerry waved off my apology. "You're young. And as far as I know, cancer hasn't touched your lives. At least Steven's never mentioned anyone in your immediate family. Think about it. You still have the luxury of skepticism. I've been there." He paused, drawing his lower lip inward. "I don't ever want to go there again. And I wouldn't wish it upon anyone else in the whole wide world. So you see—I've lost the luxury of skepticism."

I felt an enormous need to apologize over and over to this man. Of course he saw things differently than I did. An image of myself as an infinitely selfish child registered behind my eyes, and I pushed it away with a shake of my head. I feared remembering the pain Alyssa had suffered would, for me, forever taint any good associated with this breakthrough treatment.

I swallowed, building my resolve.

"Jerry, have you talked to Alyssa since she left?"

"No, I'm sorry to say I haven't. I really should be ashamed, I guess, not checking in on her. I very much enjoyed having her around while she worked for me—it was kind of like having a teenage daughter again. I don't mean that bad, mind you—just she was so energetic, on the go, always caught up in the next health craze or what have you."

Jerry's description of Alyssa brought a smile to my eyes, until I remembered my last conversation with her. The person Jerry was describing was carefree, fun-loving; the person I had last seen was distraught, heartbroken, confused, and filled with paranoia. I had to ask myself if I really believed that last part. I had used the same word to describe myself recently, but I wasn't completely convinced that a healthy dose of paranoia wasn't justified these days. Maybe that was even truer for Alyssa.

Jerry continued. "That was a good thing you did, helping her get to the hospital and all. Steven told me."

"Yeah," I said, looking down at the floor. "You know she got a letter."

I looked back up at Jerry, wondering how he would react to my cryptic statement. For a moment, I thought he wasn't going to react at all. His face displayed nothing that revealed a true reaction. Within seconds, though, he broke into a consummate Jerry smile, his weathered cheeks bunching into twin apples under bright hazel eyes that were only slightly squinted.

"Letter," he said as if testing the word.

"She has an appointment today."

"Oh, that letter," he said, a grunt of a laugh escaping his throat.

"She's not thrilled about the process. I think she feels like giving blood at the last drive had something to do with her ..." I had to pause to stop myself from finishing with the word miscarriage. "... trip to the hospital," I finished.

"I didn't know that," he said. "Did her doctor say how that might have triggered her problem?"

"No," I said flatly, deciding to err on the side of truth if not traveling there wholeheartedly. "They didn't seem to think one had anything to do with the other. I can't blame her, though, for making the connection. So you can see why the CURE program isn't for her. She was a little worried about what might happen if she didn't show up for her first appointment. I assured her, of course, that it was completely up to her. Obviously, she has a choice," I said. My toes were already in the test waters. Why not wade in a little deeper?

"She should keep the appointment. Maybe you could talk to her, convince her it's for the best."

"How can I do that if I'm not convinced myself?"

Jerry pressed his fingers against his forehead as if staving off a migraine. He pulled an extra chair over next to him and motioned for me to sit down. His expression was so intent, his brow so tight, I thought he was going to scold me, or fire me, or at least tell me to mind my own business.

"Would it be enough if I told you Alyssa *needs* to keep her appointments?" he asked, staring directly at me.

I shook my head, a simple but honest answer.

"I could lose my job for telling you this," he said blankly.

I simply nodded.

"Alyssa has tested positive for the breast cancer gene. She *will* get cancer one day," he said slowly.

A soft whistle passed my lips.

"She never told me that," I said finally.

Jerry sat a little straighter. "She doesn't know."

My response popped out, unchecked. I couldn't have held back even if I'd had time to think. "Then how do *you* know?"

"Remember, my job could be on the line here."

"You tested her blood?" I asked, then took it a step further, "Without her consent!" I was instantly appalled at the invasion of Alyssa's privacy. It was official. From now on, I would embrace every fear, suspicion, mistrust, and unreasonable obsession that so much as knocked on the door of my psyche, instead of passing off my mind's warning signs as paranoia.

Jerry reached out to put his hand over mine. Intellectually, I saw it for what it was—a fatherly gesture meant to reassure me—but I yanked my hand away anyway.

"Not me," he said, folding his arms across his chest.

"You. The clinic. LifeShare. Whoever. Never mind losing your job, Jerry. This can't even be legal. It's definitely not ethical," I spat, my voice trilling to a higher octave.

"You're missing the point."

I shook my head frantically and rolled my chair back a few inches, distancing myself from the man in front of me.

"Missing the point? What about me? I've given blood here. And Steven. What's wrong with us? What kind of anomalies do we have lurking in our DNA? Oh, wait! Maybe we don't want to know. Maybe if we wanted to know, we would give someone permission to run tests on us, maybe we would—"

"Lower you voice, Emmalyn," Jerry said sternly, cutting me off.

My mouth clamped shut of its own volition, an ingrained reaction to elderly authority. I took a few deep breaths and glared at him.

"I can't believe you are a part of something like this," I

finally said.

"Did you know I had a daughter once?" he asked, surprising me.

"Don't change the subject," I snapped back.

"She died … in a car accident. Seventeen. Bled to death," he said.

The phrase made me cringe. At the same time I felt my anger diffuse by a small increment. The pain in his voice was evident.

"Her injuries were brutal. There was a blood shortage. The hospital didn't have enough of her type, and she just …"

He let his sentence trail away, but my mind finished it too easily.

"Don't you think I would have done anything to save her? That's what brought me to LifeShare in the first place. I'm just an old computer geek, but working here I feel like I'm part of the solution. And now we have *the* solution—CURE. You know I have to be a part of that."

I opened my mouth, half-hearted protest poised on my lips, but he held up his hand.

"Believe me," he said evenly. "Everything you are thinking, everything going through your head right now, I've considered. I'm not the kind of man to jump into things lightly. I weighed what I know against the greater good and I made my decision."

"It's criminal," I whispered, my body suddenly too tired to muster up my previous resolve. "People come in here to give a part of themselves—their *blood*. To help others. They have a right to know what LifeShare is doing with it."

"Don't you see?" he said. "We're about to cure cancer. Nobody's going to care that LifeShare might have run a few tests without permission."

The smile that crossed his face sent shivers down my spine because I knew without a doubt that he honestly believed that what he was saying was true. I pictured a world of healthy people, forever freed from mankind's most dreaded disease, burying LifeShare in the throes of litigation. Cancer, no cancer, CURE or not, that, at least, LifeShare would deserve. The company would deserve it, I corrected myself, and quickly pulled myself back from the vengeful daydream. What about LifeShare's employees? I wondered. What about Jerry?

What about Steven?

"This data I'm inputting?" I said, holding up my reports from the clinic. "What does it mean? Have I been filling LifeShare's databases with unlawfully obtained information?"

"Emmalyn, you're putting in the same information LifeShare has always kept on file."

"Nice noncommittal answer, Jerry. Don't spin me. What else am I inputting?"

There was no humor left on his face. "I'll be honest. Ninety-nine percent of it is run-of-the-mill stuff you'd get if you went in to see a doctor for a physical. Cholesterol, lipids, triglycerides, sugar levels, that kind of thing."

At least he had confirmed what Steven and I had worked out the night before regarding the codes.

"I won't even ask why LifeShare, or anyone else for that matter, should store that kind of information. What about the other one percent? That would be information like you have on Alyssa?" I asked. "Why?"

"I told you I think of her like a daughter." Jerry reached into his back pocket and pulled out his wallet. He slipped his thumb into one of the slots and pulled out an old picture, tattered around the edges, of a teenage girl in a cheerleader uniform, her body strong and athletic. The wind had caught the girl's long blonde hair and the photograph had captured it flying wildly around her head with the sun reflecting off the golden strands. It looked a little like a halo.

The resemblance was uncanny. The girl in the picture could have been Alyssa in her teenage years.

I handed the photo back to Jerry and he tucked it carefully back into his wallet.

"I'm the one who asked for Alyssa's test," he said, shifting to one side to slide the wallet into his pocket. "I knew about her mother and her grandmother. I couldn't stand the thought of losing her to the same fate, not when we can prevent it. I swear to you, most of the things we tested for were generic, like the cholesterol. But some of us—a few of us who work here requested certain other tests for family members, people we love, like I did with Alyssa. I wished the test had come back negative, but I'm grateful it won't matter now that we have CURE."

I was beginning to hate that word and how it fit so naturally into our vocabulary even though its meaning was now irrevocably distorted for me.

Mist flooded my eyes. I slowly nodded, blinking away the moisture. "I understand."

His face relaxed. He looked relieved, as if what I thought might actually matter to him. I had to look away as I calmly laid the stack of test results on the desk beside him. My next gesture was probably meaningless coming from me, but I offered it anyway. I put my hand over his, holding it there while I looked into his sad but hopeful eyes.

"I can't work here anymore," I said.

CHAPTER NINETEEN

My limbs felt lifeless as a zombie's as I traversed the maze of corridors at LifeShare, maneuvering my way to Steven's office.

I waved at the faces I recognized behind glass windows along my way. I nodded at anyone who passed me in the halls, intermittently pasting what I hoped passed as a friendly smile across my face. They all waved or nodded in cordial response.

Just another day.

I kissed my husband longer than was appropriate for the office, clamping my hand to the back of his head, holding his warm lips against mine while I savored the taste of something reassuring, the one person I had to be able to trust. When I pulled away, dropping into his extra chair, he only looked at me and waited.

Steadily, I talked. And he listened.

Some of it he already knew, but I filled in all the blanks. I talked about Alyssa, the connection she placed between LifeShare's blood drive and the loss of her baby—and yes, I believed there had been a baby. I talked about Alyssa's letter, the CURE appointment she had no intention of keeping, about taking blood and giving blood and unauthorized tests. I talked about Jerry, about his daughter's death, how he was instrumental in having Alyssa's blood genetically tested without her knowledge and how he believed that was the right thing to do.

I talked about Samantha and the vague, fuzzy truth about what had happened in the tunnels. Because despite Professor Kendall's strange instructions, I did believe she had died there, and at the hands of some kind of animal, although my mind still would not allow a clear image to form. And because I told him what I believed, I told Steven the last words Alan Kendall had told me before disappearing with his niece. *What you believe happened ... did not happen ...*

And then I talked about black cars with tinted windows and a young man with silver eyes, unnaturally white skin, and lips the color of black cherries. For the first time, I talked about Isaiah. About the part he played in the tunnels.

And his warning.

"I'm coming home with you," Steven said finally as he gathered me close and a tear escaped down my cheek.

Temptation seeped into every cell of my body, to let him be there for me, to hide behind his loving shield against the world and the chaos in my mind. But purging myself of the craziness that had swarmed my mind for the past weeks gave me a kind of strength I didn't know I still had.

"I'm okay," I told him.

There was one more thing I needed to do.

I didn't call.

I rang Alyssa's doorbell and waited.

Memories of that other day I had appeared on her doorstep flooded back. The blood, the frantic trip to the hospital, the confusion about what the blood meant.

I began to shiver, thankful that the rain falling softly against my skin gave my shaking an explanation other than fear.

I was about to turn away when Dillon came to the door. His young face sagged with fatigue. When he looked into my eyes, the corner of his mouth quivered.

"She left," he said and turned his gaze to the floor.

"Left?" I said, hating to pry even though I had to. "When? Where?"

Dillon managed to meet my eyes again with his own, now

glassed over with tears. He crossed his arms across his chest defensively, and this seemed to give him the courage to speak.

"This morning," he said. "I don't know where she went. She said … all she said was that she just couldn't do it. She couldn't stay."

I laid my hand over Dillon's arm.

"I don't think she meant you," I said, and hoped it was enough.

For a while I just drove, alternately away from and back into town, wanting more than anything to be anonymous, to escape the town where I lived, much like Alyssa, I assumed. At the same time I longed to be grounded, to have a safe haven, and if that wasn't here, with Steven, then it couldn't be found. Even the tunnels called to me—their cool silent refuge—and I felt an overwhelming urge to find my way into them again. I should have been revolted by the very thought of those clay corridors, but I wasn't, and I found myself feeling grateful that Samantha's mangled body had been found at the creek. I could almost pretend she had never been down there with me.

After several hours, I grew weary and headed back to the house. I didn't need a psychiatrist to tell me I was attempting to find a substitute for my hikes into the tunnels. Driving, no matter how fast or how far, would never satisfy my particular need for escape and adventure combined. And my place was at home.

The drizzle of the morning gave way to steady rain as I approached my driveway. Not wanting to brave the wet, I pulled alongside the mailbox and grabbed the mail before pulling into the garage. The steady drumming against the roof did at least dampen my desire to explore the tunnels. I didn't know for certain whether the entrance behind the church had already been closed off, but since I never went into the tunnels during this kind of rain, I could at least set that notion aside for the remainder of the day.

Hunger growled inside my stomach as I closed the garage door behind me, went inside, and tossed my purse and mail onto the counter. I had missed lunch and had intended to grab a snack to hold me over until Steven got home for dinner, but my appetite vanished in an instant.

I recognized the official white envelope sticking out from between the bills and junk mail for what it was without really getting a good look at it. My heartbeat sped to wild thumps as I pulled the envelope out from the stack. My fingers trembled but I managed to slide them beneath the flap and remove the letter.

Two days. The date stamped on my letter was two days from today. Like I would drop whatever I was doing and fall obediently in line for my dose of the CURE.

Like I would let those people at LifeShare anywhere near me. Near my baby.

I yanked open the nearest kitchen drawer and crammed the letter in amongst a scramble of spoons and knives, then slammed the drawer closed and turned my back on it. If I couldn't accomplish getting this ridiculous summons out of my mind, I could certainly get it out of my sight.

I stood before the mirror in only a small tight tee-shirt and panties, intending to pull on my favorite pink sweats. I stared at the rounded white expanse that had become the core of my body. It seemed to grow bigger day by day. I had definitely reached the point where there could be no denying that I was carrying a baby inside me. I placed my hands protectively on either side of the mound that contained our child.

From out of nowhere, Steven came up behind and wrapped his strong arms snugly around me, cradling my middle by wrapping his fingers into mine. I hadn't even heard him come home. He kissed my neck and freeing one hand from mine, he stretched the neck of my shirt to one side as his lips traced along the top of my shoulder and back up to the outline of my jaw.

I turned into him, grabbing his face with my hands and greedily drawing his lips to cover mine. His hands, rough and seeking, roamed freely over my skin, setting my every nerve on fire. I tugged the bottom of his shirt over his chest, my fingers working fast, reluctant to separate his arms from me even for the second it took to yank the fabric over his head, and threw the wadded shirt onto the floor. Eyes closed, I let my hands return to read the contours of his body, my fingers trailing over every fiber of muscle, every dip and curve and hard edge of him.

For a moment, I felt a sense of betrayal—mine, not his. Weeks ago, hadn't I closed my eyes in this same way, used my hands in this same fashion to explore the miniscule variations in the tunnel walls? Knowing Steven didn't approve of my being there, I had nonetheless run my fingertips along those dirt walls, feeling for what I couldn't see, searching for those subtle differences in the surface of the dirt, trying to discover something hidden, a passage to the side corridor that had been carefully crafted to conceal that thing someone didn't want me to find.

I had to believe Steven had nothing to hide. Working for LifeShare did not make him the enemy. He could not be part of the conspiracy that threatened my every thought.

I opened my eyes. He was here, with me, completely vulnerable, nothing hidden.

Little by little, my mind emptied itself of everything but the warmth and strength of him and the electricity of our bodies tangled together as we stumbled to the bed.

The rain continued to fall throughout the evening. Several times, I found myself standing at the window, looking out into the night at the wavering curtains of water. Occasionally, a sheet flung itself against the glass. I watched the splatters beat spots against the relative safety of the panes, then collapse into random rivulets as the rain and wind backed away from the window for a reprieve.

Beyond, the usual scurrying business of the world seemed to have gone on hiatus for a time. I looked for cars passing by on nearby roads but found them quiet. Along the streets, squares of light from the neighboring windows alternately refracted into starbursts and melted into swaying rectangles.

I fell asleep to the first distant rumblings of thunder.

My mind had disintegrated into a blissful fog when a deafening crack pierced my sleep. In unison, Steven and I jolted upright. Out of reflex, my hand shot out in the dark to seek out any part of him, landing on his forearm. I closed my fingers around the strong muscle there, immediately relishing the security of his skin against mine.

"Storm." His voice croaked, barely finishing the single word before morphing into a groan. I heard the first beep from down the hall at the same time that he swung his legs over the side of the bed. The beeping was from our smoke alarms. The power was out.

I gathered the covers into my balled fists, tugging the edge of the blankets under my chin. My heart banged inside my chest, again. I forced myself to breath steadily while the banging gave way to a rambling of frenetic flutters. I could hear Steven wrenching the plastic shield away from the smoke detector, looking for the button to quiet it.

Outside, more rumblings sounded in the distance, short growls that bounced first from the north and then the west and rebounded back to the north in angry conversation. I settled back against my pillow, letting my eyes drift shut.

A sudden bolt of lightning bathed the room in a blinding flash and the image of Isaiah's pale face burned into my mind's eye, a nanosecond snapshot there and gone. Thunder instantly pounded my ears. I shuddered against the deafening force that shook the walls around me.

Darkness engulfed the room, and white afterimages floated across my vision. The spots morphed into ghostly faces, all staring at me as they drifted across the room, white ovals with shining silver orbs for eyes, smears of black voids where the lips belonged.

Seconds later, more flashes rocketed through the room, blinding me, and his face was there, then gone. I blinked, rubbed my knuckles into my eyes, scoured every inch of the room around me, searching for him, for the pale face, for Isaiah. Nothing registered but furniture and knick-knacks and paintings—I saw nothing in the darkness of my bedroom that shouldn't be there.

I let out a long sigh and tried to shake off my sleep stupor.

Another round of pounding reverberated around me. The thunder seemed disconnected from the lightning. It wasn't until I heard voices downstairs that I realized I hadn't heard thunder at all but the sounds of fists banging against my front door.

Not even stopping to grab a robe, I hurried down the stairs in my baggy tee-shirt and shorts.

Three men stood at my door, rain streaming down over their bodies. Jerry stood in the center, his thinning hair spread across the crown of his head in plastered wet ribbons. The two men flanking him wore dark jackets with hoods pulled far over their foreheads. The house was so dark, I couldn't recognize either of the shadowed faces.

"Where is she?" Jerry said when he saw me appear around the corner. His words seethed against clenched teeth.

I felt the urge to recoil. Instead I slid in next to Steven, who put his arm across my body.

"If you know where she is, you need to tell me," Jerry spat in my direction.

Steven sidestepped in front of me. "What in the devil's name are you talking about, Jerry?" His steady, almost friendly, voice contradicted the tension I could feel in his body.

"She knows where Alyssa is." Jerry tore his angry gaze away from me to look at Steven.

"I don't," I whispered defensively. I wasn't sure if anyone but Steven could hear the strained breath that passed as my voice.

"She doesn't know anything," Steven echoed. "And what business is it of yours anyway?"

The rain fell harder, thrumming. I could barely hear myself think. And yet, from behind me, I thought I heard—or felt—a shuffling of movement. A chill spread over me. My bare knees shook, threatening to collapse underneath me.

Jerry pointed an accusing finger at me and made a move to step into the house. Steven grabbed his arm and forced him back into the rain. "If you're worried about Alyssa," Steven said, one careful word at a time, "I understand. But this is not the way to handle it, Jerry."

The rain kicked sideways, slapping into the men, who swayed. The two hooded figures looked around, cocking their heads in unison. It was the first time they had moved, and there was something familiar about the way they carried themselves, something that gave me the creeps.

They both twitched, the openings of their soaked hoods pointing toward my kitchen, and I heard a rustling near the garage beyond.

I jerked my head in that direction, then back to the men. I wanted these men gone, Jerry included.

The man to Jerry's right leaned almost imperceptibly toward him and spoke something I couldn't make out amidst the driving rain.

"We know she was here," Jerry insisted.

I spoke the truth in a clipped, angry staccato. "She hasn't been here."

"You need to leave," Steven added in a voice that came across infinitely more reasonable than I knew he felt. "In the morning, we would be happy to make some calls and find out if Alyssa is all right. If," he hesitated, "that's really what you're interested in."

Jerry's eyes slowly roamed away from Steven's face to find mine. An almost pleading expression had taken over.

"*You* know what I want," he said. He spoke only to me, and I thought I knew what he meant.

"I know what Alyssa wants. Leave her alone," I demanded.

The man's eyes darted first to the hidden face on one side of him, then to the other, before resting again on mine. "I can't do that," he said.

Steven stepped forward, and Jerry's bodyguards shifted toward the door.

Jerry held his hands out to either side as if permitting the two men beside him to back away. Silently, the three of them turned and walked back out into the rain. With his head lowered and eyes squinted against the rain, Jerry glanced once over his shoulder to look at me.

Steven slammed the door and turned around, placing his back against the barrier of the door as if reinforcing it. I felt myself panting and bent slightly to brace my hands against the tops of my knees.

"What was that all about?" he said.

The answer to Steven's question came from behind me.

"It is part of the agreement."

My hands flew off my knees and I spun. Isaiah stood centered in the hallway behind me, drenched and dripping rainwater. Without the flashing lightning to disrupt the night, my eyes had readjusted to the dark. This time I knew the anemic face I saw before me was no illusion.

"They will not find her," he said.

"Is she in danger?" I managed to ask through the constricted muscles of my throat.

"Grave," he answered simply.

Steven grabbed my shoulders and tried to pull me back. I could feel the heat of anger pouring off him. For a moment, I had forgotten he was there. Yes, I had told him about Isaiah, but only now did it occur to me to wonder if he had believed my story about this unusual man who liked to appear out of nowhere only to disappear again without a trace.

I raised my arm, blocking Steven's forward motion. It mimicked Jerry's signal to the men he'd brought with him and it was just as effective. Steven stood behind me, still but alert. Streams of his labored breath pounded the side of my face.

Isaiah was the first to speak. "We must protect her."

Silence hung in the air. I couldn't find any words, and Steven seemed temporarily dumfounded. Isaiah waited, his eyes transfixed on my face.

Finally, Steven spoke, nodding his head toward the door. "From them?"

"Yes," Isaiah answered. His eyes never left mine.

"I don't understand any of this," Steven said. He rubbed his hand over his face, fingers crackling against the stubble of his beard. "What in the world could they possibly be planning to do to Alyssa? And why? We should call the police."

"I will lead them in the wrong direction," Isaiah said, ignoring Steven.

I stood silent. The events of the last weeks—months, however long it had been—came rushing back to me. *Don't let them take your blood.* Isaiah's warning words rang in my head.

"How?" I asked, a sudden memory twisting my stomach in a sickening flop.

"The towels," he said.

I touched Steven's arm. It was enough; he could trust me, even if he couldn't trust the man who shouldn't be standing in the front hallway of our house. "Stay here," I told him, and I led Isaiah to the garage. I couldn't bring myself to actually pass through the doorway or to open the trunk to my car. My keys were lying on the kitchen counter. I pushed the button on the key fob while Isaiah stood at the rear of my car, waiting.

He didn't take his eyes off me but reached in and picked up the grocery bags filled with the bloody towels from Alyssa's trip to the hospital. How many times had I intended to ask Steven to throw them away for me? How many times had I forgotten?

I shielded my nose against the coppery smell of dried blood as Isaiah came back through the doorway and walked over to where Steven waited in the foyer.

"When I return," he told Steven, "be ready to leave."

The two men—my tanned, organic, wild-haired, bare-chested husband in pajama pants, and the contrasting young man sheathed in black with skin as pale as the emerging moon—both turned to look at me: tired, frightened, disheveled, torn from sleep, standing with my hands plastered symmetrically alongside the curves of my belly.

"We must protect her." Isaiah repeated his earlier words.

He turned his silver eyes on me. I felt certain he was no longer referring to Alyssa.

Steven stalked throughout the house, checking the locks on every door and window. "How did he get in here?"

"I don't know. It's what he does," I said. I followed him around the house as he bolted from one opening to the next.

Steven threw open the door to the nursery and stopped short at the last window. "Locked," he said, dragging a hand across the top of his head. "He breaks into people's houses? That's what he does?"

"No." I stared at Steven for a moment. "I think he's just … there." I couldn't find a way to explain the seed of understanding that had not had time to completely form into an explanation inside my own head.

"You're not going anywhere with that guy." Steven barreled past me and across the hall to our bedroom. I followed.

"I can't explain what's going on here," I finally said after a short staring match. I couldn't believe what I was about to say, and I worried that he might think I had finally lost it after all. "I think it's connected, though. Me. Alyssa. Isaiah. The blood drives. CURE," I finished, aware that my voice was filled with animosity.

When he didn't respond, I went to the closet and took out an overnight bag, yanked open the top drawer to my dresser and began tossing clothes onto the bed.

"You can't be serious." Steven leaned forward, planting his hands on the bed.

"Come downstairs with me," I said, and without waiting, left the bedroom and went down the stairs to the kitchen. I opened the drawer and pulled out the piece of paper I had shoved in with the utensils. I held it out for him to see.

Steven took the letter. I saw understanding cross his face when his eyes made it to the middle of the page. My appointment dates were there. Two days. I was scheduled to have the first of my blood drawn in two days. He had to know that after Alyssa, after tonight, there was no way I was going to let LifeShare or anyone else take any blood from my body, especially not while I was carrying his child.

CHAPTER TWENTY

Isaiah returned in less than an hour. Steven and I sat hunched together on the bottom riser of the stairs, waiting and resolved. The arm around my shoulders squeezed me tight enough to hurt.

I jumped when the doorbell rang. I suppose I had been expecting Isaiah to simply appear before us. The formality of him standing on the front stoop waiting for us to open the door was disconcerting.

"Alyssa will be safe now," he announced. His normal demeanor, at least the one I was used to, had dissolved into something more frenetic and more energized than the stiffness and control he had always displayed. The silver in his eyes danced in the dim light when he shifted his gaze between Steven and me. It reminded me of the way a lifeless plant springs back to life after being watered.

"Where are we going?" Steven accepted his explanation, more concerned with our next step.

"Emmalyn will go with me. You must continue with your daily routine, so as to avoid suspicion."

Steven shook his head. "She's not going without me."

Once again, Isaiah stood perfectly still, expressionless, as he apparently did when mulling things over. "Then you may accompany her, to see that she is safe," he relented finally. "I will return you home once you are satisfied."

We didn't discuss it further. Steven and I piled into the backseat of Isaiah's SUV. The rain had stopped but what was left of the night was still shrouded in leftover humidity and a stifling blackness made even blacker by the extreme tint of the car's windows. My body shivered involuntarily. Even after Isaiah turned on the heat—a ridiculous notion by the standards of any Georgia summer—and pointed the fans in my direction, I felt an unmistakable chill in the air. Steven moved next to me, blanketing me with his arms.

We were in the car for maybe fifteen minutes. The first ten seemed directionless, so that between the meandering path through town and the enhanced darkness I had no idea where we were going. After a moment or two, I hunkered in against Steven, not caring where Isaiah was taking us, but I felt the shift in terrain when we left the asphalt and turned onto a dirt road I could never have found again in daylight. The car bounced and bumped against the rough path, joggling and splashing through the wet woods until finally we came to a stop.

Isaiah got out first, then opened my door. The remaining clouds had grown wispy, riding the night sky on a high breeze so that the moonlight filtered down now in an ethereal glow. Remnants of the white house reflected the grey light enough for me to recognize it. We were behind the back field of the LifeShare property, and the house that stood before me was the same one where I had fallen against the stairs and bruised my back. I wondered briefly if coming here was part of a game, if Isaiah had brought us here as some kind of cruel move to drive a wedge between Steven and me, but dismissed the idea when I remembered that Steven had no knowledge of where I had been when I'd hurt myself.

I caught Isaiah staring at me and felt my cheeks blush against the night. Somehow, I felt sure he knew I had been here before.

"I own this house," he said, offering an explanation neither of us had sought. "It was once my home." He turned quickly toward the house, as if he had felt it necessary to give us this information but wanted to elaborate no more.

I tried to imagine, if he had lived here, how the house had fallen into such disrepair so quickly. Perhaps he had inherited the house from his family and it was already in poor condition. A storm? The librarian I had talked to had mentioned a tornado, but that, I remembered, had been decades ago.

We silently followed in his footsteps, Steven holding my arm beneath the elbow lest I fall, I assumed. Now wouldn't be the time to let him know that I had walked over these paths before. I stepped onto the exposed floorboards. The wood creaked beneath our feet and I had to push down pangs of guilt. I felt like I was betraying both these men, Steven for pretending I had never been to this place that had become a source of the danger he wanted me to avoid, and Isaiah for having trespassed on his land and home.

Isaiah went straight to the cellar steps, the very ones I had traversed with the sun beaming down on my shoulders. Steven and I paused at the top, listening while he unlocked the bolt to the heavy wooden door below. I looked around me, into the night sky and the shrouded woods, then stepped down onto the brick stairs with Steven close behind.

Isaiah had entered the cellar before us and disappeared into the dark, but the moment I took my first tentative step toward the cellar he reappeared, holding a lit candle he held out to illuminate my way. I avoided looking at his face, rendered sickly yellow by the candlelight, and concentrated on finding my footing on the narrow bricks.

Once we were inside, Isaiah pushed the door back into place and threw a series of bolts to lock it tight.

The cellar, though mostly empty, looked much as I had imagined, lined on one side with crude shelves, a wooden table the only furniture. The smell of the earth struck me with reassurance, conjuring the familiarity of the tunnels, and I embraced the memories of that space that I loved—the quiet solitude, the sense of being surrounded by the earth, and the comfort I felt with being underground. I wanted to fall onto the dry red dirt and carve a spot for myself where I could rest.

I was surprised when Isaiah carried the candle to the shadowed corner perpendicular to where we had entered the cellar and wrenched open another door I hadn't even noticed. Exhaustion nearly overwhelmed me when I realized we were not planning to stay here in the cellar.

"We must go," Isaiah said, sensing my reluctance, and so I took a deep breath—hoping to find some hidden store of energy—drew myself up straight and stepped into the corridor behind him.

Steven and I had no more than passed the wooden door when Isaiah pulled it closed. It landed against the earthen jamb with a combination of soft whoosh and heavy thud. Isaiah blew out the candle, and darkness fell around us like a smothering weight.

Then I heard the clink of metal and another door opened immediately before us, revealing the distinct grey walls and beige tiles that could only be a part of LifeShare.

Revulsion overwhelmed me.

Steven must have felt some of what I felt, or at least sensed my discomfort, because suddenly he lunged, maneuvering past me, toward our guide. His face was contorted in a way I had never seen, as if he could rip Isaiah to shreds.

"What is this, some kind of joke?" he spat.

I shrunk against the cold wall, bracing for a fight. I wasn't used to seeing this side of my husband. We were changing, he and I. I wondered when, or if, we would go back to being the people we had been before all this craziness had started.

Unalarmed, Isaiah sidestepped easily, and Steven slammed against the wall behind him.

"It is the most confusing place," Isaiah said calmly.

"I don't want to be confused," I said, a quiver in my voice. "This is exactly where I do not want to be."

"Yes. But this is the place where no one will find you," he assured me.

So Isaiah had an entrance to LifeShare from the cellar of his fallen home. Who knew why, or how it had come to be. What we were doing had to be considered breaking and entering, at the very least. Even so, the simple way he spoke, for some reason I couldn't analyze right now, made me want to believe we were doing the right thing.

"I will explain," he said.

Steven and I looked at one another for a long moment. I saw his original reluctance give way. He trusted me. Good or bad, and I had no way of knowing which way things would go from here, he trusted me. That was something.

We gave Isaiah no signal, no confirmation. He simply shifted his silver gaze from me to Steven and back and proceeded down the corridor.

We followed him silently, until he stopped at a side door, where the lock had apparently been opened for our benefit. All traces of Isaiah's organic earthy cellar evaporated from my senses as we stepped deeper into the building that served as the symbol of all my recent fears. I gave our new friend a questioning glance.

"Arranged," he whispered by way of explanation. He pulled the door shut and I heard the engaging clang of a lock I couldn't see. A small keypad instantly glowed green in the dark, previously disabled, back on guard.

"Arranged?" I whispered under my breath.

Isaiah acknowledged me with a nod.

A chill swept over me. At first I thought the fear of getting caught had infiltrated my resolve to do this … whatever it was we were doing … but the farther we moved along the corridor, the deeper the chill set in and I realized that this section of the building was refrigerated. Only then did I pay attention to the walls on either side of me.

The hall itself was wider than the upstairs hallways of LifeShare where Jerry and Steven worked. This area was less like a hall and more like a small room, not unlike the size of our nursery at home, I thought as another shudder rocked my body, but much longer. The walls had been segmented into a grid that stretched from floor to ceiling. The grids looked very much like file drawers with dual locks, similar to the safe deposit boxes in the vault at the bank.

Or like crypts, my mind interjected.

And that was the only impetus I needed to begin imagining

what might be stored behind those doors.

Blood.

My brain began an automatic calculation—the number of stacked doors multiplied by the length of the room multiplied by the number of doors with glowing green keypads like the one we had come through. I could not fathom the sheer number of pints that might be stored behind those file drawers, but the enormity of it made my head spin.

Real or imagined, my nostrils began to detect a faint hint of copper in the air. I must have swayed on my feet, because Steven grabbed me by the elbows, holding me steady. Only then did I realize how wobbly my legs had become.

Isaiah had turned to face us. He was eyeing Steven in a curious way. I remembered him coming to my rescue in much the same manner at the grocery store not so long ago. I couldn't tell if his expression indicated jealousy, or admiration, or something completely different. Perhaps he thought he was the only one capable of swooping in quickly to stop a girl from falling out flat on the ground at the sight—or thought—of a little blood.

No one spoke throughout my little episode. It was as if we had made a pact to remain silent. From then on, I made a concentrated effort to look directly forward until we finally reached the end of the long room. I had convinced myself that the coppery smell I had first associated so strongly with the scent of blood was simply the large amount of metal in the drawers lining the walls. This made me feel at least a little better.

Mind over matter.

A lone emergency light spread its thin glow over the corridor, its corona fading as we approached the far wall. The darkness grew so deep, I was grateful we only had to walk forward in a straight line. Anything more complicated would have been difficult to maneuver.

I stopped short, squinting at the squares in front of me. I couldn't believe that this was a dead end—I had thought Isaiah knew where he was going—but all I could see before me were the same square grids I had seen all along. It reminded me of the metal door I had discovered in the tunnels, the one Samantha had tried to bully me into opening. I closed my eyes against the memory, fearing I might faint again, when I heard the pop of a latch. Isaiah had pulled back what looked very much like the thick vault door of a bank and was motioning for us to follow him. This last wall of drawers was nothing more than a façade, yet another secret entrance into the inner sanctum of LifeShare.

I wondered how Isaiah knew about this. And what purpose it served. And who had designed it into the architecture.

During my reverie, the door closed silently behind us. The whoosh of air created by its silent closing sent the loose strands of my hair flying around my face and once again, we were in complete darkness.

Isaiah flipped a switch and I squinted against the shock of warm light. Bunk beds lined two of the walls and an overstuffed chair sat in the other corner next to a second door that I hoped was a bathroom. A small refrigerator sat beside the chair, topped by the lone lamp responsible for the light. A large painting hung against the far space, spanning almost the entire height of the wall. It was completely out of place for the otherwise sterile environment, perhaps an afterthought in an attempt to liven up the place. Strangely, the painting was that of a corridor—one less institutional than those we had just traversed—constructed of stacked grey stones. Creeping vines of green and brown wound their way through the cracks in the mortar, the occasional pink and purple flower bursting to life in what tiny rays of sunshine broke through larger cracks along the top of the never-ending stone archway.

It was a beautiful depiction of a bizarre subject.

Another time, I might have laughed at the irony.

"Tonight I will explain the agreement," Isaiah said in words as flat and cold as the linoleum beneath my feet.

"Tomorrow," he continued, and the gaze of his eyes focused in on me, "if you cannot believe what I tell you, I will show Steven the proof. I think Emmalyn can be convinced without seeing."

CHAPTER TWENTY-ONE

I sank into the overstuffed chair, grateful for the soft comfort that enveloped me after the cold bleakness of LifeShare's corridors. Steven perched on the arm, sticking by my side, while Isaiah stood across from us, his back straight against the side of the bunk beds. We were all silent. The only sound in the room was the slight hum of the small refrigerator.

"Let's hear it," Steven finally said. Just in case anyone thought him agreeing to come here with me, and Isaiah, meant he wasn't skeptical, we now knew exactly where he stood. An edge of anger painted his voice.

Isaiah leaned forward almost imperceptibly. He seemed to be reading my features, possibly gauging how I might react to whatever it was he was about to tell us.

I tilted my head in a nod, urging him to begin.

"I am a member of the special population," he said.

I flinched, tensing. At the same time a kind of relief spread through me. Steven looked down at me. "What?" he said, less in response to Isaiah's statement, I thought, than to the conflicted look that must have spread over my face.

"CURE." The word was a hiss on my breath.

"Yes," Isaiah confirmed.

"It doesn't really work, does it?" This had been one of my foremost fears, that millions of people were subjecting themselves to some kind of global guinea pig test that would ultimately turn out not to be the answer to their hopes but instead a huge disappointment. All that faith shattered. The miracle debunked. I couldn't imagine the kind of mass depression that might generate.

"It works." A tight frown creased Isaiah's brow. It was the first time I had seen anything but stoicism on his pale face. The line that formed between his eyes was like a fissure that not only cracked the porcelain of his face but also the shield I had barely managed to hold up against my doubts and fears.

"Explain," I said evenly, steeling myself against the very explanation I asked for.

"Three appointments. There is a reason." He seemed to know my thoughts.

"To make room?" I repeated the words I had spoken to Alyssa. I still had no idea what they meant.

"The blood is a reserve to be used at a later date, not unlike storing one's blood for a planned surgery. The room we came through," he said, waving toward the corridor of file drawers, "is filled with those stockpiles. The first chosen for the procedure is not based on need or proximity to death, as you might think it should be, but rather on whether enough blood has been placed in the silos to complete the procedure."

"Someone who has given blood before," I said. "Like Alyssa."

"Yes, and yourself," he replied.

Until I had become pregnant, I had donated blood at least three times a year. I imagined bags of my blood sitting inside those crypts on the other side of the wall. A shudder spread through my core and along my limbs. My hands quivered. Steven scooped them up and sandwiched them between his.

"What about me?" he said, hanging on to my hands a little too tightly. "I've given more blood than Emmalyn. Certainly more than Alyssa." He was no doubt remembering her many excuses for avoiding the blood drives.

"There is another criterion for who is first chosen," Isaiah said.

"What is it?" I whispered.

He paused. The black-red slash of his lips quivered, much like my hands, before he spoke. Something inside him seemed to be pulling him back as he searched for what he wanted to say. The vertical line etched along his forehead ironed itself away as he pushed his next words through tight lips.

"It is a matter of taste," he said carefully.

"Taste," I repeated, my head spinning with the possibilities. An image of the package of meat I had picked up at the grocery store flashed before my eyes. The juices—*blood*, I corrected myself—that ran from beneath the cut of meat inside the package, how it had made me sick to my stomach. How that same piece of meat would appeal to someone with the right appetite.

I stared at Isaiah, my eyes pleading with him to continue, to take my mind away from that memory.

He obliged. "Taste," he said again, then went on quickly, although he no longer seemed content to stand still in his usual countenance. Isaiah began to pace, letting his hand slide along the wall at hip level. I couldn't take my eyes off his hand, the fingers lightly trailing across the surface. How many years of that would it take to wear a smooth line onto a rough clay surface? I wondered, unsure where the thought came from.

"The donations were tested," he said finally. "Sampled, if you will. By us—not all of us—but by some of the special population. It is in the agreement. As Emmalyn knows, I am not in agreement." His eyes cut swiftly from Steven to me before he turned on his heel to pace in the opposite direction.

I could tell he was trying to ease us into whatever point he was trying to make. To say he was uncomfortable would be an understatement. Speaking about this seemed to torture him in some way.

Pulling my hands away from Steven's, I stood up and took a step toward Isaiah. As if moved by a spell, he stopped his pacing and tilted his jaw, turning his head so that the silver eyes stared out at me like beams from a lighthouse.

"Just tell us," I said gently.

A grimace passed over his face, distorting his lips into a crooked line. His eyes bore so intently into mine, I felt an inexplicable pull like gravity.

"We have preferences," he said. "And to answer Steven's question—why he has not yet been chosen—many of us prefer the blood of a female. Like you, with your cakes and candies, we are not above indulging in a sweet tooth."

Steven bounded off the chair and yanked me away from this young man with his pallid face. I was hardly able to believe the implications of Isaiah's words, but I was not afraid of him.

"This is crazy," Steven spat. "*You're* crazy."

I touched Steven's arm, hoping to calm him. "So you are ..." I couldn't find the words to finish.

"What?" Steven shouted. He stepped toward Isaiah, his arms pulling away and slightly back, bent for a fight. "You're a vampire? Is that what you're trying to tell us? You're an idiot!"

What happened next was reminiscent of the flashes of lightning that had accompanied the night's storm. I blinked and Steven's back slammed against the opposite wall. The rest was impossible and yet there it was before my eyes. Isaiah's body defied gravity; he crouched, mid-air, over my husband, his hands and feet planted against the wall on either side of Steven's larger body. He yanked a fistful of Steven's hair, pulling his head to one side, exposing his throat. A growling hiss escaped Isaiah's throat. His teeth, long and sharp and startlingly white against his dark lips, hovered an inch away from Steven's neck.

"No!" I screamed, scrambling to get around the chair.

Isaiah let out another hiss. His eyes darted to mine. A line of darker grey seemed to outline the shining silver irises. With what appeared to be great effort, he folded his black lips back down over his teeth, jerked his head back to face Steven, and pounced backward from the wall, landing once again with his back against the supports of the bunk bed.

I ran to Steven, clutching him. His arms folded around me. His heart beat wildly inside his chest.

"No more of that!" I screamed, as if I had any control over this ... creature.

"I had to make you believe." There was no hint of anything but calmness in Isaiah's voice.

"We believe," I said. I pulled Steven back to the chair with me, holding on to him in hopes of settling the mass of coiled muscles. He had to know he was no match for Isaiah if it came to that, but his body language said differently. He perched on the edge of the chair, leaning sideways to shield me. It made me want to cry.

"Just finish," I said to Isaiah.

"Sweetness is not the only indulgence among our kind," he said matter-of-factly. "Some enjoy a bit of fat in the drink, much like preferring a filet mignon to a breast of chicken."

I could not help the disgust that overtook my expression.

"I am sorry," he said, "but that is why the information on cholesterol and blood sugars is catalogued. As far as the CURE itself, we are not the type to offer of ourselves. We have negotiated an exchange. We do not age. We cannot be killed—for lack of a better description—easily. Our bodies have the ability to regenerate, and scientists—our scientists, not yours—have found a way to transfer that ability to the human body. Without effecting a change," he clarified. "We are not interested in increasing our numbers. But we, as a group, have found a way to indulge in a privilege that many of us have denied ourselves over recent years. It is a simple bartering system. You are receiving a great gift in return for our satisfaction—satisfaction that requires no carnage."

"You drink our blood." I couldn't believe this was coming from my own mouth. I swallowed hard.

"We have always drunk the blood of humans. We crave more. The experience of pouring refrigerated blood from a bag into a glass does not fully satisfy our basic needs, and many have become restless over the years. It has become more difficult to contain our instincts. The agreement will help with that."

I shook my head. "And the blood reserves?"

"The reserves are necessary to prevent complications." He paused, but when neither Steven nor I interjected, he went on. "One complication would be death, the other conversation. We wish to avoid both."

My mind could guess at what he meant, but I couldn't bring myself to formulate it into an absolute thought within my brain. "Transfusion?" I muttered, almost unaware that I had spoken.

"Exactly," Isaiah confirmed. Approval seemed to register on his face and I felt very much like the type of excellent student teachers long for in a classroom.

Encouraged by my involvement, he no longer minced words. "We are allowed to drain the body. To near completion. It is our natural instinct to gorge, without stopping. Under normal circumstances, that would, of course, result in the death of our ... subject. However, because the donors have stored enough blood for rejuvenation, there is little danger of death. The transfusion must take place quickly, hence the necessity of clinics like the one here at LifeShare. The legends as you may have heard them are true—a single drop of a vampire's blood shared with a human will bring about transformation. That is why we cannot offer any of our own blood in return. The blood used for the transfusions has been treated with a modification of our blood. An ounce is all that is needed to alter the DNA of a human, but it must be administered in several minute increments. The first, a mere gram, is given at the first donation, a slightly larger amount the second donation. The largest dose is returned with the last complete transfusion. This allows the patient to become acclimated without shock. Anyone undergoing the treatment is guaranteed cellular integrity. In that respect, what you call CURE is indeed that—a cure for cancer."

"Side effects?" I voiced a concern that had plagued me since I had first heard of CURE.

"None, well, other than a brief sense of euphoria. Some will experience a short-term increase in strength or speed, but we have found that this is usually expressed as a general feeling of well-being or hyperactivity. By the time a patient might make a connection, the side-effect has passed. Scientists—neither ours nor yours—have not been able to connect the euphoria to the actual treatment. That may be purely the result of the human emotion called hope. We no longer experience such emotions," he clarified.

Steven spoke up. The edge had not left his voice, although he was trying hard to contain it. "What about Alyssa, and others that refuse the treatment? Why did Jerry show up at our house looking for her?"

Isaiah paused, weighing his response. "There is no contingency in the agreement for refusal. If I may put it rather crudely, what occurred tonight was the result of someone missing a much anticipated meal."

"That's barbaric." Steven's observation encompassed my overall opinion. Barbaric—the description could not be limited to only the last part of the incredible explanation Isaiah was sharing with us, although it was certainly the most shocking thing I had ever heard anyone utter.

"We are not generally described as a patient species," Isaiah offered. He seemed to recognize the excuse as flimsy.

"And Alyssa's baby?" I asked. The fingers of Steven's hand tensed against my shoulder. I stared directly at Isaiah, refusing to look away. The question was like a disease I had carried with me since that horrible day I had found Alyssa with the blood streaming down her legs. Isaiah had been with me at the hospital. He knew the answer. The time had come for me to know it too.

He pressed his lips together in a stern line, silver eyes bearing against my own.

"Most of my kind have forgotten the importance of procreation. An unborn life," he glanced at the small mound of my belly, "holds no significance to our kind. Perhaps you can understand why." This last was statement and question mixed into one, but not one I felt I needed to answer.

"To put it more clinically, we needed test subjects. To make sure the transfusion would properly rejuvenate before we committed fully to the agreement. We could not permit the complication of death on any noticeable scale; it would jeopardize the agreement and our population. The fact that Alyssa became a test subject was purely random."

"So her blood was drained?" I demanded. "All of it."

"The body is never entirely void of blood. New blood is allowed to enter before drainage is complete, to keep the vital organs functioning. But in essence, yes."

"And the baby's?" I asked, nearly choking on the words.

"I am afraid so." A hint of sadness colored Isaiah's otherwise rigid expression. "The transfusions apparently cannot rejuvenate an unborn child."

A flurry of nausea washed over me. Someone—some *thing*—wanted my blood, my *sweet* female blood, wanted to drain every drop of it from my body, and that someone could not care less that in doing so, they would be killing my unborn child.

Steven seemed to channel my thoughts. He leaned protectively over me. He laid his palm against my cheek and pulled my face up so that he could connect his eyes with mine. Beads of sweat broke out over my brow.

"We're not going to let anything happen to you. Or the baby," Steven said, his words almost scolding in their intensity. "We must protect her. Right?" he said to Isaiah.

"We will protect you both," Isaiah said, assuring Steven but speaking to me.

"And coming here?" My mind wandered back to why Isaiah had chosen to bring us to the very place where these gruesome experiments were taking place. "Hiding in plain sight?"

"The LifeShare building is filled with the scent of blood. It should be very difficult to differentiate one particular meal from so many."

CHAPTER TWENTY-TWO

As morning drew near, we agreed that Steven should leave before the halls of LifeShare sprang to life. It would not be unusual for me to spend the day at home, or run errands, or do a million other innocuous things that would keep me out of the sight of prying eyes, but Steven needed to be seen going about his day as normally as possible.

The first few minutes after I watched Isaiah and my husband leave without me were the worst. Claustrophobia took over for a while. I found myself pacing the room, much like Isaiah had done only hours before. I stood in front of the second doorway for at least a half hour before I had the nerve to reach for the knob. To my great relief, it did turn out to be a bathroom, but after I used it, I discovered I was afraid to flush the toilet for fear of someone behind the thick walls hearing the tell-tale sign of my existence.

I stretched out on the bottom bunk for a while, thinking I might sleep. Every fiber in my body screamed out for rest, yet my eyes stubbornly refused to cooperate, instead fixing on the cross-hatch of mattress springs above me. Finally I gave up on the idea. Instead I took a plush blanket from the stack at the end of the bed over to the chair and cuddled it around me, relishing the warmth.

My mind played tricks on me, first telling me that everything that had happened—all that Isaiah had told me tonight—was nothing more than a dream, a ridiculous figment of my imagination. In the next second, I would have to yank myself back to focus on the nondescript little room that confined me—my cell—to reign myself away from visions of vampires, fangs against skin, and dripping blood.

Legs curled into the chair, I eventually dozed. I awoke to the slowly churning calculation of what time it must be. Too exhausted even to find my cell phone, I let my mind count back into the night, to what time Jerry must have shown up at our doorstep, then factored in travel time and how long it must have taken Isaiah to conduct his lecture on Vampire 101. Of course I had no idea how long I had slept, but took a guess that it had to be early evening. Five o'clock, maybe.

The LifeShare clinic closed to the public at six. I wondered how long the most dedicated employee would linger in the building. Realistically, I could not imagine Steven and Isaiah returning before the middle of the night. I also could not imagine spending more than a few more hours trapped alone in this disguised dungeon of a room.

I dragged myself up off the bunk and went to the refrigerator. Isaiah, I assumed, had stocked it with cold cuts and bread, a bowl of fruit and tray of vegetables, and bottles of water. I rummaged further and found milk and a carton of lemonade toward the rear. Cross-legged on the floor, I carefully assembled a sandwich consisting of bread layered with two slices of ham, a piece of cheese, and a slice of turkey. Twin tears dripped from my eyes at the same moment I managed to get the sandwich to my lips and bite.

Two days, I thought. Back in our kitchen, when I had shown Steven my letter, the appointment date had registered as two days away. Now that evening was upon us again, I realized, day one was drawing swiftly to an end. When morning came, it would be day two, and someone—some*thing*—would be expecting me to show up at the LifeShare clinic to prepare me for dinner.

Despite these thoughts, I managed to get the sandwich down. Fatigue clawed at me and I burrowed against the chair. I awoke an immeasurable time later to the soft whoosh of the faux wall opening. A burst of cool air swept over me when Isaiah came through the door. I stared up at him from where I had fallen asleep, sitting on the floor with the blanket loosely draped over my shoulders, my head propped lazily against the cushion of the fluffy chair.

"Where is Steven?" I said the moment it registered that Isaiah had returned alone.

Isaiah kept his eyes fixed on the opposite wall. He seemed to be studying the tall painting that hung there. It was the first time he had ever avoided eye-contact with me.

"He was not able to come." The words slipped reluctantly through those dark lips. He still did not look at me.

I climbed to my feet, ignoring the tingling needles that stabbed my lower limbs. With great purpose, I positioned my face in front of his, forcing him to look into my eyes. He had never had any trouble staring at me before, in fact had never given a second thought to how uncomfortable it had made me. If something had happened to Steven, I intended to make sure he looked me straight in the eye while delivering the news.

"What exactly does that mean?" My question escaped slowly, sliding over my tongue like the hissing of a snake. I sincerely hoped Isaiah could fully detect every molecule of my venom.

"Exactly? I cannot say." With what appeared to cost him great effort, he met my gaze head-on. "But your husband is a willful man. He wishes to make sure you are safe. I should not have told him everything I knew."

I wasn't sure if this was supposed to make me feel better, but it definitely did not.

A fleeting idea of trying to bolt past Isaiah, to find my husband, flashed through my mind. Then I remembered the speed with which Isaiah had pinned Steven against the wall to demonstrate the skills of his kind—the *special population*. I could only imagine what else they were capable of.

"Find him," I ordered.

Isaiah's pasty lids fell over his silver eyes in silent agreement. Without a word, he walked back through the door he had entered.

The door swung back toward me and met the jamb with a pop followed by a buzzing hum. I knew I was locked in.

The scream that boiled up inside my throat came out as a choked sob. I wanted Steven. I wanted out of this place. I wanted this craziness to never have happened.

I fell to my knees and grabbed the blanket from where it had fallen on the floor. I tore at it with my hands, ripping and yanking at the coarse unyielding fabric, unable to find any release from the frustration boiling through me.

Infuriated, I smashed the blanket against the floor, forming a lumpy ball. Scrambling to my feet, I scraped my knee against a torn piece of the cheap linoleum but barely felt the slight stab of pain. I reeled back and heaved the blanket across the room. The ridiculousness of the gesture was apparent as I watched the blanket float out of the tight formation I had worked so hard to achieve, layers of it riding the air and undulating into something more akin to a magic carpet than the missile I had intended it to be.

Plates would have been better. Mugs of scalding coffee. Books. Lamps. Anything, but at least the blanket did not completely lose its forward motion before slamming against the painting. The frame drummed against the wall and slid sideways, swinging on the axis of whatever hook it hung from, then settled back with a final thump. The rectangular shape now clung to the wall at a thirty degree angle, revealing a triangle behind it that was a slightly deeper shade of grey than the surrounding walls.

I slid my feet across the floor and gripped either side of the heavy painting. Groaning with the effort, I lifted the oversized painting up and flung my weight to the side, hoping I could free it. The slab wobbled toward me. The mass of it was more than I had bargained for; it had to have been hanging freely from the wall for the blanket to have even budged it, but it held stubbornly in place now. The vision of myself lying on the floor with this enormous plank flattened over my body brought on a shiver of hysteria I forced myself to ignore. I stepped back, increasing my leverage and let my hands slide along the outer edges until the bottom of the frame crashed against the floor. The top of the frame, as if in deference, fell toward the wall, landing with a thud.

I took a deep breath and positioned myself to the right of the frame. Bracing my feet at an angle behind me, I pushed the painting aside, uncovering the grey sterile door that had been hidden behind it.

Trembling, I touched the handle.

All I could think about was the fact that Steven had not returned with Isaiah. The combination of that and being trapped here was quickly elevating from frustration and concern to horror. What could possibly keep him away? Each scenario I turned over in my mind was worse than the one before it. I hated the idea of what it might mean that Isaiah could not find him. He had certainly never had any trouble locating me. Of course, that might have something to do with the scent of my blood, I thought as fresh terror coursed through my veins. The dread I felt wasn't only for myself, but for my entire family.

Looking down, I raised one foot to step through the doorway, and noticed the blood that smeared the top of my shoe. I traced the source back to my knee, where I had scraped it on the torn linoleum. Frantically, I yanked the shoes from my feet and threw them behind me. My hands were shaking. I turned around, my jaw aching with the tension of trying not to run, and grabbed the water bottle I had left on the floor by the chair, doused one edge of the blanket, and used it to clean the blood off my knee and shin. Pressing a dry section against the wound, I forced myself to count to twenty. When I pulled the blanket away, the scrape was no longer oozing and the dried blood was cleaned away.

That would have to do.

The corridor behind the painting was consummate LifeShare— long, grey, sterile walls and more of the linoleum that had covered the floor in my hideaway. I glanced back to the relative safety of the yellow light and forced myself to move farther into the dark tunnel before me. The floor was smooth and cold. The bones in my feet began to ache as I picked up the pace.

The corridor grew stiflingly dark until I had to walk with my hands in front of me for fear of walking into a wall. The silence would have been suffocating if not for the echo of my heartbeat in my ears. No matter how far I went, I didn't seem to be going anywhere. I knew LifeShare was expansive. That fact had never registered as fully as it did right now.

All of a sudden, I felt so tired. The stress was catching up to me. I leaned against the wall, drawing deep breaths. I was starting to doubt my decision to leave Isaiah's little hidey-hole. What had I hoped to accomplish? I wasn't going to find Steven this way. I didn't know when, or even if, I could find my way out of this maze.

I let my head drop back against the wall, hoping to calm my nerves, clear my head. When I heard the hushed whispers, I thought for a minute they were nothing more than my own throbbing pulse strumming against my temples.

I held my breath. By remaining very still, I was able to distinguish the difference between the sounds of my surging body and what I thought were voices bouncing off the walls around me. I stood straighter, cocking my head from one side to the other, listening more intently than I had before.

They were voices, I finally deciphered, coming from above my head. I lifted my hand in the darkness and felt a cool breeze wafting down from above. I remembered the air conditioning system that Professor Kendall had shown me and wished I had paid better attention to the labyrinth of air ducts.

A vent.

I jumped away from the wall and froze. The realization that I was lost in the depths of LifeShare hit me as a wave of vertigo set in. I threw my hands out to my sides and spun around, searching like the newly blind, and finally banged my wrist. There was no way of knowing what I had found, I'd become so disoriented. If I followed the wall, would it lead me back to my hiding place? Shouldn't I have waited there in case Steven came back? I squinted back into the darkness but I didn't see any trace of the glowing light I had left behind.

"… long day … more syringes … don't know … so cool …"

The whispered snippets filtered down through the vent in waves.

"blood … not if they knew …"

I could feel the heat of fear and bad decisions rising to the surface of my skin, the tears collecting in my eyes. My hands danced across the surface in front of me and my fingers closed around what felt like a bar. Without thinking, I pulled and the invisible door opened to a dingy stairwell leading up.

Muted light shone down like the glimmer of water in the desert, pure temptation.

I had to follow it. What choice did I have?

Seven steps up, the stairs turned to reveal another set of seven heading in the opposite direction. Stepping lightly—as if my cold bare feet would make any sound against the concrete—I hurried up the second set only to find that they ended at another door. I had been forced into a decision: go back the way I had come and hope to find the room again, or continue ahead.

Show us what's behind door number three? I thought ridiculously, Bob Barker's famous game show line clattering my senses.

Yes, show us, I said to myself, mustering all the courage I could find. I cracked the door in front of me and jerked back, squinting.

The bright light stung my eyes. I flinched, and the door slipped from my hands, nearly banging shut. I clawed at it, finally getting a grip just as it was about to crash into place. Afraid to move, I listened through the opening.

The whisperings I had heard on the level below were more prominent now. They were coming from down the hall to my left.

I put my ear to the crack in the door, straining to make out what they were saying.

"… imagine if this got out. I'd almost be willing to break the gag order if I thought there was enough money in it."

A second voice: "Yeah, dude, you'd be the richest idiot down at the state penitentiary."

"Know what your problem is?" the first guy said. "You ain't got no gumption."

"Gumption?" The other one laughed. "What is that? Some kind of hillbilly lingo? Just get the blood already. You know these guys aren't what you'd call patient."

"Yeah, I got it," the hillbilly said. I heard a door clang open to my left and two young men in blue scrubs bounded into the hallway and headed away, their backs to me. The one on the left kicked the door shut as they walked away. I eased my door open another inch for a better look. They were carrying a cooler between them, each man gripping one side to support the weight.

I waited until they turned the corner at the end of the hall and then I followed them, my heart hammering with adrenaline.

"Answer me something," the second one, the hillbilly, said, "since you're so much smarter than me."

I judged plenty of distance remained between us by the sound of his voice and moved forward to where the hallways met. I stopped, planted my back against the wall, and waited. All I could think to do was go the same way they went, but not until I was sure they wouldn't catch me.

"Lay it on me," the first guy said, his cocky voice growing mercifully softer.

There was a slight pause during which I found myself holding my breath. When they weren't talking, I had no way to gauge where they were heading.

"Say we wipe out cancer. I'm just wondering what's going to kill us now. We can't all live forever." The voices dropped another decibel.

"Dude, we'll always have heart attacks and plane crashes." Both men found this extremely funny and their laughter rang softly along the hall until another slamming door silenced it.

I peered around the corner, disappointed—but not surprised— to find that the door the two men had just gone through contained a glass window. The door they took was the first in a series of six identical doors.

Options? Dead ends?

The blue of their scrubs disappeared beyond the glass.

This was it. I would either find a way out or I would be caught. I might be the one to wind up in the state penitentiary, I thought, and felt an unwelcome pressure in my chest. I forced myself to take a deep breath and blew it out so slowly it made no sound at all.

Hugging the wall, I scurried down the hallway. From a distance, I could tell the glass door had a security keypad similar to the ones Isaiah had bypassed on our way into the lower floor of the building. Not that following the men through it would be a good idea. Obviously the door led in some way to the clinic, which was the last place I wanted to be, but at least from there I knew my way out of LifeShare.

I took another steadying breath and approached the door, praying no one would see me as I leaned to peer through the window.

In an instant I wished I had made another choice, *any* other choice. My mind screamed at me to retreat—shrink back, move, anything—but I couldn't.

I was horribly mesmerized.

CHAPTER TWENTY-THREE

This was the back hallway of the clinic, the one that stretched off behind the line that Lucy guarded so nonchalantly when I'd gone to pick up more forms for data entry. The fancy new examination rooms. Rooms where the mystery of CURE could unfold in cloaked privacy.

The men in the blue scrubs flanked an examination table, the one on the left removing a bag of blood from the IV pole, the other guy handing over a replacement from the cooler.

I stared, helpless to look away, as they exchanged one pint after the other, until I lost count, hanging enough blood to rejuvenate—*bring back to life*, my mind demanded—the person on the table. One of the guys moved, revealing the limp wrist that hung off the edge of the table. The color of that skin was so grey, so translucent, so lifeless, paler even than Isaiah's skin. A streak of blood smeared the man's wrist, and I instantly knew that whoever he was, he was dead, if only for a moment.

I blinked, revulsion tingling through me in spasms, but my eyes traveled upward of their own accord, settling on the gruesome, self-satisfied, lusty face watching the men in the blue scrubs take down the last bag and wipe the bloody wrist.

I couldn't tear myself from that familiar face, so similar to Isaiah's but so much more menacing. I knew what Isaiah was—he had told me, *shown* me—but I had never seen blood dripping from the slash of Isaiah's bottom lip or witnessed the snarling smirk of his upper lip drawn back over blood-stained teeth as he stood over a person he had just fed from. My stomach roiled and for a moment, my mind went blissfully blank. I recognized the dense feeling of stupidity that spread over me for what it was—a coping mechanism—and I fought against it, forcing myself to register everything I had seen, to comprehend it, to allow every revolting nuance of what I was witnessing to emblazon a memory on my brain.

I needed to gather the strength to survive, to protect my unborn baby, but I had no idea how to break the friction that glued my feet to the floor. I stared through the window, absorbing every detail of the scene as leisurely as if I were a patron in an art museum, studying the work of a grisly master painter. As if I had paid my price for entry and was therefore entitled to a perfect memory.

Except I had no intention of paying any price for viewing this particular canvas. Especially not the price that had apparently been negotiated on my behalf. No knowledge, no consent, just part of the agreement, like Alyssa.

Remembering Alyssa helped. My eyes unlocked and the images before me shifted.

Several things happened at once.

One of the men—I wondered crazily if he were the hillbilly—started counting the empty blood bags.

The arm hanging from the table, now flush with the tones of live pink flesh, twitched.

And the vampire slowly cranked her head in my direction, turning her fiery gaze on me.

I felt myself gasp at the intense amber of Lucy's eyes and shock blasted through me, not because it was Lucy, but because I realized that in the second before I knew it was her, I had expected those eyes to be silver—like Isaiah's; or black—like the legends described; or blazing red—like the child of the devil's eyes surely must be.

Instead the perfectly average rusty brown irises rendered me unable to move. Everything lapsed into a slur of motion.

A macabre grin spread over the vampire's—*Lucy's*, my

conscious insisted, over *Lucy's*—face.

The two guys who'd delivered the blood twisted in identical slow pirouettes until they saw me. Matching expressions of shock transformed their faces.

And Steven sat up from the table, raising the arm that Lucy had used to drain his blood dry, and dragged his fingers through the dark strands of his curly hair. His eyes met mine.

The vampire sprang.

The window rattled inside its frame and Lucy's face was inches from mine, the amber eyes narrowed to slits, the black lips curled back so I could see that every edge of every tooth was outlined in the crimson of my husband's blood.

I ran.

I bolted, not back the way I'd come, but left, past the five additional doors, my brain struggling to map out how these hallways must work. I had to be on the back side of the exam rooms, windows here so the CURE fanatics could all see what everybody was up to, no windows on the other side, a charade of privacy.

Lucy. She'd lusted after my husband, not for his body, or his attention, but for his blood, for the taste of it. She must have smelled it on him every time she got near him.

And there he lay, submitting to her desires. My disgust could not have been more powerful if I had discovered them making love.

This fueled my already aching heart and lungs, and I bounded through the first door I encountered, sliding and skidding into the halls of LifeShare—the halls I knew, ones I had traversed enough to know where I was.

I floundered only for a second, my logical side begging me to seek out the exits where I knew I could get out, but deep inside I felt determined to squash the voice of logic.

Images of Lucy filled me like a deteriorating virus as I ran—her sweetsy smile, her girly voice, that snide look on her face when she realized I was pregnant, the way she had taunted me when she caught me testing one of the side doors of this very corridor.

A cog turned over, my last thought clicking into place. I stumbled to a halt, nearly tripping over my own feet. It took only a split second to get my bearings.

I had passed that same door, only a few yards back.

I doubled back, grabbed the door handle, levered it down, and pushed.

The door resisted, and I felt panic lock down on my chest.

I pushed again, unable to fathom that it could be locked from the other side. The door handle turned. This had to be the only way. It had to be the reason Lucy had caught up to me and kept me from going through it on that last day before I quit LifeShare. Because she knew something she didn't want me to know.

A draft of cold air swept down the hall from the direction of the clinic and a weak sob crept up my windpipe. I threw my weight against the door and recoiled from the pain in my shoulder, barely stifling a scream.

But the handle was still flipped down, firmly gripped in my hand. The door opened while I fell backward.

P - U - L - L—Push.

My dad's old joke for working the door the wrong way flitted through my mind … and cut through my hysteria.

I rushed through the door, yanking it closed behind me and felt the change under my feet as the world went black once again.

I was blind in the heavy darkness but forced myself to keep moving. I stuck my arms out to either side and immediately found the walls formed a narrow passage where I could touch on either side. The floor didn't seem level but felt like it sloped downward. And something else … it smelled differently here, somehow safer than LifeShare's antiseptic halls.

I had a flighty ridiculous moment, turning while I ran to sneak that last over-the-shoulder confirmation of safety, saw nothing in the dark, and slammed into the end of the passage.

I fell to the floor, a shriek bursting from my throat before I could stop it. I clawed my way back to my feet and felt along the barrier I had run into, spreading my hands frantically over the surface of the cool metal until I felt the lump of a bolt under my fingers.

A dry laugh escaped me when I heard the thunk of the bolt retracting. A mechanical hiss resonated behind me, from the other side of the LifeShare door. My laugh died on my lips, but I was vaguely aware that the muscles of my mouth remained pulled back in a mocking grimace. I felt insane, but I wasn't. No, you're completely, wonderfully rational, I told myself. My mind had swallowed down some very important information in the last few moments and it was coughing that knowledge back up just when I needed it.

The door at the top of the ramp opened and light spilled down long enough for me to get my bearings, then disappeared back to black. Warm air turned frigid around me, tumbling over and around me like waves in a storm. That terrible hissing spread along the space like wildfire.

P - U - L - L—Pull! I thought. I wrapped my fingers firmly around this handle and yanked the door toward me.

The metal door opened with a grumble, and I lunged head-on into another barrier where the doorway should have been wide open. This was no door, no wall. This was dirt. Dirt! The sheet of it gave way when I pushed. Pellets and shards of clay pelted my skin as in rained down around me.

I dropped my head, shielding my eyes from the avalanche.

Earth! Sweet earth. A cloud of it filled my nostrils, and I lapsed into a coughing fit that did not remotely threaten to slow me down.

Forgetting the door, I took off through the corridor, the fingers of my right hand trailing the close walls of the side tunnel of the corridor, instinctively finding the smooth ridge drawn along the wall, my left hand out in front of me so I would know when I got to the end. I had no way of knowing which side tunnel this could be—one I had been inside or one I hadn't yet discovered—but the end came up quick.

Struggling with the dust in my lungs, I dragged my hands wildly over the surface and found the familiar crevice that both Samantha and I had squeezed through the last time I'd been in the tunnels. Except I had barely gotten the swell of my belly through even then. Allowing myself one step back, I drew my knee up and slammed my foot blindly against the wall, threw my arm across my nose and mouth as another spray of clay tumbled around me.

I grabbed the edge of the widened opening and pulled myself through, turned right, and took off.

The main corridor felt cavernous and claustrophobic at the same time, the darkness oppressive while the open space left me disoriented.

I had the horrible notion I wasn't moving at all, until the side wall met my wrist with a snap that sent a shot of pain up my arm. I forced myself to move forward through the black, mentally conjuring the tunnel my eyes couldn't see. My own breath played a wheezing harmony to the sound of my fingers swooshing against the dirt, the thudding of my naked feet an irregular drumbeat, marked by sporadic groans when I tripped over the rough surface or stepped down on a rock, all of it sweet music because it drowned out the hissing shrieks that followed along behind me, drawing closer with every step and pushing cold air onto my heels.

I tried burying the memories of Samantha that were popping to the surface, but I couldn't. I could *smell* her here. The metal tinge of her blood had seeped into the ground when she'd been attacked, and it was all around me, making my stomach pitch and roll.

Suddenly I stopped and spun around. Something was wrong. My foot slid into a dip in the floor, my ankle twisted, and I tripped forward. I realized what the problem was a split second before my arms sank into a mound of loose dirt. They'd filled it in. I had made it to the church entrance, but my escape no longer existed.

Panic seized me. Tears streamed from my eyes, cutting tracks through the mask of dust over my face. My lungs screamed in pain. My wrist sent stabs of agony through my body.

Cold laughter filtered toward me from somewhere in the dark tunnel.

And it made me angry.

Gritting my teeth, I fought against the soft dirt. It tried sucking me down. For every inch I managed to dig out with one arm, the other sank in half that, until finally I loosed one arm and rolled, scurrying sideways on hands and feet like a crab. My spine hit the wall and I bit back the wail of exhaustion that came over me.

Of course there was nowhere to go from here, my mind screamed at me in panic, even as my arms flailed around me for some magical release. This was where she had fallen for the last time, Samantha, and I was about to follow—literally, ironically—in her footsteps.

That horrible hissing filled my ears, invading my every nerve. It could have been a thousand voices, or one, a maniacal acoustical trick, barreling toward me like a freight train, or easing down on me on tip-toes. I couldn't comprehend it, and it didn't matter.

My feet scrambled against the dusty floor, pure reflex to get back, ridiculous because I had nowhere to go.

The sound that filled my ears was so loud now, so *hideous*, the air that accompanied it so, so cold.

I turned my head and squeezed my eyes shut, steeling myself for whatever was coming my way.

Felt the crash and the wall behind me break away.

CHAPTER TWENTY-FOUR

Dim, sputtering light spilled out from behind me and sent my shadow looming toward the faces in the dark. I heard the laughter of children and just as quickly realized that the cheerful sound was nothing but a memory I'd made from that day at Vacation Bible School, forged along with the memory I would never shed of Samantha's ripped and bleeding throat. I scrambled backward through the hole and across the cold uneven floor.

I had no idea where I was going until I came to the end, till I reached the stone support column and pressed against it, knowing that not another millimeter of retreat existed for me.

The church. This must be the foundation of the church. What else could it be?

Drenched in sweat, caked in dirt, every muscle in my body screamed out at my smallest movement. Ragged breaths tore from my lungs, riding waves of stinging pain as I sucked in new air— thick, dusty, disappointing gulps of it that made my chest ache with the effort.

I folded my hands over my belly, fully aware that the feeble gesture meant nothing to the aberrations surrounding me.

They were there, hidden beyond the dim grey-green pool misting down off the flickering fluorescent above. I wished they would show themselves already, instead of taunting me this way. I had seen with my own two eyes the blinding swiftness of Isaiah's movements, the lightning speed with which the vampire—*Lucy*— had launched herself across the examination room at me.

Whoever—*whatever*—was out there could have overtaken me a hundred times or more.

This must be part of the game, then. Stalking the prey. Their idea of fun, part of their *satisfaction*. I felt a well of hysterics bubbling just beneath the surface of my skin.

"Cowards," I spat.

My first word. It tore itself from my throat like a growl.

Instantly, I regretted my audacity. A cacophony of snarls, hisses, rumbling growls that made mine sound like the coo of a dove ricocheted off the surrounding stone. The air seemed to move in tandem with the threats, icy waves slapping against me as the echoes reverberated from one side of the room to the other.

One by one, as they crept forward, the shadows gave way, revealing deranged ghostly faces to my right, my left, impossibly—but no, not really impossible, hadn't I seen Isaiah hover over my husband—above my head. My eyes darted from one to the next, my mind cataloguing each horror that revealed itself. Teeth glowing against the darkness. Hungry eyes piercing the night, a rainbow of daggers pointed directly at me.

Steeling myself against the inevitable attack, I pressed against the stone, inching my way up in tiny, painful increments until I was standing. I moved my cold, tattered feet one step forward. I would face this head-on, at least. After all of this, *I* refused to end it as a coward.

"This is all that matters," I said, holding the roundness of my own body—my baby, Steven's baby—protectively within my fatigued arms. "I won't give it up."

"I don't want you to," he said. The frost that tainted Steven's voice brought instant tears to my eyes.

Slowly, his face, glowing as lifelessly as the others under the sprinkling light, eased out of the darkness. I wasn't sure if he was truly there or if my mind had snapped.

My heart plummeted. I searched his beautiful eyes. The green was there—hearty, moral, healthy green, the same green that had always been there—but now I knew that meant nothing in the world of vampires and demons.

I raised my hand to touch him, touch his face, just to see if he was real, and his green eyes faded into a black fury.

"Emmalyn, don't move." His voice was hard as iron. Steven lunged at me, his strong arms raised, his lips torn back in a snarl.

I opened my mouth to scream, and waves of death pounded me from every direction.

Steven moved too fast to be human. In an instant I was pressed against the wall and his back loomed in front of me, his stance wide, crouched, arms spread as far as they could reach to shield my body. Deathly neon faces darted in and out of the cool darkness. Steven's body coiled, swiftly shifting in response to the taunts.

The scream died in my throat. He was protecting me.

There were at least five of them. Each moved with lightning speed, swooping in to tease me with a cool burst of air against my burning skin. They bounded from one spot to the next, impossible to follow—though I tried, tried to spot Lucy among them, to distinguish that face I suddenly hated amongst the others. But they moved so fast, landing sometimes with a heartbreaking thud, other times coming down without any trace of sound, like the soft padding of cat's feet on carpet so that they were there and then gone before my eyes or mind could register their presence.

The silence was the worst. At least when they hissed or snarled at me, they became less surreal, more like an animal I might stand a chance of fending off.

Something brushed against my hand, raising the tiny hairs along my fingers. Repulsed, I shrank back against the stone. Uncontrollable tremors racked my body. I drew my hands in close to my breasts, twisting to mimic the shifting shield my husband created.

"Uhmmmm." I now knew the sound for what it was: an appreciation for something delicious tangled up in the sizzling murmur of a snake's hiss.

Against my will, a groan gurgled up from deep inside me.

A tongue flicked out so swiftly I didn't have time to see it, but I felt the wet slap of it wash against my skin. One of them had tasted the knee I had scraped, the wound reopened and bleeding freely.

An appetizer, my mind jeered. The muscles in my legs softened to jelly.

Steven's elbows jutted back on either side of me. I grabbed his strong arms, willing myself to stay upright.

"We had a deal," Steven shouted. His voice sounded as hoarse and ragged as mine felt.

"Ah, but I never imagined she would taste so sweet." The face loomed in so close, the cold breath of death billowed over my chest. I tried to turn my face but I was frozen in place. Even in the dismal light, I recognized the amber eyes.

Lucy let her head roll back and laughed. Jealousy burst through me. I hated her for feasting on my husband.

As if she knew my thoughts, the monster jerked her head so that her bared teeth, still tinged with bloodstains, hovered over Steven's neck.

With a resolve I could not fathom, Steven turned his head in a mirrored movement to stare at her. "You had my blood," he seethed through clenched teeth. Layered in the words was regret that he had somehow betrayed me. I felt it as clearly as I felt the chill that poured off Lucy's body.

"Dinner," she said snidely. As if she had been yanked by a rope tied about her waist, she flew backward. Out of nowhere, another appeared at her side, landing with the toe of one shoe propped against the ground, that leg crossed before the other in a regal stance. He curled one hand into a loose white fist, as if admiring an expensive manicure.

"And how *was* your supper, Lucinda?" he asked her, his words slithering through the air.

"A rare steak," she said matter-of-factly. "A bit gamey for my taste." She rolled her eyes to look at me, mouth spreading into a yawning grin. "Though rich in flavor, I'll admit. Deal?" She seemed to ponder the concept.

Her jaw moved first, frame replaced by still frame, followed by the sinister brown eyes that swept over Steven in delicious admiration before settling on me. Then suddenly she was inches away.

"So sweet," the vampire mocked. "I've decided I would like dessert."

The regal one appeared like a flash behind her.

"She's mine, but I would be willing to share," he sneered.

A streak of movement smeared my vision, followed by a thunderous whack of bodies on stone. Lucy was gone, and the other one with her. My lungs acted on their own, sucking in great sobs of air.

Cloaked by the darkness, another voice rang out. "You have had your fill, Lucy. And you, Caleb, shall have nothing." I recognized the voice at once as Isaiah's.

The others—they were still there? —left pattering echoes in their paths as they scurried to the opposite side of our little battle ring. Like the scuttling of insects running from the light, I thought, and cringed once more.

"She is mine. I ordered her!" The vampire's voice sang out, angry, whining—anything but regal—like the pained whimper of a bratty child denied.

Isaiah's voice churned with anger. "You will not have one drop of her blood."

"We shall see," Caleb shrieked.

Lucy lunged forward, and her neck snapped so quickly under Isaiah's hands that her body had fallen to the ground before I could process what I had seen.

Isaiah's hand shot out and grabbed Caleb by the neck. One of the others moved toward Steven and me, and Isaiah intercepted, swinging Caleb through the air like a whip, cracking his body against the vampire in front of us.

The air boiled with the turbulence of their fight—flesh, if that's what you could call the sallow skin of vampires, crashed against flesh, bones cracked, teeth gnashed, snarling yelps stabbed the air when one of them fell victim to the other's attack.

I pressed one fist against my beating heart. A prayer chimed through my mind like the clanging of a bell, over and over, and I realized I was praying for Isaiah, for his safety. The irony of what I was doing nearly overwhelmed me.

A tortured squeal, ear-deafening in its horror, rang out against my head, behind me, beneath me, and overhead, throughout my very core. The last of it, in the seconds before it tapered to nothingness, reached a pitch so high I capped my hands over my ears, desperate to block out the horror of it.

I felt the tension fade in Steven's body before I realized that the screams had given way to blessed silence.

He moved, and I clawed at his shoulders, wanting desperately to hold him in place.

"It's okay," he said. He whirled and his hands grabbed me and pulled me against him.

My head shook involuntarily side to side. I started to protest, unable to believe in his words, but the figure that eased into the edge of the light silenced me.

"You are safe," Isaiah said. He seemed so perfectly calm compared to my consuming fear that anger began to boil irrationally inside me.

I looked at Isaiah's pale skin, bathed mottled green by the fluorescent bulb, but what I saw was Steven's limp arm hanging from the edge of the table in the LifeShare clinic.

"You killed him." It started as an accusation, but only relief colored my croaking voice. Tears flooded my eyes then. For five solid minutes I gasped and sobbed.

When I finally got control of myself, I had slumped back to the hard ground with Steven crouched in front of me. My hands were folded into his. I stared at them, his hands wrapped around mine, couldn't seem to move my eyes from that sight. I craved light—stabbing bright, blinding rays of sunlight—so that I could tell if his hands still carried the ruddy complexion of a man whose skin reddened under ultra-violet before it mellowed to a golden tan. Or if that skin was gone forever, replaced by …

The image of Lucy, with her lustful amber eyes, standing over him, Steven's blood dripping from her lips, invaded my vision.

I lashed out, yanking my hands away from my husband's, if that's who he was anymore, and swung at his face, his shoulders, his chest.

"What did you do?" I screamed. My voice was nearly as shrill as Caleb's had been in the moments before his death.

I said it again, barely more than a whisper this time. "What did you do, Steven?"

Understanding crossed his face and he lifted his chin, turning his face to the blue-green glow of the fluorescent, before he dropped his eyes again to face me. It was enough for me to tell that, outside of the artificial hue of this light, his lips would still be the same shade of pink as the day he had first smiled at me.

A choked sob escaped my throat. My shoulders crunched forward.

Steven's hands shot out again. He pulled me into his lap, wrapping me up in his arms.

I closed my eyes against his chest. "They move so fast. How did you—"

Isaiah's calm voice crept out from a corner of darkness, interrupting me. "Stubborn. He would have been helpless against Caleb's groupies."

I nearly laughed. It was the first informal thing I had ever heard Isaiah say.

I thought of the faces—the ones besides Caleb's or Lucy's—of the vampires that had followed me here. My eyes darted frantically from Isaiah to Steven to the invisible corners.

"They are gone. Rebels, they call themselves." A cold smirk pulled at Isaiah's black lips. "Your word was more specific."

My expression remained blank.

"Cowards," he said.

Had I actually said that? When this was over, Steven should slap me for my stupidity.

Steven.

"What did you do?" I repeated the question, but for Isaiah this time.

The smirk was gone from Isaiah's face. "I shared only one drop with him. To give him our speed. And strength. He would have come anyway. He would have been vulnerable."

I bounded to my feet, squaring my shoulders. "But you said it only took one drop to …"

I couldn't make myself finish.

"Only if given during the process." When I didn't understand, he added morbidly, "Only if we share a drink from ourselves at the same time that we partake of the drink." His eyes narrowed slightly to see if I comprehended.

"Only in death," he said after a moment, making himself perfectly and horribly clear.

Another streak in the night—the last, I hoped—caught my eye at the same moment that Steven swept me up in his arms. An eavesdropper retreating?

"I can walk," I said, my protest ridiculous since every nerve in my body roared with fatigue.

Isaiah's black lips curled ever so slightly at the edges. He said to me, "Your husband's newfound speed and strength are temporary. Shall we let him enjoy it?"

EPILOGUE

Sometimes I dream that the world has gone back to normal, that people aren't flocking in droves to be cured of cancer with no idea of the violation they are allowing to take place against their bodies in trade for peace of mind.

I dream a lot about cold stone under my feet and the hissing snarls of predators hiding in the dark. Often, when I close my eyes to go to sleep at night, the phantom splashes of light that dance behind my eyelids sprout sinister eyes. Gashes slice across the images, creating the tell-tale cherry-black lips. I have only to imagine the hungry teeth behind those lips, tools for tearing into our flesh, and then I can't sleep at all.

Today I am dreaming of the future. Steven's voice is soft but prodding. I open my eyes, slowly processing my surroundings, and smile.

"Margie's here." He is leaning over me, touching my hair. He has been extremely protective of me lately.

"Mom?" I say, but she isn't even looking my way. She is gazing down at the beautiful baby boy lying in the bassinet rolled close to the bed. He represents a small victory in all this. The CURE was amended, thanks to Isaiah, to exclude pregnant women.

"Look at how perfect you are," she says to our baby, then to Steven and me, "You did good."

I laugh and hold out my hand. Wrapped in her arms is the ice green baby book she picked out on the day we went shopping. That seems like a very long time ago. "Let me see," I say, and she is all too willing to hand over the book so that she can pick up her grandson. She looks sheepishly at us, anxious for permission.

"Go ahead," Steven tells her. He slides a look my way. We both know she can hardly contain herself.

Mom gathers the tiny bundle into her arms and immediately begins to bounce and coo and flutter her fingers at his soft chin.

I almost can't take my eyes away from him. He is so perfect, so amazing, and came so close to not being with us—a true miracle. I remember the book in my hands.

"Come sit here, Mom." I pat the side of the bed and she climbs onto the edge next to me. Steven comes around to the other side and sandwiches me in. I open the book, marveling. There are pages and pages of photographs, each captioned in sweeping calligraphy. So many faces I have never known but all part of the ancestry that brought us to this moment, and now there is another to add to our family tree.

"Sweet little Andrew," she says, cooing the name we had picked out for our baby if it turned out to be a boy.

"Actually …" I glance up at Steven and twin grins creep onto our faces. "We've decided to name him Isaiah."

"Isaiah," she repeats slowly, testing the fit of the new name in much the same way that she would ponder a new garden or a house waiting to be decorated. It sounds perfect when she says it.

"What a wonderful name you have," she sings to our son. I can hear something—well, something *Margie*—in her voice as her words grow in excitement. "Turn the page," she says, dropping the baby-speak.

I flip another page.

Margie's finger taps a tattered picture of a young man with dark hair and cream skin. I read the caption at the same time she tells me, "Your great-grandfather was named Isaiah. He died very young. Did I ever tell you about him?"

"No. Never," I say, mesmerized. Steven leans closer to examine the photograph with me. The tone is pure sepia, but even in the brownish hues I can see that something is odd about the face in this picture compared to the other old photographs pasted over the pages.

"His eyes?" I can't form a question any more coherent than that.

"Yes," Margie says, a hint of admiration mingling with her simple acknowledgement. "I remember my grandmother telling me about his eyes. Grey. Pale as silver, she used to say. You know, you are the only one in the family who ever came close to inheriting them. Just a few flecks of grey," she says, staring into my eyes as moisture threatens to overflow them, "but that's what makes them beautiful."

A knock sounds at the door. I look up, blinking away the tears, to see Professor Kendall standing there. I haven't seen or heard from him since that day behind the church on the first day of Vacation Bible School.

When Margie sees him, a broad smile spreads over her face. "Alan Kendall? My word, it's been forever." She looks him up and down; the sight of him must bring back memories of my father, because now her eyes are gleaming with tears. "You haven't changed one bit in all these years."

"Well, neither have you. Just as beautiful as you ever were," he fawns, hugging her over and around the bundle of my son. "So this is the bouncing baby boy, huh? Fine little fellow, isn't he?"

I laugh, despite the fact that Alan's last words to me still ring in my ears. *What you believe happened … did not happen.* They are less confusing now, after all I've learned, but I am no less confused as to why he was the one to say them.

Steven stands to accept the Professor's handshake.

"Congratulations, young man," Alan says, and reaches into his shirt pocket for two cigars. He hands one to Steven and rolls the other in his fingers. "I suspect you're not a smoker. Tradition, you know."

"Thank you, Alan," Steven says, and glances down at me.

"Margie," Steven says suddenly. "Emmalyn's had a craving for something chocolate and the pudding is not doing to trick. How about going down to the cafeteria with me. I've never been pregnant, so I have no idea what might be the best choice."

We all laugh. Mom covers little Isaiah's face with kisses and she lowers him into my arms as if he is the most priceless heirloom, which he is.

Alan walks over to the bed to admire the little guy.

"Isaiah, is it? Fine choice," he says.

I smile down at my perfect baby.

"So ..." I say after a moment.

"You want explanations," he says.

"I suppose so."

I can't even begin to voice all the questions. How he knew? How *much* he knew? If he knew, why he would give me the picture of Isaiah's house, as if he wanted me to go there? Why he didn't steer me away from the tunnels?

"Hah," Professor Kendall laughs. The sudden genuine amusement that burst forth suggests that it resonates from somewhere deep in the archives of him. He is looking at the scrapbook my mother brought us, open to the page containing my son's namesake.

"I didn't think I could reveal the truth," he says, his eyes shining, "but I suppose I wanted you to know him."

I glance at the book, at Isaiah, young and pale, a handsome vintage version of the man I had met at the hospital.

"You knew him?" I try to do the math in my head, but I can't make it work. Alan cannot be old enough to even have been a boy at the time Isaiah died, could he?

"He was in one of my classes at the University," Alan says, watching me closely as the realization of what he is saying slowly sinks in.

I can't speak, but I imagine my face would make a comical picture—eyebrows raised, jaw slack with disbelief—and yet I believe him.

"You mean you've been teaching since ... since?" I sputter when I can finally speak.

"Oh, no. Isaiah and I were university students together. Best friends," he says and draws his lips into a sad smile. He gestures at himself, inviting me to survey the length of his body, then waves his hand dismissively. "No. I've been this old man for quite some time, since about the time I met your father, I'd say. If I'd known what I'd wind up being, I might have chosen to make that change while I was a bit younger." He laughs but without much humor.

"How?" I say.

"Never mind that," he says, and glances toward the door. "Suffice to say Isaiah has a reputation for looking after the people he cares about."

Alan lays his thick hand over mine, cradling my son with me.

"He is a fine young man, your great-grandfather. A fine student, too, although he left the University to marry your great-grandmother and move here. Turned out to be a fine businessman, as well, although I can't say he built those houses of his purely out of an entrepreneurial spirit. Or the tunnels."

Alan pauses, a twinkle in his eye at remembering his friend in those long-ago days. "He knew more than he let on, Isaiah, and he wanted to save people from the dangers of the world. I suppose he still does."

I want to ask him about everything, about the sun, and the legends, and about my heritage, and what it means.

He hears Steven and my mom before I do, and cocks his head. They are coming down the hall.

He winks at me. "A little thing called zinc," he says playfully, as if he has anticipated my curiosity. "Very handy product." Then his face grows serious. "We are indeed sensitive to the daylight, but the light we truly have difficulty walking in doesn't come from the sun, Emmalyn. Isaiah found being around you challenging at first, but it seems we can evolve, for the right reasons."

Steven and my mom return at that moment, cutting off the barrage of questions I am suddenly willing to ask.

Alan holds up the gift bag he's been carrying.

"A little something for Isaiah," he says cheerfully.

I pull the tissue from the bag and remove a tiny shirt, barely bigger than Steven's palm, and hold it up. A white tee-shirt, nothing remarkable, and yet everyone in the room is grinning.

I don't mean to be unappreciative, but my face must be a blank.

"Turn it around," Steven says.

I flip the shirt around. The back is printed with letters, much like a baseball jersey. "Explorer," it reads.

I can't help but laugh. "I love it."

"We'll see," Steven says a little teasingly, but a familiar edge of concern creeps into his voice.

He drops onto the bed beside me and snakes his arm around my shoulders. The fingers of his other hand curl into the ones I am using to hold Isaiah. It's just the average strength of a man's rough fingers against mine, but it is all the support I need.

Yes, we have secrets, Steven and I. Not from each other— never that—but there is a secret we are now a part of and, at least for now, must keep from the world.

ABOUT THE AUTHOR

Sandra Hood was born in Atlanta, Georgia and graduated from Kennesaw State University, where she studied Computer Science, a discipline she finds strangely invaluable in constructing plots and weaving in side-stories. Sandra believes that in a world where bizarre, complicated, and sometimes evil agendas come into play, mankind holds at its core an inherent goodness, a trait she likes to explore in her writing. She currently lives in the suburbs of Atlanta with her two come-and-go college children and a dog who likes to stare at her while she writes.

You can learn more about Sandra at www.sshoodfiction.com, where she occasionally blogs and shares short stories, or follow her on facebook at: Sandra Hood, author.

www.ingramcontent.com/pod-product-compliance
Lightning Source LLC
Chambersburg PA
CBHW030022180626
46810CB00001B/172